DEADLINE IN DALLAS

BROKEN CHORD
A MUSIC ROW MYSTERY

DEADLINE
IN
DALLAS

Alice A. Jackson

WordCrafts

Manny Zammorra was a man of long standing habit. He glanced at the clock on the bedside stand. 11:30 p.m. Zammorra closed his book, a subjective critique of the newspaper business by a former White House press secretary turned Harvard professor. So far he had drawn little wisdom from its pages, despite the books vaunted place on the *New York Times* bestseller list. The author seemed oblivious to the competition of online news outlets to the traditional printed newspaper.

Reaching over, he clicked off the lamp, slumped back on the double pillows, tucked a husky arm under his head, and ran his free hand through thick black hair liberally threaded with gray. He stared at the shadowy overhead light fixture and waited for sleep to overtake him.

This was the time of night he dreaded. The time he most missed Alicia. He still slept only on his side of the bed. The other side was undisturbed except for those times at night when he would awake and reach over for her, only to feel wrenching disappointment. Alicia was not there. She would never be there again.

Friends assured him the terrible void following Alicia's death from cancer three years ago would lessen. It hadn't. Instead, it wrapped him in a shroud of ache and longing each night.

As pronounced as were his habits, Manny Zammorra's discipline was even stronger. After his wife's death, staffers at the *Brownsville Daily Leader* saw little variation from his daily routine. He had politely spurned the gentle advice of friends and co-workers to get away for a while. He had chosen instead to return to his office the week following the funeral.

He turned on his side and slid his hand under the covers to the vacant side of the bed. It stayed there until sleep finally abated his nocturnal mourning.

Zammorra blinked awake, unsure what had disturbed his sleep. He glanced at the clock. 1:15 a.m. It was then he heard it—the sharp creak of wood on the stairway. Then again, and again. He had been meaning to get under that stairwell for years and securely screw cross supports under the steps to silence the creaking noise.

Who would be coming up the stairs at this hour? Maybe his son Joseph who had a key to the front door.

"Joseph, is that you?" he called out.

No response.

He pulled the covers aside and reached for the switch on the bedside lamp. A figure stood framed in the doorway. Behind that figure, the shadowy outline of a second figure. A question was forming on his lips just as the bullets fired from an automatic weapon. The torrent of hollowpoints bored into his face and chest, eclipsing words, knocking him back onto the pillow. One ruptured his heart. Several more collapsed his lungs. Manny Zammorra was dead within seconds.

The second figure moved from the shadows to the bed and with two swift slices of a large, steel knife severed the dead man's head, then grimly positioned it back on the pillow above the body so the stricken eyes looked out toward whoever entered the room.

It was his oldest son who found him later that morning. Joseph received a call at his law office from the *Daily Leader's* concerned managing editor. In all his years at the newspaper, Manny Zammorra had never been late for work.

2

The email message was cryptic to all eyes but his. *The news is good.* He deftly deleted the email before picking up the telephone to dial his pilot. "Have the helicopter ready in an hour," he instructed, in a voice barely above a whisper.

Christo rarely raised his voice. It was a discipline he taught himself many years before, after reading about an American president who admonished his fellow countrymen to speak softly and carry a big stick. Such counsel appealed to his pragmatic nature.

Now he must hurry Bette. It could be 15 minutes; it could be two hours. Whatever! It was never enough time for his beautiful Bette. An hour would just have to be ample. He was due in Dallas this evening for a reception and dinner hosted by The Greater Dallas Commerce Association—the GDCA as the group's letterhead boldly declared in red and gold letters. Cocktails would begin at 7:00. A non-drinker by preference, he found he often learned far more at such gatherings listening to the informal chats over drinks than from conversations during the dinners which followed.

A thin smile creased Christo's lips as he pulled shut the door to his office. He had been courted by the Dallas businessmen's group shortly after he made a subtle inquiry about the availability of dilapidated warehouse space. The space had been jettisoned by a bankrupt company onto the city's abandoned-property list a year before.

The mayor's Office of Economic Development had been the first to respond. Then came the letter from the GDCA. The net result—lucrative incentives, making the expansion of his operations into Dallas a reality, and draping those operations with a cloak of legitimacy.

Christo silently applauded his success. With or without the generous tax abatements, the warehouse complex would have been acquired. Located adjacent to one of the city's poorest barrios, the discarded warehouses promised another advantage for his new enterprise; an abundant source of undocumented Hispanic workers. *A perfect fit*, he mused silently; much like his marriage to Bette, the only child of his mentor, Jacoby.

Christo strode out of his office and bounded up the curving, marble stairway and down the veranda hallway overlooking the vast, ornately tiled and landscaped courtyard below. From the large marble fountain in the courtyard's center, gleeful cherubs spouted a geyser of water that spilled over the sides like a drenching rain into a large round basin.

At the end of the hallway, carved wooden double doors stood slightly ajar. He pushed one door wider and walked across the expansive bedroom to the exquisite reflection smiling at him from the large mirror. He bent and brushed his lips against the porcelain skin of one bare shoulder and felt the familiar rush of pride and lust. She never failed to take his breath away. He whispered in her ear, "Bette, my love. We leave for Dallas within the hour."

3

Lesley Rowan glanced at the large round face of the clock on the wall across from her desk. She had less than an hour to finish the story confronting her on the computer screen before she was due in makeup for the five o'clock newscast. *Damn!* Time seemed ever-short, given the demanding deadlines of television evening newscasts. The familiar pressure of panic knotted in her stomach. She reached for a paper cup beside her computer. It was empty. *Damn!*

Lesley walked over to a blue bottled water machine and filled the slightly crumpled cup. The water cooler was a newsroom perk, albeit a newer one. The City of Dallas water, coming from an aged, rusted water fountain, tasted so brackish, drinking water had become a continuing source of discontent with the staff. *Something new to carp about besides who was getting the most face time on evening newscasts*, she mused silently.

Lesley was not one of the complainers about the old water fountain. But she silently applauded those who had, and the small victory they had won with the parsimonious station manager, Bart Henderson. He grudgingly paid for the newsroom water perk out of his zealously guarded travel budget; a budget he fervidly reserved for the golf outings planned with fellow attendees during the annual gathering of the National Association of Broadcasters in

Las Vegas each spring. Without a trace of remorse Henderson left it to his top assistants to attend the seminars and other convention events. He considered playing golf with other station executives a rite of passage for a sales manager turned station manager.

As Lesley walked back to her office, her attention was drawn to the bulletin bell ringing on a computer atop the vacant desk of an assistant producer. She glanced down at the screen and her eyes fixed on an Reuters story marked "URGENT." The story was datelined Brownsville, Texas. Her eyes raced across the page.

Brownsville Daily Leader Editor Manuel T. Zammorra, 58, was found brutally beheaded in his suburban Brownsville home this morning in what police are calling a cartel-style slaying. A police spokesman said Zammorra was cut down by multiple bullets fired from a high-caliber gun, then savagely beheaded.

The decapitated body was discovered by his oldest son in the upstairs bedroom of the journalist's modest, two-story home.

Lesley pressed her fingers to her lips. "Oh, my God," she whispered as her eyes raced across the computer copy.

Sources close to the investigation say members of Mexico's powerful El Poder Cartel are suspected in Zammorra's killing. Beheadings are common with the notorious Mexican cartel, often as a means of sending a warning.

Police speculate the editor's murder may be retaliation for an investigative series run by the Brownsville Daily Leader in recent week, detailing cross-border drug smuggling by the cartel and the bribery of high-ranking municipal officials in Brownsville and Matamoros. The newspaper series quoted sources who said cocaine and marijuana shipments were being smuggled through Brownsville to major Texas cities, and as far north as Chicago and Detroit.

The editor's slaying comes in the wake of an escalating turf war between the El Poder cartel and its smaller rival, the Cortez cartel, a rivalry that has spilled across the border into Brownsville neighborhoods and business districts. Several high-ranking members of the Cortez Cartel have been killed in recent weeks. The bodies of two cartel members were discovered along a busy road just south of Matamoros last week. Both had been beheaded.

A federal grand jury has been impaneled to investigate both the growing violence between rival drug gangs and the alleged political corruption.

Tears broke through Lesley's tight emotional guard and trailed down her cheeks. She swallowed the last gulp of water and crumpled the paper cup in her hands.

Manny dead. Dear Manny.

It was the summer between her junior and senior year at the University of Texas that Lesley had interned at the Brownsville newspaper. When she was introduced to Zammorra by the city editor she found him distracted and aloof, and unfairly attributed the editor's natural reserve to unfriendliness.

A week later, Lesley wrote her first front-page story, a milestone for an intern. Swallowing her initial misgivings, Lesley approached Zammorra's office. It seemed an oasis of calm at the far end of the cluttered newsroom. Too many desks were crammed back-to-back in too little space. The tight fit of desks and people was exacerbated by the cacophony of voices and ringing telephones.

She had stood awkwardly in the doorway until the Zammorra finally looked up distractedly from a computer screen. A brief smile eased the frown on his features. He dismissed her apology for interrupting him and listened patiently while she requested he review the story she had just written.

From that day on, the soft-spoken editor had critiqued her stories with a seasoned eye for making each better, in a manner always constructive, never belittling. Lesley became a eager and attentive protégée. She incorporated his suggestions for improving her news writing into the style and substance of each report.

Manny Zammorra evolved in her mind into a father figure. He epitomized the paternal figure she had created in her imagination as a child, a replacement for the father she never knew. That figment of her daydreams was a gentle man who carried her on his broad shoulders, laughing deeply as he circled around a lush, spacious yard; a man who hugged her often, who praised her flawless report cards, who approved her prom formal in the most flattering terms.

That man did not exist in Lesley's real world. Her father absented himself from her life before she was barely out of diapers. And he never returned.

Her mother, a registered nurse, was left to raise Lesley alone. She worked nights, and slept while Lesley attended school. There were no child-support payments in the mail. When her father left for the excitement of a new wife, he severed all financial and emotional responsibility to his first wife and child. He was a hero only in Lesley's imagination.

Lesley honed her writing skills quickly under Zammorra's quiet tutelage. His demeanor was so different from the newspaper's harried, Alka Seltzer-swigging city editor, Ed Woods, who barked his disfavor with any shortcoming in her copy, unconcerned who might be listening. Other staffers feigned disinterest by lowering their heads whenever Wood railed at whoever was the target of his wrath at that moment, thankful they were not on the receiving end of one of his curt admonishments.

Lesley brushed away sudden tears with the back of her hand. That simple movement forced her focus back to the sad reality of the final paragraphs of the news service story, which listed Zammorra's many journalism honors, ranging from an expected Pulitzer nomination for the drug series to dozens of state journalism awards, including being named to the Texas Journalism Hall of Fame just a year ago. He had been the first Hispanic-American to be inducted into that hierarchy of legendary Texas newsmen.

Following the induction ceremony Lesley and Zammorra participated on a panel reviewing news ethics, sponsored by the University of Texas and broadcast statewide on public television. Unlike other members of the panel, Zammorra offered no showboat answers to the problem of balancing strong news ethics with the increasing pressure to make newspapers and television newscasts more tabloid-like in their coverage and presentation.

Zammorra's ethics were inexorably planted in the 1970s. It was the period that followed Watergate, when the journalism profession had taken the ethical high-road following the unraveling of the Nixon administration. When Zammorra was appointed editor of the Brownsville newspaper, he stood as restrained bastion against the influence of Rupert Murdock and his ilk on newsrooms throughout the country. The investigation of cartel drug smuggling and political corruption by the *Brownsville Daily Leader* was an example of Zammorra's chosen ties to that commitment.

"Something big?" The raspy voice of the news editor, Bill Burton, interrupted her sad reverie.

"The editor of the Brownsville newspaper's been murdered. It just came across," she added, without looking up, resenting his intrusion on her grief.

"Whoa, big stuff," exclaimed Burton. Noticing a tear still sliding down her cheek, Burton asked, "Did you know him?"

"I worked for him in Brownsville one summer during college." The murdered editor's gentle face swam before her.

"Sorry, Les." Burton nodded and quickly headed toward his cubicle office, just steps from where they stood. Before she made the turn toward her own desk she saw his fingers dancing over the computer keyboard and heard the immediate response of the adjacent laser printer. As Lesley settled into her chair she saw Burton rocket out of his office, heading toward the news director's office at the far end of the newsroom, gripping a paper copy of the story.

Lesley knew the lineup for the five o'clock newscast had been set an hour ago. No doubt Burton, whose nervous energy always propelled him at a more frenetic pace than the rest of the newsroom, would want the editor's slaying inserted into the upcoming news line-up—if Mac Withers approved. Disparaging staffers sneered at Burton behind his back, saying he couldn't wipe his butt without Withers' approval.

Lesley returned to her office to confront her own computer screen. She needed 30 seconds of additional copy on the upcoming Dallas mayoral election. Her eyes raced over what she had already written about the Republican incumbent, Grantham Stewart II. He had emerged from political obscurity four years ago to wrest the mayor's office from long-entrenched Democrats. Now Stewart was the entrenched incumbent being challenged by a wily veteran of the state legislature, Dennison Davis—'Denny' to his friends. Her eyes raced across the words already on the screen.

Stewart is the scion of an oil-wealthy family. His grandfather discovered some of the most fertile oil fields of East and West Texas in the 1920s and 1930s. The 90-year old family patriarch came to Texas in his teens, hungry and ambitious.

Like so many of his wildcatting contemporaries, little is known of his roots. What is told is mostly old speculation, which, over several decades, has grown into legend and has assumed the aura of truth.

More words rushed onto the computer screen, some gleaned from information in a resume provided by the mayor's press secretary. Lesley noted with amused cynicism that the press release did not mention Stewart's family estate. She glanced at her own notes taken during an interview with the mayor last week.

The 20-acre Stewart compound is surrounded by a high wrought iron fence, and dominated by a multi-gabled, Tudor-style stone mansion his grandfather built on the highest point, at the center of the wooded acreage. In the shadow of the mansion, obscured by large oak and pine trees, stands the smaller home of the mayor. The home was a wedding gift from his grandfather when Stewart brought his young, Texas-educated wife to Dallas more than a decade ago. Sarah Stewart and their two children have remained in the house following the couple's separation and divorce.

Even with no juicy details to relate, the couple's divorce had still rated several paragraphs on the front page of the morning newspaper. Lesley was content with her shorter account.

"Les, could you come to my office right away? It's important." It was the news director's voice, rasping at her through the intercom on her telephone. The intercom clicked off before she could respond.

Damn, she cursed silently. The piece on Stewart needed to be finished before Hal Crockett, the executive producer, came looking for it with his typical, constipated look.

Burton, Crockett, and the five o'clock producer, Jerry Simms, were already sitting around a tightly fitted conference table in the news director's sparse office when Lesley arrived from across the newsroom. Behind his large, cluttered desk, Mac Withers evinced his impatience by absently tapping a pencil against the desk top. His perpetual frown smoothed a little as he nodded a silent welcome to Lesley and motioned her to a seat near Burton.

Withers liked Lesley. She was the antithesis of the average anchor. Good-looking enough, that she was. Beautiful by any measure—tall, leggy, with shoulder-length black hair and emerald-green eyes that could fire when she was keen on pursuing a story or masking anger—anger she seldom gave vent to, unlike her two male counterparts.

The difference, thought Withers, as he watched Lesley slip gracefully into a seat, *is that Jed Thompson, the five o'clock co-anchor, and Tom Fitzgerald, who holds down the same spot at six, are readers. They don't know shit about reporting. Lesley does. She was journalist first; anchor second. That's why she is here, co-anchoring both evening news blocks.*

It was her writing and reporting that first caught Withers' eye when he was judging entries in the annual Texas State Television Association Awards program two years ago. Lesley was then a reporter at a small West Texas television station. The story submitted by her station was by far the most compelling he'd reviewed, even among the multiple entries from stations in the state's larger markets.

That story flashed across his memory as he watched her approaching. He recalled the distraught man, holding a wailing toddler, standing in the partially-opened doorway of the steamy hovel, the tip of a butcher knife pressed against the baby's throat, demanding in a voice slurred by drugs and alcohol to talk with the media—not police.

It was Lesley who volunteered to go in, over the vehement objections of the local sheriff. It was Lesley the man allowed through the door. Long minutes later, she emerged with the child clutched in her arms just as a shot rang out from inside the two-room adobe structure.

SWAT team members found the man dead. *A better choice*, he had told Lesley, *than returning to prison.*

The night Lesley accepted her award at the annual dinner in Austin, she also accepted Withers' offer to co-anchor KDLL's top-rated evening news.

4

W ithers stepped from behind his desk and took his usual seat around the conference table

"Les, you saw the story on Manny Zammorra, right?" he began, his gruff manner reasserting itself. The other male faces trained on hers.

"Yes," she answered hesitantly.

"Bill tells me you worked for Zammorra."

"Yes. For two summers as an intern. Why?" she asked, her curiosity piqued.

"This could be a hellava story. I think you should go to Brownsville and cover the funeral and the investigation. That series the *Daily Leader* ran went national. And the chaos down there is getting worse, particularly at that border crossing. The governor announced at his news conference this morning he's sending additional National Guardsmen to beef up security along the border there. Bad situation."

Lesley's and every other head around the table nodded agreement. "We'll send a satellite truck with you. I'm putting Jack Reilley on the story at this end. He's already been following up with the Dallas cop shop about the drug connection here that the *Daily Leader* cited."

Mac paused to read her reaction. She looked back at him

impassively, veiling the rapid fire images pounding her brain, recalling the story she read only minutes earlier and the face of Manny Zammorra on the Austin news panel. She wondered with growing horror if the bullets had obliterated the face now focused in her mind's eye.

"When do we leave?" she asked. It was the response Mac expected. "You want me to coordinate with Jack on the drug angle from down there?"

"Yeah. If Zammorra was taken out by tha El Poder bunch, that could bring the feds into the investigation. I'm sure they'll concentrate the probe down there," Mac surmised, his attention focused solely on her. "You only have two or three days, so you'll have a lot to do. Coordinate with Hal and Bill. Keep us posted on what you're working on so we can promote the pieces. I'm sending Pete Kannady and Hector Morales with the satellite truck. Morales speaks the language. That might come in handy down there. You'll have Hank in the field with you. Okay?"

He knew the answer before he asked. Hank Bottoms had been field producing for Lesley nearly since the day she joined the KDLL news staff. She was the only reporter who seemed able to communicate well with the moody, introverted producer. Tall and thin, Bottoms had an almost hawk-like appearance, with a long face punctuated with deep-set eyes and a large nose shadowing thin lips.

From the beginning there had been a synergy between the brooding producer and the young anchor which brought out the best of Bottoms considerable creativity in the field. Outside of Withers and the payroll department, Lesley was the only person who knew Bottoms was married and the father of a young son.

Mac Withers looked at his producers and news editor for the first time. "Any questions, gentlemen? Anything further you need to tell Les?" He was answered with silent nods from the three men.

"Get us a good story, girl." Mac's voice softened slightly as he looked at the eager affirmation on Lesley's face. He knew he was sending one of his best reporters. She would get the job done better than just about anyone on the news staff. Lesley wanted nothing more than to validate his confidence in her.

Back in her office, the message she spoke into the distant answering machine was short. "I can't make it tonight. Sorry. Mac has me on the road to Brownsville first thing in the morning. I'll make it up to you as soon as I get back."

Christo impatiently swilled the remaining 7-Up masquerading as champagne in the plastic flute. Scorn darkened his hard features as he glanced around the room at the Brooks Brothers and Armani-suited men and the designer-gowned women at their sides. The din of their inane conversations assaulted his ears. He had already had enough of this charade. And there was still the dinner ahead. His eyes continued to discreetly circle the packed room looking for one man in particular. That person was nowhere in his range of vision.

Patience, he reminded himself and glanced over at his impeccable Bette. Sensing his eyes on her she sought his face and smiled. Her thick, raven hair was secured in an elegant chignon, giving even more depth to her dark eyes and sensuous lips. Her beauty never ceased to impress him. Never more so than now. She was his Helen of Troy in this fortress of Dallas commercial power he had come to conquer.

Christo noted a rustle of movement behind him and turned just as two men approached. One he knew. The other he was eager to meet. The younger man could have been a mirror reflection of the older man 30 years ago; both tall, both with high cheek bones that gave their lean faces a strong, chiseled handsomeness.

The older man grasped Christo's hand warmly. "Juan, it is so good to have you in our fair city." Turning to the man beside him he said, "I'd like to introduce my son, Grant Stewart, the mayor of Dallas." Pride rang in his voice. "Grant, this is my friend, Juan Christo."

"Welcome to Dallas, Mr. Christo," Stewart said warmly as he extended his hand. "The project you propose for our city will be a source of future pride, I'm sure."

"Thank you. And it is a great pleasure to finally meet you, Mr. Mayor," Christo replied in a thick Hispanic brogue. "May I present my wife, Bette."

The smile that widened the lips lighted the dark eyes of the woman standing next to Christo. Grant Stewart found himself drawn immediately into the circle of her beauty and warmth by the delicate hand that slipped effortlessly into his. "My husband and I are so honored to be here this evening." Her voice was soft, her English flawless, with only a hint of an accent.

"The honor is ours, Senora Christo," he returned graciously, feeling the delicate hand subtly slip from his.

Blaine Stewart turned to his son. "I wonder, Grant, if I could leave you to entertain this lovely lady while I introduce her husband to some others I'd like him to meet?"

"Certainly, if Senora Christo doesn't mind my company?"

She smiled her assent as the elder Stewart took Christo by the elbow and steered him through the crowd to a more secluded area of the ballroom, nodding to several couples he knew as they made their way across the crowded room. Glancing discretely around him as they walked to ensure no one was nearby, Stewart said in a low voice, "I received a call from our friends in Chicago. We may have a problem with our pilot. Let's find some privacy and I'll tell you about it."

5

The pipe organ trumpeted the ancient Gregorian requiem from the choir loft above the crowded cathedral. Its haunting tones sorrowfully draped the senses of those sitting quietly in the wood pews. The intense sadness of this occasion was palpable to Lesley, seated near the back of the cavernous Catholic cathedral beside Hank Bottoms.

The front pews had been roped off for the friends and family of Manny Zammorra on one side, and the *Daily Leader* staff filled in the three rows across the aisle. Seated just behind the family were the governor, two senators, one congressman, and several pews full of Brownsville community and government leaders.

The aging Monsignor called the funeral Mass a celebration of Manny Zammorra's life. It was a celebration met with silence by most who listened—with tears by those closest to the slain editor.

When the long solemn service ended, Lesley stood with other mourners watching the flower-draped casket being rolled down the tiled, center aisle of the church. Zammorra's sons followed the casket. They gripped the arms of their wives and hugged their young sons protectively against them, their eyes swollen and reddened by grief. The two grandchildren had known their grandfather well. Campouts and fishing trips became a refuge from his own loss, cementing a closeness he had fostered even while Alicia was still alive.

Watching them pass, Lesley thought it would probably be the grandchildren who would miss Manny Zammorra the most.

As the slow procession of mourners filed toward the vestibule and outside into the blinding sunlight of mid-morning, Lesley reached for her small clutch bag. She felt something next to it. Looking down, she saw a funeral program with the top of an envelope above the fold.

Instinctively, she glanced around her. All of the nearby faces were watching the parade of mourners waiting their turn to file out of the pews and exit the church. No one appeared to be looking her way or seemed interested in her discovery.

There was one face that did. As she slipped the crumpled bulletin into her purse, the face turned away from its obscured vantage point. It slipped back into the protective shadow of a huge column in the choir loft, further into the shadowy darkness of the church's heights. A thin smile creased the mouth, reflecting relief that Lesley reacted discreetly after noticing the envelope near her purse.

He had spotted Lesley just minutes before the long service started. Her sitting on the far end of the pew made it easy to slip, unnoticed, into the seat behind her and the tall, stooped-shouldered man accompanying her. He was one of the three men who had entered the downtown hotel lobby with her before each checked into their rooms. It would have been more difficult to get the message to her at a hotel where all the room entrances were on the outside of the building. Not enough cover. This had worked perfectly. Now the waiting would begin.

Once inside the station's satellite truck, Lesley was able to open the envelope as her colleagues busied themselves loading camera gear into the back. The message was a mix of printed and cursive letters and appeared to be written by someone who'd either never fully learned penmanship, or wanted to disguise the handwriting.

Don't waste your time in Brownsville. You won't find anything here. The killers are safe across the border. The man behind the killing is not here. You need to look in Dallas. The money is there. Matamoros is a decoy. If you look for oil you will find drugs. That is what this is all about. I will be at the city park near the main bridge over the Rio Grande at ten p.m. I'll find you. Come alone.

Lesley felt a chill of fear. *I'll find you.* She debated showing the strange letter to Hank but quickly decided against it. Whoever it was seemed to know she was working on the motive behind the killing of Zammorra. She wondered if he had heard any of the promos on KDLL billboarding the series she would be reporting from Brownsville.

If you look for oil, you will find drugs.

Lesley could recall no mention of an oil connection to the drug smuggling in any stories in the *Daily Leader* series she and Hank had pored over. The two-week series detailed drug trafficking through Mexico to Brownsville, and north into the Southwestern and Midwestern United States. Dallas was singled out in the stories. She had interviewed the three *Daily Leader* reporters for more than an hour about their investigative series. The stories alluded frequently to one confidential source. Only one of the reporters actually talked with the source—a source the reporter seemed hesitant, almost fearful, to discuss.

Federal drug agents on both sides of the border were openly quoted in the newspaper series. The confidential source was never quoted directly: only mentioned as verifying some of the routes used by the smugglers and the different methods they utilized to disguise the drugs. Someone who obviously knew. Was it someone close to the El Poder cartel? That was never established in the *Daily Leader* series.

Lesley closely questioned Tony Gomez, the reporter who talked directly with the anonymous source. Gomez refused to say how the source first contacted him. Under her probing scrutiny his dark eyes shifted away. He apologetically refused to give any information about the contact. Could that source be the author of the note?

Dallas connections? This intrigued Lesley. Gomez insisted that information had come from a confidential source. But he also conceded the source could provide very little supporting evidence.

Even more intriguing to Lesley was the source had claimed to Gomez that the Dallas connections were influential and powerful. The *Daily Leader* investigative series did cite more substantial evidence of numerous Brownsville connections to the notorious Mexican cartel, from bribed border guards to greedy city officials fingered by other workers who Gomez claimed were jealous of their fellow employees and supervisors financial payoffs for cooperating with the cartel.

Lesley remembered the newspaper had prominently displayed photos of expensive homes; detailed luxury vacations, and private-school educations for the children of several high-ranking Brownsville municipal and law enforcement officials whose salaries could not support such lifestyles. Several officials were placed on paid administrative leave or outright suspension following the *Daily Leader* revelations. The allegations were now the focus of investigations by federal and state grand juries. Some alleged offenders were being offered immunity from prosecution for their cooperation. "Flipping" is what Gomez termed it.

Mexican officials reacted with the fervor of sleeping turtles. No arrests so far on their side of the border. And none were expected, according to Gomez. It was a reaction the three *Daily Leader* reporters who bylined the investigative series attributed to systemic, long-standing corruption among Mexican police officials and civil servants. Gomez stated flatly most were on the payroll of the cartels, facts he ascribed to unnamed sources. Those on the Mexican side of the border, who might have knowledge of drug smuggling, remained silent out of fear of the brutal retribution meted out by the cartels to any who shared their secret operations with police or the media.

Lesley fed her reports live from Brownsville for the five and six o'clock newscasts and taped a separate report for the late newscast. It was Hank Bottoms who suggested the backdrop for the reports. Bottoms seemed to have a sixth sense for finding the right location to enhance the mood of the story. The cramped and somewhat chaotic newsroom of the *Brownsville Daily Leader* was the backdrop Bottoms chose.

Meticulous by nature, Bottoms even faxed the two evening anchors questions they could ask Lesley on air during the early newscasts. While generally not a judgmental man, Bottoms accepted the reality that spontaneous discourse was not the forte of the two KDLL evening anchors. So, he left nothing to chance.

Lesley seldom questioned the quiet producer's decisions. Bottoms approached his job with an almost religious zeal, feeding well-written and well-reported stories from the live locations to which he was assigned.

In Lesley, Bottoms found an empathetic and willing accomplice. Intelligent, glib, with a photographic memory for names and dates, she was a field producer's dream. She was able to write, succinctly and quickly, the portion of her story that could be put on the field camera teleprompter. Even when the teleprompter occasionally malfunctioned, Bottoms could not recall her stumbling in the two years since they began working together. Her smoothness and professionalism were qualities he believed would one day bring her an offer from one of the major networks. Lesley had revealed to him an approach by Fox News Channel, which she adroitly declined while at the same time leaving an opening for a future approach.

When the field work was completed and the KDLL team arrived back at the hotel Lesley pleaded a headache and retreated to her room. She checked her computer and ordered a rental car be delivered to the hotel by 9:00 p.m. Two hours later, after placing a do-not-disturb sign on her outside doorknob, Lesley quietly closed the door and headed down to the front lobby. The car was there, just as the desk clerk promised. She paid with a personal credit card and asked sweetly for directions to the riverfront area. The eager young clerk told her more than she ever wanted to know about Brownsville's riverfront park, delaying her departure by at least five minutes. She squelched her rising impatience and even managed to offer the clerk a compliment and slip him a generous tip.

Lesley pulled to a stop in the park's nearly deserted parking area. It was 9:30. She was in place well ahead of the note writer's suggested meeting time. It was early enough, though, to allow tension to roil inside her. She felt in her shoulder-purse for the cool steel of the handgun she had carried since her car was nearly jumped by three men at a West Dallas intersection a year ago. Luckily, she had spotted two of the men running toward her car in the side-view mirror. She had been slowing for a red light at an approaching intersection and had failed to see a third man rushing her car on the passenger side. A black ski mask covered his face, a baseball cap on his head, and he was wielding a baseball bat. He had jumped in front of her car, forcing her to brake instantly before he leaped on the hood. She acted instinctively. The sudden acceleration of her car sent the man sprawling to the pavement. She had never looked back to see if he was hurt and was too panicked to care.

Texas law was one of the most liberal in the nation on carrying personal weapons. The gun was a compact .38 caliber, "powerful enough to stop anyone within short range," promised the burly instructor at the firing range. The gun's kick nearly knocked her over the first time she fired it. She could now hold it with both hands and aim without fearing kick-back. And it was always the man in the ski mask with the baseball bat she saw through the barrel's sight.

Lights illuminating a walkway along the Rio Grande River cast an amber glow on the murky water. Lesley had seen the Rio Grande several times and was always surprised at how narrow the distance was from the Mexican shore to the United States side, and how little water it contained during dryer months. In the movies, the fabled river was always wide and deep. Even as far west as El Paso the river was often not much more than a putrid creek during periods when rain was scarce. It reeked of the waste dumped into it from the Mexican side where municipal environmental considerations held a lower priority.

Lesley adjusted the side-view mirrors to ensure a better view of anyone approaching from the rear of the car. She glanced at her watch. Fifteen minutes to go. She felt a flutter of nervousness and tightness in her stomach. *Fear,* she admitted silently and instantly regretted her decision to come alone. As if to reassure herself, Lesley pulled the handgun from her purse and pushed the safety off, tucking the weapon between her thigh and the center console, out of view but close at hand.

Lesley felt the man's presence before she saw him approaching from a copse of trees near the parking area. She momentarily pondered how long he might have been watching her from the covert darkness of those trees. He was tall and angular, with a large, felt, western-style hat pulled low over his forehead, partially occluding his face. Tinted glasses hid his eyes. Glancing around, he tapped lightly on the window. She rolled it partially down.

"Thanks for coming. I wasn't sure you would." A thin smile creased his lips. "It's kinda scary here, but the best place to meet." His voice was low and somewhat gravelly as if he had just awakened from sleep. The voice of a man no longer young.

"That editor you talked about earlier. He *was* murdered by a Mexican cartel. I can vouch for that. But the real story you should be after is in Dallas. I pretty well know who's behind the drug-running for the El Poder cartel." He looked nervously toward the back of the car. "I pretty much know how and when they're getting the stuff into the States."

She could see only his profile as he glanced away again to scan the area around the car. Watching his profile, Lesley could see the man's back jaw muscles pumping as he fell silent and leaned his thigh against the car door.

"Why haven't you gone to the police or even the FBI?" she asked.

His response was a deep sigh before he finally answered, "What you're asking is, why I'm telling you and not them? Very simple. If I go to them, I'm dead. And it could endanger someone close to me."

"Are you involved with these people—these drug smugglers?"

Another deep sigh. "Yes."

"How?"

"I'm a pilot for them. Getting the drugs overland is getting harder, so they've started flying drugs to a drop-off near Tyler. There's a private airstrip in one of the old oil fields. It's just south of Tyler off State Road 18. Place called the Henson field."

"Henson? Is that who owns the oil field?" Lesley scribbled the information into her reporter's notebook.

"No," he replied. "The wells are owned by a Dallas outfit. As I pointed out in my note to you, there are some powerful folks behind this. So when you start nosin' around be *real* careful," he warned, "because it could put me and my..." He turned away abruptly, realizing he was might be revealing something, or someone, he appeared hesitant to disclose.

"I understand your concern. And I promise you my complete discretion. But I need more to go on," Lesley said, almost pleadingly. "Like how sure are you that the cargo you're bringing into that airstrip is illegal drugs—which drug; marijuana, cocaine, what? And which cartel you fly for, how often they're flying drugs into that Tyler location, names of the powerful people in Dallas..."

"Look," he interrupted, as he leaned his arm on the door. She could smell cigarettes on his breath and saw apprehension mixing with fear on his face. "Look," he repeated, "the people behind this are forging production records on a bunch of oil wells that were shut down in the eighties and nineties, when the oil business went south. I'm guessing that's how they launder the money. It's the way they cover their ass for the money they're making from the cocaine and fentanyl I fly in." He withdrew his arm from the partially open window and turned away for a moment staring silently toward the river before turning back toward her. "I don't know most of the particulars. But I can tell you where the oil wells are. I've seen some of those records from Tyler and down near Midland.

"Do you have any of the records with you?"

"No. You'll have to do your own checking on that. It's an outfit called Althea Oil & Gas. That's about as much as I know for sure right now."

"Okay. But how can I contact you?"

"You can't. I'll get in touch with you... Shit!" The expletive hung in the air as the man bolted away, melting into the dark shadows of the trees from which he had emerged only minutes before. Stunned by his sudden departure, Lesley sat gripping the steering wheel trying to rehash the brief conversation that hinted at so much with so exacerbating few details. Who was he protecting? Certainly himself. He said someone close to him was in danger. Who was the other person? So many questions and concerns swirled her mind. And why had he chosen to speak to he? Lesley did not recognize his face and was certain they had never met, which only added to her uncertainty. There was one fact that he seemed sure of—Althea Oil & Gas. It was a start, albeit a thin one.

Lesley started the engine and when she turned to back out, she spotted the headlights for the first time—a police cruiser. It was heading slowly toward her and must have been what the man had seen that sent him fleeing so hurriedly.

As Lesley backed out, the police car pulled alongside her rental. The window of the Brownsville Police Department cruiser rolled slowly down. A handsome young Hispanic face leaned toward her. "You okay, ma'am? You parked alone down here?"

"Yes, officer. I'm fine. Just enjoying the river view."

"All right, ma'am. Have a good evening." The cruiser pulled slowly away. Lesley could feel her heart pounding in her chest so hard she wondered if the police officer had heard it. As she reached for the gear shift, she felt the gun lodged tranquilly against her leg. She pushed the safety lever back into place and slipped the weapon into her purse before driving out of the parking area.

Lesley was pulling under the front portico of the hotel before her breathing and heartbeat returned to normal.

Lesley stared at the towering Dallas skyline on the screen saver as it weaved across the monitor. For the last 15 minutes she had been debating showing Withers the note and describing the subsequent, abruptly terminated meeting in the Brownsville park. Still wrestling with her dilemma, she was startled by Withers' voice behind her.

"I didn't mean to scare you. I guess it's my Frankenstein face," he said, grinning down at her. Slightly less than medium height, on a stocky, muscular frame, Lesley thought Withers had the intimidating stance of a bulldog. She learned shortly after arriving at Channel 15 he had just such a reputation among the staff.

He came to the station from the *Dallas Morning News*, a no-nonsense reporter who had been seasoned in his early days on the police beat and matured into the newspaper's top political writer. Following a divorce and a year of battling depression with beer, he took a leave of absence from the newspaper. Where he went and what he did during those few months he shared with no one. When he returned to Dallas, it was to the newsroom of KDLL as news director.

Within six months many of the faces populating the newsroom changed, to the silent chagrin of the station's old guard headed by Bart Henderson and top sales staffers. Withers hired a cadre of fresh faces recruited from top journalism schools and newspapers to replace several of the meticulously coiffed, smoother-speaking former reporters. Young and fiercely competitive at times, often looking somewhat rumpled on camera, the new faces created an aggressive news image for the station.

Under the contract he hammered out with Henderson, Withers had been given a free hand to operate the news department for one year on his terms. Henderson kept his part of the bargain over the several month course of the newsroom overhaul. He tried to intervene during those first weeks of the purge, when handsome face after handsome face came angrily to his office seeking a sympathetic ear for their complaints against Withers or pleading to get their job reinstated. Mac Withers would suffer no interference. He made that clear the first time Henderson strolled into his office to diplomatically demand the news director back down from releasing a reporter who was an after-hours drinking favorite of Henderson and his sycophantic sales manager. Withers listened without comment, his face expressionless, then dismissed Henderson's appeals with a blunt, "My decision stands."

Bart Henderson was a consensus maker. At least that was how he portrayed himself to the after-hours regulars who gathered most evenings in the posh Outrigger Lounge. The construction of a large hotel so near the station had been fortuitous. Not only did it provide a convenient watering hole where Henderson could hold court, but it provided him a suitable place for corporate executives to stay on their semi-annual sojourns to KDLL from the conglomerate's Manhattan headquarters. Henderson never mentioned the trade worked out with the hotel chain. In exchange for advertising, the hotel covered the cost of those semi-annual stays—and Henderson's running bar tab—which in turn helped keep his expense account plump.

The usual group nodded empathetically when Henderson described how distraught he was for those impacted by the newsroom changes. He would run his left hand through his wavy, salt-and-pepper hair, furrow his brow in a sympathetic frown, and declare with self-righteous resonance—he was being forced to back Withers by the higher-ups at corporate.

At the time Withers came on board, KDLL's daily newscasts were languishing in the cellar among the four network-affiliated stations. "But just see how fast the tables turn if the ratings don't improve," Henderson had promised ominously, tipping his martini to the "here-here'" of the obsequious gathering. Henderson silently vowed to fire Withers at the first opportunity if he failed to deliver.

Firing his news director was the furthest thing from Henderson's mind when the book for the second major ratings period arrived following Withers' hiring. It showed a leap to second place in the early news block and a respectable gain for the 10 p.m. newscast. When Henderson renewed Withers' contract at the end of his first year with the station, it was for three years at the salary the news director requested.

Henderson doggedly reserved one important decision for himself. He would have final say over who anchored the improving newscasts. There was no disagreement from Withers on that score, except when Henderson vetoed Lesley Rowan to replace a departing male anchor. Two male anchors suggested strength and stability to the audience, Henderson argued. Consistency. That's what the newscasts needed to keep the ratings momentum building. After Henderson finished laying out his case he leaned back into the plush burgundy leather of his desk chair with his arms folded behind his head.

"Lesley Rowan is the best choice," Withers stated calmly. "She won't disappoint." The news director, who never sat down when he went to Henderson's plush office, turned abruptly and walked out the door leaving Henderson awash in silent anger as he stared at Withers' back. The news director had not even bothered to say goodbye. *Pompous bastard!*

Lesley Rowan debuted with each of her two male cohorts a month later. She also served as a primary replacement on 10 o'clock newscasts when a regular anchor was absent.

Lesley looked up at Withers. She had worked for him just over two years and still knew little about him. He was demanding, but supportive; his news judgment unfaltering; his well-honed journalistic talents vaulting the station to prime competitor status in the Dallas market. KDLL stories often broke ahead of the newspapers. Those scoops became a strong source of pride for the news staff and a strong selling point for the advertising staff. It was a pride in which Lesley shared. Her initial admiration for Mac had only grown during her tenure at the station.

Withers debriefed Lesley closely about the information she gleaned from her sources on the Zammorra killing and the murderous turbulence scarring Brownsville. She withheld only one key aspect: the note, and the brief meeting with the man who wrote it. Withers' expression was circumspective as he studied her face. She appeared somewhat edgy since returning from Brownsville. A little more withdrawn than usual. He offered her a day or more off. It was an offer she declined.

"Everything all right, Les?"

"Sure, why?"

"Just checking. You've been working pretty hard lately. Maybe you need to take me up on that day off. Maybe a long weekend."

"Maybe I will." She smiled and turned back to her computer screen and its twirling lines. "Thanks, Mac."

He laid his thick hand on her shoulder, gripping it lightly. She lifted her left arm and patted his hand in response, feeling the warmth of his hand lingering on her shoulder even after it was withdrawn.

Lesley heard the text ding on her cell phone. She fished it from her purse. It was a message she was expecting. "Come by the apartment tonight. I've got a Texas-sized heartburn from missing you so much."

It was sent from his private phone. Lesley felt a stir of excitement ripple through her as she deleted the text. Too many curious eyes in the newsroom. Email and texting were their most private means of communication. All telephone calls into the station were still answered until 11 p.m. by switchboard operators, who acknowledged callers with sugary salutations laced with vinegar retorts if the caller was discerned to be a fan instead of a person having real business with the newsroom. His voice might be recognized. So texts sufficed. She would only answer if she couldn't be there.

The sultry evening air wrapped around Lesley like an electric blanket on high as she stepped out the back door of the station building into the parking lot. Dallas was like a desert in summer, without benefitting from the nighttime cool-down afforded by low humidity levels in more arid areas of the far west. It was well past rush hour. Still, the temperature hovered in the low 90s.

Lesley's faded blue Mustang convertible was parked next to the high chain link fence that enclosed the rear of the station where several news vehicles were parked under a large, metal, protective canopy and spaces were marked for employees and visitors.

The Mustang had nearly 100,000 miles. It was a surprise high school graduation gift from her long-absent father, the only gift she ever remembered receiving from him. It arrived without a card or even a note, delivered by a salesman from the Paris, Texas dealership where the Mustang was purchased. It was the salesman who let slip who had purchased the car. There was no return address to send a thank-you card. She had been unable to acknowledge her father's one and only gift.

As the Mustang sputtered somewhat grudgingly to life Lesley silently promised herself she would look for a new car soon. Finding time was the problem. And the mechanic who had tuned-up the old horse in April declared the car in extraordinarily good shape which had forestalled its possible retirement. It was just enough excuse to put-off looking for a replacement.

As Lesley pulled out onto the broad street running in front of the station, another motor cranked more smoothly to life, not moving until she turned the corner heading for the freeway three blocks ahead. Weaving in and out of the thinned-out late evening traffic, the driver easily followed the Mustang, keeping enough distance between his car and Lesley's to remain unnoticed.

Lesley seemed to drive almost on autopilot, her thoughts preoccupied with Withers, her failure to share with him the note left in the Brownsville church pew, and her meeting with the mysterious man at the riverfront park. As she circled off the freeway, she resolved to speak with Withers tomorrow. She had held off informing the news director hoping the pilot would contact her again. The man had disclosed so little in those moments before spotting the police cruiser approaching. It left her anxious for another meeting and frustrated at not being able to arrange one.

She assumed Withers would admonish her for keeping her crew in the dark and going to the meeting alone. Lesley conceded the criticism would be justified. A familiar uneasiness clawed at the pit of her stomach for the umpteenth time.

She had begun checking out Althea Oil & Gas even before returning to Dallas. It was the one concrete piece of information the pilot had revealed besides the location of the drug drops. So far she had learned little. The scarcity of information on the company only raised more qualms about not disclosing the note and its writer sooner. Althea Oil & Gas, at least on the internet, had proved to be an almost phantom company. Another reason she should have informed Withers. She knew of his history as a veteran investigative journalist—and the awards he had garnered, including sharing in a Pulitzer Prize. Lesley admitted she would need Withers' input to help her define the possible consequences of the information imparted by the pilot, however thin it might be. And—of more personal consequence—why it had come to her. She felt an almost visceral relief at her decision to see Withers first thing tomorrow.

Lesley turned onto a widened street. Its lushly landscaped boulevard was lined with enormous trees spaced at generous intervals. The long branches stretched across to form a natural canopy on both sides of the thoroughfare. Brick and stone townhouses and upscale condominiums flanked the spacious boulevard on both sides. Lesley slowed as she approached a three-story, 1930s vintage apartment building that had been reclaimed by developers. In a five-year effort that won them the cover of *Architectural Digest* and national prominence, developers had transformed this aged and blighted area near downtown Dallas into prime real estate. She pulled around a corner and quickly swung the Mustang in between a Lexus and a Ford Explorer. *You will hardly be noticed*, she thought with silent mirth as she turned the key to the car's ignition off.

Seeing her round the corner the driver who was following slowed but kept moving ahead. Parking was barred on the boulevard, giving him no cover on a street illuminated by gaslight-era fixtures. Darkness was slowly effacing the retreating daylight. He turned at the next corner and quickly pulled in behind the first car, ignoring the warning of the yellow, painted curb, prohibiting parking. Glancing carefully around him, the man walked back to the main street. He saw Lesley ascending the wide steps of the front entrance to a building in the middle of the block with distinctive Art Deco styling. From the shadows of a large tree he observed her pick up a key from behind a potted plant on the left side of the oversized oak, then cross to the stained-glass double doors. She unlocked the right-side door and replaced the key in its hiding place before disappearing inside.

He walked slowly toward the building with his hands burrowed casually in the pockets of his jeans. As he came nearer he strained to see the number above the wide doors of the front entrance. The apartment building looked familiar. He recalled driving through the area several months ago. He had been pulled by a gnawing curiosity to scout the home of the newly-estranged Dallas mayor after reading of the city official's separation from his wife. He stopped momentarily in front of the steep steps that Lesley had ascended and peered up at the address. Even in the opaque light on the porch it was now clearly visible—1218. He felt his stomach lurch.

"You son-of-a-bitch," he hissed.

$$7$$

"I've missed you, lady." He whispered the words into her ear as he gently pushed soft strands of black hair away from her face, his lips lightly nibbling each ear lobe, sending a rush of feeling down her spine.

"Me, too."

"I picked up a bottle of your favorite Zinfandel. How about I get you a glass?" he suggested, biting her lip playfully between sentences.

"Bribery, sir. Shameless, unadulterated bribery. But it works. Make mine a big glass."

He looked at her intently. It was so unlike her to drink more than a single, small portion of wine, and she almost never had a second glass. She did look tired tonight. *Must have hit a rough patch at work.* He smiled. "Coming right up, ma'am."

She followed him into the small kitchen and watched as he deftly uncorked the slender bottle of rosé wine. It was her favorite. He was always attentive to what she liked best in almost every aspect of their relationship. Then he opened himself a bottle of beer.

He handed her a nearly full glass and looped his arm through hers. "Here's to a beautiful lady," he said softly, tipping the bottle against her glass. He set his bottle on the marble counter and pulled her into his arms as he lifted the glass from her hand. His tongue teased each side of her neck before hungrily seeking her mouth.

She answered his passion with equal hunger. The sound of the telephone ringing startled them apart. He sighed with resignation as he lifted his mouth from hers. "Damn phone! Who in the hell would be calling this late in the day? Let's see how urgent." He made no move to answer the telephone.

The intrusive ringing ended and a deep, male voice announced, "Hello, this is Grant Stewart. I can't answer right now. Your call is important to me so please leave a brief message and your phone number, and I'll get back to you as soon as possible." The message was immediately followed by two beeped tones, then a longer tone.

"Your whore is no secret anymore, you son-of-a-bitch," came a man's voice, slightly muffled as if he were holding something over the mouthpiece. "You'll pay big time for this." Then a sharp sound as the caller abruptly clicked off his cell phone.

"Oh my God, Grant! Who *was* that?" There was instant alarm in Lesley's voice. "Someone must have seen me come in."

Grant Stewart walked over to the telephone sitting on a mahogany table. He pressed the replay-button and listened intently as the rude message repeated itself. Lesley stood beside him staring at the telephone. No number was illuminated in the bar just below the day, date, and time to give a clue to the caller.

As if reading her mind, he turned and said, "It may have been from a disposable cell phone."

"You're right, of course." Lesley turned, clasping her arms to her chest and lowering her head. Grant pulled her close and gently turned her to him, lifting her chin with his hand.

"Hey, Les. Quit worrying," he instructed gently. "I get crank calls all the time. It comes with the territory." Grant began soothing the worry lines furrowing her brow with his lips. "It's probably the *National Enquirer* trying to increase circulation by getting us to run to the nearest grocery store next week and buy a copy to see if it's about us."

"This isn't funny, Grant," she said looking at him despondently. "Why would somebody be following me?"

"I don't know, Lesley." A frown replaced his smile. "But we'll find out. I'll get Steve Myers working on it in the morning."

"No!" The word possessed a vehemence that surprised even Lesley. "You can't bring the police in on this. Especially Myers! He would just assign it to someone below him and even more people would know I was here tonight."

"You may be right," he said, relief at her rejection of the police chief's assistance smoothly hidden in his reaction.

"I know I'm right. Police departments are hotbeds for rumor-mongering. They'd have a field day with this one—mayor bedding anchor."

"Bedding. That's as Shakespearean a term for sex as I've heard in a long time."

She laughed and immediately felt some of her tension melt away. She had been discovered. That was a fact. What the caller would do with the information was yet to be seen. Which gave them time to come up with a rational, plausible reason for her being in his apartment at eight o'clock at night.

A thin shiver of fear ran through her at the realization, again, that someone may have followed her here. Who? She recalled stories of stalkers on the news—mostly mentally-deranged fans of celebrities. Some consequences of stalking had been tragic.

And that voice. Even muffled, it had a familiar sound. It was a voice she had heard before. But where?

"He's targeting me, Lesley, not you," Grant said, again seeming to read her thoughts. "That's apparent from the phone call. Remember me? I'm the guy running for reelection."

"Perhaps you're right. But what if we are being watched by someone? It could hurt your reelection." She looked back at him and smiled wanly. "It could compromise the Southern Baptist vote."

"Well, we can't do anything about it at this moment. So why don't you come over here and sit down," he said, pulling her toward one of the couches, "and drink your wine. Getting you inebriated sounds like a perfect plan for getting in your pants."

She smiled more broadly as she took a sip of the smooth wine. "Men! Even in a crisis you have only one thing on your minds. I'll stick to this one glass of wine, thank you very much."

Lesley sat pensively, sipping the remaining wine, feeling his closeness. She turned instinctively toward him as she felt his eyes on her.

"By the way, have I told you, you look marvelous, darling?" he murmured in a poor attempt at Billy Crystal. "I'll get the bottle. You need a refill."

"And you need to take this more seriously."

He hesitated before sitting down. "Maybe coffee is a better choice tonight."

"I think you're right."

The smile faded slowly from her face as she watched Grant walk back to the apartment's small, utilitarian kitchen, with its black and white tiled floor and ceiling-high cabinets, all painstakingly restored by workmen. A sense of foreboding enveloped her again—akin to fear. It tasted in her mouth and throat like a floating cotton ball.

It was so different from the sensation she had felt on their first evening together. The dinner invitation was a surprise. It had come as she stood in the center of his private City Hall office. She was awed by the plush, yet tempered formality of the office. Despite the muted grays and blues, accented with soft burgundy in the chairs and drapes, it was a room with a distinctive flavor and character—his.

Lesley flushed with embarrassment at her own transparent curiosity when Grant Stewart began explaining how he redecorated the office. He had paid for the updating. The wide-topped, rounded, mahogany desk was custom-built and sat in the center of a thick oriental rug that he had obtained in the Middle East during a trade mission the previous year sponsored by the State Department. Laughing, he explained the trade mission failed at drumming up markets for Dallas businesses. And his purchases had only added to the national trade deficit. He then pointed to two wall hangings purchased along with the rug.

"How about dinner tonight? After the newscast, of course."

She had been turned away from him appraising a handmade tapestry. It depicted a dashing, saber-wielding sheik riding a spirited Arabian horse.

"Everyone who comes in here is struck by that tapestry. I won't take *no* for an answer." There was an irresistible firmness in his words.

She said yes.

After dinner at a quaint Mexican restaurant, cubby-holed in a row of near-downtown buildings, resurrected from decay by an aggressive urban renewal program in the early 1980s, they strolled through the area, wrapped in the welcome warmth of a winter evening. Dallas was often treated to such breaks from winter by an indulgent Mother Nature, whose mood could turn quickly wrathful with springtime tornadoes followed by scorching summers. The clear sky that evening was bathed in moonlight and lavished with stars.

On one of the corners of the restaurant district stood an elderly street vendor selling steaming tamales wrapped in cornmeal for one dollar. His crinkled face reflected the difficulty of his lot in life; selling tamales to people with mostly full bellies. Despite the temperate evening, a red wool cap was pulled down snugly over his ears, and the collar of his worn, brown parka was pulled up around his neck. Like the man himself, the tamale cart was worn, the once-bright printing on its sides long faded. Prior prices were still evident. There were painted X's through *fifty-cents* and *seventy-five cents.*

Stopping at the tamale cart became a regular event after each dinner, as much a part of their growing relationship as the love-making that followed. If the old man recognized the mayor or the television anchor holding hands before him it never showed on his inscrutable face.

Then came a night when they found the old man and his cart absent from the familiar corner. Just over a month later he was back, standing beside his cart, shivering in the frosty night air that had clasped Dallas in a wintery hug. It was only when he stepped from the side of the cart, to hand the tamale wrapped in a paper napkin to Lesley that they noticed the crutch supporting his right side and the lower pant leg pinned behind his right thigh. They knew then why he had been absent from his corner. The bills Grant had pulled from his pocket were discretely reinserted. From a zippered section of his wallet Grant drew several $100 bills and pressed them into the old man's mitten-covered hand. The weathered face stared at the bills. When he looked up, his lips quivered and tears misted his milky brown eyes. A whispered "thank you" was barely audible.

"Hey girl, you're far away."

Lesley looked up, welcoming the intrusion of Grant's soft voice from the kitchen doorway into the sadness that had enveloped her as she recalled that cold night.

"Coffee's on."

"Good." She smiled reassuringly to lessen the look of concern on his face. Within minutes he was back, handing her a thick mug of the steaming brew. It smelled delicious.

"Here's to a sleepless night," said Grant, raising his cup, "for more reasons than caffeine."

It was well after midnight before Grant turned and slipped almost immediately into a deep sleep. He had not mentioned the caller again and his lovemaking had cleansed thoughts of the caller from Lesley's mind, at least temporarily.

She lay silently awake beside him listening to the evenness of his breathing, the satisfaction of their coupling still coursing through her. Grant Stewart was only her second sexual experience. She had only Bobby Morris to whom she could compare Grant's sexual prowess.

Handsome, muscular, fun, insistent, Bobby Morris was the college football player she had succumbed to in the back seat of his red convertible, after an hour of passionate kissing and heavy petting. Panting, he promised gentleness but did not deliver. The experience left her hurting and emotionally empty. Morris never asked her out again which only increased the shame and guilt she felt at the cavalier manner in which she had forsaken her virginity. When Lesley would run into Morris on campus, walking to classes or passing in a hallway, he always acknowledged her with a wave or friendly greeting, but never another date.

Occasionally, she would lay awake in her dorm room at night wondering how many of his athletic buddies he bragged to about screwing the virgin editor of the campus newspaper. She imagined herself the butt of ribald jokes and could feel her face flush warmly in the protective darkness even now as she remember her humiliation.

It was not just the ignominious loss of her virginity to Bobby Morris that was keeping her awake at this moment, but the caller's voice and the threatened impact to her future. She had told no one of her relationship with Grant. They agreed from the beginning with the need for discretion and secrecy. His divorce had been finalized. But the conflict of interest of a journalist sleeping with a high government official haunted her during moments of harsh self-reflection.

Grant Stewart faced a tough reelection race. He faced an electorate that had become increasingly critical of misdeeds or even the hint of impropriety by public officials at all levels of government. An affair could prove an insurmountable roadblock to a second term for a candidate who won office with a platform steeped in traditional family values, particularly if that affair was with a highly visible television news anchor. Not to mention the affair could threaten her future with KDLL.

Withers would consider the relationship a breach of ethics on her part. His face drifted into focus, his perpetual frown deepened by disappointment and sadness. Mac Withers took journalistic ethics seriously. It distinguished him from his newsroom competitors. All news employees were required to sign a stringent ethics code. It prohibited accepting gifts or favors from public officials or other news sources, or doing anything that could compromise the journalistic integrity of the station. She signed the code willingly and may now be just as willingly abrogating that code.

When Grant stirred shortly after five o'clock she was still wide awake. He had turned only once to sleep briefly on his back, snoring softly. His breathing quieted minutes later. Lesley envied his ability to turn off the looming troubles she could not vanquish in favor of rest. This would be a long day.

"Hi, beautiful."

"Hi, yourself, handsome." She smiled as he leaned over and kissed her softly on the lips. "Ouch, you need a shave, bristle man."

"That can wait. I have other things to do right now." He pulled her on top of him, pushing her disheveled hair back from her face before he lavished it with kisses.

Giggling, Lesley sat up straddling his firm stomach. "I would like to comply with your demands, but if I do, you will be late for work. Your secretary will be worried. Probably call the police. They will break down your door and find us in a most compromising position. You will be impeached. I will be fired. And this story will not have a happy ending."

He laughed. "Party pooper! My other girlfriends just tell me politely they have a headache."

"I'm not that original."

"I'll make coffee if you want to shower first," he smiled, slapping her rump smartly.

The shower was appealing. She waited until he disappeared out the bedroom door before slipping out of bed and heading for the oversized corner shower stall, enclosed on three sides by etched-beveled glass. The multiple massage shower heads propelled the warm water in a pulsating flow, helping relax her knotted shoulder and neck muscles. She let the water work its magic on her weariness for several minutes before the shower door opened.

"That looks like fun. Can I join you?"

"Only if you come bearing coffee."

"I do." He pressed a large mug into her hand. She sipped the aromatic liquid while the water pelted her back. She handed the mug back to Grant. "I'll just be a moment and you can have the shower."

"I think I would like to shower right now." He laid her cup on the vanity and stripped off his pajama bottoms. His body was quickly wetted by the shower flow as he ran his hands over her glistening skin.

"I've heard sex in a shower rates a 10." His mouth covered hers before she could respond and she could feel his urgency pressed against her. What was it about morning sex that so aroused men? She had been coming to his apartment for several months and seldom left without making love in the morning. He was unhurried, waiting until she responded to the pleasure of his hands and his mouth before he lifted her. She wrapped her legs around his waist as he penetrated her with a strong thrust that arched her back with erotic pleasure. It was over in moments. She felt his breath coming in heaves as she buried her head in the hollow of his neck.

"God, that was good. Have I told you lately that I love you?"

Lesley lifted her head and looked searchingly into his face. "It's the first time you've told me."

"I do love you, Lesley. You must know that by now. I want you with me every morning, just like this."

"Sex fiend!"

"I'm serious, Les. I love you. We have to find a way to be together."

"We are," she answered lightly, unwinding her legs as she slipped to the shower floor. "I would call this togetherness, wouldn't you?"

"Be serious. I want some long-time togetherness. I want to marry you."

His words momentarily stunned her, wiping away the smile and quieting the glib answer forming on her lips. She felt the water gently pounding on her back. His words were completely unexpected. Their relationship had been voluntary, relaxed, non-committal up to this point. Lesley's discipline had never allowed her to picture a future for their relationship. Her pragmatic nature refused to contemplate any long term commitment.

Now, looking into his strong face—with its high cheekbones, deeply grooved cheeks, and thick black eyebrows—Lesley saw the sincerity and intensity of his feelings reflected in his dark brown eyes, affirming emotions she had stubbornly abnegated, but could no longer avoid. She loved him and had known it since early in their relationship. Denial had protected her from rejection, from pain, from admitting the depth of her own emotions. No more.

"I love you, Grant. God knows I sometimes wish you had any other job but the one you have, or I was not paraded before a television news audience five nights a week. Our lives would be immeasurably less complicated."

"The important thing is you *do* love me despite my employment. And yours." He smiled broadly. "If you refuse my proposal I promise to start sending you tacky pink roses every day. And I'll call a news conference to tell the world you refused my proposal. I'll cry right there on live television. Loudly, too! It may not get me you, but it sure as hell will get me the sympathy vote. Great strategy, huh?"

"You political maggot. Let me out of here," she laughed, playfully pushing him away. "Look," she said holding up her hands, "I've been in this water so long I'm turning into a prune."

"It's okay. I love you, waterlogged or dry. Makes no difference, ma'am."

She dried quickly while he finished showering. She handed him a fresh towel before slipping out the door to dress in the same clothes she wore the night before. She was not expected in the newsroom until 10:00 a.m., so there was ample time to go to her apartment and change before heading to the station.

Lesley was sipping a second cup of coffee, heavily laced with sugar, when Grant emerged from the bedroom, shaved, in a beige shirt, fitting the final loop on a narrow-striped, silk tie. He dressed with smart taste. His appearance underscored his good looks and business demeanor. She flashed a smile of approval.

"Where's my coffee, woman?" he demanded, kissing her and licking the taste of coffee from her lips.

"Sugar or calorie-free?"

"Plain suits me," he responded in an exaggerated drawl. "You know us Texas men like our coffee strong and unpolluted."

As she crossed to the coffeemaker, her eye caught the telephone on the table in the living room. The threatening voice crashed back into her consciousness. Grant saw her momentary hesitation.

"What's the matter?"

"The caller. Grant, what are we going to do?" Again, she experienced the nagging awareness she had heard the voice before.

The caller had been in his thoughts, as well. Grant was certain it was the same voice he had curtly dismissed several times at his home during the years he was married to Sarah. He had protected Sarah from the caller. He must protect Lesley as well.

His back was to her when she turned around, his face hidden as he answered. "Don't worry. He won't bother you anymore. I think I know who it is." Grant wondered why the man would be following Lesley. He would damn sure find out.

C hristo swept a satisfied glance over the mountain plateau. Each flattened terrace his eyes lingered over was covered with coca plants laden with greenish brown leaves, awaiting the pickers making their way upward through the shrubs on the lower steppes.

The morning sun would soon burn off the soft haze still hovering around the coca plants. *A good crop,* he calculated. *Maybe ten metric tons.* It would take another two days to complete the harvesting. Another seven days for processing before the cocaine would be ready for shipment. The cocaine they processed would supplement the synthetic fentanyl his factory was also producing. The opioid could be cheaply produced. He had learned that by studying a clandestine report on Chinese fentanyl production. It was proving a fruitful lesson learned. The relatively low cost to expand customer bases in the United States and Europe was rapidly making fentanyl his most lucrative product. Except for the Chinese, there was, so far, little competition for the fentanyl market.

A thin smile creased Christo's face, equally browned by his Indian heritage and the sun. As his eyes swept the lush coca crop, he considered how pleased his greedy Mexican partners would be at the output. Just the harvest from these mountain fields alone would go a long way toward easing the scarcity of cocaine in the States, a shortage manipulated by the El Poder cartel to heighten demand on the streets and ensure top price for their export. Christo silently conceded producing the products was no problem. Getting the products to customers in the US and Canada was now the greater concern. That concern forced his thin smile to dissolve into a frown.

Christo's biggest worry was with the savage methods being used by his Mexican associates to defend their drug domains. Six members of a rival cartel had been brutally slain by El Poder henchmen who dumped the bloodied and beheaded bodies in an alley in Brownsville. *Why beheadings?* he questioned silently. *Dead was dead. What satisfaction was there in wreaking more violence on a dead body? Such violence was unwarranted,* Christo had lamented to the cartel leaders. *The murders would only attract more attention.*

A warning. That was the terse explanation given by the heads of the El Poder cartel. A warning not just for rivals, but made implicit to the foot soldiers that carried out the orders of cartel leaders. It ensured loyalty. *Money was not always enough*, his partners had explained in dismissing his concerns. Disloyalty was the ultimate offense in their eyes. It undermined their business model.

Christo knew when to keep his own counsel, and he did so. *They are inviting more government retaliation*, he reflected silently during the conversation. His fear was realized when he heard several weeks later that the American president was sending troops to bolster efforts to curb drug smuggling and violence along the Mexican border and keep illegal migration in check. The building of a wall along that same border could prove a future impediment, but the presence of troops was a real and present threat. The killing of the editor was an even more stupid act. Christo grimaced recalling details of the murder that would undoubtedly attract more unwanted attention on the drug trade from the American side of the border. Christo shook his head silently.

The small man standing deferentially at his elbow looked at Christo with alarm. "Are you not pleased with our work, Senor Christo?"

Startled from his thoughts by the fear in the voice beside him,

Christo patted the man's arm reassuringly. "Yes, yes, Manuel, I am pleased. This will be a very good harvest. It will bring wealth for your village."

The old man shook his head affirmatively and flashed a tooth-less grin at his mentor. "Sí. I am glad you are pleased, Señor. The harvest is good. It will warm our winter."

Christo grasped the wizened man's shoulders affectionately before turning away from the terraced fields and striding toward the black Mercedes parked under a grove of trees. He was followed silently by the two stoic, burly bodyguards who shadowed him wherever he went. This was Christo land. This was his village. San Luis. He had left it many years ago a young, penniless boy. He had returned its benefactor.

As the big car headed down the steep winding dirt road leading out of the village, Christo leaned back in the leather seat and felt a deep sense of satisfaction. He was rich beyond his wildest expectations. And he was sharing his wealth with the village where his parents, and four of his ten siblings, were buried. They had died too soon, before he could return to the village to share his new wealth. Their graves were now marked by large, granite monuments, the only thing he could give them in death.

Christo turned and glanced out the rear window at the terraced hillside, partially shrouded by the choking dust stirred by the car accelerating down the steep road. He had purchased the land and put the village to work. *They were his partners,* he had told them benevolently, *and would share in the proceeds from the coca crops.* They applauded enthusiastically. Only the young priest, Father Diaz, who journeyed up the mountain road to the village on Sundays to recite Mass, demurred. He had warned the villagers in his gentle voice that their labor would be spent on the Devil's work, growing coca for the white powder.

The following Sunday was the priest's last trip to the village. He was killed when his aging, battered station wagon hurtled off the steep road leading from the village down the mountainside and crashed into a tree. Father Diaz had died instantly, reported the medical examiner. The accident report concluded the car's brakes had failed. No one had examined the car or brake line closely enough. Small punctures in the brake hoses went unnoticed.

With the grateful consent of the bishop, Christo arranged for the priest to be buried near his parents, erecting a granite monument fit for the grave of a revered priest.

In the three years since the priest's death Christo had become a hero to his former neighbors. A younger brother, Eduardo, was installed as overseer, supervising the planting of the coca shrubs on the terraced vistas carved out by bulldozers. Working with a well-paid, pliable agronomist from the university in Bogota, the coca plants flourished in the warm moist earth of the mountainous Colombia terrain.

Despite the new-found economic boost from the coca crops, only the main street through the village had been paved. Most of the villagers still lived in small adobe houses with sod roofs scattered along the dusty side streets. A white picket fence here and there was the only indication of new spending, except for the school at the end of the main village, a gift from Christo. He eyed the building benevolently before turning and resting his head against the plush leather.

The school was the tallest structure in the village; a handsome building constructed of brick and stucco and fronted by white columns that gave it the appearance of a diminutive university library.

Christo even hired the teachers, a husband and wife from a small town just outside Bogota. The coca crop paid their salaries and purchased their discretion, providing the first education opportunity for the children of the harvest workers. Poor and illiterate, the villagers were at first skeptical of Christo's plan for a primary school for the village.

They were Indians. For centuries, their culture dictated children learn from their elders, not teachers from a large city. What ideas would be placed in their children's heads? Parents feared their children would turn from their Indian culture, from the old ways, and espouse new lifestyles, alien to the inhabitants of the village.

Exactly, Christo promised silently. The children would learn. Like him, some would leave the isolation of their mountain village for a better life. But unlike him, they would leave with their heads filled with learning, to help them enroll in university, get jobs, and rise above the poverty imposed by adhering to a culture that kept his people wrapped in garish, hand-woven blankets and ignorance.

He had left of his own volition when he was only 10. Had worked hard and caught the eye of Jacoby that fateful day outside Bogota a year later. He warned the big man of the police who waited in ambush along the road leading to the Jacoby villa, perched high on a distant mountain.

Christo was hoeing weeds to earn his evening meal in one of the large vegetable fields on both sides of the highway when he saw the first police cars speed by and stop just around a curve above the fields. Trucks loaded with more armed police rumbled beyond the curve, followed by a camouflaged jeep with three men who looked like Americans.

Boys on the streets talked about the presence of American Special Forces, and of federal drug agents sent to help Colombian police crack down on drug trafficking. From the distant protection of trees above the roadside Christo had watched the police preparations. Savvy beyond his young years, he recognized the ambush being prepared. Christo heard many stories about the great man who lived on the mountain, far above the fields, in the pale, rose painted villa. He was told it was an impregnable fortress, surrounded by a high stucco wall some said was more than a foot thick and patrolled by armed men who guarded wealth beyond the reaches of his imagination.

Like the other youngsters who lived on the streets of Bogota, Christo was wary of police. They were the perceived enemy, to be avoided, to be castigated, to be ridiculed, to be feared. He felt no remorse in hailing the big man's caravan of black Mercedes and warning them of the police trap ahead. The bodyguards were skeptical, roughing up the young messenger who had waved them to a stop from the middle of the road, until a stocky man stepped out of the car and ordered them to stop.

His name was Alejandro Christo Jacoby. Christo watched Jacoby approach him. He knew of the man from the street boys' glowing descriptions of his power and wealth. As the big man stood before him, languidly pulling on a thin cigarillo, Christo knew in his young heart fate had interceded.

"Let the kid go," Jacoby ordered in a sharp voice.

Christo felt the rough restraining hands loosen their hold on his tattered clothes. The big man scrutinized him from several feet away, his dark, expressionless eyes betraying nothing of his impression of the painfully thin, disheveled youngster. Jacoby knew a street kid when he saw one. This was one.

"What's your name?" he demanded, lifting the cigarillo he held nonchalantly between his thumb and index finger to his thin lips.

"Christo," the boy replied, looking unblinkingly into the drug lord's face.

"Interesting. I thought I was the only man with that name." He turned abruptly and got back into the car without another word, signaling Christo to follow. Juan Christo became his name. After so many years, it was hard to even recall his birth name, Emmanuel Sepulveda.

Christo never returned to the vegetable fields. He accompanied Jacoby back to Bogota, to await the helicopter that took them safely to the villa, far above the clutches of the waiting police. Circling the expansive grounds of the villa before landing on the concrete pad some distance from the main house, Christo looked down on a world he never imagined; a world of lush gardens, fountains, shrub-bordered walkway, a soccer field, and a village of smaller homes that bordered this palatial estate. The walled hacienda sat atop the highest point of the massive grounds, a stucco and tiled edifice so large it took Christo's breath. The awestruck youngster's expression prompted a rare smile from Jacoby.

"It's my home," Jacoby said without emotion. "Work hard and you'll always be welcome here."

With the street smell scrubbed off his skin and outfitted in new clothes, the clothes of a man, Christo became Jacoby's hardest working disciple.

The wealth Christo first observed as a boy was now his. Christo lit a cigarette and relaxed back into cushioned leather, a thin line of smoke emitting from his narrowly opened mouth.

Within two weeks the newly harvested cocaine would be processed and ready to move, along with a large quantity of the synthetic opioid. He would personally deliver the shipment to its first destination; not a trip he looked forward to making, but still, a necessary journey.

Shipping the drugs overland into the States was now compromised; stupidly compromised by what he suspected was treachery from within the El Poder cartel. He had little respect for his Mexican partners. But they were necessary to his operation, as necessary as his American partners in Dallas and Chicago. The difference was the Americans were more disciplined and tacit—qualities he often found lacking in his Mexican partners. His contempt for the Mexican cartel had grown since newspaper stories uncovered much about the cartel's overland pipeline to the States. Those revelations were forcing the Mexicans to begin shipping drugs aboard the oil company aircraft.

So far, no problems. But it was less safe. And weather could be a major factor in delivery schedule. There was the danger of one of the DEA's AWAC planes homing in on the plane. If the DEA became suspicious of the aircraft or its owner, it could place his Dallas connections in danger; connections Christo himself had created and nurtured during the several years of their association. His decision not to share this Dallas connection with the Mexicans was proving a wise move. Better they were kept in the dark. It was an assurance he gave his Dallas friends. It was a promise he kept. Like his Chicago partners, Christo valued discretion. He sat at his computer, and in the cipher he had developed to insure secrecy, sent an email to Matamoros.

Greetings Diego,

I will arrive on the seventh of next month. I look forward to being with you and your family. Bette is also looking forward to the visit. We have reservations at the Del Rio and trust you have secured our box for the bullfights. Until then, my friend, may God hold you in His hand.

Christo

The drugs would be shipped on the seventh of the following month. Christo intended to make sure the product reached its customers.

9

Lesley swallowed the last gulp of tepid coffee, trying to find reassurance from the sugary liquid coursing down her throat. Since her early teens coffee had made mornings more bearable. She was on her third cup and reminded herself to drop an extra dollar or two into the coffee kitty. Bart Henderson's perks for the newsroom stopped at the water cooler. He steadfastly declined to pick up the monthly coffee service tab for a newsroom filled with what he derided as coffee-energized zealots.

Mac Withers looked up as Lesley knocked. With a quick flick of his hand he waved her to a seat. He had noted when she slipped into her newsroom office an hour before and absently wondered what had brought her to work early. A sanguine smile creased his mouth. He figured he was about to find out.

"Got a minute, Mac?"

"Sure, what's up?"

"Can I shut the door?"

"Go ahead. You'll make everybody's day, speculating about what we're discussing behind closed doors."

Lesley eased the heavy door shut and sat down in a chair facing Withers' desk. He watched patiently as she gripped her hands together in her lap and noted the obvious distress on her face. Something was wrong, but he hesitated to press her. He sat back in his chair and waited for her to begin. When her attention still seemed focused on her clenched hands, he prompted, "What brings you to work so early?"

She finally looked up. "Mac, when I was in Brownsville, something happened. I should have told you about it, but I wasn't sure what to make of it." She hesitated, her attention diverted to perusing several items on Withers' desk and avoiding his face. "I hoped I could follow up on it myself."

Then the words tumbled out—some after prolonged hesitations—about the note in the pew by her purse blaming Manny Zammorra's murder on Mexican assassins; of the urging to check oil well records; of the powerful Dallas connections; of the interrupted meeting with the man in the park; of possibly being followed last night. She made no mention of going to Grant's apartment or the message on his answering machine.

When her narrative appeared finished Withers leaned forward and said, "He hasn't contacted you since you got back?"

"No."

"And you're sure no one followed you this morning?"

"I'm pretty sure," she said.

"Maybe we should call the police," suggested Withers. "This seems to be something they need to look into. This guy could be dangerous."

"No, Mac." There was an edge of panic in her voice. "I don't want the police involved. At least not yet. I think the guy is trying to give me information about a story. If we involve the police he may be frightened away."

What she said made sense. Withers leaned back in his chair again and clasped his hands behind his head, looking at Lesley thoughtfully. It was uncharacteristic of her to hold anything back involving a story. He had a nagging sense there was still something she wasn't sharing with him. "Maybe the best course is to wait and see if he contacts you again. We sure don't have much to go on if he doesn't." Withers added, "If he does, I want to know right away."

Lesley had turned away and was silently staring out the window to the side of his desk. His face softened. "I think this has scared you a bit. That's good. Next time you'll let me know sooner."

"You're right, Mac. I am a little spooked."

"Keep your cell phone handy. If this guy contacts you outside the station, call me at home. Have you got my number?"

She nodded. Withers rested his chin on clasped hand and looked intently at Lesley. "Les, I mean that. Don't take a chance. Call me immediately. I don't want you hurt." He grinned, easing the tension. "Even a Peabody's not worth that."

When she finally turned back to face him it was with a slight smile. "Not to worry. I'm a very obedient girl," she replied. "At least sometimes."

Lesley rose to leave but turned back to Withers before opening the door. "I just hope he contacts me again. My curiosity is killing me," she said, trying to infuse lightness into her tone.

Watching her walk across the newsroom to her small cubicle Withers made a mental note to contact the night security guard to check for cars parked outside the station. Lesley was scheduled to fill-in for a vacationing anchor on the late newscast next week.

The car was parked near the station that night and the next three nights. The driver had maneuvered the vehicle to sit at an angle from the entrance to the station parking lot, where his car was partially occluded by a large tree across the narrow street. The leafy canopy of the tree's wide branches enfolded the car in protective shadow. The driver watched warily each evening as the guard dutifully patrolled the perimeter of the station property, but seemed to take no notice of the vehicle parked only a block away.

Each night the man had followed the aging Mustang. It was an easy target to keep in sight in the diminished late evening traffic. Each night he followed her, she drove directly to her apartment, deviating only briefly the first night when she pulled into a convenience store just off the expressway. He noted she pumped the gas herself. And from his vantage point a half block away he monitored the front lights of her upstairs apartment. They were usually off by midnight. She had not returned to the mayor's apartment. Why? That puzzled him. Had it been just a one night stand? This piqued his curiosity. Quickie sex with a beautiful news anchor? That would probably be par for Stewart. Just the style of a handsome, well-to-do man who wielded the kind of power Stewart had by virtue of his personal wealth and elected position.

On the fourth night the man left his car parked a block away and hugging the concealing shadows of the tree-lined sidewalk, he approached Lesley's apartment building. The ornate, glass and steel front door opened into a narrow hallway. The right side was lined with mailboxes. Above each mailbox was an intercom button and speaker, which allowed visitors to reach tenants and for tenants to buzz visitors through another door leading to a small elevator.

The sound of the buzzer startled Lesley. She placed the herbal tea she had just brewed down on the coffee table and stepped over to the intercom after glancing at the clock on the fireplace mantle. It was 11:30. Who could be trying to see her at this hour? Grant never came to her apartment. They always met at his condo.

She pushed down the intercom button with rising trepidation. "Yes?"

"I'm sorry to come by so late, but I need to talk with you. May I come up?"

She recognized the voice immediately—the man from the park in Brownsville. But she still asked, "Who is this?"

"We met before. In Brownsville. Our meeting got cut short. If you want the story we need to talk." His voice was calm. "You're gonna have to trust me. I mean you no harm. Look, I can't stay here in the lobby any longer. Can I come up or not?"

Lesley felt an immediate spike of panic. He was a stranger. She could barely remember his face. Her common sense battled with her curiosity. This man was the key if she wanted to pursue the story. "Yes," she heard herself reply almost as if it was an out-of-body being pushing down on the button to unlock the entrance door. "When you come through the door take the elevator to the fourth floor. Apartment 410."

"Thank you."

Shaking, Lesley reached for the cordless telephone on the glass-topped coffee table. She had programmed Mac's home number into the phone. He answered on the second ring.

"Hello?" The voice was husky with sleep.

"Mac, its Lesley. He's here. The man who contacted me in Brownsville. He's coming up right now. Can you come over?"

"I'll be there in 15 minutes. Don't let him in until I get there."

Lesley told Mac she had to hear the man out. Anyway, he was already on his way up.

"Don't be a fool, Lesley," Mac shouted, his voice ringing verbal alarm bells. "Don't let that guy in."

Too late. She gave Mac her apartment number and pleaded with him to hurry before hanging up. By the time she grabbed her handgun from a desk in the bedroom the doorbell was chiming. She slipped the weapon into a purse next to the couch and rushed to the door.

The man was taller than she remembered, and older. The expression on his weathered face was bland, his deep-set hazel eyes unrevealing. Strangely, she did not sense danger.

"I'm Lesley Rowan," she said, extending her hand as he stepped inside the apartment. "We didn't have much opportunity to get acquainted at our last meeting."

"No, ma'am, I'm afraid we didn't." He glanced around the room with a practiced eye as he grasped her proffered hand. "Before I give you my name, I've got to know you're not going to talk to anyone about this meeting. You can't tell anyone who I am. Do I have your word on that—as a journalist?"

"You have my word." She hesitated. "But I must tell you. I just called my news director while you were coming up from downstairs.

He insisted on coming over." She paused, waiting for his reaction. His face was inscrutable.

"Can he be trusted?"

"Yes. I've already told him about the note, about going to the park in Brownsville, and about what happened." Flustered by his piercing scrutiny, she lowered her eyes. A wave of doubt washed over her. She should have followed Mac's advice and not let this man in. How foolish. Instinctively, she glanced at the clock. Mac would be here shortly.

The man perceived her sudden apprehension. At the same time, he felt his own rising. It would be foolish to be seen by a second person. This meeting was risky enough. "Shit," he muttered.

Lesley flinched at the softly spoken expletive, almost as if he had hit her. The man searched her face. "I have to believe it was your news director, and not the police, you called. It wasn't the police, was it?" he demanded harshly.

"No," she replied, looking directly at him. She was telling the truth. Of that he was suddenly certain. He had been trained to spot liars, something he could do intuitively after all these years. She was clearly afraid, but no liar.

"I took a big chance coming here."

"Why did you?"

A slight smile creased his thin lips at the direct question, deepening the crevices in his cheeks stretched taut over high bones. His was a strong face, with the look of a man who spent a good deal of time outdoors.

"As I told you in Brownsville, I'm a pilot for an oil company. Most of my runs involve taking equipment and supplies down to Mexico."

"Won't you please sit down." Lesley pointed him to a chair across from the couch.

"Thank you, ma'am." Even seated, he appeared tense, like a coiled wire ready to spring.

Lesley sat down across from him and reached for a legal pad and pen she kept near the telephone on the end table by her chair.

She had seen the purse as she reached for the pad and drew a sense of comfort from its close proximity.

"Who do you work for again?" She was direct. He liked that.

"I work for Althea Oil & Gas. It's a small outfit. They drill mostly in Texas and Mexico. I always fly to an airfield between Matamoros and Reynosa."

He glanced nervously at his watch. "Look, I don't have much time. Have you checked out the oil fields in Tyler I told you about?" She shook her head. "You need to see how much oil they're reporting on their books. See how many of their wells are actually pumping oil. It will probably tell you a lot."

"Do you know who owns Althea? I could find almost nothing about the company on the internet. I was waiting to talk with you before pursuing it further."

"I don't know about that. I got the job through an ad in the Dallas newspaper. I'm an ex-con, so I was just glad to get back in the saddle. A few weeks ago I recognized a guy I used to work with a long time ago on one of the runs to Mexico. That was the first time they loaded drugs. He remembered me, too. He thinks I'm still working for the government. Turns out he's a DEA plant. We've talked a couple of times since, while the stuff was being loaded. He told me the cartel he's working for is hooked up with another bunch headed by a guy named Christo. No first name. Thinks this Christo is in Colombia. At least that's where the cocaine is grown and processed. From what he said, Christo ships the stuff overland into Mexico. He thought the fentanyl was also produced in Colombia. They only started flying the drugs into Texas after those stories started coming out in the Brownsville paper."

"Is that why Manny Zammorra was murdered?"

"The Brownsville paper named names and got too close to things. The Mexicans always send a strong message when they're displeased. They don't like a lot of light being shined on their enterprises. That's probably why they took out the editor."

"How do you know its drugs you're bringing back to the States?"

He laughed with a smoker's wheeze at the question. "You can tell by the weight and the smell. Trust me. It's drugs. There's always an Althea truck, kinda like a big dump truck, waiting when I land. It's been there every time the last four weeks. I land at an airstrip in Smith County, just south of Tyler off FM 60—that's a farm-to-market road in case you didn't know."

She did know about the farm-to-market roads which cut through much of the rural area of Texas but said nothing.

"It's in a big field of old oil rigs. Where the stuff goes from there, I don't know. I suspect to a distribution warehouse somewhere. Probably Tyler or Dallas. After we unload the cargo in Tyler we take the plane to an airstrip on a ranch outside Weatherford. We unloaded a shipment there two weeks ago. First time. Nothing there since. But they've put me on stand-by to fly down to Mexico sometime next week. Didn't say exactly when. I didn't ask." And he added in a sardonic tone, "They pay in cash, and it more than covers the bills."

He saw the question forming on her lips. "They also pay me for my discretion. If those Mexicans ever find out I'm talking to anyone, I'm history." He pulled a pack of cigarettes from his shirt pocket. "Mind if I smoke?"

"No, of course not." Lesley did object but sat silent while he lit a filtered Marlboro. She pulled a crystal ashtray from a drawer in the end table—one her mother had used the only time she had visited—and handed it to the man.

"So why are you risking talking to me? You don't even know me."

He looked at her reflectively for a moment. "That used to be one of my jobs a long time ago, planting stuff with the media. I called that editor that got killed in Brownsville. He said he didn't have the manpower to send anybody from his office. So he recommended I call you."

"Manny recommended me?" Lesley was incredulous.

"Yeah. He said you were a *digger.*"

"Dear Manny," she whispered before looking across at the pilot.

"You appear to be very concerned about the Dallas connection. Do you know who that might be?"

He shook his head. "Not for sure. When I read about a powerful Dallas connection, I kinda thought I might know who it is." He drew deeply on the cigarette and smoke wafted out of his nostrils and mouth. "The DEA guy got a peek at one of the Mexican's phone when he left it on a crate. It had texts to someone in Dallas. Said they were coded messages. All he could decipher from the two he read was whoever received the texts was in the oil business. And—there was a high up political connection."

"Did he provide you a name or phone number?"

The craggy face relaxed in a smile. "No, ma'am," he said with an exaggerated drawl, as he took another pull on the cigarette. "I know someone who might be attached to a high up political connection in Dallas. Hope I'm wrong. But that's why I left you that note when I saw you at the editor's funeral." He took another long pull on the cigarette. "It's somebody I've got to protect. The only sure way to do that is to get someone to check and see who that political guy is."

"Who are you protecting?"

His eyes pierced the distance between them. "My daughter."

"How might she be involved in all this?"

"She isn't. That's not important anyway," he added dismissively. "But some folks she has to associate with are important."

"And those *folks*—who are they?"

"Can't say. It's my gut talking to me. Like I said, I'm hoping you can check it out. The political connection I have in mind is in city hall."

Lesley looked up sharply. *City hall.* Her throat seemed to close up as panic swelled in her chest, sending her heart racing. "You suspect there's a connection with Althea by someone high up in city government?"

"Yeah. I suspect the name you find on Althea's records might just match a high up person in city hall. Maybe someone connected to that official." He continued, "This guy in Mexico—the DEA mole—said he thinks Althea is doctoring production records to show more oil than their wells are pumping. Probably laundering drug proceeds through those Tyler oil fields. Maybe the oil field outside Midland too." He took another draw on the cigarette before crushing the remainder in the ashtray. "The name you need should be on those records."

"If he *is* a DEA plant as you suspect, why did he trust you by telling you all this information?"

"He and I—we're both ex-Army. Special Ops. I guess he felt a connection. He may have been trying to warn me to stay clear. Who knows?" Smoke billowed from his nostrils. "Last time we talked—a coupla weeks ago—he was kinda fidgety. Said he's scared his cover might've been blown. Doesn't know for sure, but he's asked to be pulled out. If they do yank him, he's afraid the investigation might get deep sixed—that means dropped, ma'am."

Lesley smiled and tilted her head to acknowledge she knew the meaning. Then he added grimly, "Whichever way that wind blows, I just hope they get him out in time."

The door buzzer blared, startling them both. The man turned abruptly toward the front door. "Where's the stairway out of this place?"

"At the end of the hall, but…"

"Which door?" he demanded, rushing toward the front door of the apartment.

"Door on the left. It's marked."

The door buzzer sounded again. Lesley pushed the intercom button. "Is that you, Mac?"

"Yeah. You okay?"

"I'm fine. Take the elevator to the fourth floor. I'll have the door open," she said, holding her finger on the buzzer long enough to allow Mac to enter the downstairs door.

She looked over at the pilot who was standing in the breach of the doorway. "Wait! How can I contact you?"

He turned toward her, his lean face shadowed by the hall light. "You can't. I'll contact you. Good hunting." He narrowed his eyes and stared at her without blinking. "And for godsakes, don't say anything about this to your boyfriend or you'll sure as hell regret it." His tone was harsh; his warning ominous.

How did he know about Grant? She suppressed the fear that rose like bile in her throat and asked, "You didn't tell me who your daughter is."

"I don't want to involve her. She doesn't know about any of this."

"Then how is she linked to all this?"

"If I told you, you wouldn't believe me."

$$11$$

Lesley's stomach lurched. Her hands shook. There it was again—fear. It danced on her skin like tiny needles. The man loped swiftly down the dimly lit hallway and disappeared behind the door opening to the back stairs, just as the elevator light dinged softly, announcing its arrival.

"Over her, Mac." Lesley waved him inside.

"Hey, girl. You okay?" She looked pale and shaken. He glanced around the room instantly.

"He's gone, Mac," Lesley said, answering his unspoken question. "He didn't want to wait until you arrived. He seemed really wary of anyone else knowing about this."

"You look scared, Les. Did he threaten you?" Mac searched the face of the young woman before him.

"Not with life or limb," she admitted with a self-deprecating smile, aware of his scrutiny. "Please, come and sit down, Mac," she said, motioning him to the same chair where the pilot had been sitting just moments before. Lesley sat down stiffly on the loveseat across from the stocky editor.

"What did he tell you?" Mac's voice forced her thoughts back to the mysterious man who had exited her apartment so abruptly.

"He pinpointed where the drugs are being flown into Texas. To an airstrip in Smith County near Tyler mostly. He said it was an old airstrip in the midst of an oil field." Lesley checked her hastily scribbled notes. "It's just off FM 60."

"How does he know that?"

"He pilots a plane for Althea Oil & Gas that is flying the drugs in from Mexico. He said he's on stand-by to fly down to Mexico and back next week."

Mac remained silent, mentally absorbing what Lesley just said. *Jackpot! They now had a direct source—even a possible where and when.*

"Did he say if this Althea outfit is involved directly, or just being used?"

"He didn't say."

"Did you ask?"

Lesley hesitated before finally answering, "No." A flush of embarrassment heated her face. "He wouldn't give much information. He did suggest we check Althea production records for wells in those fields near Tyler. Said it may give us the Dallas connection." She ran her finger down her scribbled notes. "He also said he met a man in Mexico he's sure is a DEA agent. He described him as a mole. Or plant. Said the DEA agent saw some papers with those oil fields on them and thinks they might be laundering drug money through Althea."

Withers absently scratched the stubble of beard sprouting on his right cheek. "Did he say why he picked you to contact?"

Lesley lowered her head and turned away from Mac. "After the stories appeared in the *Daily Leader*, he called Manny Zammorra. Manny said he didn't have the manpower to check out the Dallas angle. It was Manny who suggested me," she added with a trace of sadness.

Withers stood up. Sighing heavily, he walked across to where Lesley sat, touched her shoulder lightly, and sat down next to her.

"Jesus. I'm sorry, Les. I know how much you thought of Zammorra."

"Mac, I asked the pilot why he was doing this," Lesley said, turning to Withers. "He said he was protecting his daughter. He wouldn't tell me her name. He wouldn't even tell me *his* name. He did mention he was an ex-con, but nothing more about himself."

"What did he say about the Dallas connection?"

"Only that if he told us we wouldn't believe him."

Mac looked at Lesley sharply. "Does he know who it is? Does he have any proof? Or is he just trying to send us on a wild goose chase?"

"I don't know, Mac. He seemed sincere. He also seemed a little nervous and apprehensive. When I told him you were on the way, he got really skittish. Said he would contact me later and bolted."

She did not add the man's admonition not to tell her "boyfriend." That he might know about her affair with Grant Stewart was unsettling. Particularly so, as she was now certain it was his voice she heard on Grant's answering machine a week ago. And Grant had said he recognized the voice. *Maybe Grant was mistaken,* she thought absently.

"Well, girl, we don't have much to go on," Mac said, his voice more mollified as he stood to leave.

"I'm sorry, Mac. I didn't prove much of a Woodard or Bernstein with this Deep Throat." She smiled apologetically and added, "I promise I'll do better next time."

If there is a next time, Lesley thought morosely as she stared at her hands, clenched tightly together in her lap. What a disappointment this must be to the veteran journalist standing in front of her. She had a rare opportunity—a potentially huge story dropped in her lap—yet she accomplished so little in her brief meeting with the source who sought her out. She felt a great sense of defeat knowing it was Manny who had recommended the pilot contact her. Why had the man gone to such lengths to impart his suspicions about a Dallas link to a Mexican drug operation, only to give her such sparse details? She felt certain he knew more than he was telling her.

Withers felt something akin to sympathy as he watched the tangle of emotions play out on Lesley's face. The same traitorous feeling he had earlier today crept into his thoughts. Lesley was holding something back. She seemed too taut—wound too tightly.

With a pragmatic pursing of his lips, he decided not to push her right now.

She was his most instinctive reporter, Withers acknowledged silently as he studied her strained face. Her reportorial talents became evident in Lesley's early days at the station. He recalled sending a young nurse practitioner to Lesley's office after she had complained no one in the city's health department would take her concerns seriously. She had information, she said, about a noxious discharge into a drainage ditch at the back of a small plant in South Dallas.

The ditch ran alongside ramshackle homes near the plant, in one of the poorest barrios in Dallas. Harried physicians, who treated neighborhood children and their parents at an overcrowded public health clinic near the plant, were too overwhelmed by sheer numbers of patients to notice the coincidence. It was the nurse practitioner who first questioned why children living in homes bordering the ditch had similar burn-like abscesses on their skin and hacking coughs. The nurse said her appeals for help to investigate her suspicions about the source of the children's symptoms were met with patronizing disinterest by city health officials. They appeared unconcerned about the suspected lead and acid contamination spilling into the ditch from the battery recycling plant. The nurse practitioner found her first sympathetic listener in Lesley Rowan.

The station paid for a private laboratory to test the discharge taken from the ditch. The tests confirmed the nurse practitioner's worst suspicions. Lead levels were dangerously high. And lead was only one of several toxins discovered in the samples.

Calls by Lesley to the plant were not returned. An attempt the next day to interview plant officials on site was spurned by a man who identified himself only as the plant manager. Amid a vociferous hail of obscenities, he ordered two security guards to escort the KDLL crew off plant grounds, an order they carried out with unnecessary roughness, injuring the audio man.

Withers remembered Lesley tenaciously tracing ownership of

the offending plant to a holding company in New Jersey, primarily involved in garbage collection and disposal. Waste Reclamation, Inc. operated under a variety of names in several northeastern states, where it held licenses to run landfills and waste incinerators. It was a name familiar to staff lawyers in the offices of attorney generals in the states where it operated. She learned the New Jersey firm and its various offshoots faced a growing mountain of legal actions for waste disposal violations. Staff attorneys in the affected states, with whom Lesley spoke, confirmed they were investigating possible links between Waste Reclamation, Inc. and organized crime.

When confronted with the facts uncovered in the Channel 15 report, Mayor Grant Stewart acted swiftly, pledging the full resources of the city to halt the pollution and force the company to clean up the contaminated areas around the plant. An emergency injunction halted the toxic discharge and the plant closed abruptly. Within weeks the abandoned plant and the ditch were fenced off by city hazmat crews as a temporary measure and the entire site placed on the Texas Superfund list. A legal battle was launched to force Waste Reclamation, Inc. to pay for the clean-up. It was a battle still deadlocked in the courts. But it did garner Lesley and KDLL a top award from the Texas State Press Association.

Lesley interrupted Withers' reverie when she finally lifted her head and looked up at him. Withers sensed her discomfort. She had been frightened, he conceded, but still had met the man on her terms. She had spunk. More than that, she had strong instincts. The Waste Reclamation story had proven that.

Mac pushed his fists into the pockets of his trousers. "We don't have much to go on, Les. Let me think about how to approach this. We'll talk when you come in tomorrow, okay?"

"Sure. Thanks for coming so quickly, Mac."

Sleep eluded Lesley until just before dawn. She fell into a restless slumber that pulverized her psyche with dark dreams of malevolent, unseen forces, trapping her in a dark place where no one could hear her calls for help. She awoke shaking, more tired than before her brief sleep. A protracted, steaming shower and three cups of black coffee later, she felt ready to head to the station. Dressing quickly, she was on the bypass heading for work shortly before nine, grateful the headache she had awakened with was finally fading, and morning traffic was thinning.

As she walked into her small office she spotted a note on her computer. *See me immediately. I have a proposal. Mac.*

She glanced toward his office. He was behind his desk, the office empty, a rarity at this time of day. The door was open.

"Good morning," Mac said as he looked up from the stack of mail he was sorting through. His penetrating look missed nothing. "You look beat." He stretched back in his leather chair, and as was his habit, clamped his arms behind his head while Lesley sat down in one of the chairs in front of his desk. "I've warned you about keeping late hours with strange men."

"Mac, I blew it. I'm sorry." The words flew out, the same words she scourged herself with during the sleepless hours of the night. "I've been over and over the meeting, thinking of all the things I should have asked and didn't."

"You didn't blow anything, Les," Withers responded gruffly, sitting upright and clasping his hands in front of him on the desk. "Quit kicking yourself. You got us a big chunk to sink our investigative teeth into. That stuff about looking at oil production records for those fields.... Where were those fields again?"

"Near Tyler. He also mentioned near Midland."

"Yeah, Tyler is closer. Midland not so much. Anyway, you don't have time. And you don't have the knowledge to comb through legal records."

Before he could draw breath to continue, Lesley said, "If you're pulling me from the story, I understand. I don't blame you. I—"

"Les." Mac sat up straight in his chair. The frown on his face eased slightly, thinning the deep furrows in his brow. "I'm not pulling you off the story. I want you working on it full time, with every minute you can put into it between newscasts. And I've got someone who can help with the research. You won't like him, Les. But if there's a guy who can find whatever it is we're looking for in those records, he's the guy. And he knows the oil business."

12

Mac was right. Lesley did not like Witt Terrell when they met two days later in the news director's office. A ruddy, pitted nose looked almost elephantine in the center of his emaciated face. His eyelids partially covered bloodshot eyes, and the pinched red in his cavernous cheeks was a dead giveaway. This man was never far from booze.

Although slightly rumpled, his clothes were clean and he did not smell of liquor. That was the only thing she could find even slightly favorable about the man she had been assigned to work with for the next few weeks. "A former cop turned journalist" was how Withers described Terrell. A long-time acquaintance. How long? Withers didn't say. Nor did he mention where Terrell was currently employed, if at all. She didn't ask.

"It's nice to meet you, Mr. Terrell," she said, extending her hand with all the graciousness she could muster.

Mac suggested they talk in the small room adjacent to his office where they would be screened from the rest of the newsroom.

Terrell listened without comment as she recited what she knew, while he scribbled occasional notes in a small, worn spiral notebook. It looked as old and rumpled as the man writing on its pages.

She felt certain Withers had briefed Terrell on the story already. When Lesley finished, she waited for questions. There were none.

Instead Terrell seemed engrossed in the brief notes he had been scribbling, flipping the pages of the tattered notebook and scanning them again. Lesley sat quietly, feeling mildly uncomfortable.

"Mr. Terrell, what is checking production records of Althea's wells going to tell us?" she asked, hoping to refocus his attention.

He looked up from his notes, his watery, reddened eyes still partially hooded. "It should tell us how much oil those wells are producing." Hesitating, he thumbed through the rumpled notebook before continuing. "Then we'll check a few of those wells ourselves to see if they really are pulling anything up. That should tell us if Althea's plumping up its production records to launder the drug money through the books of its oil operations." He leafed through another page of notes. "And it'll give us a start on tracing who owns Althea—like the name of its board—when it was incorporated. And maybe give us some leads so we can start peeling back the layers of shell companies." Terrell looked over at Lesley. "My guess—if these folks are doing what we think they're doing, it might take a road atlas to follow." A reedy chuckle sounded from deep in his throat.

"Maybe even a GPS guide," she countered. Her attempt at levity was greeted with a blank stare. Did this man not know what GPS was? His expression indicated he did not. GPS aside, Lesley suddenly felt a grudging respect for the soft-spoken man sitting across from her. She had not told him that was the same conclusion drawn by the man in her apartment three nights ago. "I must admit I'm naive, Mr. Terrell. I thought drug money was always laundered through banks offshore."

"That's the usual way. Could be where the money from this operation is ending up." Terrell looked down at his notes again. "A lot of those Tyler fields have been bone-dry for years. If Althea's still reporting production on wells that aren't producing a drop, that will pretty much cinch it," he emphasized. "We'll see."

"When do you plan to go to Tyler?"

"Not right away. I'm going to nose around in Austin first. See if

I can find out who Althea Oil & Gas is and a little about its corporate structure. There's no listing for the company in the Dallas area. If it exists, that's where the records will be. Depending on what I find, then I'll head to Tyler."

"How will we keep in touch?"

"Mac's giving me a cell phone and a credit card. I'll call Mac direct. Keep you posted through him."

Lesley looked puzzled. "Mac has a direct line. Harder to trace," he explained. "Calling him will keep anyone from tying the two of us together."

And calling Mac direct will retain Terrell's anonymity with the rest of the staff, she thought, *but it will be a little impractical having to relate everything through Mac. What if Mac is out-of-pocket? Not likely,* she quickly concluded.

Mac seemed to have no life beyond the station. Still, if they were going to work together, there should be some method for direct contact. She would press that point later.

"How soon do you think you'll know something?" She left unsaid her concern about what she would tell the pilot if he contacted her, to assure him they were acting on the information he had provided.

"Don't know, ma'am." Terrell picked up his pen. "Tell me about the pilot who contacted you. You know, what he looked like, what he said about himself. Anything you can."

He listened attentively, at times scribbling furiously, showing no visible disappointment at how little she could tell him. No name, no place to contact the informant, only a promise he would contact her again. Even her physical description of the man seemed limited. "I'm afraid this isn't much for you to go on," she concluded.

"He didn't give you much to go on, ma'am. We'll just have to do the best we can with what we've got." For the first time, a slight smile lighted his stark face. Tucking his notepad inside his worn khaki jacket Terrell rose to leave, nodding a silent goodbye before crossing back into Withers' office. Despite his somewhat rumpled, bizarre appearance, Terrell slipped out of the newsroom a short time later, unnoticed by staffers hunched over computer keyboards or talking on the telephone. Even the small group gathered around the coffee service table failed to observe the disheveled man slipping out the door leading to the rear parking lot.

Lesley's email and telephone message lights were on, reminding her how long she had been away from her desk. As she opened her email, Terrell fixated in her mind. He was an alcoholic. Of that she was certain. Maybe a recovering one, but an alcoholic none-the-less. Just the look of the man defined a hardcore alcoholic, the type she would expect to find in a flophouse or sheltered at a downtown mission. Yet, she admitted, again grudgingly, he evoked a sense of confidence in his ability. His questions were pointed—his attitude without reproach, despite her dearth of information and detail.

Among the several emails was one from Grant. *I'm home this evening. The champagne will be on ice.* Her heart leaped at the words. He was back, after a week away, attending the U. S. Conference of Mayors meeting in Washington. The frequency of his interviews by C-SPAN and the other news networks covering the annual gathering, tagged him as a rising star within that prestigious political group.

Several snippets of the national interviews had been played on the evening newscasts. Some of the interview snippets were even inserted by the late news producer near the top of the newscast. It was a welcome departure from the usual overload of murders, robberies, and crash fatalities on which late news viewers seemed to thrive—if the ratings books were to be believed. It was a rarity for anything political to compete with Dallas's nightly quotient of criminal mayhem. Viewers seldom went to bed disappointed by the content of KDLL's 10 o'clock news.

During the six o'clock news, she watched a minute-long interview with Grantham Stewart on the monitor to the left of one camera, feeling secret pride. He radiated the wealth he was born to and the part for which he had been educationally nurtured at the University of Texas and Harvard—a handsome, poised, knowledgeable attorney-turned-politician. Thanks to gavel-to-gavel coverage by C-SPAN, Grant was gaining national attention.

Their week apart had been a period of reflection and revelation for Lesley. An emptiness pervaded her days. Grant's face, his voice, his absence invaded her dreams. His declaration of love threatened the emotional barrier she had constructed. Because of the absence of her father throughout her life and her cavalier treatment by Bobby Morris, she had built a comfortable barrier meant to hold off involvement, commitment, even love. As an only child, raised in a single-parent household, she had been denied the opportunity to achieve the comfort level with men accorded girls raised in two-parent households or with brothers. Without a father-daughter, brother-sister relationship to draw upon, she admitted, in her more candid moments the past few days, she distrusted men—even feared them. Above all, she feared revealing herself to anyone. Her privacy was her sanctuary, her protection. Yet she knew Grant would expect an answer tonight.

†††

Grant met her at the door with a proffered glass of her favorite wine.

She tilted the glass to him before taking a sip of the chilled vintage. "Hi."

"Hi, yourself." He took the wine glass from her hand and placed it on a foyer table, then lifted her into his arms, kissing her as he turned and swiftly kicked the door shut. The length and intensity of the kiss left her breathless as he placed her back on her feet.

"What a nice welcome," she whispered.

Lesley did not leave until the first pale-pink hues of the new day filtered through the sheer drapes of the bedroom windows, invading the darkness that cloaked their lovemaking. He did not reiterate his proposal of marriage. She left more troubled by that than by the answer she had not given him.

13

"*Stupido!*" Christo crashed the telephone receiver down savagely, giving vent to his fury while he cursed the caller under his breath. The pilot could be dealt with. It was the timetable that must not be interrupted.

Christo walked to the large window behind his desk, a scowl lingering on his face, his thick hands clasped firmly behind his back. He stood looking out at a wide panorama of towering mountains, their highest points still veiled by tropical mists. Higher clouds, journeying languidly across the early summer sky, cast large shadows over the sides of the mountains, providing the viewer with a kaleidoscope of ever-changing greens.

It was a scene that never failed to soothe his frustrations and compress his thinking to the pragmatic side of his nature; allowing reason, not emotion, to direct his thought process. Containing his volatile temper was something he learned from his late mentor. Observant as always, he had often watched as Alejandro Christo Jacoby dealt with problems that threatened the day-to-day efficiency of his wide ranging empire.

Nothing was lost on Christo's youthful eyes. Jacoby would listen without comment to most problems brought before him, extrapolating the solution often before the narrative of the difficulty, faced by one or the other of his managers, was completed. In a manner that demanded deference and obedience, Jacoby would quietly order a solution to be carried out. To not do so begged instant punishment for the men entrusted to run his businesses—both legitimate and illegitimate—with ruthless efficiency. Christo had learned well. His management style mirrored his mentor's.

The pilot must be silenced, but only after those sent to carry out that fatal sentence extracted the reasons for the pilot's activities, to determine if he was a government agent.

Christo quickly repressed a rising frustration at not having the answers before him now. Why had the Dallas faction been allowed to hire the pilot in the first place? They should have done a more thorough background check. Americans put such value in tracing the past involvements of prospective employees. It was an easy process in the climate of instant access to information accorded by the internet and the open society of the United States.

Frustration was empty anger. It served no purpose except to spawn more anger. His American partners could provide few answers. They knew the pilot had served in the army, joined the FBI, and spent time in prison on federal racketeering charges stemming from taking payoffs from a Mafia syndicate. On the surface, the pilot appeared to have a perfect background for the work he was now doing. Still—a mistake. In this case—a regrettable mistake. Christo could only hope it was correctible. Or the retribution would go well beyond the pilot.

He gave grudging credit to the Mexican cartel's operatives for spotting the pilot among the mourners at the editor's funeral. His brother, Eduardo, had acted appropriately, ordering the pilot be watched. No contacts with police were observed. But why the two contacts with the Dallas television anchor? These actions puzzled Christo. Could the pilot have been the informant who interested the Brownsville newspaper in the Mexican cartel's activities? The newspaper's investigation was troublesome, Christo observed thoughtfully, but any harm to the cartel had been quickly neutralized. What could the pilot be telling the Dallas woman? The

Althea plane had never been used for transporting drug shipments until recently. Did the pilot even know what his plane carried?

Christo reached around and drew a slim cigarillo from the wood humidor on his desk, lit it slowly, and drew deeply on its aromatic smoke. He had no intention of changing the timetable for the flights from Mexico to the States. The pilot would make a flight as scheduled, the day after tomorrow. Only the landing location would be changed. And only after they were in the air. Then they would learn why the pilot was so friendly with journalists.

There was a small, but worthy welcoming party on the tarmac to greet Christo as he descended the short steps from the rented jet. It consisted of Eliud Mendosa, Pietro Salador, and Vincente Estavar—the head of El Poder cartel. Mendosa and Salador were Estavar's cousins and top assistants. Christo expected this kind of reception, but was still flattered they were here. It spoke to his importance in their eyes. The handshakes were warm, the words cordial.

At his side, Bette looked stunning in a two-piece silk suit of soft coral that drew out the amber highlights in her shoulder-length hair. Her beauty was measured in the appreciative appraisals of the three men as each greeted her with effusive warmth.

Estavar raised Bette's hand to his lips, lightly kissing it as his eyes lingered on her face. *Christo has done well. She is a beauty, this daughter of Jacoby, my late partner.* Estavar remembered the gangly adolescent with the shy smile and flowing hair, who played the piano with such finesse. Although her playing lacked concert quality, it was joyful and spirited. He enjoyed the sprightly rush of her fingers along the ivory keyboards. He had paid as fulsome a tribute to her musical talent then as he now paid to her beauty.

The charcoal asphalt shimmered in the midday heat as the convoy of Mercedes sedans and large SUVs swept along the highway. It passed through the southern edge of Matamoras, to the countryside dotted with adobe shacks, each marked by a front door of once-colorful paint, most faded by the sun. Christo knew these were the homes of workers who tended the rows of citrus trees on Estavar's sprawling farm. Citrus exports helped provide the cover that camouflaged the flow of illicit drugs across the border, to an eager and ever growing customer base in the States.

"A good crop this season?" Christo inquired.

"Oh, yes. We sent all we could north this last harvest. Top price," beamed Estavar, warming to the topic of his large fruit-export operation and its success. "Citrus crops in Florida were damaged during by an early hurricane and a late freeze. So the Americans need more of our fine Mexican oranges."

A look of satisfaction flashed on Estavar's broad, brown face. He took Jacoby's suggestion years ago to purchase land and grow crops; a legal business to provide a natural cover for the export that transported him from poverty to enormous wealth and power. His growing wealth had also added weight and a social conscience to the pretty, nubile girl he'd married so many years ago. She harped constantly about the small dwellings housing his workers. In his angry retorts, Estavar reminded her of the nearby, shabby hovel in which he'd spent his formative years. His workers were well-paid and well-housed compared to the families of his youth.

His home was an extravagant contrast to those of his workers. It sat in a lush oasis of green lawns and trees, surrounded on all sides by citrus orchards pointing like hundreds of green fingers to the horizon. The two-story adobe mansion was designed by a Spaniard inspired by the Moorish influence in his own country. The four-sided, salmon exterior of the adobe was accented by a thickly tiled roof and by the second-story balconies that circled around the upper interior of the hacienda. From the balconies, guests could look down into a garden courtyard with a colorfully tiled fountain that never failed to elicit profuse compliments.

To Christo, it was a fairy tale scene. It charged his imagination to draw upon the stories of colorfully robed Moors on spirited, Arabian stallions, like those his mother described in the bedtime stories she told to coax her brood to sleep. Those stories were the extent of his cultural enrichment as a youngster. Seeing the lush garden and the magnificent fountain, with its flowing streams of water dancing over the colorfully tiled pathways, never failed to remind him of his mother and her stories—the single pleasing memory of a sad childhood from which he had escaped so many years before.

†††

Christo awoke early the next morning. Refreshed by a cold shower, he lightly brushed Bette's forehead with his lips as she slept serenely. He descended the wide stairway to the cool front of the home where the three leaders of the El Poder cartel awaited him behind the arched wooden doors of the library. He was warmly welcomed into the company of Estavar and his two lieutenants and offered a Cuban cigar and a glass of Spanish brandy. Christo swirled the burnished-colored liquor in the round glass and inhaled the smooth warm aroma. An excellent choice.

After Christo prepared his cigar, Mendosa lit it with a long match. Christo pulled the sweet smoke contentedly past the brandy's path and into his lungs before sitting down across from the Mexican trio.

In his more reflective moments, Christo admitted admiration for the kinship displayed by Estavar toward Mendosa and Salador. Christo sought no such relationship with his own henchmen, even his four brothers now employed in his operation. He held himself apart from all top associates. Always his dealings with them were at arm's length, in the context of an employer with employees. He was mistrustful and wary by nature, elements of his personality honed on the hard streets where he spent his early youth. Even his siblings could not get close to this solitary man, who wielded power in the same impersonal, methodical manner of his mentor.

"Always maintain the wide view, the long look," Jacoby instructed him. "You see more that way. Your view is never obstructed by emotions."

Remaining removed from interpersonal relationships with those who carried out the day-to-day operations of his drug empire allowed Christo that unobstructed view, and the unfettered ability to take whatever measures necessary to protect the empire his mentor bequeathed him as the favored son-in-law. Only Bette was allowed to view his soul and share the machinations of his keen mind.

She was her father's daughter, in every respect his equal. Only gender prevented her from inheriting the mantel of leadership Jacoby wrapped around the strong shoulders of her husband. With Christo, she was a discreet partner, the shadow leader, the only trusted confident. Jacoby had seen the sexual attraction and mental synergy between the two young people. He skillfully encouraged it to the final embrace of marriage. Into Christo's strong hands Jacoby entrusted the business he spent a lifetime building—the partnerships he fused in Mexico, the United States, Italy, and the Middle East—and the only person he had ever truly loved, his oldest daughter. As he lay dying of the cancer invading his bones and brain, he never doubted his choices.

Christo eased back in his chair to listen to the three men, the unwelcome nature of their discussion abated somewhat by the congeniality of the brandy and cigar. He was a good listener. It was another lesson learned from his mentor.

After listening for a time without comment, Christo finally spoke. "The plane will land on an airfield near another oil field owned by our partner in Dallas," he instructed. "It is remote. There is no danger of being observed." He looked around at the three men. Their expressions were impassive. There was no disagreement with his plan.

"I would like two of your top men on board. They will help unload the shipment onto an Althea truck. It will be driven to the same warehouse in Dallas. Arrange for another pilot to take the plane on to the original destination. The pilot is to be dealt with. I want to know why he's been contacting that television woman in Brownsville and then in Dallas. We need to know what he's been telling her. When we know, dispose of him. Make sure the body is found and the murder made to look like a street killing. The journalist may then realize we are aware of her meetings with the pilot and it might frighten her away. Your men will return on commercial flights to Matamoras, one at a time. Are their passports in order?"

The three men nodded assent. Christo's incisive instructions had been greeted with nods of silent approbation. Estavar then voiced the concern that hung in the air between the Colombian and Mexican partners, "What do you think is going on, my friend?" he asked mildly.

Christo took a long pull of the mellow cigar. As the expelled smoke evaporated above his head, he looked pointedly at Estavar. "I don't know. But I fear our American partners have made us vulnerable. It is a feeling I don't like. I assume you feel the same."

The malevolence in Christo's tone was not lost on Estavar, who nodded agreement. He knew Christo to be a man who suffered no disloyalty, no weakness. To do so invited unhesitating retribution. It was the same indissoluble seal that had held Jacoby's empire—now Christo's—together.

14

A hard fist slammed his stomach. The force of the blow roused him from the brief darkness that had descended on him just moments before. Why would they not let him slide quietly into the peaceful darkness? It beckoned him with a fleeting promise of remission from the wracking pain. The bullets that shattered his knee caps had sent agony screaming up his thighs. The two gunmen had quickly crippled any chance of his escape. He was now resigned to his lack of options and wanted only to be enveloped by the darkness.

A hand pulled his head back roughly by the hair. Another hand waved ammonia under his nose that taunted the pilot back to fuller consciousness. *Why did you contact the Dallas news anchor? What did you tell her? Who are you working for?* He told them what he had been trained to tell such voices so many years ago—to deny whatever they insisted he knew—deny them the answers they demanded.

Another hard fist punched his stomach, unleashing a shrill cry of pain from his throat, followed by a rasping cough that forced more blood through his clenched teeth. Blood seeping from his mouth already coated the front of his shirt. He was going to die. Of that the pilot was certain. If only his body would resist the ammonia and return to the darkness and its promise of freedom from the pain the two men were inflicting so intensely on his body.

Maybe if he told them something diverting they would be satisfied. Anything to halt the punishment, to give him a rest, however brief, from the torturous blows. The pilot's lips moved. The sound they made was so slight the larger of the two men had to bend close to the bloodied face.

The pilot's nose leaned grotesquely toward the left side of his face, swollen and blood-caked, rendering it almost unrecognizable amidst the other damage from the initial beating.

"What did you say, amigo?" his antagonist demanded. The pilot's swollen lips labored to form the words. The strong smell of ammonia floated once again on his senses.

"Tell us again, amigo?"

The words came now, in a rasping whisper. "His wife is my daughter."

"Whose wife, you son of a whore?" His head was pulled back sharply and the pilot could see the brown face hovered over him, inches from his, the man's breath reeking of soured beer and bologna. "Who are you talking about?"

"My daughter... married to the mayor of Dallas. He's screwing the television lady. I was trying... to scare her off."

The man pushed away from the bloodied face before him and looked at the second man standing to his left. "What's he talking about?" He was answered with a shrug from the other man.

"Gringo, you're not making much sense." The brown face hovered in front of him, so close, the pilot could smell the man's breath again.

The pilot struggled to speak again. "My daughter… she's married to the mayor of Dallas. He's screwing the television lady." His voice faltered and it took all the strength he could summon to force the words out. "I was trying to get the bitch to leave him alone…" The pilot's tongue flicked across his bleeding lips. "I wanted him back with my daughter." The blue eyes, reduced to slits, pleaded for acceptance of his words.

The name appeared to register with the large Mexican standing over him. "You caught the TV lady screwing the mayor, your daughter's husband?"

The pilot nodded slightly.

The acne-scarred face with its wide nostrils disappeared from the pilot's blurred view. He heard the two Mexicans talking in low voices, but was unable to make out what they were saying. He cared only that they believed him long enough for him to die and escape the penance he knew would descend on him if they doubted his explanation. The darkness was reaching out to him again, offering respite and relief from the agony. He wanted to sleep and never wake up. To die. He knew that would be his end this day. He had known it since this morning when his mind was torn between conflicting feelings of alarm and curiosity.

Just before taking off, a man the pilot had not seen before on any of his previous trips to Matamoras, handed him the coordinates for the trip and the landing site, then introduced him to a burly, pocked-faced man who strapped himself into the co-pilot's seat and a second beefy Mexican who took the seat directly behind the pilot. The man explained they were oil field workers returning to their jobs. The pilot's gut told him differently.

Diverting the flight to an unfamiliar airfield west of Dallas had triggered his initial alarm. The two men sitting beside him and behind him only added to the pilot's uneasiness.

The man who had handed him the map and coordinates spoke with a more urbane Spanish dialect, which puzzled the pilot. He wondered idly if this was the infamous Christo he had heard whispered about by some of the Mexican cartel henchmen. The man spoke in a soft but commanding voice, offering only instructions that he also wrote on the map which he had laid between the two seats in the cramped cockpit. "Diego is familiar with the landing strip where you are going. He will help you," he had said, before stepping down from the footstep below the door on the pilot's side.

Moments later the pilot had turned the plane into the wind, and it lifted effortlessly into the azure sky before heading north.

The cargo strapped down in the plane's cargo hold had not shifted during take-off. The pilot had checked the straps to be sure they were secure and knew then what he was carrying was not oil field equipment, as the manifest they handed him stated. Strapped securely in the aircraft's hold were two tons of cocaine.

As the Cessna Caravan 675 cruised at a comfortable speed just above sporadic trails of cirrus clouds, the pilot wondered silently how much his cargo would sell for on American streets. *A DEA canine would have no problem sniffing out this shipment,* he mused silently.

Several feeble attempts at small talk by the pilot had been met with stony silence from the man sitting next to him, only adding to his foreboding. When the man did speak it was to bark out the coordinates in thickly accented English.

A weathered, ramshackle storage building marked the site of the airfield, in the center of acres of stilled oil pumps. A tattered wind jacket near the building hung limply on its pole. After circling the airfield, the pilot found landing tricky on the level but overgrown terrain.

The heavily loaded plane bounced sharply at the first touch of the wheels on the hard ground, jarring the pilot and eliciting crude oaths from the passengers seated behind the cockpit. By the time the plane rolled to a stop, a large truck, with Althea Oil & Gas emblazoned on its sides, was already lumbering toward the airplane.

The pilot stood several yards from the plane, dragging silently on a cigarette, attempting to look disinterested in the unloading activity around him. His two passengers and the driver heaved the large boxes through the plane's narrow rear door into the back of the truck backed up to the plane. The pilot did not offer to help with the unloading, and his help was not solicited. Watching the work in the blazing afternoon sun, he felt a creeping disquiet, and sorely wished he had risked detection. He could feel the comforting weight of a .45-caliber gun in a holster under his arm. He never carried his old service revolver when he flew, fearing a surprise check of his credentials by a zealous FAA official. Being an ex-con who was still on probation with a gun invited an end to his job and a return to prison. Today had been different. When he was advised of the change of landing location, the pilot had slipped away long enough to retrieve the gun and holster from his glove compartment.

Pulling deep on the remains of a second cigarette, the pilot surveyed the area around him. It was old habit to reconnoiter any situation. The terrain was open and flat. There was no place to run. A large padlock secured the only door visible on the storage building.

After the last box was shifted from the plane to the truck, the driver pulled a canvas canopy across the top of the truck, hiding the contents beneath. He jumped down from the back of the truck and scrambled into the cab. His helpers made no move to join him in the cab. As the big truck pulled slowly away from the plane, the pilot's attention was drawn to the two passengers now walking deliberately toward him. Each man held an automatic weapon. The pilot stamped out the cigarette he had just lit, knowing whatever action he took now was probably too late. He would be dead before he could pull his gun from beneath his jacket. Before he could consider any response the first bullet tore into his left knee, shattering the bone. The second bullet bore into his right thigh, just above the knee. Pain seared his senses, tearing a scream from his throat as he fell to the hard ground.

While the two Mexicans pulled him into the shack and were binding his arms behind a stout wooden chair, he heard the engines of the airplane revving up and then take-off shortly afterwards. Whoever was piloting the plane had remained well hidden.

Each beating evoked deeper suffering. The pain eventually sapped the strength to even scream. Each time he had attempted to move toward the beckoning blackness, the rude smell of ammonia drew him back and the beating resumed. His slumped body strained at the duct tape binding his wrists behind the chair. The voices of his two tormenters were becoming more distant. On a cell phone, one was speaking rapidly in Spanish. Much of what the man with the foul breath was saying, the pilot could not comprehend through the fog that clouded his mind. When the voice fell silent, he heard their approaching steps. For only an instant he felt the cool metal against his head before the sound exploded in his ear, and the blackness he sought enveloped him, ending his hours of torture.

Lesley shuffled through the sheets of stories for the six o'clock newscast, to ensure they were in the same order as the producer's rundown. She glanced at the first page of copy, the lead story. The temperamental teleprompter had taken to stopping suddenly and remaining stubbornly still in the middle of newscasts, forcing the anchors to switch quickly to the large-print paper copies shared with them by the producers and directors. The best efforts of the station's two engineers could only temporarily repair a piece of studio equipment still in use well beyond its normal life span. She felt a surge of irritation, wondering how many more drinks and golf games Bart Henderson enjoyed by forestalling the purchase of a reliable teleprompter.

Jed Thompson slid into the cushioned seat next to her. "Hi, beautiful," he beamed, as he deftly clipped the small Sony microphone to his tie. "Ready to kick butt?"

Lesley gave him a smiling thumbs-up. She liked Thompson. He was flirtatious in a breezy, don't-take-me-seriously kind of way. His contract would be renegotiated next month. A strong showing in the current ratings sweeps would give him a better bargaining chip with Henderson. Even though Lesley suspected her two co-anchors made a good deal more money than her, she harbored no envy. Lesley was doing far better financially than she ever expected to do so soon out of college and monthly counted the blessings of her six-figure salary she increased her growing investment portfolio.

"Thirty seconds," intoned the floor director. The two anchors straightened in their chairs and shuffled their copy one last time. "Stand by." Both watched the floor director's fingers count silently down from five to start. A red light flicked on the front camera. Flashing a broad smile, Thompson welcomed viewers to this edition of Channel 15's *Action News* at six. Lesley wished viewers a good afternoon as she smiled warmly into the camera in front of her before launching into the lead story—her story—an exclusive about a multi-million-dollar development in downtown Dallas that was being formally announced at a news conference tomorrow morning. Grant's friendship had some ancillary benefits.

The teleprompter rolled faultlessly. At the end of the first commercial break, Thompson read first. Off-camera, Lesley quickly previewed her next story and listened only absently to Thompson's rich voice.

"The badly beaten and decomposing body was identified by the Dallas County Coroner's Office as 57-year-old Bradley Stephen Collins. Police sources say Collins is a convicted felon who was currently employed as a pilot. Deputy Coroner Dell Martin attributed the cause of death to a single gunshot wound to the head, but said the man appeared to have been badly beaten. Police have little information on Collins and have been unable to track any next of kin."

As Thompson was reading the story, a short clip of video showed a black body bag being hoisted into a county coroner's van as blue and white lights circled like streaking vultures in the background. Yellow crime tape roped off what appeared to be the entrance to a dark alley.

It was the word *pilot* that triggered Lesley's attention. In the monitor she saw a driver's license photo of the pilot in a box to the side of Thompson's head. Lesley felt her chest contract and the air seemed to rush out of her lungs.

"Anyone with information about Collins is asked to contact the Dallas Police Department at the number below."

Lesley watched, stunned, as the police number was projected on the studio monitor below Thompson. Her mind was immediately a jumble of racing thoughts. Was this the pilot who had contacted her? He was 57. She recalled the pilot had looked at least that old.

The floor director's arm, and the soft click of the light on camera two, forced her attention back to the slow-moving teleprompter. She began reading almost mechanically. The words were recited flawlessly, with the conversational intonation she perfected in countless practice sessions before the large mirror above her bathroom vanity. The words were meaningless. Like a well-programmed robot, Lesley completed the newscast and quickly exited after the floor director signaled clear and gave his usual salute, "Good newscast, everyone."

Lesley sought the privacy of her office and tried to call Terrell. No answer. She left a detailed voicemail and a shorter text, then rushed to her car. Like the stories she had read through the remainder of the newscast, she drove mechanically, as if on autopilot. After pulling into her designated parking space, she reached for her cell phone and dialed Mac. He was just opening his back door when the cell phone rang.

15

I have a little surprise planned for the weekend. It starts early, so you have to take Friday off. No excuses. Or I'll call your boss and remonstrate directly with him. Then, my sweet, as Doris Day used to sing, your secret love won't be a secret anymore. Blackmail works. Trust me. I know. I'm a politician.

Lesley deleted the message and excitedly dialed Grant's home number. A surprise! What could it be? The answering machine at the other end of the connection clicked on. Before the tone ended, Lesley impatiently requested Grant call her back. Within seconds her telephone was ringing.

"Hi."

"Hi yourself, beautiful. Why aren't you here instead of over there?"

"You didn't invite me."

"An oversight. Come on over and I'll make my amends in the best way I know how. Deal?"

"No deal. Anyway, you know I prefer flowers and where can you get a dozen roses at this hour? Sorry!" Lesley laughed into the receiver. "Anyway, you're stalling. What's the surprise?"

"If I told you, my dear sweet dodo bird, you wouldn't be surprised. Can you get Friday off?"

"I'm sure I can. I've got a ton of vacation time built up."

"Pack a bag, with at least one absolutely gorgeous evening dress.

Bring shorts, skimpy tops, and a bathing suit, and leave the pajamas at home. I'll be waiting outside your apartment at 6:00 a.m. on Friday. Don't be late."

"Grant," she asked excitedly, "where are we going? Tell me, or I'll yell 'kidnapping' when you roll up outside my door at that ungodly hour."

"I'll not say one word more, except I love you, and I will be there to whisk you away at the crack of dawn Friday. Don't forget what I told you to bring."

"Grantham Stewart, you rat." Her words went unheard. The line was already dead at the other end.

He was taking her somewhere. But where? It must be warm with water, since he told her to pack shorts and a bathing suit. But the evening dress? *Oh, well,* she thought pragmatically, *I'll just have to be surprised*. Her elation over Grant's surprise slowly dimmed as she remembered the call she must make to Witt Terrell. Lesley glanced at the number for the cell phone Mac had given Terrell and dialed it on her own cell phone. That was the emphatic condition imposed by Terrell for contacting him. By pay phone or cell only. The connection had a cavernous sound, typical of cellular connections not close to a cell tower, as the warbling ring sounded in her ear several times. Finally, a husky voice answered.

"Hello."

"Mr. Terrell, this is Lesley Rowan in Dallas. I'm sorry to disturb you." She hadn't expected to find him asleep this early. Or was he just hung over? There was only silence from Terrell's end. Lesley finally plowed ahead. "I found out this evening that a pilot was found beaten and shot to death in Dallas overnight. Police said he was a convicted felon employed as a pilot."

She hesitated a moment before continuing, "I'm afraid it may be the man who contacted me."

Again, silence at the other end of the line. "Hello? Hello? Mr. Terrell?"

"I'm here, ma'am. I'll check it out. Tell me what you know."

Lesley related the facts in the story read by her co-anchor. She realized how bare the information was.

"I'm sorry I have so little to tell you. That was all we had in our story tonight," she added apologetically.

"It's okay, ma'am. It's enough to get started. I'll get back to you. By the way, does Mac know about this?"

"Yes. I called him earlier. Oh, and Mr. Terrell," she added hastily, "are you coming back to Dallas soon?"

"Next day or two, probably. I've got to tie up some loose ends here first." He was gone without a goodbye. She had not been able to tell him she might be out of town when he returned. That was something Mac would have to deal with.

Sleep eluded Lesley, held at bay by the excitement that coursed through her about the surprise planned by Grant, and the more ominous concerns about the murder of the pilot. She could not escape the still unanswered question: was he the same man who had first contacted her in Brownsville? If he was, could his contacts with her have precipitated his brutal murder? How did Grant know the voice on the answering machine? He had not mentioned the caller since that night. Why? So many unanswered questions. It left her uneasy and wide awake.

If the pilot's murderer knew about the contacts with her, where did that leave her now? She bleakly wondered if the killing could place her in danger. Lesley decided to see Mac at the office first thing tomorrow.

St. Michael's chimes sounded on the stately grandfather clock which dwarfed the other furnishings in the apartment's compact living room. Standing nearly seven feet high, the massive cherry timepiece had been an impulse purchase at an overpriced furniture store in an upscale Dallas suburb. The chimes struck five times.

Later, as she sat sipping a steaming cup of black coffee, the soft light of the new day invaded through a small, east-facing window above the kitchen sink. Sleep was hopeless now. Gripping the cup in both hands, she sipped gingerly, feeling the warm liquid melt away the weariness dragging at her since she had exited the bed an hour ago.

Pulling on a pair of jeans and a tank top, Lesley slipped quietly out the door and went down to the lobby to get the morning newspaper. Buried inside the local section was a three-paragraph story on the murdered pilot. The body was found in an alley behind a bar, in a garishly neoned area of Dallas's downtown, dominated by strip bars, massage parlors, tattoo parlors, and adult book stores. Police had long ago nicknamed the area Naked City after a 1948 movie that epitomized the *film noir* genre of dark, low budget detective pictures popular in the 1940's and 1950's. It was an area of Dallas tourists would not find on points of interest maps distributed by the city's Chamber of Commerce. The story of the pilot's murder read like just another killing in the crime-ridden area. The victim's wallet was found discarded in a nearby trash bin, any credit cards, cash, and identification missing. He was identified from fingerprints on file with the FBI.

After leafing through the rest of the newspaper, Lesley poured the remains of the coffee into her cup. She strolled over to the patio door leading from the dining room onto a small balcony on the back of her apartment and pulled open the drapes. The rising sun cast long, spindly, westward-reaching shadows from the tall trees at the rear of the apartment building. It was a time of day when she should feel renewed. Instead, a dark foreboding screened out any communion with the new day. Gnawing inside her was the still unanswered question: was the pilot just a victim of street thugs, or was he killed because someone knew he had been talking to the news media about what the plane he flew was bringing across the southern border?

Showered and dressed by eight o'clock, Lesley would talk to Mac in person. She had gone to work with little or no sleep before. Make up would cover any tell-tale signs of sleeplessness. She could crash tonight.

Withers listened without comment as she hesitantly laid out her suspicions. "It's too early to speculate," he cautioned. "Let's wait to see what Witt comes up with. And, yes, you can have Friday off." Lesley left his office without assuaging his unspoken curiosity about why she was making the request.

Withers turned to his computer and emailed a message to Jack Reilley. He asked the police reporter to see him when he got in. Reilley was one of Withers' plum snares from the morning newspaper; a loner, recondite in his dealings with producers, acerbic in his dealings with just about everyone else on the staff; who worked long, often irregular hours and refused overtime. It was the stories he turned in that forced reluctant tolerance of Reilley by the rest of the staff. Concise, well-written, detailed, and factual, Reilley's stories could be depended on to be one step ahead of the competition. The only people he seemed at ease with were cops and Withers.

Reilley balked at cooperating directly with Lesley after her return from Brownsville. No amount of cajoling, even by Withers, could alter the crusty police reporter's attitude. But left to his own instincts Withers knew Reilley would latch onto whatever information was available.

Shortly before noon, Reilly walked, unannounced, into Withers' office. He eased his tall, angular frame into a chair across from Withers and faced his boss with the permanently pugnacious scowl that offset his otherwise handsome face. "What's up?" he asked.

Reilley was a man of few words, and he took few pains to hide his perennial impatience at any newsroom meeting. Producers and news editors had long since accepted his absence from staff meetings.

"What do you know about the man killed in Naked City early yesterday?"

"Lived in Dallas. Flew for that outfit—Althea Oil & Gas. He's an ex-con. Hasn't been out long. Served time on a federal rap. Former FBI. Maybe CIA. He was charged with being on the take with the Nevada mob. Convicted on a lesser charge. A couple of detectives remember reading about the case. They think he took a fall for someone. Can't find anybody here who knows the guy, or ever saw him. They think he was killed elsewhere and dumped in Naked City to make it look like a mugging." Reilley paused and stared down at the floor. "He might've been working undercover. Don't know yet if, or on what. Dallas cops may call in the feds to help."

"They don't know much, it looks like," said Withers.

"You're right. Why the interest?"

Withers shrugged. "Just curious."

Reilley stood up and walked toward the door. He turned slowly back toward Withers. "There is something kinda interesting, Mac. Jack Denton let me go up to the guy's apartment last night while they looked around. I saw a picture of Mayor Stewart's ex-wife. It was in a frame in a dresser drawer. I don't think the cops recognized her. She was a lot younger when it was taken. Maybe a teenager. Can't figure why the guy'd have a picture like that."

"Yeah," Withers agreed. "How do you know it's her?"

"She was at North Texas University when I was there. A knock-out. Wasn't surprised when she married big bucks."

"Interesting coincidence. Keep me posted, will you?"

"Sure."

Withers pondered what Reilley had just said. Why would an ex-con have a photograph of a woman who was the former wife of the city's mayor? It made no sense, and yet there was something nagging at him. What? His mental search was interrupted by Hal Crockett, the executive producer, ready to go over the preliminary lineup for the early afternoon newscast. After Crockett darted out with the revised lineup, Withers strolled over to the coffee machine and refilled his grimy cup, never washed and only briefly sterilized by each fresh portion of the hot brew. Seeing Lesley bent over the computer, he walked slowly toward her office.

"Les, what was the reason the pilot gave for contacting you?"

Lesley looked up from her computer where she was composing an acceptance letter for an upcoming speaking engagement at a small college. She looked momentarily perplexed at Mac's question.

"He told me it was because he was trying to protect his daughter," Lesley responded. "He wouldn't tell me why or even tell me her name."

Withers nodded. "That's it. I couldn't remember. Thanks."

"Why do you ask?"

"Just curious."

Withers walked back to his office without seeing the troubled expression on Lesley's face that followed his departure. Back behind his desk, Withers pondered why an ex-con, working for a suspected drug running outfit, had a framed picture of the mayor's ex-wife from her younger days? Could she really be his daughter? It was something for his friend to check out. Withers fished a cell phone from his briefcase and dialed Witt Terrell.

16

Lesley watched the flaming ball of the setting sun lowering toward the horizon at the edge of the ocean, and wondered absently why it looked so much larger and brighter at day's end, slipping into the water with such a garish last hurrah. She felt Grant's arms tightened around her shoulders. She nestled against his chest, feeling his chin resting lightly on her head. How protected she felt in his embrace. How content, as the gleaming boat swayed gently to the rhythm of the ocean's soft undulations.

The voice invaded her reverie, speaking deferentially in Spanish. "He says we have to get back before dark," Grant interpreted. Their brief days together would end before the sun next set in the western sky. Tomorrow they would board the private jet for the flight back to Dallas. All that remained were a few hours. Time would not stretch. She whimsically pictured a large clock in Greenwich, with their names hanging from its ornate metal hands. It ticked away, indifferent to their impassioned pleas to slow its staunchly regular progress.

"How about having dinner sent up to our room? Or would you rather go out?"

"In our room," she replied in a languid tone. "But later. I don't want to leave where I am right now. I'm so cozy." Lesley felt his arms pull more snugly around her. "I don't want you to ever let me go."

Grant kissed the top of her head, inhaling the floral scent of the shampoo lingering in her hair. He felt the familiar urge to make love to her. His need seemed insatiable. To silently telegraph what he was feeling, he squeezed her gently and softly kissed the side of her neck. They were still standing on the deck when the boat pulled slowly into a docking bay at the marina near the hotel on Grand Cayman Island. It was a place he had come to love, with its gleaming white houses set against neat green hillsides. Unlike other Caribbean islands, Grand Cayman hid its poverty, showing visitors only its British-instituted tradition of politeness and deferential efficiency.

Grant had discovered Grand Cayman in his youth, when it had been a sleepy gem in the western Caribbean. He came here frequently enough that he considered acquiring a home on one of the island's lush hillsides overlooking the turquoise bay.

Darkness was descending as the crewmen secured the sleek sailing vessel to its moorings. The blazing sun slid below the horizon, leaving only traces of soft, orange hues to remind the two passengers of the riotous ball's descent that slowly ushered in nightfall.

Grant tipped Lesley's chin upward and bent to brush her lips with a kiss. "Did you enjoy yourself?"

"Very much," she whispered in reply. They had spent the afternoon snorkeling off a secluded cay, viewing an exotic assortment of fish, turtles, and coral.

An hour later, dinner was wheeled into their suite by a white-jacketed waiter. He lifted silver lids from the plates, revealing lobster tail lightly brushed with a lemon butter sauce, and small filet mignons surrounded by a colorful variety of steamed vegetables.

A portion of each item still untouched on her plate, Lesley leaned back in her chair and lazily stretched her arms above her head. "I'm stuffed."

"Tsk, tsk, tsk! Didn't Miss Emily Post teach you that saying you're stuffed is very bad manners, and very un-Texan-like."

"Would she be less offended by, 'I'm full'?"

"Probably not," Grant laughed. He pushed his chair back and stood up, taking her hand and pulling her to her feet. "I'm fed and happy, woman. There's just one thing more I need."

"And what would that be, Mr. Stewart?"

"A distinctive dessert that only a woman can serve to a man."

"Pecan pie. I hear it's a favorite of most tall Texans."

"I'm more in mind of a sex soufflé, ma'am."

"Really! I'm not sure I know the recipe for that dessert. Maybe you'll just have to teach me how to make it, Mr. Stewart."

"My pleasure."

He swept her up into his arms and carried her into the suite's bedroom. With a free hand he pulled back the silk floral coverlet and laid her on the lavender sheets beneath. Bracing his body above hers, he kissed her longingly. Lesley felt the need for him circuiting through her groin, and the instant wetness that announced her need. His lovemaking was tantalizingly deliberate, until her body screamed for closure. It came quickly after his penetration, wave after wave of orgasmic pleasure that faded only after she felt the wetness of his own release.

Early in their relationship Grant had overcome her reticence, patiently dispelling her frigidity with persuasive foreplay. His reward was an intense sensual response that surprised Lesley and left him happily exhausted on many of the nights they spent together. He seemed never to get enough of her.

Grant reached for a cigarette from the unopened pack on the bedside table. He mostly had quit smoking, a habit that had peaked at two packs a day while he was an undergraduate at the University of Texas. After leaving that pressure-charged campus, he found it easy to cut back and eventually to quit. Now it was only after sex he felt a need to light up and felt no guilt in this self-indulgence. He tapped the bottom of the firm pack, pushing one of the Marlboro's up above the rest. "Mind if I smoke?"

Lesley shook her head sleepily and snuggled closer and was quickly asleep. He flicked the gold-plated lighter his father gave him on his 18th birthday and rested his head back in the cradle of his left arm, feeling the top of Lesley's disheveled hair beneath his hand. She did not smoke, but seemed never to mind this ritual following their lovemaking. *She is so different from other women I've known over the years,* Grant thought. Unless they smoked, they objected to him smoking. Even Sarah.

His former wife's face flashed in his mind: young, pretty, silky-blonde hair cascading down her back, her luminous grey eyes alight with laughter. The laughter faded following the births of their son and daughter, and was replaced by a glum, pouting indifference. The happiness of the early years of their marriage slowly disintegrated into an eventual marital purgatory for them both. What had happened to change their lives? He knew the one word answer—politics. His ambitions differed from the idyllic lifestyle Sarah envisioned for herself. Having children. Sharing time with her comfortable circle of friends, who frequented the Shepherd Hills Country Club to play bridge, sunbathe, sip Singapore Slings in the afternoon, and arrive home just ahead of their executive husbands. Politics was not part of Sarah's lifestyle equation. It interfered with her routine. Hence, the dissatisfaction—the moodiness—the sexual indifference. Then divorce.

It was for him an acute embarrassment. For her, he sensed relief. Sarah continued to find solace in her circle of friends. They found her eligible dates for weekend events at the club. And Grant instinctively knew she was happier without him—a thought that stung, even now, months after the divorce was final. He viewed his marriage a failure. Failure was alien to the aspirations of the world he had built for himself since childhood. But even with their differences, somehow he and Sarah had remained cordial, making a difficult situation far more tolerable for their children and his parents.

His father's unsmiling, critical face—so much like his own— undulated into ghostly focus in the smoke he softly expelled. He refused his father's advice to keep up the appearance of a marriage. *For your career,* reasoned Blaine Stewart. *For our business.*

His father suffered no appearance of contention or disunion. Any differences must be kept within the family. To do otherwise would invite unwelcome attention. That could be embarrassing, even damaging, his father warned. Sarah and the children remained in the home his grandfather built as their wedding gift—within the family compound—within the benevolent constraints his parents erected around Sarah to insure against any unwelcome attention. The closeness forged early between his parents and Sarah remained undaunted by the divorce. They treated her as a favored daughter. She delighted in the attention from her in-laws, attention she complained bitterly to close friends, was never given her by their son.

Sarah was right, Grant admitted to himself. *I did neglect her.*

Grant inhaled deeply on the remains of his cigarette. Sarah's shallowness appalled him from the beginning. She showed no interest in those things which intrigued him, stimulated him. He speculated often, in the time since they separated, how he could have been so blind to the superficiality of her brain and her spirit. In the beginning, she faked pleasure during intercourse. After the birth of their daughter six years ago, she refused him altogether for a time, claiming postpartum depression, then, tearfully raging when she suspected him of dalliances. There were none, something Sarah refused to believe. When he finally left, he was content to take the blame in the eyes of his parents and the public. A small price, he reasoned, to free Sarah and free him.

He visited with the children every weekend, either at their home or at his condo, and attended as many of their school activities as his schedule allowed. Those were the best times with his son and daughter, who appeared precocious and well-adjusted, despite their parents' failed marriage. He grudgingly conceded Sarah appeared an involved, nurturing mother, serving on the board of the private day school they attended, carpooling with other mothers, accompanying the children to a daily regimen of lessons from ballet to piano to drums—even serving as a Cub Scout Den leader for their nine-year-old son.

He took one more draw on yet another cigarette and snuffed out its remains in an ashtray next to the clock. Two o'clock. He needed to get some sleep. They were flying out that afternoon. Lesley stirred next to him. He rolled over and softly kissed her cheek. Her eyes fluttered open and a slight smile creased her soft lips.

"Hi," he whispered.

"Hi, yourself. What time is it?"

"Not time to wake up. But since you are..." The rest of the sentence was silenced by his lips covering hers.

An hour later, Lesley stepped out of the shower, refreshed, her face flushed from the warm water, her wet hair matted to her scalp and neck, a towel only partially covering her. He had stepped out of the shower while she washed her hair, and lay on the bed taking in the breathtaking beauty of her near-nakedness. It was another small victory, won in their early days together, replacing her shyness and self-consciousness with a smiling insouciance that allowed him to make love to her with a light on, and feast on her nakedness at moments like this. She was everything he ever desired in a woman. Marrying her would make him complete. Of that he was certain, as he watched her pull on a pair of white shorts and a blue tank top sans bra.

"I can't sleep. Let's walk on the beach."

"I like that idea, ma'am," he drawled.

An hour later, they returned to the hotel room for breakfast. The first hint of day was appearing, shyly at first, lavishing a pale, pink greeting across the distant horizon. Their cherished hours together were counting down.

Lesley was pensive on the return trip, her thoughts riveted on the answer he sought before they checked out of the resort. When could they be married? Assuming the reason for her contemplative withdrawal, Grant took the seat across from her and busied himself with reading faxes from his office and listening to voicemails. When he finished, she was still staring out the small, round widow.

"A penny for your thoughts? Maybe even a nickel."

"I'm just thinking about us—us together, all the time." She smiled and reached over to hold his hand.

By early evening they were landing at Love Field, the remnants of the retreating sun simmering on the concrete as the plane glided smoothly onto the long runway, toward the reception area of the Stewart Oil Company hangar. As the plane came to a stop, Lesley's answer crystallized. "I would be honored to marry you as soon as you'll have me."

17

Lesley slipped the green carry-on bag from her shoulder and punched the play button on her telephone. There were five messages, all from Mac Withers. Glancing at the handsome grandfather clock, she dialed Withers' home number. 9:20 p.m. Lesley pictured Withers sitting in front of his television, swilling bourbon and waiting for the late news to come on. He answered on the first ring.

"Hi, Mac. It's Lesley. I just got back. What's up?"

"Witt Terrell got back in town yesterday. He should be sobered up by 10 tomorrow morning. Let's meet in my office? He's got some interesting stuff."

"Sure. I'm on pins and needles. See you tomorrow."

As with every other telephone conversation she could remember having with Mac Withers, his goodbye, like Witt Terrell's, was the sound of a dial tone. It was rudeness, in Lesley's estimation. Mac just seemed not to find any need to formally end a conversation with a ritual goodbye.

✝✝✝

Lesley was at her desk before nine, and spent the next hour answering a variety of emails and voicemail messages; everything from viewers wanting more information about her recent health report on a new diet drug produced by a Dallas-based pharmaceutical company, to a reminder from a neighborhood dry cleaners about clothing she had dropped off nearly a month before. Another email from her dentist's office offered to move her six-month teeth-cleaning appointment to tomorrow. *Good thing I wasn't gone for a week,* she glumped. *Or, god-forbid, two.*

When Lesley poked her head into Withers' office shortly before 10 a.m., she could barely discern Witt Terrell's thin frame, nearly swallowed by the large leather chair where he sat in a corner of Mac's office. He looked terrible. Mac was wrong on one point. Terrell did not appear to have sobered up yet. His pallor was ashen, the facial skin pulled taut over bones that stood like twin peaks above his sunken cheeks. She felt instantly sorry for the man.

"Hi, Mr. Terrell," she said, feigning cheerfulness as Withers waved her to a chair near his desk.

Terrell nodded slightly to acknowledge her salutation.

"I filled Witt in on that pilot's murder before I called you back," Withers said, "and what he told you the other night."

"Has Reilley found out anything more about the dead pilot?" Lesley asked.

"Not the last time we talked. I'll check with him when he comes in." Withers cracked a derisive half smile. "You know Jack. He declares squatters rights to my office anytime he's working a big story." Withers leaned back in his chair, clenching his hands behind his head in his ritual stance. "Witt's had an interesting trip to Austin. Tell Lesley what you found, Witt."

"Well, ma'am, as I told Mac earlier, Althea Oil & Gas was started a few years back, 13 years to be exact, by an attorney in Killeen by the name of Danford Pearson. Seems Pearson took over some oil leases. Interesting thing is there's no record he ever paid for the leases. And he was the only person listed on the original charter when it was filed. He's listed as both president and secretary. The annual renewal of the corporation's charter is up-to-date. Filed by a law firm in Chicago the past few years."

Terrell did not voice his suspicions about why a Chicago law firm would be used for a Texas corporation—when there were plenty of renowned attorneys in Dallas or Austin or Houston specializing in the legalities of the oil business.

"Checked that while I was nosing around Austin. Got the lease numbers on all the wells listed for Althea Oil & Gas. Seems they're pretty prodigious producers according to the outputs listed on state reports." Terrell looked down at his bony hands, folded in his lap, pondering his next words. "Problem is, Mr. Pearson's been dead for five years and I can't find hide or hair of a will or any kin still living."

"You're kidding!" Lesley's attention was distracted from Terrell's gaunt face to his hands which he was nervously clenching and unclenching in his lap. She suspected he needed a drink badly and wondered if he was abiding by Mac's mandate of no drinking, at least on the job. "So who actually owns the oil company now?" she inquired.

"Don't know yet, ma'am. The fact that a dead man is still listed as the owner sends up all kinds of red flags. Althea has shell company written all over it. But I need to do more checking. I came back to let you know where I am, and to ask if you want me to keep going. Mac says keep at it till we get some firm answers."

"So where do we go from here, Mr. Terrell?"

"For me, back to Austin today, ma'am. After that, Tyler, to check out some of those wells listed by Althea. See how many we find still pumpin' oil and whether they're producin' what those state forms claim they're puttin' out."

Lesley smiled at the emaciated man slumped in the hollow of the tufted, burgundy leather. "You *have* been busy, Mr. Terrell. What can I do to help?"

"Nothin' I can think of right now. Let's see what I find. I'll come back here, or at least give you a jingle with that little phone Mac gave me."

Withers pushed forward, absently rubbing his thick hands together. "Better call us here at the office, Witt. If I'm gone or Lesley's not here, the operator knows where to reach me. Lesley, too. One of us will call you back."

Lesley thought Mac's suggestion about calling them only at the office and not at home a little strange, but said nothing. "Good luck, Mr. Terrell. Let me know if there's anything I can be doing to help at this end."

She slipped out of the office, hearing the low voice of Terrell without being able to make out what he was saying, as she closed the door behind her.

Back in her office, Lesley stared at the computer screen and the aesthetic Dallas skyline that served as her screen saver, and mentally reviewed what she had just learned. *So what if the owner of Althea Oil & Gas died five years ago? That didn't explain why the pilot was killed or show any link to the drug trade.* Those were the answers she was seeking: the answers to the allegations made by the pilot; allegations she suspected had cost him his life. What role Althea Oil & Gas played in any of this was still unclear from the information Terrell had turned up. *But it's a start,* she conceded silently. The story was riding on Terrell's back at this point.

"Les." It was Withers' voice crackling on the intercom.

Lesley picked up the telephone. "Yeah, Mac."

"Come back by my office when you get a chance before lunch."

"I'll be right there."

This time she stood in front of Withers' desk and he made no motion for her to sit down.

"Jack Reilley shared something that might be of interest. He's been checking it out to get the police take on it."

"What's that, Mac?" she asked, her curiosity piqued.

"Seems the cops found a photo of a woman in the apartment of that pilot they found murdered last week. Jack said they think it's a picture of Grant Stewart's ex-wife… when she was a lot younger."

The shocked expression that flashed momentarily on her face was not lost on Withers.

"Didn't you tell me that pilot who contacted you was trying to protect his daughter?"

Lesley's mouth went dry. She opened it to speak, but the words were trapped in her throat. She felt Mac's piercing look. "Yes." The word was barely audible. "Yes," she repeated, "he did tell me that. I can't believe someone like him would be her father. You know… the mayor's wife… ex-wife… the pilot being an ex-convict and all…" Her voice trailed off.

"Yeah, it is hard to believe. That's what Reilley said." Withers felt an edge of discomfort watching Lesley. "You okay, Les?"

"Sure. It's just rather incongruous." She shrugged her shoulders to underscore her doubts.

"Well, I just wanted to let you know about that. Keep it under you hat until Reilley gets it checked out, one way or the other."

"Right! Thanks for letting me know."

Lesley turned and walked quickly out of the office, feeling Withers' eyes following her. This information had caught her completely off guard. Sarah Stewart, the daughter of the dead pilot? It seemed unfathomable—her father, the murdered pilot involved in a drug-running operation. She rejected the connection immediately.

Lesley saw Sarah Stewart occasionally in the local section of the newspaper, smiling and beautiful, promoting this charitable event or serving as a volunteer for another worthy cause. She was active in the Dallas Junior League and sat on the board of at least two philanthropic organizations. Then there was the video of a somber Sarah Stewart gripping her children's hands as she led them up the front steps of the exclusive school they attended—video shot the day after Grant Stewart's office had issued a short statement announcing the couple's separation. Lesley recalled the quiet dignity with which Sarah Stewart had handled the intrusive reporters and cameras. Her efforts to shield her children had evoked Lesley's admiration long before she and Grant had begun dating.

Lesley felt a wave of melancholy wash over her, knowing she was now planning to marry the man with whom Sarah Stewart had shared 10 years of her life and given birth to his two children.

Any remaining thoughts of how she would deal with Sarah Stewart after she married Grant were abruptly dispelled moments later by Jack Reilley approaching from across the newsroom. She quickly repressed the irritation that seemed to always to bubble up in her when she had any contact with the lanky police reporter. She found him curt, egotistical, and supercilious, along with a host of other negative adjectives.

"Hey, Lesley. How's it going?"

She doubted he cared much. "Good," she responded, trying to ignore the mocking tone of his greeting. "What's happening with you, Jack?" Lesley looked up into his smug face with those deep-set, mocking, brown eyes. He seldom shared pleasantries with any of his fellow reporters. But it was the station's several news anchors for whom he saved his most acerbic criticism. Reilley appeared to view them as under-worked, over-paid prima donnas. Herself included. She silently resented Reilley lumping her in with some of her fellow anchors whom she also viewed in the same disparaging way.

"Did Mac mention to you about the picture police found in that murdered guy's apartment? It *is* the mayor's ex-wife. A detective confirmed it. Said they're going to question her about it. Anyway, Mac wanted to make sure you know."

Lesley felt her heart race. She stood up and fumbled with the file that held her rapidly expanding notes on the drug-running story. "Mac mentioned you knew Sarah Stewart?"

"Yeah. Back at North Texas. She was a looker even then." Reilley leaned against the door frame and shoved his hands into his pant pockets before adding, "And she caught herself a big, rich fish," his tone clearly cynical. He lingered as if waiting for her to add something to what he had just disclosed. She looked over at Reilley who was eyeing her curiously.

"Something else, Jack?" she asked, trying to quash the panic she felt rising inside her.

"Heard a rumor last night. Seems one of the off-duty cops working security at Love Field saw you getting on a plane with Grant Stewart. Anything to it, Les?"

His blunt question hung in the air between them before she finally answered. "Yes."

Reilley seemed to be waiting for her to say more. When she didn't, he said, "Okay then," ducked his head, waved a flippant goodbye and strolled back to his desk.

Jack Reilley watched her from under hooded eyes as she walked briskly toward the news director's office. *Great ass*, he thought, watching her cross the newsroom and get waved into Withers' office. He had come in early to confront Lesley with the rumor about boarding a plane with the mayor.

Thing is, he thought, *she didn't deny it. Was it an interview—or something else?* He glanced at the wall clock. Time to hit the cop shop. Whistling softly under his breath, he took a short cut between desks manned by reporters, whose faces were pivoted on computer screens. Jack Reilley wondered why the hell Mac insisted Lesley be told about a picture found in a murder victim's apartment. And her strange reaction when he confronted her with the rumor. Reilley prided himself on reading faces. She seemed almost frightened. Like a deer in headlights. *Must have something to do with the story she's working on involving the murder of that editor in Brownsville. But how?* Like most things that baffled him, he filed it away in his mind to consider later. He felt sure Mac would fill him in at some point.

When Lesley returned to her office she immediately fished her cell phone from her purse and saw Grant had called earlier. She dialed up her voicemail and listened as he said, *Hi, gorgeous! I'm leaving the office early. Some campaign appearances to make this evening. Probably won't get home till late. I'll call you. And don't make plans for this weekend. Mom and Dad have invited us to dinner Saturday. It's about time they meet my fiancée.*

18

Lesley was nervous, imploring her face and hands not to betray her. Standing in the center of the expansive, white-marbled foyer below the largest crystal chandelier she had ever seen, Lesley felt like she had during her initial newscast more than two years ago. At the first commercial break, an engineer had rushed onto the set and began checking wiring around and under the anchor desk.

"We're hearing a strange noise," he had explained in a muffled tone, as his head disappeared under the large desk on Lesley's side. When the floor director warned "ten seconds to air time," the portly engineer was forced to stay put, while she and Jed Thompson finished the next segment. It proved enough time for him to discover the source of the subtle noise heard by the technical director—Lesley's left knee knocking gently against a wood brace that separated her side of the desk from the co-anchor. Mystery solved. It took several more newscasts to conquer her nervousness, and much longer to overcome the acute embarrassment of being the brunt of newsroom banter.

Grant squeezed her hand reassuringly, seeming aware of the internal turmoil she battled as they stood in the entrance to his parents' elegant mansion. High, arched entry ways led to large rooms on either side of the foyer. In the center of the grand entryway, a wide stairway curved to the second floor, where the thick, carved balusters stretched across the entire length of a wide hallway lined with works of art of various sizes. All were in ornate, gilded frames with brass lights illuminating various scenes of Western life captured on canvas. The effect was spectacular to Lesley, who felt she was standing in the entrance to a museum gallery rather than a private home.

"Hello, Lesley. I'm Grant's mother, Grace. Welcome to our home." She reached for Lesley's hands while lightly kissing Lesley's cheek. The warmth of the greeting momentarily overwhelmed Lesley, who could only smile in return, as she found herself looking into one of the loveliest faces she had ever seen. Soft, gray-blue eyes appeared like small saucers in a heart-shaped face, framed by platinum hair pulled back in an elegant chignon at the back of her head. Her youthful complexion was only lightly touched with makeup.

"Thank you, Mrs. Stewart. I'm delighted to be here."

"Please, my dear, call me Grace," she beamed. "After all, you're almost part of the family." Still clasping Lesley's hands, Grace Stewart turned to her son. "Grant, why don't you introduce Lesley to the rest of our family?"

A wide smile crossed his face. "You've met the heart and soul of our family," he said with obvious affection, bending over to brush his mother's cheek with a brief kiss. "That handsome gentleman to her right is my father, Blaine."

"Hello, Lesley. I join my wife in welcoming you to our home," he said graciously.

His rich, deep voice matched his face; strikingly handsome and a reflection of what she could expect Grant to look like in his later years. Only the eyes were different, somehow more obtuse, not reflecting the friendliness in his voice. There was no outward reluctance on his part as he offered his hand. Perhaps it was wariness she sensed, a holding back, as if he was reserving opinion regarding his son's choice for a spouse. She felt dejection wash over her momentarily, an emotion quickly dashed by the hearty greeting of Grant's brother, Elliott, and his wife, Emily, whose hair was styled identically to her elegant mother-in-law's. The younger woman's green eyes danced to the light of her smile.

"Come, Lesley." Grace took her arm. "There is someone in the library who is anxiously waiting to meet you."

Lesley was steered through a spacious sitting area dominated by floor-to-ceiling windows and decorated in soft hues of yellow. They moved through open double doors into a high-ceilinged room with mahogany bookshelves rising from base cabinets on three sides. A massive atrium skylight allowed the last vestiges of daylight to center light onto two large, burgundy leather couches facing each other. It was there the aging patriarch sat puffing contentedly on the remains of a cigar. He appeared oblivious to the commotion created by the arrival of Grace, Lesley, and the family entourage.

Grace stood directly in front of her father-in-law before she spoke. "Daddy, this is Grant's intended, Lesley Rowan."

Grantham Stewart drew deeply on his cigar and did not acknowledge Grace, staring past her at the leaded glass paneled window on the far wall. "Daddy's a little hard of hearing," Grace whispered in Lesley's ear. "He's 92, you know. Daddy!"

"I heard you the first time, Grace." There was a slight hint of irritation in the old man's voice. The aged face now turned directly on Lesley, observing her keenly. "How are you, young lady? Glad to have you to supper this evening."

"Thank you, Mr. Stewart. I've looked forward to meeting you."

"Why?" he asked. The demand in his voice was unmistakable.

"Daddy!" Grace exclaimed.

"She can speak for herself," he said gruffly. Grantham Stewart's curmudgeonly demand prompted a smile from Lesley. "Grant has told me about many of your adventures when you first arrived in Texas," she said. "You've had an exciting and interesting life."

"I'm flattered you think so, young lady." The old man crushed his cigar out in an ashtray and rose slowly from the couch.

"Let's eat. And I will sit by this young lady and let her satisfy an old man's curiosity. Unhand her, Grace," he ordered with a sly smile. "Take my arm, Miss Rowan. I need a little more help these days. The legs aren't what they used to be when I was wildcatting. Come on, Grant." He tossed the words like dice over his shoulder, acknowledging his grandson for the first time. "Show us to the dining room. We're puttin' on the Ritz for your young lady."

Grant grinned at his grandfather and winked at Lesley. "Let's go, you old charmer. I know you're just trying to win her away from me. I'll warn you right now. It's too late."

His grandfather chuckled and patted Lesley's arm. Lesley gazed around, transfixed by the room into which she was led. Colorful murals, depicting the battle of San Jacinto and other moments of Texas history, rose from the mahogany wainscoting to the ornately-carved crown molding.

Sensing her awe, the old man patted her arm approvingly. "This is my favorite room. A fellow I knew down in Houston painted this many years back. I never tire of it."

"I can see why. It's magnificent," she added, putting her thoughts into words as her eyes swept the length of the mural.

The diners were clustered together at one end of the long, gleaming mahogany table. Flickering candles from the several large crystal and silver candelabras added a warm ambiance to the meal of stuffed pheasant, surrounded by wild rice and topped with a light brown sauce. Having never tasted pheasant before, Lesley found it delicious. The aroma of corn pudding stirred memories of her grandmother's holiday cooking, which always included the baked vegetable dish.

The old man monopolized her attention. Responding to her slightest urging, he talked expansively about his early days in Texas, wildcatting in the newly discovered oil fields of east Texas, and later in the western part of the state. Those had been long days of back-breaking, dangerous labor, of sweat and hope, but for many of the comrades of his youth, bitter disappointment. It was a lifestyle of boisterous excess by his colorful description. His rowdy lifestyle was finally quelled after accumulating great wealth and marrying the heiress of a socially prominent Dallas family. At the mention of his late wife, the old eyes, still clear, watered slightly, reflecting the energy of his mind as he took Lesley back in time to his youth. The grief he felt for his wife was as transparent as the skin drawn tightly over his long, thin hands and his stooped, thin frame.

From across the table Grant watched her, surreptitiously pleased at her engaging interest in his grandfather and his grandfather's obvious warming to Lesley.

"She's lovely," whispered his mother, seated next to him. "I wish Daddy would share your young lady with the rest of us."

"You'll have plenty of time to get to know her better, Mother," he whispered. "She's obviously enjoying Grandfather."

His mother nodded an end to this avenue of conversation, rather than an affirmation to her son's tactful admonishment. In the nearly 20 years Grace Stewart had lived in her father-in-law's home, following the death of his wife, she maintained a stoic truce with the aging patriarch, who continued his wary dislike of his oldest son's choice of a wife since their introduction nearly five decades ago. The pain of his disapproval vanished long ago. In the ensuing years she replaced her mother-in-law as mistress of his home. She left her father-in-law no opportunity to complain about the management of his home or his life. When Blaine insisted their second son be named for his father, she consented graciously, having won the first war over names: their oldest son bore her father's name. Despite the shackle of his grandfather's name, Grant was the child of her heart: so affable, so different from Elliott, who had inherited her face and his father's aloof personality. From her youngest son, Grace received the flattering attention and affection she so craved from her husband. Her darling Grant. So handsome. So successful.

Watching the smile play on and off Lesley's glowing face as she listened to the old man, Grace's mind focused on the appropriateness of this future daughter-in-law. Beautiful, yes. Grant inherited her eye for glamour. Good manners, yes. Essential for the wife of the mayor of one of America's most influential municipalities.

But Lesley's career? That was the question mark in Grace's mind. Sarah had been a homemaker, a mother—a woman who did not seek status to compete with her husband, only a status that complemented her husband.

The picture of Sarah, penetrating her thoughts, stirred the hurt still gnawing at Grace's core over the failure of her son's marriage. Those vows were sacred. After all, she had countenanced Blaine's apathy for years. It was the face they presented to their friends and business acquaintances that mattered. In that effort she exemplified perfection, as she did in all things in which she took an interest. Only with Sarah had Grace failed. *Be more tolerant*, she had encouraged her willful daughter-in-law. *Stewart men need more freedom. Look at the tree from which Grant branched,* she urged. *Like father, like son. It is a good life, if a wife practiced tolerance.* Sarah refused. So, she was alone. And across the table from Grace was the woman who would replace her. How sad for Sarah. If only she had listened.

Grace's introspection was interrupted by Alicia, serving bread pudding swimming in a rich vanilla sauce. The rotund cook beamed a smile so wide it appeared to divide the upper and lower portions of her face. "Enjoy," she said merrily in her thick Hispanic accent as she placed a bowl of the pudding in front of Lesley.

"It looks delicious."

"It is," said Grantham Stewart, his spindly fingers reaching for a spoon. "It's the pride of your kitchen, isn't it, Alicia?"

"Sí, an dis family like my bread pudding." Her deliveries of the dessert complete, Alicia swept happily back through the doorway leading to the kitchen.

"The best part of having Alicia, my dear, is her ability to cook American," remarked Grace. "At this skill, she could now be native born. However, it did take me sometime to teach her that dinner rolls should replace tortillas."

Light laughter greeted Grace's comment.

Lesley thought the remark condescending, but she smiled politely and caught Grant's wink. Lesley felt a swell of trepidation as she glanced at Grace Stewart. This woman would be formidable, she decided, and turned her attention back to the old man.

The sip of brandy was surprisingly smooth and warming as it cleared her throat. Lesley had never tasted the liquor before. Generally inexperienced with most alcohol, Lesley normally avoided liquor in favor of wine.

They were enjoying the brandy in the mansion's formal living room. Silently saluting the decorator, Lesley approved of the soft yellows, with a sprinkling of subdued blues and pale corals which gave the room an appearance of warmth and hospitality that in no way detracted from its formality and elegance.

"This room is beautiful," complimented Lesley, turning to Grace.

"Thank you, my dear. This room was one of my first challenges when Blaine and I moved in with Daddy. It was so darkly formal before. The house needed—what is it young people say—to lighten up." Grace tipped her brandy snifter slightly and smiled appreciatively at Lesley. *The girl has good taste*, she thought. *Remarkable, given her background.*

"Now that you've met Grant's mother and father, tell me about your parents, dear," Grace said.

Lesley managed only the barest remarks about her long-separated parents. She dismissed her father by saying bluntly she had never met him. She described her mother as shy and intelligent, a dedicated registered nurse who worked in the neonatal department of a large hospital in Austin. She had moved there when Lesley was still a toddler.

"Your mother sounds like a remarkable woman. I look forward to meeting her," Grace said graciously. "Do you see each other often?" Grace noted the uncomfortable expression that flashed across Lesley's face.

"No, unfortunately we don't. Only on holidays. I do try to spend a weekend with her around her birthday." Lesley glanced away from Grace's piercing scrutiny. "I suppose the press of our jobs doesn't allow us much time together," Lesley explained, the last few words barely audible.

In voicing those words, Lesley felt the full weight of guilt she harbored deep inside over her lack of closeness with the woman who gave her life and raised her. Throughout her childhood years, Lesley could never remember Katherine Rowan angry or ecstatic or enthusiastic or demonstrative in any way. She was simply a quiet person, draped in a sweet sadness that no one, not Lesley, not even her mother's parents, could penetrate. *She has been deeply hurt*, her grandmother once explained to silence Lesley's persistent questions. *And she never got over it*, Grandma Nell had added, without explaining any reason for her mother's pain.

When Lesley was older, she attributed the "hurt" to her mother's failed marriage and longing for her lost lover. She fantasized about her mother and father, young and in love, romping through the hay fields of her grandparents' farm—her mother's raven hair, long then, streaming in the wind as she raced across the field behind her father, the two of them kissing under the shelter of the thick, old, oak tree standing solid and alone in the center of the hay field, happiness radiating on their young faces.

In reality, Lesley seldom saw her mother smile. At the same time, Katherine Rowan never complained and was attentive to her sprightly young daughter's every need. Lesley could not recall her mother ever taking a vacation. The only trips she and her mother made were to her grandparents' farm.

Katherine Rowan altered her work schedule frequently to attend school events. She never missed any part of Lesley's young years. And Katherine was in the audience for several high school plays in which Lesley had a leading role under the encouraging, but strict, tutorage of Mildred Stevens. Mrs. Stevens was the drama teacher who wrestled through Lesley's inherent shyness to tap a wellspring of thespian ability. Lesley attributed her anchoring ability to experience of performing on stage in high school.

"I hope we can meet your mother very soon, dear." Grace's words interrupted Lesley's reverie. "How did she react when you told her you were marrying my Grant?"

"I haven't been able to reach her yet." Lesley ducked her head momentarily lest anyone note the prevarication in her words. She had not yet attempted to contact her mother who knew nothing of her relationship with Grant. Lesley made a mental promise to call her mother tomorrow.

The remainder of the evening passed congenially until a ringing telephone in an adjacent room intruded on their conversation. Moments after the ringing stopped Alicia beckoned to Blaine, who excused himself to take the call. When he did not return for some time, Grant appeared restless and suggested they leave. It was well past 11 p.m.

After joining in the polite protests, Emily rushed over to exclaim excitedly she wanted Lesley to be her guest at the country club for lunch. "If we're going to be sisters, we need to get to know one another. Grandpa kept you mostly to himself, tonight," she said in a sweetly complaining voice, while flashing a wide smile at the old man, now sitting alone in the cavernous living room, pulling contentedly on another cigar.

"Emily, darling," Grace interceded. "Let's not overwhelm Lesley. There is plenty of time to get acquainted. After all, she's a well-known broadcaster and I'm sure has a lot of demands for her time."

"Come here, young lady. I want a proper goodbye." Grantham Stewart's voice immediately silenced the other voices. Lesley walked back to where the patriarch sat absorbing the social exchanges between his family members and their guest. He parked his cigar on a large ashtray on the floor next to his wingback chair and took both of Lesley's hands in his liver spotted hands and held them in a grip that would have hurt had Lesley been wearing rings.

"You'll bring new spirit to this family, young lady. We need it," he told her in a voice pitched low enough not to be overheard by the others. "Give me a hug and come back real soon, you hear."

"I will. Thank you, sir." Lesley bent and wrapped her arms around the thin wrinkled neck and felt a light kiss on her cheek. "Goodbye."

Grant was at her side and shook his grandfather's hand. "I gather you approve."

"You're damned right I do," the old patriarch said brusquely, as he bent to retrieve his cigar. "Make sure you don't screw this one up," he admonished, shaking a gnarled finger at his grandson with obvious good humor.

Grace linked her arm with Lesley. "I'm so sorry. Blaine must still be tied up on the telephone. Let me see you to the door."

Just as Grant opened the huge oak door, Blaine stepped out from the library, pushing one hand through his hair as if to brush away the source of the agitation displayed on a face—a face shrouded in a deep frown as he pulled the door closed behind him. He seemed momentarily startled by the sight of the group near the opened front door, then appeared to gather himself as he strode toward them.

"Sorry for the interruption. It was a pleasure meeting you, Miss Rowan," Blaine said somewhat distractedly, extending his hand. Lesley felt sweat on his palm.

Turning to his son, the elder Stewart bid his son goodbye with a handshake. "Call me in the morning, if you will."

"Sure, Dad," replied Grant, sounding perplexed by his father's request. He too had seen the exasperation on his father's face when he exited the small study off the large living room. The phone call had obviously upset his father. *Something to broach with him in the morning when I phone him,* Grant made a mental note.

A rush of warm air greeted their exit as Lesley and Grant stepped outside, holding hands, onto the wide steps leading to the paving stone driveway circling in front of the mansion. Grant's silver Jaguar sat bathed in pale moonlight, giving it an almost ghostly hue. *The color of Blaine's face,* Lesley thought, as she slid into the low leather seat. She wondered silently what had been said in the telephone conversation that so upset Grant's father. *A puzzle,* she concluded.

19

W itt Terrell took a pull on the pint of Jack Daniels, carefully
screwed on the cap, and tucked it back into the back pocket of his
jeans before rubbing the back of his hand absently over his mouth.
The warmth of the liquor penetrated all the way to his stomach.
He should not be drinking. He promised Mac no liquor. It was
a promise he knew he wouldn't keep when he made it. Whatever
Terrell was *not*, he *was* a man of his word—except where liquor
was concerned. He could taper back. That he was doing. And he
would not get drunk. He would drink just enough to hold off the
demons and the shakes and maybe a little of the boredom.

Terrell watched through the murky pane of a window, his only
view to the outside from the dusty confines of a weathered, empty
storage shed where he had been sitting since noon. Down a dirt
road 50 yards or so a dump truck had pulled up about an hour
before and parked. It had high, slatted sides and *Althea Oil & Gas*
painted in faded, but still-recognizable letters on the side of each
door, nearly identical to the truck that had been here two days ago.
Terrell felt a brief sense of satisfaction. He had two locations for a
stake-out. When the first truck rumbled into view along the dirt
road leading to the field, he knew his gut had been right.

That first truck had arrived at about the same time. It caught
him off guard as he was writing down numbers off pumps at the

far end of a hundred acre or better field. There were dozens of oil pumps grinding tirelessly, their heavy steel arms rising and falling with an unaltered cadence. He had dived behind the base of the nearest pump, his heart thumping loudly in his chest. For more than an hour he lay there while the truck motor idled and daylight thinned. Whoever came in the truck remained inside. Just before sunset he had heard the drone of plane engines. Minutes later, a larger twin-engine plane made a jerky landing on a makeshift air strip in the middle of the oil field, bumping to a stop near the truck, which promptly backed up to the middle door of the plane. Binoculars hung around Terrell's neck; they were a precaution for scanning the field periodically to be sure he was not being observed.

Terrell watched two men jump down from the truck's cab. There were two other men who alternately came to the doorway of the plane, handing down large wood-crated objects—each about the size of a half-dozen egg crates—to the two men on the back of the truck. To an untrained observer, the objects looked like small equipment crates. Terrell suspected otherwise. He was half a field away, too far to hear their voices over the drone of the plane's engines and the clattered idling of the truck that sounded in need of muffler repairs.

The unloading was completed in less than an hour. Only the top of the sun still peeked about the horizon to light the operation. After the unloading was completed, the plane's door was quickly secured, its engines revved, and it was taxied to the southern end of the landing field where it took off toward the south before slanting back to the north. Even in the dimming light Terrell could make out the now familiar Althea Oil & Gas logo on the plane's tail.

Raising a thick cloud of dust, the truck lumbered slowly away on a narrow dirt road, which meandered through the oil rigs, many of which Terrell suspected were pumping from wells long depleted of oil.

It had been dark for some time before he stood up cautiously. Shaking the stiffness from his legs and shoulders, he had walked to where the old Pinto was hidden, a half-mile away in a thicket, off a road so overgrown it was barely discernible. Mac had given him $5,000 to purchase a car and some clothes. The 1980 Pinto had relatively low mileage, coughed and spat like a tubercular patient when he turned the ignition over, but was a steal for $900.

Terrell had driven back to Tyler and fallen into a restless sleep at a cheap hotel on the edge of the city. He had returned to the oil field yesterday and again today around noon to observe the landing area from the shelter of the dilapidated storage shed. From there he was now peering through his binoculars at what looked like the same truck parked under the shade of a large oak tree.

Feeling the familiar pull within, Terrell fished the pint bottle out of his back pocket and took a long gulp. He knew it would not make him drunk, which is what he really wanted to be at this moment—not sitting here in a wood and tin enclosed furnace, sweat dripping from every pore of his thin frame. *Helluva way to make a living. Even the FBI was never like this.*

Wrong, he thought, recalling International Falls.

That was the pits in those early days; bitter cold and dreary, reminiscent of Thule, Greenland, the icy no-man's-land where he had spent a lonely year on duty with the Air Force. He left the Air Force after four years, expecting greener pastures with the FBI. Instead, he got border duty in the number one hellhole for agents. "An assignment for rookies," he was reassured by the special agent in charge—a veteran agent who finally acquiesced to his superior's refusals of his annual request for a transfer, and resigned himself to spending his FBI career in upstate Minnesota and not in the cushier confines of a Washington office. That was when Terrell had started drinking.

Even after all these years, the liquor still burned as it went down. Terrell stuffed the pint container back in the pocket of his jeans.

Beams from the late summer afternoon sun reflected off the dust-caked window, making it more difficult to view the field across the road. He glanced at his watch. It was nearing five p.m. About the time the plane arrived yesterday. Terrell shifted uncomfortably on the small, portable canvas seat he had purchased at an army surplus store in Jacksonville, just a few miles down the road from Tyler. It beat kneeling or standing, but not by much.

Another hour passed. Still no sign of the plane. The lowering sun streaked the western sky with a gaudy mixture of pink, orange, and reddish hues, filtered by thin clouds. His savvy eye measured another hour or so of day light remaining. Apparently, it was enough.

Terrell's sharp ears picked up the sound of the truck's cranky engine sputtering to life. By the time the truck slowed on the edge of the makeshift airfield, he could hear the plane approaching in the near distance.

A thin smile creased Terrell's lips, knowing his long, sweltering vigil was finally being rewarded. He lifted a video camera from the case at his feet. The camera had been Mac's idea, and he had personally instructed Terrell on how to use it. Small and lightweight, the camera was state-of-the-art surveillance equipment, with a lens that could deftly narrow the distance between the storage shed and the objects it viewed.

Terrell fitted the camera atop a small tripod, removed the lens cap, and pressed the camera against the left corner of the glass. Lowering his eye to the viewfinder, he pulled the truck and its occupants as close as the telephoto adjustment would allow. That had the effect of moving the big vehicle from a small portion of the viewing screen to nearly full-screen, then back again as he waited for the plane to land from the south. A flashing red light inside the viewfinder alerted him the digital camera was rolling.

Within minutes he saw the twin-engine plane distantly in the viewfinder. He panned the camara to follow the plane as it landed and zoomed in as the truck pulled abreast of the cargo door. The transfer of the familiar wooded crates took longer than the unloading yesterday. This delivery was considerably larger. By the time the plane was emptied, the crates were piled nearly to the top of the truck's wooden slates. A canvas cover was stretched across the load. Before the truck had pulled away, the plane was already disappearing into the southern sky.

Keeping the camera rolling, Terrell zoomed in on the truck door's logo and on the dust-covered license plate dangling precariously underneath the truck bed as it lumbered away. The license was secured by two thin wires. *Probably used for more than one truck*, Terrell speculated. He noticed no other identifying numbers or marks on the truck, details he would look more closely for when he viewed the tape later.

Again, Terrell waited patiently for full darkness before carefully easing the short, narrow door of the shed open. Its hinges squealed in rusted agony as he ducked his head out into the open.

The silvery shadow of a partial moon hung high in the east sky, drifting lazily westward between the lingering clouds, lighting his way back to where the car was concealed. Two hours later he pulled into the driveway at Mac Withers' home.

After viewing the video Mac turned to Terrell. "You think those crates hold drugs?" Mac knew the reply he would get before posing the question, as he scrutinized the man sitting across from him, gripping a large mug of coffee with both hands. A day or two's growth of beard shadowed Terrell's gaunt cheeks. His eyes were red-rimmed with fatigue, blending the man's face with the rest of his untidy appearance. Mac had smelled the liquor when Terrell stepped into the slate foyer. He said nothing, offering instead to make coffee. Terrell gulped down the oversized mug of the brew while Mac inserted the camera's 64-gigabyte memory card into the monitor and began watching the drug transfer in silence.

"I'd bet my last dollar it's drugs," agreed Terrell, keeping his eyes fixed on his coffee mug.

"What's the next step to find out?"

"I need to follow the truck next time there's a connection." Terrell raised the steaming coffee to his lips, sipping gingerly, grateful for something to hold onto to keep his hands from shaking. He felt sure Mac had smelled the Jack Daniels on his breath. "I might need someone to drive while I tape where it goes from the drop area to where the stuff is stored. Know anyone willing to come along?"

"I'm sure we can arrange that. How soon?"

"Hard to say, Mac. Two drops in three days." Mac shook his head. "That's pretty close. If those crates do contain drugs, they must need to move a lot of merchandise in a hurry."

"The word we get from our police sources is there's been a drought on the streets lately. So the market's primed, at least in Dallas."

"That may explain the back-to-back drops. If that's the case, my guess is another could come in the next day or two. That's supposing there are a lot of anxious buyers."

"When do you plan to head back to Tyler?"

"Tonight. I want to be there before dawn, just in case the bad guys change their flight schedule."

Mac set his mug on the large coffee table separating two over-stuffed beige sofas flanking a brick fireplace which scaled the wall to the ceiling. "Look. It's late. Why don't you stay here tonight and leave in the morning? You look like you could use some sack time."

The invitation was appealing. Terrell had planned to sleep in the back seat of the small car tonight, feeling it prudent to avoid being seen too often in the Tyler area. Muggy temperatures still lingered in the low 70s at this time of the year in Texas, even at the coolest hour of the early morning. And he would face the insatiable buzzing of flies and mosquitoes to make his cramped sleeping quarters even more uncomfortable.

The prospect of a soft bed, air conditioning, a hot shower, a shave—it was tempting. Terrell stared into his coffee cup. But he was a man who followed his instincts. Hunches seldom failed him. His gut was urging him to return to Tyler tonight.

"I'd better get back. Thanks, anyway." Terrell swallowed the last of the now tepid coffee. "How soon can you send somebody up to Tyler?"

"Probably not before tomorrow morning. Jack Reilley is who

I'll send if he can be pulled off his beat. Where do you want him to meet you?"

"There's a truck stop about a mile west of Tyler on Route 31. It's big and it's busy. I'll check in with you at the office and we'll figure out a time."

"Sounds good," said Mac, rising slowly. "When you call I'll tell you what car to look for. I'll get him up there as soon as I can."

Terrell looked over at Mac. "I think our Mexican friends will be on a different schedule just to keep the chances of being detected lower. Have to be worried about being detected by the Border Patrol or the FAA. Good chance they might fly in early tomorrow. When the plane pulled away this evening, it kept going south instead of turning north like is usually does." He rubbed the side of the coffee cup as if attempting to draw assurance from its warm sides. "Any chance you could arrange somebody tonight?"

Mac stared at Witt Terrell's craggy face. They had worked together at the Dallas newspaper, Terrell a reporter, Mac a city editor. Terrell often came to work hung over, but it never detracted from his work. His instincts about a story were uncanny. If he had a hunch that plane would be landing tomorrow early, with another load of drugs, Mac knew his friend well enough not to question his instincts.

"Stay put. Let me call someone."

"Sure."

Mac ran his finger down the list of Channel 15 staffers' home telephone numbers until he stopped on the one his eyes were searching for. He hesitated momentarily before lifting the receiver and dialing the number, still debating the decision he had just made walking from the living room to the kitchen. After the fourth ring, Mac was about to hand up when the ringing was interrupted with by breathless, "Hello?" at the other end.

"Les, you all right?"

"Oh, hi Mac. I just walked in with a load of groceries when the telephone rang. I've been out shopping. What's up? Something wrong with the newscast?" There was a tinge of worry in her voice.

"No. The cast looked fine." He drew in his breath. "I've got an assignment for you."

"Great. What is it? When?"

"Now."

A minute later her cell was ringing Grant. When he didn't answer, she left a brief message. "Sorry, can't come tonight. I'll tell you about it tomorrow. Love you."

20

To Lesley's delight the Mustang motor purred as it sped down the dark interstate. Its more recent death rattles had been allayed by a young mechanic at a Texaco station not far from her apartment. The mechanic's head was shaved bald and his dark work clothes smelled of grease. The oversized jumpsuit he wore was so dark the grease stains appeared to have vanished into the rough fabric.

Her Mustang was now happily removed from her nightly prayer list. The reason—Jesse Combs who had truly proved to be a gift sent from God in her mind. He would listen intently to the engine for what seemed long periods with his head bent under the hood. What sounded improved to her ears often required a tweak or two to meet a standard of perfection only his ears could discern. *God,* she decided, *would drive a Mustang if he ever did return to his earthly kingdom, and he would place it in Jesse Combs overly-caring hands. It beat riding a donkey, but not by much,* she concluded, bouncing along uncomfortably on worn seat springs the mechanic promised would be his next refurbishing project.

Lesley could well afford to trade cars. It might be cheaper in the long run. Parts, and the labor to install them, were costly. It was not the money that held her back. It was her father. This was her one and only link to the knight in shining armor of her childhood daydreams. For the time being she would ride into whatever battles lay ahead in her faded-blue Mustang convertible.

A huge, lighted billboard on the interstate announced the truck stop, with instructions to take the next exit. Mac told her to look for Terrell's old Pinto. *Amazing*, she thought, as she pulled slowly into the main entrance to the truck stop, *that anyone who still drove a Pinto had lived to tell about it.*

Look for it on the left side of the restaurant, Mac had directed. She threaded slowly through lines of trucks parked on either side in back of the sprawling main building. It was a gauntlet of low-rumbling motors. Turning at an opening, Lesley saw the small car at the back edge of the building, the last of three cars parked next to the restaurant. She pulled into the vacant parking space beside the Pinto. Terrell's head lay back against the headrest. He appeared asleep, but the appearance was deceptive. He had heard her car pull in and park and the door open.

Mac promised Lesley that Terrell would smell better this time. After a brief tug of words, Terrell had reluctantly showered and shaved before heading back to Tyler.

As Lesley approached, Terrell got out of the Pinto and leaned against the driver-side door. The short-sleeve shirt he wore looked like a half-full sack with his thin frame inside. Probably a loaner from Mac. His eyes betrayed a lack of sleep. She had slept only two hours herself before the alarm sounded, rousing her into the shower and onto the road.

Terrell awkwardly extended his hand and offered her a smile that barely extended his lips. "Hi, Miz Lesley. Looks like we're a reporting team today."

"Looks that way, Mr. Terrell." She smiled to ease his obvious discomfort. "You've done a great job up here. Mac says you may be on to something big."

"Yes, ma'am. Could be. Then again, might not." Terrell pulled the stub of a cigarette from his breast pocket and lit it with a match. "We'll see." He took several long pulls on the cigarette stub, held protectively between his thumb and forefinger before throwing it to the ground. The toe of his boot rendered it harmless. "I guess we better head out to the field."

He silently measured the view of the Mustang from the front of the building. This appeared to be where employees parked. It would not be as noticeable there. "Why don't we go in my car, if you don't mind? It's easier to hide at the field."

A new sun remained shyly out of sight, just below the horizon, its presence betrayed only by random hues of soft, pinkish-orange now muting the night darkness to a soft gray. The sky above was quiet except for the loud bawling of a hawk, up early, as it scanned the ground for breakfast. The bawling stopped as it flew downward to raid the nest of a convenient lark sparrow, whose melodious trills were turned shrill by the panic of chasing the raider across the pre-dawn sky. But it was too late to save the baby sparrow clamped firmly in the hawk's jaw. Sadness tugged briefly at Lesley, watching the life and death chase and the desperate courage of the small sparrow trying to rescue its doomed offspring by diving at the invader.

Terrell had not spoken since hunkering down near the lone window of the dilapidated storage shed, which was still rank with the odor of urine sprayed on walls by prior visitors. He seemed impervious to the stench as he fastened the video camera on a tripod. She felt nauseous and willed her mutinous stomach to not embarrass her.

"Mind taking first watch?" he asked in his reedy voice. "Just keep an eye on that landing strip to the right. The trucks have been coming off that dirt road just to the left. And whatever you do, keep your head down low as possible," he instructed gruffly. As he scooted over to lean against the side wall, she took his former position under the window.

Terrell had made no attempt at conversation on the ride to the oil field. She had not liked him before and less now. But her dislike was tempered by a natural sympathy for his loneliness. It made her more curious about why he was here and what brought him to this state in life. *Alcohol, no doubt.* Maybe the bottle was to blame for his past—although she noted appreciatively he was not drinking. Mac had mentioned a promise he elicited from Terrell, a promise Terrell was apparently keeping, to her relief.

Each time she stole a surreptitious look at Terrell he appeared to have his eyes closed. His breathing remained even, indicating he was not asleep, maybe just dozing. Or ignoring her. If a plane were coming, it would have to arrive quickly to beat the daylight now garishly blooming across the eastern sky.

Dawn stretched into mid-morning and the heat and stench in the shack was becoming unbearable. Lesley took another gulp of water from the half-liter bottle she'd had the foresight to purchase at the truck stop along with a package of Twinkies. She had not seen Terrell drink or eat since they arrived. She wondered absently if she should offer him some of her water. Her mind drifted to Grant and the smile that would trace across his lips as she pictured his reaction to his fiancée sitting in this hellish hovel staking out a possible drug drop. It was the barely discernible sound that wrested her mind back to reality. Lesley whispered, "I think I hear a plane approaching, Mr. Terrell."

"Yes, ma'am, I hear it." Lesley moved away from the window as Terrell hunkered down and peered out through the foggy glass. *It must be flying low*, he thought. *Yeah, definitely an airplane. But no sign of the truck.*

The plane passed over the field, heading north. Terrell could not see the plane and only guessed at its direction from the sound of the engines. Maybe some other plane heading into Tyler's airport, although he had checked earlier. This was not a regular flight path for aircraft landing there.

"False alarm?" Lesley asked, as she leaned forward to peer out a corner of the small window. Terrell shrugged. Long minutes passed. Then they both heard it again, the noise of a plane's engines approaching from the north. The aircraft was shortly overhead and

Terrell waved impatiently for Lesley to crouch lower down. The plane then banked sharply in the south sky and began descending toward the grassy landing strip. As Terrell cautiously peered out the window, a truck rumbled into view, raising a cloud of dust in its wake, moving faster than the truck had yesterday. *It must be late,* Terrell surmised, *which explains why the plane didn't land on its initial flyover.*

Lesley heard the passing truck stop with its motor idling. She raised slowly, her eyes just above the window, as the driver maneuvered the old GMC into readiness to back up to the plane. The plane bumped down several hundred feet away, skipping precariously on the first touchdown, and once more before its wheels gripped the ground and it began slowing.

There's more rush in this drop, Terrell thought as he rested the small camera against the glass to defuse the dust and movement and punched the on button. His video from the last landing was good quality; maybe even good enough to use as evidence in a court of law. With full morning light, this could be even better.

As the truck's passenger came around the driver's side, there was a brief exchange with the two men framed in the cargo door of the plane. The man on the ground finally shrugged his shoulders, walked back to the truck, lowered the truck's gate and waited sullenly as the driver backed up to the cargo entry of the plane. He then climbed up over the side and stood in the truck bed and was joined by the driver. The loading took less time than it had the day before. The cargo was packed in large canvas duffle bags instead of crates and appeared heavier for the men heaving the bags into the back of the truck.

Terrell guessed it was marijuana or cocaine. *Maybe both,* he surmised as he kept the camera rolling on the scene.

Even before the plane circled to begin its takeoff the truck was already heading out of the oil field on the rutted access road. Dust stirred up by the departing truck obliterated it from sight. Only the lingering dust marked its path. Terrell was counting on that hovering dust cloud to guide them in following the truck to a paved county road, which intersected with the dirt road winding through the oil field.

When they were sure the plane was headed south and the truck out of sight, Terrell and Lesley bolted for the Pinto with the video equipment. Terrell had hidden the compact car under the protective branches of a thicket where he had hacked an opening the first time he explored the oil field.

"Get in and buckle up," Terrell ordered tersely, stuffing the camera into the back seat. By the time they reached the intersection with the paved road, only a hint of dust lingered in the air. Would it be enough? Terrell spun the little car north in the direction of the interstate. If they lost the truck now, this trip would be in vain. And if they came upon the truck too quickly, they could be spotted by the driver or his passenger. It was going to be dicey. Terrell pushed the accelerator to the floor.

Lesley felt her heart racing with the car, silently urging him to go faster, fearing they were losing the truck on the winding track. Still no sign of it ahead. A half-mile before they reached the intersection with a main highway, they spotted the truck ahead, waiting to exit onto a paved county road.

"We'll hang back," Terrell muttered. He slowed as a sign announced the approaching intersection where the truck had been waiting just seconds ago. At the neck of the intersection Terrell spotted the truck. It was heading north, toward the I-20 loop that would take it east to Tyler or west to Dallas, whichever was its destination. He pulled onto the two-lane highway after waiting for a slow-moving car to pass and within a minute had the truck in sight on the flat highway. Terrell silently shared the relief he saw etched on Lesley's face as he checked traffic in both directions.

Where the road fed into the interstate the truck headed west toward Dallas. Keeping to the posted speed, never varying more than two or three miles per hour, the truck attracted no attention from a state trooper sitting in a grassy median with his radar gun pointed in their direction. *If he only knew*, Lesley thought, as they passed the patrolman moments later. The truck was high enough that Terrell could keep it in sight even as he hung back behind three other cars traveling in the right lane. He was a hundred or more yards behind, but did not want to risk being spotted by the truck's driver.

Following Terrell's instructions, Lesley reviewed the video he shot from the shed through the tiny viewfinder. It was all there—the plane landing, the truck backing up, the duffle bags being tossed from the plane to the truck, three dozen or more. A fortune waiting to be collected. Lesley snapped in a fresh battery. They were set for the next opportunity to video.

Traffic thickened as they approached Dallas, which provided both a better cover and a menace for Terrell. They lost the truck for more than a minute, while the Pinto was trapped in a lane slowing for cars backed up near a turn-off.

Using Terrell's old FBI binoculars, Lesley strained to see ahead, above the high-profile semis. They had gone more than two miles while her panic rose, with Terrell whipping from lane to lane, before she finally spotted the canvas-topped bed of the truck. She heard the man next to her sigh heavily in audible relief.

Terrell now stayed to the faster left lanes on the expanded interstate. "He's turning," Lesley shouted. The truck headed down an off ramp, into a sprawling industrial area less than a quarter-mile ahead. "Hold tight," he ordered, whipping the old car across three lanes, maneuvers greeted by irate horn honking. Then he darted intrusively into the line slowing for the off ramp, fervently hoping the truck driver's attention stayed focused on the road ahead, and ignored the honking vehicles behind him.

The truck was no longer in view, after turning at a traffic light onto an arterial road at the bottom of the off-ramp. Which way? Terrell patted his steering wheel impatiently. *Does this goddamned light ever change?* He turned left, accelerating ahead of the three cars in front of him, slowing at each interior street. As he slowed at the fourth street, Lesley spotted the truck about four blocks down. Terrell skidded the Pinto sharply around the corner before slowing behind two cars and a delivery van in line some distance behind the truck.

"He's turning left."

"Okay. We'll hang back."

Both watched the truck, moving slowly down a feeder street lined with warehouses on both sides, banked by loading docks. Terrell drove past the street. At the end of the block, he U-turned, circling back, and turned down the same feeder street. The truck had disappeared.

Ahead, streets curved between the ubiquitous steel buildings, differentiated only by brick facades on some of the warehouse entrances. Like the main road leading in, a median now separated the lanes, where young trees, sprouting upward from a heaping circle of black mulch, offered a pseudo-environmental viewshed for those peering out from the occasional windows in the bleak, shapeless steel buildings lining the road on both sides.

"Shit," Terrell swore under his breath. Lesley shared his frustration but kept silent.

Terrell wound through street after street in the sprawling complex of offices and warehouses. Nothing. He drove to the end of a street that rambled for several blocks before an interstate ramp divided it from an area of ramshackle homes that stood between two-story, drab gray clapboard apartment buildings.

Terrell turned onto a street at the far end of the industrial area. Lesley saw it first. In faded letters above an office entrance door at the end of a row of loading docks was written, *Althea Oil & Gas*. Vacant docks lined the loading area. The building looked abandoned from the outside. A narrow alleyway separated it from the adjacent building and was lined with commercial dumpsters.

"They're probably in the back. Let's park here," Terrell said, pulling into a parking spot at the side of an adjacent building amid several other cars. "You stay here. Let me check it out first. Okay?"

Before she could voice a protest, he grabbed the camera and was out the door.

Waiting was not something Lesley did well. She checked her wristwatch. It was close to one p.m. She would check in with Mac and let him know where they were. She called on Mac's cell phone. No answer. She decided against leaving a message.

An hour passed. Sweat trickled down her back and dampness oozed under her arms. Even with the windows rolled down, there was no relief from the afternoon heat.

Where in the hell is Terrell? Another ten minutes passed. Still no Terrell. Lesley fished the cell phone from her purse and was dialing Mac again when Terrell opened the door and without a word slid into the driver's seat, turning the key in the ignition at the same time he closed the door. The cold motor turned over twice reluctantly, and then sputtered to life. He swung out of the parking lot and sped toward the main road.

"Check the video," he snapped. His face was red and damp with sweat. His left hand had a death grip on the steering wheel. The hand holding the camera was shaking like a flapping flag in a stiff wind.

Lesley rewound the tape and squinted into the viewfinder. What played on the small screen churned up excitement in her stomach. It was here. Large duffle bags being carried from the truck into a darkened warehouse, the name, *Althea Oil & Gas, Dock 4*, in view above the activity. But it was the next video that stirred even more excitement. Despite the absence of anything but daylight streaming down from high windows along the outside wall of the warehouse, the ambient light was enough to show the truck's contents scattered on the concrete floor of the warehouse. Two beefy Hispanic men were seen counting the duffel bags, pulling a vinyl wrapped package from one bag, sniffing the tightly wrapped block before tossing it back in, checking the contents of each duffel bag before zipping the bags closed and marking a sheet on a clipboard. Lesley could hear one of the men ask, "Everything look okay, amigo?" The response was in muffled Spanish.

She glanced at Terrell. His face was pale, almost ashen. Sweat trickled down the side of his face into a shirt collar already damp. "This is great stuff you got. I can't wait for Mac to see this," she said.

Terrell turned toward her. A look of utter weariness pervaded his dark eyes. "They saw me."

21

The voice at the other end of the line spoke in Spanish, the tone agitated but at the same time apologetic. They did not see the man until the truck was unloaded and began pulling away from the dock. He was holding a small video camera. It was pointed at the dock. What should they do?

Stunned silence greeted the question.

"Compadre?"

"I'm here. Did you recognize the man? Dallas police maybe?"

"No, I didn't recognize him. Could be police. I don't know. They don't usually work alone."

"How did he get away?"

"We couldn't find him. We looked everywhere. He just disappeared." There was a rising note of apprehension in the voice at the other end of the connection.

"All right. Sit tight till I call Estavar." Edmonds felt a new rush of panic. He had to make sure they covered all their bases. He searched his mind for any loose ends and remembered the security cameras the guys in Chicago had had him install. He wasn't sure if the Mexican bunch even knew about them. "There are security cameras in the corners of the warehouse and above the outside entrance and the truck dock. Pull the tapes out of the cameras. And clean the truck real good. No trace of anything, understand? Comprende!"

"Yeah! We'll take care of it."

"I'll head out there to pick up the tapes. Don't forget—six cameras. So I need six tapes. Got it! Maybe we'll get lucky and get a look at this spook." He bit his lower lip hoping that would be the case. "Hustle your asses. Inmediatmente!"

"Yeah, yeah! Consider it done. What about us?"

"I'll call Estavar." There was a pause. "I'll arrange with him to have you picked up. No more screw ups, savvy?"

He hung the telephone up slowly. "Shit!" This was too close to home. Walt Edmonds felt his stomach lurch. "Shit," he repeated. His mind was racing. He slammed the desk with his fist. A warehouse full of drugs and someone snooping around with a camera. Panic filled his throat with bile. He dashed to the restroom in his office and unloaded the Danish and Starbucks coffee he had enjoyed less than an hour before. Edmonds' carefully nurtured, tanned complexion was paled by the vomiting and panic. He sat down glumly at his desk, turning to look out on the flowing, concrete fountain five stories below, surrounded by a meticulously landscaped plaza entrance into the downtown Dallas highrise where he maintained his office.

He picked up a cell phone to call Vincente Estavar. The message would be verbally coded. Estavar would know what to do. They were *his* drivers. What about getting the drugs to Chicago? He knew they would have to be moved quickly. Could they risk it if the cops might be on to them? Was there a choice?

Shit, he repeated silently as his cell began ringing the distant number. Beads of sweat dampened Edmonds hairline as he pressed the phone to his ear. *A chink in the armor of their operation. With any luck, maybe only a small one.* The phone rang a second time. *No breach of security would be tolerated.* The ringing stopped after three and an impatient voice at the other end demanded, "What now, my yankee friend?"

A bead of sweat began a slippery path down the back of Edmonds' neck. Estavar would have to decide what to do.

"Shit! Sorry, Les." Mac turned to Terrell sitting across the desk from him, looking directly into the sunken eyes, red-rimmed with fatigue.

"Did they get a make on your car?"

"I don't think so. I hid until I thought the coast was clear to get back to the car. We didn't see anyone who seemed to be following us."

"Okay. Maybe we got lucky this time," Mac said, clasping his hands behind his head and leaning back in his high-backed chair. "They can't spot you a second time, Witt."

Mac's admonishment was answered with a silent nod. The news director sighed heavily. He wanted the story. But he didn't want anyone hurt. The brutal murder of the Brownsville editor and the pilot were evidence of what could happen. No story was worth that.

"Witt, you go to my house. Get some food, a shower, and some rest. We'll talk this evening."

Withers turned to Lesley. "I hate to ask this, girl. But I want you on the air on your regular newscasts. Can you do it?"

"You betcha," she smiled, doing her best mimic of the female sheriff in *Fargo*. "I keep a change of clothes in the make-up room. And I can sponge off the reek of this assignment in the ladies' room. No problem."

She turned in the doorway. "I'll put notes on everything we saw on my laptop at home tonight so I don't forget anything."

"Good idea. See you later, Les." Withers pulled open a desk drawer. He grasped a set of keys and handed them to Terrell. "You'll need these to get in, Witt."

Lesley pushed the buttons on her cell phone to access the answering machine in her apartment. Seven messages, all from Grant, disappointed she couldn't come to his place last night. His words were playful, sexy. By the last message his voice was more serious, his concern evident. Where was she and why had she not returned his calls from this morning?

The private line answered on the first ring. "Grant Stewart."

"Theeee Grant Stewart of mayoral fame?"

"Where have you been? And more importantly, who were you with?"

"Suspicions, suspicions! I was on special assignment. I can't tell you with whom. It's a deep, dark secret that will be revealed in an upcoming broadcast. You'll just have to watch if you want to know."

"What the hell kind of special assignment keeps you out all night and away from my bed?" Grant demanded, feigning irritability.

"My, how grumpy we are today. I've been told it comes from being constantly horny. We need to do something about that, Mr. Stewart."

"I plan to tonight if my beautiful news lady is available."

"Well, your prescription for alleviating horniness will be filled tonight. Is it a date?"

"Yes, you vamp. Come wearing a rib protector. I plan to tickle the truth out of you about your whereabouts last night, my fair maiden."

"Such chivalry, Mr. Stewart. What maiden, fair or not, could resist such a charming invitation? Where do I get a rib protector?"

"Check with the Dallas Cowboys."

"I'll see you tonight after the six o'clock cast. But you have to promise no tickling. It stems my sex drive."

He laughed. "In that case, Miss Rowan, I pledge no tickling. Love you."

"Love you. Bye." Then she remembered the promise to make written notes of what had transpired in the past few hours. Note writing could wait!

The Waterpik shower head pelted her skin with invigorating pulsations. What a great idea to have a shower in the make-up room. It was the station's make-up artist who showed her into the shower closet when she went to retrieve the spare outfit she kept at the station for just such a situation as today.

God, it feels good to get clean again, she moaned silently as she washed away the sweat and grime of the last few hours and let the warm water address her fatigue. What would she tell Grant about how she spent her night? He would certainly ask again. She would just have to think up a credible lie. Telling him the truth was not an option.

It was just after five when Witt Terrell awoke, perspiration soaking the pillow despite the air conditioning. *Fear.* He could taste it. *Palpable* was the way his instructors at the academy described it. They were right. What if they found him? He would be killed. And maybe Lesley, too. That was the last time he was taking the girl with him. He didn't need a partner tracking this story. He worked better, *and safer*, alone. Mac would just have to understand or get someone else. A new plan formed in his mind as he relaxed back on the pillow, staring at the ceiling. He eventually nodded back off to sleep.

It was an hour later when he awoke again. He called Mac, but there was no reply. After a quick shower, Terrell rummaged through the small, battered suitcase that contained his meager wardrobe. He pulled out a crumpled pair of jeans and an even more wrinkled T-shirt. At least they were clean.

Mac had told him to stay put until he got home. He left a note on the kitchen counter. There was something he had to do.

After pulling into a Wendy's drive-thru for a hamburger and coffee, Terrell pulled back into the evening traffic. Minutes later he turned the Pinto into the cutoff for the warehouse used by Althea Oil & Gas Company. He pulled into a parking lot at the rear of a one-story building across from the oil company warehouse and waited until darkness fully enveloped the area.

The back door of the warehouse was secured with a deadbolt. He had no fear of triggering an alarm, silent or otherwise. He reasoned there was no alarm company guarding this building—not with what was stored here. What he had to fear were cameras that could reveal his presence. He had spotted two on the outside, over the front entrance and the loading dock where the truck was parked earlier. It was a chance he would just have to take.

Picking a lock was a skill he could also credit to his law-enforcement training. His instructor had insisted the good guys should know at least as much as the criminals. Slipping quickly inside, Terrell stood still, controlling his breathing, allowing his eyes to adjust to the dark, cavernous, hollow interior. It was deserted. Hundreds of square feet of nothing. No people, no truck, no drugs. He clung to the walls as he walked through the empty space, noting four mounts where security cameras looked down on the warehouse interior. The lights on all four were off, indicating they weren't operable. If he was a guessing man, he would say the tapes had been removed, if they were ever there in the first place.

Terrell continued cautiously through the building. The small office just inside the front entrance was empty. No desks, no furniture of any kind, completely bare. Reflections from the street light out front cast long shadows up the walls of the abandoned office area. "They got the hell out of Dodge in a hurry," he muttered to himself, walking back to leave the way he came in.

22

Mac knew instinctively what he would find when he turned the key in his front door lock. He had been unable to reach Terrell by phone to explain he would be late because of a dinner meeting with corporate honchos from the New York office. Terrell's note was on the kitchen counter.

I have gone to Austin. Want to find out who really owns Althea Oil & Gas. While I am there I will check out some other information on the oil wells that are pumping nothing. I will keep you posted.

Witt

Mac clicked the remote control to catch the midnight replay of the late newscast. He tilted a cold can of Bud Lite to the television screen before gulping down its remains. He liked the new opening the recently hired producer had designed. *Young hotshot knows his stuff,* he conceded as the skyline of Dallas paraded across the screen before dissolving to the anchor team. He had hired the guy away from a Chicago station; a real coup considering Chicago was a bigger media market than Dallas. Luckily, salary wasn't a factor. The guy just wanted to move to Texas. *Dallas had vitality,* Trace Abernathy told Mac during their initial interview. *Chicago was stale.* He had been on board less than a month and Mac could already see marked improvements in the look and pace of the late newscast.

Abernathy had been putting in 10 to 12 hour workdays at the

station since joining the Channel 15 staff. And then went out drinking with the late cast anchors almost every night. Mac envied that kind of stamina; to put in a full day even after being up most of the night. He had that endurance once. Only most of the all-nighters in his younger days were spent dealing poker or hell-raising at a bar near the newspaper—activities that eventually wrecked his marriage. Now it was all he could do to stay awake through the 10:00 p.m. newscast.

He wondered absently where Witt was tonight. Probably holed up in a cheap motel somewhere near Austin, making up for the expense of renting a car. Mac had found the Pinto as he pulled in, parked around back on one side of the double garage, out of sight. Scribbled on a pad by the wall telephone in the kitchen was a number for Enterprise Rent-a-Car. He hoped Witt would call and let him know where he was staying. Witt was the last picture in his mind before it was expunged by sleep.

"I want to announce our wedding. Tomorrow."

"But we haven't set a date, Grant."

He braced himself on an elbow looking down at her face, her raven hair disheveled on the pillow, her emerald eyes radiant. She was beautiful, never more so than like this, basking in the afterglow of their lovemaking.

"I would like to make you my wife the first Saturday in September." He softly touched her lips with a finger. "Before you say, 'no, it's too soon,' I want you to know I've already planned our honeymoon. It's set and I can't change it."

She kissed his finger. "What about the election?"

"It waits for no man; but for a beautiful woman, no problem."

"I'm serious," smiled Lesley, reaching up to kiss him lightly on the lips.

"I want you by my side for the campaign. All my internal polls tell me you will be the margin of victory."

"What polls?" she asked doubtfully.

"The ones in my head and in my heart."

"You do say the most romantic things, Mr. Mayor," she said in an exaggerated Southern drawl. "It sets my little ole heart all a flutter."

"If that's the case, then the first Saturday in September it is. We'll announce it tomorrow."

"Grant. Be serious. If I marry you before the election, I'll have to take a leave of absence. Campaigning with you would present just a small conflict of interest, not to mention depriving me of just about every ounce of journalistic integrity I have acquired."

"Be serious, Les. Take the leave. Be at my side. I want you now, and for the rest of my life."

Her eyes searched his face. He was completely serious. Her finger traced the tightened lines of his handsome face. As it brushed past his lips he held it, kissing it, than nibbling it gently with his teeth. "So where are you taking me on my honeymoon?" she asked.

"You minx," he laughed, biting the tip of her finger hard enough to evoke a yelp. "I take the honeymoon inquiry as a yes."

"Yes," she replied, flinging her arms around his neck tightly as she pressed her lips against his eager mouth.

An hour later, he lay exhausted on the pillow, Lesley curled up beside him, already asleep. It was uncanny, her ability to fall asleep immediately. *A clear conscience*, he mused. Actually, he had only been half joking about the polls. The most recent internal poll taken by his campaign organization showed his popularity slipping. Marriage might distract voters from the hard reality of higher property tax bills arriving in the fall mail. *A necessary tax increase*, his advisors insisted. Dallas inner-city neighborhoods were growing, feeling the pressure of a ballooning Hispanic migration, mostly from Mexico and the three countries on its border, Guatemala, Honduras, and El Salvador. The migration filled the shortfall of workers in construction, the fast food industry, even the city maintenance department. But the increasing swell of this migration of mostly families was stressing the Dallas school system. Employers demanded more

English classes for their non-English speaking workers—classes those employers expected the city schools to provide.

Sewer ruptures were becoming more frequent in the city's aging waste-water system. Public health services had risen sharply on his watch, pushed by the increasing migrant population. It was Bill Clinton who had opened the borders under the banner of free trade. It was Dallas and other cities in border states that were dealing with the reality of the exploding immigration—legal and illegal.

Only his campaign manager and one of his closest friends knew he was dating Lesley. Both men had tentatively broached the suggestion of marriage. *Nothing like a wedding to move property taxes off the front pages of the Dallas newspapers,* observed Strand Newman, his no-nonsense campaign director. Armed with political savvy honed in the halls of the state capitol, Newman was a former state senator who had quickly gained a reputation as a power broker and consensus maker in the backrooms of the Texas state house. It was a position Newman came to take for granted after four elections. No polls predicted the humiliating defeat voters handed him on his fifth attempt to remain in Austin. If his ignominious removal from public office left Strand Newman wary of polls, he still paid apt attention to their findings. *They are a necessary evil,* he preached from his bully pulpit at Grant's campaign headquarters. *Mind the polls,* he admonished his candidate on more than one occasion. Strand could be insufferable, but he was seldom wrong.

Grant wanted to marry Lesley. He glanced at her face, sleep erasing the fatigue he had seen there when she arrived shortly after seven. Why not now, rather than later? Lesley had agreed. He continued to watch her, lifting a strand of stray hair from her cheek, silently transfixed by her beauty. She would be an asset. Even his mother agreed on that. Lesley had passed her scrupulous muster. His grandfather encouraged the match with avidity. As usual, his father offered no opinion.

He would put the announcement in Ben Henning's hands. His chief of staff could handle the wording. In the morning, they would decide when Lesley would take leave from her anchor post. He wanted her out completely. Her job and his would always be in conflict. It was the nature of the tension between the media and elected officials. The conflict of interest would always be there, especially if he was successful in the fall election. He had already been approached by state party officials about running for congress. Easing back on the pillow, Grant folded his arms under his head. But was his career any more important than hers? In his more self-reflective and candid moments he admitted her career was equally important. Lesley had worked hard to be where she was. There was no question of her talent and a future in television news that could one day carry her to the pinnacle of her craft. Grant felt the familiar tinge of guilt he always felt when he attempted to elevate his ambitions above hers. He sighed heavily. It was a battle he would leave for another day.

His mind drifted back to the voice on the answering machine some weeks ago. It was hauntingly familiar. Where had he heard that voice before? The answer evaded him, even after these several weeks. The man had not called back.

At times, Grant wished he would, so he could confront the voice and the man behind the voice. As he played the message over and over in his mind, the question inevitably arose: how did the man uncover his relationship with Lesley, and why had he expressed such vehement personal concern? No reporters had asked about girlfriends or Lesley, a relief for a man running for reelection. Announcing the engagement would end fears of being discovered in a sexual liaison with a prominent media person. It was with profound happiness and an even more profound sense of relief that he finally fell asleep.

23

Sarah Stewart opened the wide front door with a mix of curiosity and trepidation. She knew it was two Dallas detectives. The security guard at the main entrance to the compound had informed her of that when he called to announce the two policemen were headed toward her home.

"Afternoon, Miz Stewart. I'm Detective Giles, Dallas Police Department. This is Detective Hogan. Can we come in?"

"Certainly." She led the way into the formal living room off the wide foyer of the home, which, like the larger mansion in the center of the compound, was commanded by a large, circling staircase that wound to a wide hallway overlooking the foyer.

"Can I get you some coffee?" she asked, a smile masking the rush of apprehension flooding through her.

"No, thank you, Miz Stewart," answered the man who introduced himself as Detective Giles. He and the other detective seated themselves on a plush, white sofa. Sarah sat across from them in the center of an identical sofa, separated by a large white marble-topped coffee table.

"I'm sure you're wondering why we're here. We just need to ask you a few questions about a man who had a picture of you in his apartment."

Giles noted the question in her grey eyes that seemed to

illuminate her face when she smiled. Passing a five-by-seven photograph of the man across to Sarah, he mentally paid homage to her blonde beauty, wondering absently why anyone would divorce a dish like that. "Do you know this man?"

Her eyes expanded in surprise. Sarah stared at the face in the picture. There was a view of the man looking into the camera and a profile view. "No, I don't recall ever seeing this person. Why do you ask?" Sarah handed the picture back to Detective Giles.

"We believe this man is your father. And I'm sorry to tell you this, Miz Stewart. He was found murdered last month in Dallas."

She flinched. "Murdered! I'm so sorry. But I don't know this man. I talked with my father on the telephone just last night. You must be mistaken."

"We think this man may be your biological father. Do you remember him at all?" It was the first time Detective Hogan had spoken since they sat down. "Did you ever know this man as a child?"

Sarah looked stunned by Hogan's question. "Oh, gosh, I'm really not sure. My mother remarried when I was still very young, maybe three or four. I never knew my biological father. I've had no contact with him. I learned several years ago that he was sent to prison. I don't know why, and I never asked. I really never wanted to know him." Sarah looked past the two policemen to the large window that dominated the front wall of the living room. Stately oak trees stood beyond it, like rugged wood sentries guarding the front of the home. "I was raised by my stepfather, John Hilton. He was a wonderful father. He adopted my older brother and me. He's the only real father I've ever known."

"You and your ex-husband never had any contact with the deceased?" Hogan asked.

"No. My former husband did say he got a call sometime after our divorce was announced from someone claiming to be my father." She looked bewildered. "That was several months ago, if I recall. Grant told me the man was only concerned about my welfare, nothing more."

Giles' eyebrows drew up slightly. "We'll talk to the mayor about it. Thanks for mentioning it."

There was a commotion in the front hall as the door swung open and two children burst into the foyer from outside.

Drawn to the noise, Sarah stood up. "Excuse me a moment. Those are my kids getting home from swimming lessons. I'll get them settled and be right back."

Giles and Hogan watched as she hugged the boy and the girl. She must have been explaining their presence, because both youngsters peered in at the two men for a moment and then back at their mother, looking puzzled.

A rotund woman whose round jovial face beamed a welcome to the children hurried them out of the foyer to the back of the house with a promise of fresh baked cookies and milk. When the noise of their leaving stilled, Sarah turned and walked back into the living room.

"Sorry about that. They're a noisy twosome. Actually, rowdy might be a better description."

Both men were looking up at her, apparently waiting for her to say something more. She sat down and there was a long moment of discomfort caused by the tense quiet before she raised her head and looked directly at the two men.

"My children know nothing of my biological father. He vanished before I really had any memory of him. Is it necessary to draw me into this investigation?" Her voice was restrained and even. The pleading was unmistakable in her eyes.

It was Giles who spoke. "No, Miz Stewart, I don't see any reason to bring your name up. It's obvious you can't add anything to this investigation. We'll keep your name out of it." He stood up and Sarah realized what a large man he was, over six feet on a thick frame. The hand he extended to her was the largest she had ever seen.

"Sorry to have bothered you." His light brown eyes were kindly, inviting trust.

Sarah walked the two policemen to the front door. Sunlight flooded into the foyer when she opened the door. As the two men stepped out into the searing, late morning heat, Sarah asked, "Has any family stepped forward to make burial arrangements?"

"No, ma'am," replied Hogan, the smaller of the two men. "His body's still at the county morgue."

"Thank you, detectives." The door closed slowly as the two men walked down the brick steps to their unmarked car.

Witt Terrell stared at the name. It was Texas oil. Big Texas oil. Terrell had suspected he would find a holding company or worse, a trust which owned Althea Oil & Gas. It had taken him nearly two days of bleary-eyed searching to track through the convoluted maze of more than 30 holding corporations, to a board of directors that included the corporate name he now stared at.

Althea Oil & Gas also listed a Mexican subsidiary, a name that triggered suspicion. Why, Terrell didn't know. Just a hunch. There was another common thread: some of the other holding companies had the same registered agent Althea Oil & Gas used to renew their annual charters, a law firm with a Chicago address.

What was the connection between the old-line oil company and Althea Oil & Gas? Was the long-established company being used as an unwitting front? His first instinct was *yes*! Did the head of this company, a legend in Texas oil history, know about the drugs stored, at least temporarily, in the nondescript Dallas warehouse? *Probably not*, Terrell guessed. He and his family already had enormous wealth. Then why this accountant's nightmare of intertwined corporations, some Terrell strongly suspected were shell companies?

Terrell sat back in the hard wooden chair and rubbed his eyes. He was bone tired. Researching long hours, his eyes fixated on a computer screen, and scribbling copious notes, made him feel a strong need for a cigarette. Smoking was banned in the state building. He had quit smoking five years ago. But the pressure of this assignment made his undisciplined psyche clamor for a cigarette. Smoking had almost the same pull on him as the deviling need for a swig from the pint bottle in the glove compartment of his rental car.

Terrell began transcribing the names of this final board of directors onto the legal pad filled with page after page of his research. He was unhurried and meticulous in transcribing what he found. It was all here—now on page after page of notes—one suspected dummy holding-company after another, all leading back to Althea Oil & Gas and its parent company. It had taken hours to copy the legal records with the assistance of a helpful intern from the University of Texas. The copy expense was far beyond the cash in his billfold. For the first time, he used the credit card Mac had provided him.

The Windy City should be his next stop, Terrell decided. He reluctantly decided to drop off the rental car off in Dallas and hoped the aging Pinto would be up to the trip. The rental car was nice, but expensive. Mac would have to decide about Chicago after he reviewed the information that filled the pages of the yellow legal pad.

24

In Dallas, a rare summer rain was falling, without the usual noise and light show normally provided by Mother Nature. Lesley opened an umbrella and dashed out the door to the waiting, silver-blue Mercedes. She slipped inside the opened door quickly and collapsed the purse sized umbrella before shutting the door, unable to avoid getting a little wet.

"Hello, Lesley. How are you, my darling?" Grace Stewart smiled fondly as the younger woman brushed the long black hair back from her face. *She is indeed beautiful*, concluded Grace, eyeing Lesley thoughtfully.

"Hey, Lesley," Emily Stewart hailed from the back seat. "Thanks for inviting me along." She was happy to cede the front seat beside her imperious mother-in-law to Lesley. Emily observed her husband's obsequious attitude toward his mother and learned early by example. She held fawning in high regard. It kept peace between mother and son, and therefore between mother-in-law and daughter-in-law.

Mid-morning and rain. It combined to thin shoppers in the legendary Neiman Marcus flagship store downtown. The couture department was absent even lookers. Betty Worthen was behind her large, antique white French provincial desk. She was logging in more of the fall line her chief buyer had purchased at the New

York and Paris markets in the spring, before her 11 o'clock appointment arrived. She expected Mrs. Stewart would take up a good deal of what had been a scheduled day off. She had refrained from carping after Mrs. Stewart announced on the telephone yesterday she was bringing her future daughter-in-law. A pleasant surprise, she promised.

The mayor of Dallas remarrying? And she was one of the first to know. That pleased Betty. She had often been entrusted with secrets by favored clients during the thirty-odd years she had been managing this prestigious asset for Neiman Marcus. It brought her face-to-face almost daily with many of the wealthiest clients in Texas. Betty did not have customers. She never descended to that ordinary level by comment or practice. The women who walked out the double French doors of one of the world's most exclusive and expensive couture departments were clients, never customers. Occasionally she felt obliged to remind one of her associates of the difference.

There was none she liked dressing better than Grace Stewart, with her regal bearing and perfect size eight, that had never varied in all the years the oil baroness had been choosing her seasonal wardrobe from this department. Above all, Betty Worthen appreciated loyalty. Grace Stewart did not condescend to go to the designer shows in person, nor did she frequent any of the designers who competed for the lavish spending of wealthy Texas women. She trusted Betty to select most of the appropriate and flattering apparel for her seasonal wardrobe changes.

A slight creak in the hinges on the French doors alerted Betty her expected clients had arrived. She rose from behind her desk and swept forward with a smiling flourish to greet the three women.

"My dear Grace, how are you? You look extraordinary, as always," Betty said, extending both hands to greet Grace Stewart. The two women embraced, brushing each other's cheeks with air kisses. Betty turned to Emily. "How good to see you again, Emily," she gushed, clasping both of Emily's hands warmly.

"And is this my surprise?" smiled Betty inquiringly, her attention now riveted on Lesley.

"Lesley, this is a dear friend of mine, Betty Worthen," said Grace. The warmth between the two women was effusive, but genuine. "She has been guiding me and this store in the art of dressing well for more years than I care to remember." Grace turned to Lesley and took her hand. "Betty, this is the surprise I mentioned on the telephone. Please meet Grant's intended, Lesley Rowan."

Betty only feigned appropriate surprise. She had seen Lesley Rowan on the tube often. *So this is the mayor's girlfriend. Won't the newspapers have a field day when this gets out? But not from me.* Betty shrewdly sized up the girl. "How beautiful you are, my dear."

The girl *was* a beauty, and shy. A rare combination, and very unlike most of Betty Worthen's clients. No doubt her first time in a couture department. She would have to ensure it was a memorable experience. And profitable—for her and the girl.

Lesley felt overwhelmed by the ebullient greeting. She smiled to cover her awkwardness. "I'm pleased to meet you, Miss Worthen."

"Please, please, it's Betty." She linked her arm with Lesley's and guided her to one of the richly baroque viewing rooms. "Mrs. Stewart said you will need something special for your big announcement. By the way, congratulations. Grant has chosen well."

"Thank you Miss... Betty."

"Imelda, can you come here, please. I want you to meet some very special people."

A darkly handsome woman in her middle years, with a wide streak of grey through the front of her thick, dark hair—adding to an elegant demeanor—approached from an adjoining room.

"This is my assistant, Imelda Javier, without whom I could not manage," Betty added graciously.

Imelda acknowledged each woman with a smile and handshake. "May I get you some coffee mocha, or a cappuccino, perhaps?" Imelda excused herself to ready coffee mochas for all three women, anticipating in advance what the two Mrs. Stewarts would want after checking Betty's carefully maintained, discreet index card file on each client's preferences, including their favorite beverage.

If Lesley was overwhelmed by the greeting, she was more so by the elegance of the dresses she was shown, and the prices. She had once ventured into the downtown Dallas Neiman Marcus, shortly after arriving in Dallas, experiencing the smells and sounds of the fabled store. She had not been back. A small boutique in Westbrook, discovered on another early shopping excursion, carried more of the clothes that suited her taste. It fulfilled her instinct for colors and combinations that flattered her on camera.

Grace Stewart observed the reaction to the various pieces. She was visibly pleased with Lesley's choices. The girl mirrored her own taste in clothes. She enthusiastically approved both selections. The first was a lavender silk suit with a jacket, narrow at the waist, its simple lines highlighted by a paisley scarf connected to the jacket that draped over the left shoulder. Grace agreed, it looked stunning on Lesley.

The second choice, a dress in soft, green silk, would be perfect for the engagement party Grace was planning. The announcement party would be intimate and austere, with just family and close friends, the size suitable for a second marriage.

Confirming the selections with Lesley, Betty handed both garments to her smiling assistant who disappeared into the room from which they came.

"Thank you, my dear," said Grace addressing Betty Worthen as she stood to leave. "As always, you please beyond words."

Lesley reached for her purse. Seeing no cash register, she was confused about how to pay for the purchases, but more concerned about the price, which went unstated during the showings. Grace Stewart patted her arm affectionately. "They will be sent to you, Lesley. A small gift from Emily and me," she said, glancing perceptively at her daughter-in-law, trying to assuage Emily's egocentric nature, which reared itself whenever someone else was the center of Grace's attention. "I hope you will accept."

"Thank you. This is very kind of you both."

Lesley felt overwhelmed. She wanted to pay for the purchases and agreed to the shopping excursion with that intention. She felt strangely beholden, despite the graciousness of the offer.

†††

As Grace Stewart was winding the Mercedes through early afternoon traffic back to Lesley's apartment, Witt Terrell was pointing the rented Ford Taurus toward Dallas on I-35. He looked at the time on the car's screen. He faced the nightmare of hitting Dallas at rush hour, but at least he was going into the city, not out. He should be there by six. Mac would be waiting.

Terrell had tapped into several of the holding tanks at the field in Tyler before driving to Austin. All empty. The key now was to see what kind of income Althea Oil & Gas was reporting from that specific field. The company's tax statements or accounting books should hold the key to tracing Althea's source of income. But he admitted, getting a look at those tax statements or books would be impossible without a state or federal warrant. Then it would probably take a sharp forensic accountant to decipher a set of books being cleverly cooked to cover drug income. The only place he knew to find such accountants was the Texas Department of Public Safety—or the FBI.

Traffic thickened even before Terrell crossed into Dallas County—at times bumper-to-bumper—as he cursed his way impatiently to the television station. It was well after six when he finally parked the rental a block away. Mac was waiting, sipping a cup of black coffee.

"That guard on the front desk didn't like having to let me in," Terrell said as he walked into Withers' office, his eyes red-rimmed with fatigue and with his usual rumpled appearance. "Must be my casual good looks," quipped Terrell, flashing a rare smile.

"Right," Mac grinned, silently praising the security guard for being suspicious of the disheveled man, badly in need of a shave, as he took a seat across from him.

"So, do I have a story?"

"Only if you can spring for sending me to Chicago."

Terrell capsulated what he had discovered, including the Chicago law firm listed as the registering agent for several of the suspected shell companies. Mac made a mental note to check with Jack Reilley to see if he had heard of that firm or was familiar with the location of its offices.

Terrell spent the night at Withers' house and left for Chicago before dawn, leaving Mac to finish his first cup of coffee alone.

25

During mid-morning of the second day, a misty rain fell, offering just enough moisture, mixed with the humid heat of Chicago in summer, to create its own steam. Terrell eased through the traffic in no particular hurry. He had spent the long hours heading north, along the monotonous ribbons of interstate linking the Southwest to the center of the Midwest, reviewing the facts in his head. The wind beat against his face from the open windows of a car whose air conditioning remained contemptuously broken, despite a refill of pricy Freon.

The question was not if Althea Oil & Gas was a front. That seemed apparent. Terrell was convinced its source of revenue was not oil, but drugs. The bigger question was: how involved were the people running the companies above Althea Oil & Gas, which stood somewhere at the bottom of the well-layered pyramid? At the top of the myriad of holding companies, wealth was counted in hundreds of millions and listed annually in *Forbes Magazine*. These fortunes had been built during the heady days of oil depletion allowances, the 20 percent windfall that swelled the pockets of every successful oil man bringing black gold to market.

For a crime, you need a motive, Terrell reminded himself again. The question swirled over and over in his mind—*why?*

Terrell stopped at a service station to purchase a city map to aid in finding Delacourt Street. It took him just over an hour to locate the street, two blocks long and squeezed between two main avenues, in a seedy area of mostly boarded-up buildings near South-side. Numbers were scarce on the front of buildings. The only human activity in the area were street people. One sat next to a battered shopping cart with his back propped against a building. Several others were curled up on the sidewalk, asleep. The building at 415 Delacourt stood in the middle of the first block. As Terrell had anticipated, it was deserted; a dummy address for a nonexistent law firm.

Terrell tried the front door knob and found it bolted. A faded red poster alerted him the building was condemned by the city of Chicago and declared unsafe for human habitation, as were most of the adjacent buildings. 415 Delacourt was bordered by a narrow alley-like walkway separating it from the next structure. Terrell paced down the walkway, so strewn with trash and other debris it was nearly impassable. It reeked of urine and feces. He turned into another alley than ran behind the building and his nostrils were immediately assailed by a sickly and unmistakable odor much stronger than urine and feces. He pulled a cotton handkerchief from his pocket as he approached a dumpster. There was something very big and very dead in that dumpster.

Terrell held the handkerchief over his hose and mouth as he struggled to lift the heavy, rusted lid of the container and beam a small pocket penlight inside, temporarily disturbing the swarm of flies. Sunken eyes in two bloated heads stared up at him. Despite early decomposition the faces were still recognizable. Terrell felt his stomach begin to roil.

A half-hour later, Terrell watched two police cars arrive, from a vantage point around the corner, a half-block away. They had been summoned by the call he had made from a pay booth at a convenience store. The officers exiting the black-and-whites seemed in no hurry to explore the crime scene. The arrival of more police units began attracting small groups of mostly women and teens from the squalid neighborhoods surrounding Delacourt Street. There was a rising buzz of voices as more gathered over the next hour, craning to see beyond the yellow crime-scene tape now being stretched between barricades to block off the street and the alleyway behind it.

Terrell mingled at times with some of the onlookers, never lingering long enough to draw their attention or the attention of police officers patrolling the perimeter inside the taped-off area. Walking helped Terrell abate his restlessness. He badly needed a drink and could feel the familiar spasms in his hands. He wished the lackadaisical cops would get on with whatever they were doing. *Humid as hell*, he thought, wiping his face with his now grungy handkerchief.

It was late afternoon before a Cook County coroner's van pulled away with the two victims inside. After the van was out of sight, Terrell strolled over to where an older, heavy-bellied uniformed officer stood guarding the barricades, moving them as police traffic moved in or out of the blocked-off crime scene.

"What's going on?" Terrell asked nonchalantly, pointing to the several police cars parked along the first block, their lights revolving in the stifling humidity of early evening.

Terrell took a cigarette from the pack he had purchased to cover the swig of Jack Daniels he had swallowed to calm his shaking hands. "I come by here on my way home from work. Not much goes on down there usually. Cigarette?" Terrell extended the pack toward the policeman who shook his head.

"Yeah, you're right. We don't spend a lot of time here usually. This ain't nothing much though. Looks like a couple of Mexicans got blasted and got their throats cut. Probably some rival gang members."

26

Mac Withers read the news release Lesley had handed him. When he looked up, his expression betrayed his surprise. "You know how to bowl me over, Les."

"I wanted you to see it before anyone else, Mac. The mayor's office is releasing it to the rest of the media after our five o'clock cast." Lesley paused, looking down at her hands, which clasped a folded-linen envelope in her lap.

"This is for you, also," she said, handing the envelope to Mac across the desk.

"What is it?" Mac smiled warily. "I can't take many more surprises in one day."

"An invitation to the engagement announcement. It's Saturday night at Grant's parents' home." She added hesitantly, "I hope you can make it."

Withers looked away from Lesley and breathed deeply. This was a knocker. Completely unexpected. She never discussed her personal life outside the station with anyone. Certainly never with him.

"Mac, do you want me to quit?"

He leaned back in his chair and studied her thoughtfully. "I have to admit it presents a bit of a dilemma. The question is, are you ready for the kind of scrutiny you're going to be subjected to as the wife of the mayor, especially one who is seeking re-election?"

Lesley leaned forward. "I expected you to dismiss me on the spot." She smiled pensively. "Yes, I think I do know what is ahead. And I promise you I will never allow my marriage to compromise my work."

"Enough said, Les," Mac responded. "Anyway, if I let you go, Henderson would have a heart attack. Do you know what this will do for the ratings, having the mayor's fiancée anchoring our newscasts? Not to mention our anchor marrying one of the wealthiest guys in Texas?" Mac chuckled. "Hell, Les, Henderson may even give you a raise."

"That would be something to celebrate. Maybe then I could support my new husband in a manner to which he is already accustomed."

"I doubt it."

"You're right, Mac," she laughed.

Withers saw several figures moving toward his office, from cubicles lining the wall at the far side of the newsroom. He glanced at his watch: 3:05 p.m. Time to finalize the lineup for the early news. Looking down at the news release, he chuckled inwardly at the reaction he was about to observe. This was probably the new lead story.

Lesley glanced in the direction of Mac's eyes and stood up quickly to leave. "Mac." Her voice quavered. She swallowed to regain composure. "Thank you for letting me stay. I promise I will keep my private and professional lives separate and never allow a conflict of interest," she added with rising intensity.

"Les, wait." Withers pushed out from behind his desk and walked over to where she stood by the door. He reached out his hand and then withdrew it. "Come here, girl," he said, wrapping the tentative Lesley in his arms. "Congratulations," he whispered in her ear, surprised at his own emotion. "Be happy," said Withers, releasing his gentle grip.

✝✝✝

She was happy. The party swirled around her in a blur. Lights were strung merrily around the large, outdoor patio, surrounded by concrete balusters at the back of the Stewart mansion. The balusters flashed past her as she danced. White-jacketed waiters, ferrying silver trays of hors d'oeuvres and champagne among the 200 guests, came in and out of her view. The only face in focus was the one into which she now looked. Grant was so handsome in his navy sports jacket and perfectly creased beige slacks. The light-blue shirt and maroon striped tie accented his tanned face.

She rested her head against his shoulder as the 10-piece orchestra changed the musical pace to romantic, playing "Love is a Many Splendored Thing." Lesley remembered seeing the tragic love story on television as a child. Jennifer Jones lost William Holden to a war. There was no war to take Grant from her. He was here, his arms around her waist, pressing her against him. It was just the two of them. No one else mattered at this moment as he moved her gracefully to the music.

"Penny for your thoughts?"

She looked into his face and found what she hoped would always be there—love. His electric blue eyes sparkled with it. "I love you," she whispered.

He bent down and kissed her lips softly. "Me too."

"Lesley, Grant, my darlings." Grace Stewart came forward as the music stopped, holding the hand of an older man with a fleshy face, crowned by thick gray hair. The man was followed by a slender younger woman who looked to be half his age. "Lesley, this is one of our dearest friends, Walt Edmonds and his wife, Sally. Walt is the head of Althea Oil & Gas and is on our board."

The smile on Lesley's face froze and she breathed in sharply. Coughing to cover her surprise, Lesley quickly covered her mouth with her left hand.

"Are you all right, Les?" Grant asked anxiously.

"I'm so sorry," she managed to say apologetically, lowering her head and gulping to regain control. Lesley forced a slim smile and extended her hand to the man and his young wife. "How do you do? I'm so pleased you could come."

"I'll second that, Walt. How are you, Sally?" Grant shook hands warmly with the man and embraced his wife. "Well, Walt, did I do well?"

"She's a keeper, son, a real keeper." Edmonds flashed a wide grin at Lesley. Sally seemed to share her husband's magnanimity, offering Lesley and Grant effusive congratulations. They then moved away, with Sally holding on to Edmonds' arm possessively and Grace Stewart on his other side.

"You sure you're all right, Lesley?" Grant smiled down at her affectionately. "I've never seen anyone choke-up over Walt except Sally."

"It's all this excitement, Mr. Stewart," Lesley responded, in an exaggerated Southern accent. "Meeting so many zillionaires and assorted other important folks just sends my little ole system into convulsions."

"My dear, may I say, you make a lousy Scarlett," Grant grinned, lifting her chin with his finger and brushing her lips lightly with his.

"Thank you, sir. How nice to finally know chivalry is dead."

"Aren't journalists supposed to know such things? Let's dance." Lesley wanted to run, to escape, to find refuge somewhere where she could quell her turbulent thoughts and make sense of what had just happened. But instead, Grant swept her out onto the marble dance area as the orchestra launched into "Proud Mary," to the whoops of several younger couples already gyrating to the raucous rhythm. Lesley found herself in the center of the dancers and forcibly sidelined the panic she felt meeting the man whom Grant had intimated, headed or owned Althea Oil & Gas.

Jitterbugging was followed by spirited line dancing to "Yellow Rose of Texas." Lesley's head was spinning from the physical strain of dancing and imbibing two glasses of champagne on a mostly-empty stomach. The Texas favorite ended with more lusty whoops and applause from the dancers and those watching. Lesley saw Mac Withers standing alone, a plate in his hand.

"Grant, would you excuse me for a minute?" He nodded, his attention already diverted by more well-wishers.

"Hi, Mac. Enjoying yourself?"

"Sure. Great party," observed Withers, dipping a cracker into a small mound of Russian caviar. "You don't look like you're having such a great time."

"Of course I am, Mac," she replied with little enthusiasm, glancing over to where Grant stood talking to several people in front of the orchestra.

"Then why the frown?"

"I just met Mr. Althea Oil & Gas."

Withers noisily gulped down his mouthful of caviar. "Where?"

"Grant's mother brought him and his wife over to introduce us. His name is Walt Edmonds. Ever heard of him?"

"Can't say I have," he answered, glancing around the room. "Can you point him out to me?"

Lesley looked around as she sipped from her champagne flute, finally spotting Edmonds and his wife on the dance floor. "He's dancing on the left side with the blonde who is as tall as he is and much younger."

Withers spotted the couple and thought, *They'd be hard to miss. The wife appears a bit gaudy for this crowd.* The frown faded from Mac's face. "Hey, this is your party. Forget business for one night at least. We'll check him out Monday."

"All right, if you say so, boss." Lesley looked relieved. "I'd better get back to Grant. That blonde he's talking with is too cute."

"I don't think you have to worry. See ya."

Withers walked over to a linen-covered table lined with steaming silver serving dishes filled with a variety of delicious smelling choices. By the time he walked the length of the table the two servers had refilled his plate.

Walt Edmonds, Mac thought. The name did not ring a bell. Maybe a face would stir his memory. He set out to wheedle an introduction to Edmonds from Mrs. Stewart, who appeared impressed at his presence. More especially, she was impressed by the crew assigned to cover the story for tonight's late newscast. Withers had always been cynically surprised by the impact of television. Maybe it was his newspaper background.

He found Grace Stewart eagerly obliging. She appeared flattered to introduce him to a number of people whose names he recalled from the business and society pages of the newspaper. Finally, he was face to face with Walt Edmonds. It was the thick turf of grey hair that distinguished the man, not his unremarkable face or appearance. It was a face Withers would remember in the future, along with that of the pretty blonde whose arm was tightly linked with her husband's. *A sexy former secretary*, Mac speculated silently.

Several more introductions followed before Withers thanked his hostess graciously and ambled off to refill his champagne glass.

Grace Stewart stood beside her stoic husband, smugly awash in the satisfaction that the lavish party she had organized so rapidly on her youngest son's behalf was a success. "Everyone seems to be enjoying themselves, Blaine dear."

"You never disappoint, Grace."

It was the reassurance she sought. In her exacting eyes, Blaine Stewart seemed always to say just the right thing, and exemplified the good taste she expected of all those around her, from her sons to the servants. Even in a casual navy linen sports coat and tan slacks, beige shirt, and blue silk tie, he looked elegant. His attire perfectly complimented the muted colors of her long, mauve, silk dress that accentuated her narrow waist. She wore the three strands of pearls Blaine had selected from their favorite Dallas jeweler for their wedding anniversary last year. *We are an attractive couple*, she thought, in the same objective manner in which she assessed most things in her life.

Blaine smiled inwardly at his wife's fishing for a compliment. He never doubted Grace's social abilities. Her dinners and cocktail parties were always a success. He knew, only too well, to be invited was an affirmation of social prominence and power. To be left off, or dropped from Grace Stewart's envied invitation list, underscored a lack of status among the Dallas elite. Therefore, he seldom felt the need to validate her social successes with a compliment.

Blaine agreed with his wife; the girl would be an asset. He even liked her. But not the camera crew or the attention she and Grant brought to his home. He viewed their presence as an intrusion. This party should be private. Reluctantly, he had deferred to Grace and his son on the television coverage, while silently questioning if such attention was wise at this time.

27

Christo listened silently through the long explanation from Vincente Estavar, who punctuated his words with frequent and vehement profanity. Two upcoming flights were being re-routed back to the airfield of their Dallas partner's ranch near Killeen. He also was making plans to send several more shipments overland, through Matamoros and Juarez.

"And the two men who unloaded the last flight in Tyler? What of them?" Christo asked.

"They quickly left the Dallas location and took the merchandise to Chicago," came the answer. "Our partners there were extremely gratified by the rapid delivery, and very cooperative in relieving us of our problem in an efficient and expeditious manner."

"That's good, my friend."

"Unfortunate, of course," said Estavar, with no trace of emotion in the solicitous words. Such disposals were necessary at times. It was business. "I will see their families are taken care of."

"Do we know yet who the man with the camera was or who he is with?" Christo inquired patiently.

"No," Estavar admitted. Somehow a breach in the cartel he built and ran with a tight, iron fist had been exposed. By whom, he did not know. Someone had made a mistake, or worse, betrayed the cartel. Such mistakes were not tolerated by his partners. Success in drug trafficking required a sophisticated network of highly guarded, efficient partnerships, from suppliers in Central and South America, Asia, and the Middle East; to delivery routes to markets in the United States, Canada, and Western Europe. Estavar knew he must move quickly and ruthlessly to trace and repair the vulnerability in his organization or he would ultimately pay for any fissure.

"And what about the woman in the car? The one with the man."

"She has been identified." Estavar swallowed the fear that rose like vomit in his throat. "An associate of ours in Dallas looked at the surveillance tapes from another building. She does the news on a Dallas television station."

There was a long silence at the other end of the connection. The voice that spoke the next words was low and controlled. "This is an unexpected problem." Another long silence. "Determine what the woman knows. Then deal with her. I expect you to neutralize any threat she may present to our business and our partnership. And find out who the man is and who he is working for."

"I will. I assure you they will be dealt with."

"Good, my friend. Move quickly for your sake and ours." Christo's words were followed by a click at his end of the telephone line. He was gone. Christo never said goodbye.

Estavar felt his heart thundering in his chest. Failure was not an option.

†††

Mac was in his usual position, resting his head against his folded hands, watching the video of the vacant storefront in Chicago, followed by the video taken during the drug transfer at the oil field. Slowly, piece by short video piece, the story was coming together, but, Mac admitted, with a lot of gaps still to be filled in. Why had the bodies of the two drivers of the Althea Oil & Gas truck been found in Chicago when they appeared to work from a Dallas location?

Jack Reilley had made a call to Chicago police and learned the two men found in the dumpster were Mexican nationals from Matamoros, in the United States on forged work visas. And Reilley added a new piece yesterday; a puzzling piece. During an interview with detectives at her home, Sarah Stewart had admitted the murdered pilot was her biological father, but disclaimed any other knowledge of the murdered man in whose apartment police found her photograph. Police learned she was raised by a wealthy stepfather who adopted her shortly after marrying her mother when Sarah was four years old. To Sarah Stewart, the stepfather was her father, her only father. And Sarah had dropped another bombshell on the two detectives who interviewed her; Mayor Stewart apparently had a conversation with the dead pilot recently. She insisted she did not know what the two men discussed or why her long-absent father had contacted her former husband. So what was that all about? Reilley promised to keep digging. Mac agreed.

Later that afternoon Terrell was in Mac's office. "What's our next step?" Mac asked, as he studied his friend sitting in a chair across from him. If anything, Terrell looked even thinner and more tired than when he had initially agreed to help probe the allegations made by the murdered pilot.

"Next step," Terrell repeated, "has to be Walt Edmonds and Althea Oil & Gas and how the hell he ended up on the board of the Stewarts oil company."

"I agree." Mac yawned. He was feeling the pressure of the story as well. "What the hell does a guy do all day heading a company that doesn't exist except on paper?"

Terrell laughed. "Makes sure his paperwork is in order." His expression turned serious. "How much of this do we share with Lesley?"

Mac sat up and leaned his elbows on the desk clenching his hands. "Let's keep it between us for the time being."

Terrell looked thoughtful. "That girl's in for a world of hurt."

Mac leaned back in his chair and nodded agreement just as his cell phone sounded. He fished it out of his shirt pocket and answered gruffly. It was Lesley, her voice breathless, her words jumbled as they spilled out from the other end of the line.

"Slow down, Les. What's happened?"

"Someone broke into my apartment. I found my computer open. The hard drive is missing. It has all my notes about the investigation, everything that's happened so far." Her voice dropped nearly to a whisper. "Mac, they know I'm looking into this. How did they find out?"

"Did they take anything else?"

"Not that I can see."

"Why in the hell didn't you call me last night?" demanded Mac, irritation masking his concern.

"I just discovered it missing a few minutes ago." There was a long hesitation on her end of the line. "I wasn't here last night. I found all this when I came in a few minutes ago."

He guessed she probably spent the night at Grant Stewart's place, but he was too polite to pry. It was none of his damn business anyway. "Hold on, Les."

Withers held the phone away from his face and looked at Terrell, who had been listening to Mac's side of the conversation, his alarm growing. "Someone broke into Lesley's apartment last night. They've taken the hard drive in her computer. She said there are notes on it about what you two have been doing."

"Anybody named in the notes?" Terrell asked.

"Witt Terrell's in my office, Les. He wants to know if you put any names in your notes."

"Yes. I used his name, but only his last name."

"You're sure only his last name?"

"Yes, I'm sure of that. I made notes about seeing the plane land, and following the truck to the Dallas warehouse. And about meeting Edmonds at the engagement party this weekend. God, I'm so sorry, Mac. I wanted to put down details so I wouldn't forget when it came time to do the story." Her voice cracked with fear. "How did they find out I was working the story? How did they know where I live?"

"Hey! First, this isn't your fault. You had no way of knowing someone would break into your apartment. And we don't know for sure this is connected to the story you're working on."

"It's connected," said Terrell, loud enough for Lesley to hear.

"Look, you do whatever you have to do right now and let me talk this over with Witt. I'll call you back in a few minutes. Stay put," he ordered. "And lock your door."

"Mac, I'm scared."

"I know, Les," he said, unable to hide the concern in his voice. "Hey, how soon can you get here?"

"In about an hour. Why?"

"Reilley's coming in early. Let's all meet and figure where we go next." Withers laid the receiver down slowly, worry etched on his face.

Shortly after Lesley arrived, Jack Reilley walked into Withers' office, summoned there by the message blinking on the telephone on his desk. He sauntered in and plunked himself down next to Terrell. "What's up, boss?"

After hearing about the break-in at Lesley's apartment, Reilley's advice was blunt. Don't call the police to report the break-in. Regular thieves would have taken the whole computer, not just the hard drive, he pointed out. It was a conclusion already reached by the three faces looking intently at him.

"The police department's a sieve," Reilley warned. "Bringing in the cops could invite more trouble than you've already got."

Lesley agreed immediately; Withers, more reluctantly. Terrell offered no opinion, but did suggest having the lock on Lesley's apartment door changed to one that would be more of a challenge to pick, and adding a security camera.

"There's something else I've found out," said Terrell, looking up again to ensure he had the attention of the three people around him. "Our big-time oil baron, Walt Edmonds—he's got a rap sheet for fraud and embezzlement. Spent time in federal prison in Marion, Illinois."

Terrell let the implication of what he just imparted sink in. "Seems Mr. Althea Oil & Gas was in the securities business in Chicago some years back and ripped off a few hundred clients who'd invested in a couple o' scam companies that went belly-up. The indictment came from the feds. They claimed, at the time, Edmonds was thick with the Chicago mob. Of course, "Edmonds" wasn't his name then. It was Robert Petrillo. The feds never proved the mob connection. Petrillo copped a plea, got seven years and was out in less than five on good behavior. All in all, Petrillo netted himself and whomever several million bucks that never got repaid. The investors got screwed. Petrillo got lost for a while, before showing up here in Texas about five years ago as Walt Edmonds to take over Althea Oil & Gas, after the lawyer running it kicked his own bucket with a shotgun."

"Jee-sus Christ. How'd you come across that information?" Withers asked.

"An old friend in the FBI office in Chicago. I promised to share information in the future."

Lesley remained silent as the three men batted around Terrell's information. Something she had forgotten to mention to Mac the night of the engagement party—Grace Stewart had introduced Edmonds, not only as head of Althea Oil & Gas, but as being "on our board." A director of Stewart Oil. How did he wheedle his way into such a high position with one of the state's top energy companies? She would have to alert Grant at some point.

28

Alone in his office with the door locked against inadvertent intrusion, Edmonds completed attaching the hard drive to one of his computers and began pulling up its list of folders. As he surmised from the tidy elegance of her apartment, Lesley Rowan would keep any information on her computer in neat, labeled folders. He was right. He knew she was spending the night elsewhere when he entered the apartment, and had been assured by the man he assigned to tail her that she was at the mayor's condo. Edmonds knew he could be in and out of her apartment before she could get there.

Scrolling rapidly through the list, Edmonds quickly found what he was looking for, in a folder entitled KDLL Investigation. All the notes were written in narrative form, beginning with the contents of a note left in a Brownsville church pew by the pilot, the subsequent meeting in the park, and the pilot's body being found in Dallas. On the third page, he found a descriptive narrative of the plane landing in the oil field outside Tyler, and the Althea Oil & Gas truck she and the man had followed into Dallas. There were frequent references to a "Terrell" on the computerized notes. He would have to check out Channel 15 personnel to see who this Terrell was.

Walt Edmonds felt a gnawing in the pit of his stomach. The

media knew about the drug drops and about the drop site? *He* wasn't even told until a call from Mexico advised him the landing site had been changed to the Killeen ranch. He told no one except the two men driving the truck meeting the flight. It wasn't until he saw it in the morning newspaper Edmonds knew the pilot had been eliminated. And only after reading the woman's notes did he know why.

She knew about the warehouse in Dallas. So what? He could deny any knowledge of that. It had been leased for years, long before he took over Althea Oil & Gas. He would tell the police—if they came snooping around—the warehouse was never used, just a forgotten expense lost on the books. The truck had been disposed of. So had the men who took the truck to the drop site. All his bases were covered. He could only hope his partners would share his confidence.

At Withers direction, new locks were installed the next day on the two entrance doors of Lesley's apartment—the front door and the door leading in from the balcony. And arrangements were made to install an alarm system and a video doorbell that also triggered an alarm with a monitoring agency and on her cell phone. Even Bart Henderson restrained his carping to his usual gathering at the Outrigger Lounge the next evening, after getting the bill to enhance the security of the apartment of his number one anchor. He was not told police were being bypassed. Crime was rampant, he warned his rapt listeners, who were sipping the round he paid for so magnanimously. Nobody was safe these days, he proclaimed in his trademark broadcaster voice. That's why he moved to the suburbs. Not to mention, living 25 miles from the station validated a reason to stay in town for the frequent assignations that kept his sex life at an excitement level far above the expectations of his marital bed.

Later that evening, Lesley snuggled against Grant and felt his arms circle around her waist, holding her close, so close she could feel his breath on the side of her neck. Their lovemaking was always followed by feelings of well-being and relaxation. The face of Walt Edmonds suddenly intruded into her mind, expelling the contentment satiating her senses moments before. She debated telling Grant what she knew about this man, and the past machinations that landed him in federal prison. The glass of white wine, followed by Grant's lips tasting the wine on her lips, briefly pushed Edmonds far away.

She turned in Grant's arms and looked into his face resting on the pillow. "Tell me about Walt Edmonds. I met him at the engagement party. His wife. Not his first, I presume?"

"You're right. She's at least the second notch on his marriage gun. Maybe the third. She's nice, though. I like Sally. Mother doesn't, as you probably perceived."

"Actually, I found your mother to be very polite and thoughtful. If she doesn't like Sally, it certainly didn't show."

"Mother considers it her duty to be gracious to everyone who steps through those hallowed doors. She only tolerates Sally because of Dad. He and Walt go back a lot of years in the oil business." Grant raised up on his elbow. "Why do you ask?"

"Just journalistic curiosity. It comes with my territory, you know." Lesley tried to avert his attention by kissing Grant lightly on the nose. "Reporters are born with nosiness, you know. A pretty young blonde on the arm of an older, wealthy man. Great scenario. I see it on TV all the time. And I ask myself, will that be me 20 years from now, the ousted wife, superseded by a young vixen? Tell me, Mr. Mayor, is that the fate I face at the hands of Klungo?" Klungo was their pet name for his penis.

"Who knows, Miss anchor woman. I follow wherever Klungo leads! Right now, it's leading me to the head for a leak."

"Gross!" She wrinkled up her nose.

"Just the call of nature, my love." He slid out of bed and closed the door of the bathroom behind him.

Lesley lay back on the pillow, her mind immediately filling with worry. Grant clearly did not know about Edmonds' past. All the more reason to tell him what Terrell had learned.

"Why so pensive?" he asked, slipping back under the sheet beside her.

"Grant, I heard something today about Edmonds I think you need to know."

"What? It must be serious, judging from the look on your face."

"It is, Grant. Edmonds has a past you may not be aware of. He served time in federal prison about a decade ago, for bilking investors while working in Chicago."

"What?" he exclaimed, incredulity apparent in his voice.

"I learned about it only today. I can't say how or why it came up. But the source of the information is pretty reliable."

Grant lay back on his pillow. "You've got to be mistaken about Walt Edmonds. He and my dad are friends. From everything dad's told me, they go back years. You're hearing the wrong things about this guy. Better check your sources." There was a hint of irritation in his tone.

"I'm sorry, Grant. I just thought you should know. I didn't mean to upset you," she said contritely, instantly sorry she had broached the subject of Edmonds' past.

Grant turned over toward Lesley, his eyes holding hers. "Hey! Are we fussing?" he said softly. "We don't fuss. It's not allowed when two people love each other as much as we do." He pulled her into his arms and formed his lips in an exaggerated pucker. "So, give me a kiss, sweetheart."

She bit his lip playfully.

"Ouch!"

"Kiss me right," she laughingly pleaded. He did, tenderly at first, until they were fused together by the passion building within them. Lesley remained the night.

A troubling disquiet permeated Lesley's thoughts as she drove to her apartment early the next morning. Sharing with him the information Terrell had gathered on Walt Edmonds was meant to warn him of a possible future problem. The effort had been met with an unyielding defense of Edmonds. Could the facts about the head of Althea Oil & Gas be wrong? Her instincts screamed, "No!"

Lesley was suddenly consumed with guilt. She had betrayed the trust placed in her by Mac and Terrell by revealing information about Walt Edmonds to Grant. She had pledged to Mac only last week there would never be a conflict of interest. Already, she had violated that pledge.

Lesley realized, with a start, only two months had passed since Manny's brutal assassination, and the discovery of the note in the Brownsville church pew left by the pilot. He was killed even more savagely than Manny had been, as were the two men she and Terrell had witnessed unloading the truck at the warehouse. This was no coincidence.

Terrell said the warehouse was deserted. No trace of drugs, the truck, the men. Swept clean was the way Terrell described the empty warehouse. Then someone had broken into her apartment and stolen her computer hard drive. The theft left her feeling violated and vulnerable just knowing someone had been in her apartment and by now knew the contents of the hard drive. That hard drive contained critical details of the story she and Terrell were working on—what could prove to be the story of her career, she ruefully conceded. Whoever it was must have at least suspected what was stored on the computer. How did he or she know? Who was this person? Fear clutched at her chest. Needle pricks of adrenalin danced over her skin and accelerated her heart. She could still feel it pounding against her chest wall as she pulled under the covered parking area in front of her apartment.

The hand holding the telephone shook slightly, despite its tight hold on the receiver. The man struggled to speak in broken Spanish.

"It's all on the hard drive. There are several pages of notes. She talks about someone named Terrell who checked out the tanks at the Allison field in Tyler. They know the tanks are empty. This guy Terrell saw one of the drops and they've got videotape of another drop. That's apparently when they followed the truck to the warehouse. She says in her notes they've got tape of the warehouse."

Walt Edmonds wiped his neck with a handkerchief. "Jesus. We're screwed." The last three words were in English. A single rivulet of sweat trickled down each side of his face, sliding under the loosened collar of his shirt.

A third voice on the conference call responded in English. "If these fucking reporters know this much, the fucking police probably do to. Althea Oil & Gas's got to disappear. Quick. Today. No paper trail. No computer trail. Nothing. Get rid of that reporter's hard drive, along with everything else," the voice shouted in a thick Bronx brogue.

Edmonds' hand holding the receiver was shaking harder. He made no effort to argue, knowing it was futile. "Anyone looking for Althea Oil & Gas—it never existed. Not it. Not the fucking hard drive. You got it."

"Yeah, I'll take care of it," Edmonds replied, trying to still the fear quaking in his gut.

The harsh voice continued. "You're going on vacation. A nice long vacation. Go home. Pack a bag. Bring your passport. No gun. Too dangerous. I'll send our plane to take you to Mexico. We need you out of sight for the time being."

The first voice added softly in accented English, "Walt. You're right. You've been screwed. Our friend's suggestion to come to Mexico is a good way to protect you and our Dallas partners. Don't you agree?"

"What about Sally? What about my wife?"

"Leave her there for now. It would be best. We'll arrange for her to join you in a few days. Tell her you've got to leave on a business trip. Something just came up."

"She's kind of questioning. She may not buy that."

"It's up to you to see that she does." The words were spoken with a menacing finality.

Walt Edmonds gave his delighted receptionist the rest of the day off and spent the next two hours destroying what it had taken him five years to build. State reports he crafted from his head went through the shredder in seconds. By the time he finished, two large trash bags full of the spaghettied remnants of his phantom business were ready to be discarded, in the large bins at the rear of the downtown building, along with the smashed hard drives from company computers. The hard drive from the television anchor's apartment would remain hidden in his safe at home, a little insurance policy in case there was any effort at retribution against him or Sally by the people he worked for.

Even on a particularly busy day, there was little for the receptionist to do besides answer the telephone. Tomorrow there would be even less, he smirked, as he turned the key to the entrance door to the offices of Althea Oil & Gas.

Walt found the house empty, except for the housekeeper, who said Sally had gone to the hairdresser. He packed enough clothes for a week and removed a two-inch stack of $100 dollar bills from a small safe cleverly concealed behind a drawer in the large desk in his office. He crammed the money into the zippered front of a leather traveling bag that could shield the money from TSA airport scanners. There was another safe in the house—a safe he had told Sally about when they first moved into the home. It was in a wall in their bedroom, draped by a French tapestry hanging above the four poster cherry bed he shared so pleasurably with his young wife. He kept a stash of cash in this safe as well. *Never hurts to have something to fall back on if things go south*, he thought smugly, half-congratulating himself on his good planning. He turned the knob and heard the final click and felt the safe's lock release. Before shutting it, he placed the anchor's hard drive in the dark interior of the safe before closing it and twisting the knob a half circle.

On a sofa table under the massive skylight in the downstairs den, Edmonds scribbled a note to Sally saying he would be back in a few days and would call her tomorrow or the next day. He also reminded her of the combination to the bedroom safe and to clean out the safe if anything happened to him. He handed the note to the housekeeper before he left the house. It was a stroke of luck Sally was gone and not there to harangue him for not taking her along. She could be a real bitch when she wanted something.

The small private jet took off shortly before three, after refilling at Love Field on the second leg of a flight plan filed when it left Chicago. The destination was listed as Cozumel. No passengers were identified by the pilot.

Edmonds settled back in his comfortable seat behind the cockpit. This was the way to go. He felt relaxed for the first time in two days. He had not slept since discovering the hard drive in that television woman's apartment. He heard the pilots talking in rapid Spanish, but understood little of what they said. Edmonds was asleep before the small jet crossed into Mexico.

He awoke sometime later to feel the plane descending. Within 15 minutes it taxied to a stop at a private hanger at the Cozumel airport. He stepped out into disappearing daylight and down the several steps, as two brown-skinned, burly men approached the plane.

"Welcome to Cozumel, Mr. Edmonds." The taller of the two men extended his hand graciously. "I'm Pietro Salador. This is my associate, Victor Diaz." Shorter and stocky, with a thick belly, Diaz only nodded, without changing his malevolent expression, and did not offer his hand. Edmonds quickly sized up Diaz as a bodyguard, not an associate.

"We have made arrangements for you to come aboard my yacht. It's docked at the main marina only a short distance from here. I hope that is satisfactory for your stay," added Salador politely.

"Sure. It sounds great. Thanks for making such an effort on my behalf."

"My pleasure, Mr. Edmonds. This way."

As the car sped along a coastal road, only a slight vestige of sunset remained on the western horizon as night descended. The shadow of the full moon was rising in a cloudless sky. Its silver hues danced on the waves as they sped along the newer highway toward the beaches. If he had to leave and go somewhere, they had picked a perfect place for him to lay low and relax.

Neither Salador, who was driving, nor Diaz, in the back seat, had spoken since shortly after leaving the airport. His long nap on the plane left Edmonds refreshed. He was content to enjoy the drive and not converse. In all his travels to many distant places, this was his first stop in the famous Mexican resort area. This could turn out to be just what the doctor ordered. Ease the stress.

His only regret was Sally not being here to share it with him. He wondered absently what she was doing at this moment. Probably getting ready for bed. She always slept naked. It's what he liked best about her—her body—always primed, the surgically enlarged breasts waiting to be suckled. He smiled slightly at his mind's view of her silky nakedness. It was the last image Walt Edmonds saw before the wire cut off his breathing and stilled his brief struggle.

Under cover of darkness the body was unceremoniously tossed overboard from the sleek fishing boat into the shark infested blue waters of the Caribbean Sea, miles from the tourist-thronged beaches of Cozumel.

29

Jack Reilley now made it a habit to stop by Lesley's office shortly after he arrived in the newsroom from his daily rounds at the police and sheriff's departments. He needed to see if she had heard from Terrell or if there was anything new on the story.

"I picked up something that might interest you, Les." He used the nickname with the same familiarity as Mac. "There is a missing person's report on file on Walt Edmonds. Seems his wife hasn't seen or heard from him for four days."

Lesley stared at Reilley. "Edmonds is missing?" She lowered her head to hide her shock.

"Yep! Seems he left a note saying he was heading down to Mexico. Didn't say where, just that he would call. And he hasn't called."

"Do the police have any idea what's happened to him?"

"Not a clue, according to Jack Denton. He's not working the case. Lieutenant Ramiraz is. He's been checking with the Mexican authorities. Nothing so far. But the detectives just got the call late yesterday from a very worried Mrs. Edmonds. Seems he went on a vacation, and left in a hurry apparently. Denton said she's really pissed at being left behind."

When Lesley looked up again at Reilley, her face was pale.

"You okay, Les? I know you knew this guy. Sorry if I've upset you. Thought you'd wanna know."

Lesley smiled faintly. "Of course, Jack. I'm sorry. I was just thinking about something else when you came in." She turned away from her computer to face him. "This is kind of a shock. I just met him recently. And there's the connection to Althea Oil & Gas we're looking into."

"Oh, speaking of Althea—when Ramiraz and his partner went to see Edmonds' secretary, she let them look around. They found a lot of empty file drawers and no records of any kind on the company. Strange, don't you think?"

Lesley nodded. Reilley added, "The secretary apparently doesn't do a lot. Denton said she didn't seem to even know if anything was missing."

"What do the police think about his disappearance?"

"They're not commenting on the record. But they suspect he may be involved in something like that Chicago deal from several years back and just took off. They're not too sure about anything at this point." Jack glanced up at the clock on the side wall of Lesley's office. "I better get going. I told Jerry Simms I'd write the intro to my piece for the five o'clock cast." He started toward his cubicle and turned. "I'll keep you posted on anything new."

"Thanks, Jack."

He walked languidly to his desk and sat down. Lesley gazed across the newsroom. Mac was in his office on the telephone. She was due in makeup in 10 minutes. Just enough time to find out if Mac had heard from Terrell. She knocked lightly and was waved inside by Withers. Lesley was startled to see Witt Terrell hunched down in a chair in the corner of Mac's office.

"Mr. Terrell. I was just coming to see if Mac knew where to reach you." Terrell watched her with hooded eyes, his expression passive, as she related what Reilley had just told her about Edmonds' disappearance.

"I need to talk with Jack," Terrell said, as he heaved himself from the chair.

Lesley pointed to the left side of the newsroom. "His desk is over toward the studio door."

"Thanks, I'll see you a little later."

"Sure."

Mac Withers hung up the telephone. "What's up with him, Les?"

"He went to see Jack. Jack just told me the police are looking for Walt Edmonds. His wife filed a missing person's report late yesterday."

"It's leading the five o'clock. Been on the phone. Didn't have a chance to tell Witt."

"Sorry. You know yourself, if somebody lets out a silent fart in this newsroom, you know it before anyone else."

Withers laughed out loud, as much at Lesley using the word fart—so contradictory to her normally prudish nature—as at her slightly peevish reaction regarding his knowing about Edmonds before she told him. "Jack called me as soon as he found out," he explained to placate her uncharacteristic annoyance.

"I'd better get into makeup," said Lesley. She beat a hasty retreat from Mac's office.

Sitting in a makeup chair, as Ginny brushed her high cheek bones with coral blush, was normally a time Lesley found calming before a newscast. Not now. Her mind was in a whirl. *Edmonds disappears along with any records regarding Althea Oil & Gas.*

She wondered if Grant knew about his father's friend. He'd reacted angrily when she had mentioned Edmonds' prison record, but neither she nor Grant had discussed the man since then. Grant would certainly hear about Edmonds' disappearance tomorrow, when he returned from Japan where he was part of a Texas trade delegation, soliciting business in Asia. She thought of leaving a message at his condo, but decided against it. Tomorrow would be soon enough for him to get bad news.

"All done. Break a leg," said Ginny minutes later, slipping the plastic cape from around Lesley's shoulders, repeating the show business adage from old habit. Admitting to being fifty-something, Ginny Calvert learned her skills in Hollywood as a makeup artist for Max Factor after it was sold to Proctor & Gamble in the early 90s. She would be contracted out to location shoots. She had taken great pride in making actors look their best and took that same intense pride in how each KDLL anchor looked under the harsh studio lights.

Ginny found Lesley the easiest to prepare for a newscast. Her smooth complexion had even tones and only light freckles sprinkled over the nose and cheeks, easily hidden by makeup. Best of all, she had no shadows under her eyes like the male anchors. They were a pain to make up, and a pain to listen to, in Ginny's view. She tolerated their derisive, often bawdy comments about rival anchors with silence. But it stretched her patience to have to listen to their disparaging remarks directed at their co-anchors.

Lesley felt much the same about both the men with whom she co-anchored, but kept her feelings strictly to herself. She never shared with anyone in the newsroom her displeasure at their egocentric comments off-camera and petty demands of studio personnel. In her view, Jed Thompson and Tom Fitzgerald epitomized the Hollywood-fostered caricature of television anchors.

Lesley returned to the newsroom following the five o'clock newscast. She had a half-hour break while the network news aired. Witt Terrell was waiting in her office.

"We need to talk. Got a minute?" There was a heightened intensity in his voice and his eyes appeared brighter than when she had seen him earlier. *He's been drinking*, she surmised.

Lesley sat behind her desk, pointing Terrell to the only other chair near her desk. She waited for him to begin. He remained silent for an awkwardly long time, staring down at a legal pad on his lap. Finally, he began turning pages, all hand-written, she noticed.

"I found out some things in Austin," he said, his voice so low she could barely hear him. "Things that may mean trouble for some friends of yours. I haven't told Mac. I wanted to tell you first."

Lesley waited for him to continue before asking, "What friends, Mr. Terrell?"

"Your fiancé's family."

No! She could hear the word scream in her head while her lips remained tightly clenched.

"Ma'am, Althea Oil & Gas was a subsidiary of Stewart Oil, one of several offshoots, all in the oil or oil-supply business. I don't know how to put it to you easy, ma'am. Most of the companies, including Althea Oil & Gas, listed a law firm in Chicago as their registered agent. That's why I went to Chicago. There's no such firm. The building listed for their address was empty and had a condemned sign on it. And there was no such law firm listed on the internet or with the Illinois Bar. It doesn't exist except on those annual reports filed in Austin."

Lesley forced herself to focus and be calm. "What does this mean, Mr. Terrell?"

"Well, to put it to you bluntly, it means—on the surface—there's a little fraud going on. And there could be a lot more underneath."

"Like what?" she inquired hesitantly.

"I can only guess. Right now I don't have enough facts to do that. What we do know is Edmonds was probably using Althea Oil & Gas to launder money from drugs. It's an old Mafia trick. Unless the feds are on to it, nobody at the state regularly checks things like registered agents to make sure they're legit." He paused briefly, looking up from his legal pad directly at Lesley.

"Ma'am, usually company accountants file the corporation renewals each year with the Secretary of State's office. They had to get the registered agent to sign the report. Whether they knew the person signing was part of a non-existent law firm in Chicago is another thing. If it was just Althea with the fake agent, it would be one thing. But there are several subsidiaries with the same agent. Someone besides Walt Edmonds had to know."

The realization of what Terrell was intimating to her was beginning to sink in. She gripped the arms of her chair so tightly the blood drained from her fingers.

"What you're saying is, someone high up in Stewart Oil may know about Althea Oil & Gas and the drug trafficking?"

"Yes, ma'am. That's my way of thinking. Walt Edmonds was on the board of directors of the main company. He could have been fooling them though—posting income from the dry wells on Althea's books and, I suspect, siphoning off a big chunk for himself and his friends."

"Friends?"

"Organized crime, ma'am. Their stamp is all over this envelope. They're linked with the drug cartels, as the distribution arm, so to speak. It's a big business. You've got suppliers—that would be the Colombians mostly. And the transporters, like the Mexican cartels. Then you've got the distributors who get drugs to the streets. Most are big, well-run networks. I learned that during my FBI days."

"If they're as sophisticated as you say, Mr. Terrell, then it wouldn't be unusual to plant the head of one of their front companies on the board of directors of an unsuspecting parent company," Lesley reasoned, taking a devil's advocate approach.

"No, ma'am. I imagine it makes sense to infiltrate a legitimate company that way, doing just what Edmonds was doing. Edmonds was an ex-con. Seems to have been a smart guy. Could have fine-tuned his trade in prison. Probably made some different Mafia contacts there. He took over from an attorney who ran Althea Oil & Gas. That guy died some years back. Death records claim suicide. That's when Edmonds made his entrance. The strange thing is, this non-existent law firm in Chicago was the registered agent on the annual reports even before Edmonds took over."

"But it's still possible that no one at Stewart Oil may know about Althea Oil & Gas's actual source of income?"

"Possible, ma'am." Terrell stared down at the yellow legal pad on his lap and avoided looking directly at Lesley. "Not likely, though," he returned in a low voice. "Seems strange to me that only Stewart Oil and one other company had that fake law firm listed as the registered agent, and nobody knew? That's why I'm telling you all this before I tell Mac. I know you're close with the mayor and all that."

"We're being married next month."

"Yes, ma'am." There was resignation in Terrell's voice. Looking up, he saw the raw pain on the beautiful face across from him. He had debated not telling her anything before coming to her office. And Terrell left unspoken what was troubling him most; why Edmonds had cut and run so suddenly. Was there a parallel investigation by police or the FBI the station was unaware of? Jack Reilley didn't think so. Dallas police were treating Edmonds' disappearance as strictly a case of a high-profile oil man getting lost on a fishing trip while on vacation in Mexico.

Terrell stood to leave, nodded to Lesley, and walked toward Mac's office. *She's gutsy,* he thought. *She proved that when the drug flight landed. And during the chase into Dallas. She's cool under fire.* That's why he felt obliged to tell her first what he had uncovered. It would be up to Mac where it all went from here.

Mac listened raptly, never interrupting. The implication of what he was being told registered immediately. This was turning into a hell of a story. It also might be a hell of an embarrassment for Grant Stewart in the midst of an election campaign, and sadly, a hell of a heartbreak for Lesley.

Terrell left Withers' office before the end of the six o'clock newscast and headed back to Austin.

$$30$$

Blaine Stewart peered over the rim of his reading glasses at the six faces around him. His thick eyebrows were pulled together in a deep frown.

"Gentlemen, we have a problem. A Dallas police lieutenant came around seeking information about Walt Edmonds. They've discovered his rather checkered past"—he did not elaborate—"and have sagely surmised his future could be in peril. He fortuitously destroyed key records before making his hasty exit. We have not heard from Mr. Edmonds. I'm told he's out of the country and not expected to return any time soon. I have assurances of that."

Blaine Stewart allowed a brief smile to trace across his thin lips, as his eyes remained coldly trained on the men looking toward him. "This unwanted attention holds a certain peril for us as well. We must move cautiously. Any public statements must come from the head of our public relations department, and only after I have approved such statements. Do we agree?" The six heads of Stewart Oil subsidiaries nodded concurrence.

"Mr. Edmonds' character, or lack thereof, could prove an embarrassment to Stewart Oil. We will rightly distance ourselves from him and any knowledge of his past. The primary effort will be to divert attention from us." Again, the six heads nodded silent concurrence.

Blaine Stewart continued, "In the meantime, Elliott is adding Althea Oil & Gas to his duties, temporarily." He nodded solemnly to his oldest son, sitting on his left. "It will be business as usual, gentlemen." He looked directly from one face to another. "I will be going on a brief business trip. In my absence, everything will be handled by Elliott." The chairman of Stewart Oil stood up, squaring his broad shoulders. "Will you gentlemen please join me for lunch in the private dining room?"

As the six men pushed away from the long, mahogany conference table, Elliott caught the subtle eye signal from his father and lingered near his seat while the five CEOs of other Stewart Oil subsidiaries filed out of the board room. They ambled into the richly furnished dining room next door, where cherry tables were spread with white linen table clothes and set with sterling silver. Each piece of Dalton china was embossed with the familiar Stewart Oil logo, recognized around the world.

"You and I need to speak when the lunch is over. Privately."

Elliott nodded his affirmation and turned toward the dining room.

The elder Stewart picked up the telephone beside him on the conference table and dialed his administrative assistant, who answered before the first ring finished. "Rachel, would you get Grant on the line for me? I'll be in the private dining room with my associates. Thank you."

Even after a 15-year sexual liaison, Blaine Stewart was always formal and polite with the woman who guarded his office and his privacy when he was there. He could never recall having to make a request twice.

Blaine Stewart had just placed the first bite of a superbly tender filet mignon in his mouth when a soft voice on the intercom advised him his call was ready. "I'll take it in my office, Rachel, thank you." Pushing away from the table, the chairman of the board of Stewart Oil Company politely excused himself and strolled into his private office, lifted the receiver, and effusively greeted his youngest son. "Grant, Elliott and I would like you to come to the house tonight. Something's come up that could be somewhat sensitive. I think you should know about it and be prepared, in case questions are raised by the press."

"What is it, Dad?"

"Oh, nothing we can't handle, son. But I think it's best discussed at the house. What time can we expect you?"

"I won't get away from here until late. Is eight or so okay?"

"That will be fine, Grant. We'll see you then."

A frown encased Grant's handsome face as he rested the telephone back on its cradle. What was so important it could not be discussed now—but only later at the house? Grant knew his father to be a very private man who closely guarded his work and his life, sharing little of himself, even with his wife and sons. His emotionally distant father had few close friends he knew of, only a host of business and social acquaintances, accumulated over the years from his membership in the Petroleum Club and the exclusive golf club that ran along the back border of the family's 20-acre compound. A sense of foreboding enveloped Grant. He did not anticipate hearing welcome news.

"Lesley." It was Rose Harper, the front desk receptionist who answered calls coming into the station. "There's a man on the line. He's called twice and won't leave a message. Says it's real important. Do you want me to put the call through?"

"Sure, Rose." The top light on the telephone blinked as the ringer sounded.

"This is Lesley Rowan, may I help you?"

"Miss Rowan. Tony Gomez. I'm a reporter for the *Brownsville Daily Leader*."

"Hello, Tony. How are you?" She recalled the intense young man she had interviewed about the newspaper's investigative series when she was in Brownsville. It seemed so long ago, yet she realized it had only been a few weeks.

"Good, thanks." From his anxious tone she perceived this was not a social call.Got a minute to talk, Miss Rowan?"

"You bet I've got time. What's up?"

"I got a call from the informant—the one I told you about who fed us a lot of information for our series."

"I remember," she replied, pressing the receiver against her ear, straining to hear Gomez, who sounded like he was cupping the telephone receiver to shield his voice. She reached for a pen to take notes.

"I'm calling from the newsroom so I'll have to make this quick. The guy called me this morning. He's a good source—undercover DEA. Said a Dallas businessman was killed by a Mexican Cartel called El Poder. His name's Walt Edmonds. My source said Edmonds flew to Mexico on a plane owned by the Castalero family in Chicago. He also told me Edmonds' body was dumped out at sea somewhere off Cozumel. He said this Edmonds guy ran an oil business in Dallas that is a suspected front for laundering money from drug sales." Gomez stopped and she heard him take a deep breath.

"He says they know about you and the information you and someone called Terrell uncovered about Edmonds. That's the reason I'm calling you. I thought you should know." There was a long pause and she could hear Gomez breathing hard.

"I appreciate the heads up, Tony," she said with rising alarm in her voice. "Actually my apartment was broken into and the only thing they made off with was the hard drive to my computer. I had put all my notes for the story we're working on from this end on there."

"Yeah. That would explain a lot. My source said Edmonds apparently told the cartel down here he found a bunch of stuff on a stolen computer hard drive. The informant suggested I call and warn you. They may try to do to you—or to this other guy—this Terrell guy—what they did to Manny."

The warning hung in the air, propelling her heart, drying the moisture in her mouth. It was like something had come into her lungs and sucked all the air out. Her chest ached as she struggled to keep her voice even. "We have video of some of their activities. I don't think they would dare attempt to harm anyone here."

"I hope not, Miss Rowan." There was another briefer pause. "You better be careful," he said, finally. "Police here think it was the El Poder cartel that murdered Manny. And they may be the ones who decapitated a cop here who was working undercover. A neighbor found his body in the front yard of his home this morning."

"Oh, my God. How awful." Lesley made no attempt to mask the shock in her voice.

"It's really bad down here. Worse across the river in Matamoros. Even with the National Guard here and the Mexican Army working across the river, things like the cop killing are still happening." His voice choked and he shuddered as the nightmare vision of the headless body of the police officer flashed in his mind. He had arrived before the coroner's office had mercifully covered the body with a sheet. "Every day it's something like that. Nobody seems able to stand up to the cartels."

"What is it with drug cartels and Islamic jihadists that they have to resort to such gruesome tactics?" Lesley ruminated aloud.

"By the way," Gomez said, "I've given my two weeks notice. Being a journalist is scaring the shit—pardon me, Miss Rowan—is scaring my wife. We've got two kids. It just isn't safe here anymore. Especially after what happened to Manny."

"I'm sorry to hear that. Have you got another job?"

"I'm going to work for the San Antonio paper. Same beat. Police."

"I wish you luck, Tony. Your team down there has done a great job covering the border chaos. I expect your series to be a shoo-in for the Pulitzer."

"Yeah. Thanks. I just wish Manny was here to accept it if that happens." Gomez inhaled deeply. "I better get going. I've got the cop killing follow-up to write for tomorrow's edition. Just wanted you to know these people may be feeling some heat from your station, just like they did from the *Daily Leader*. You better be careful. These people are killers."

Tears misted Lesley's eyes. "Thank you for letting me know," she said, in a voice barely above a whisper. She felt a cold chill that sent an involuntary shiver through her body. Gomez was warning her she could be the next victim, a warning he was passing along from the DEA agent apparently planted inside the cartel. Could this be the same agent the dead pilot had spoken about?

"Tony," she asked with a sudden afterthought, "is there anyway you can contact the informant?"

There was a momentary hesitation before Gomez answered. "No. He calls me when he's got something. This is the first time he's called us since Manny died."

"Do you know if he might be a DEA agent?"

"We think so, but we don't know for sure. He's never really said who he works for… just that he's an undercover government agent. Manny thought he was probably DEA."

"He very well may be. The pilot who flew for Althea Oil & Gas, who first tipped me about the Dallas connection, told me he bumped into a man he thought he recognized from his days in law enforcement. He never gave me a name or anything else about the man."

"When he calls, it's always from what sounds like a pay phone. Probably when he's in Brownsville, maybe Matamoras. I never know when he'll call, but he always calls on my personal cell number."

"If he calls again anytime soon, tell him I would like to arrange to meet with him. Or at least talk with him. It sounds like he could be helpful with our series up here. Do you think he'd talk to me?"

"He might. Especially if he thinks he can trust you. I'll let him know you want to talk with him. Gotta run."

Gomez was gone before she could thank him again for passing on the warning. Then the realization of what the Brownsville reporter had said registered. He would let the informant know. Did that mean he *did* have a way of reaching him? Why would Gomez lie? Maybe just to keep her from muscling in on his prime source? Reporters were notoriously territorial and competitive.

Mac watched her walking slowly toward his office and knew

from the expression on her face something was wrong. He was still on the telephone when she walked in. He waved her to a chair.

"Witt, Lesley just came in and she looks like she's seen a ghost," Mac said into the receiver. "Come to my house when you get back. And plan to stay there. We'll talk further. It's time to go with this baby."

Mac looked up as he hung the receiver up. "What is it, Lesley?"

"I have seen a ghost, Mac. My own." She smiled wanly, a limp attempt to cover up the tumult churning inside her. "Do you remember Tony Gomez, the Brownsville reporter who worked on their drug series?"

Mac nodded.

"He just called. Said the informant—the one who fed them a lot of information for their series—the one the pilot thought he recognized as a DEA plant? She paused, and took a breath, "Well, he called Tony and told him a Mexican cartel, called El Poder, killed Edmonds and dumped his body in the ocean off Cozumel. The undercover agent also told Tony, Edmonds flew down to Mexico on a plane provided by the Castelero family in Chicago. I've never heard of them," she continued, "but I'm sure the Chicago police have. I'll check it out today."

Withers could see the tension in Lesley's face and it was underscored by her hands clenched tightly in her lap.

"Mac, it was Edmonds who stole my hard drive. They have my notes. Which confirms what we feared—they know we're working the story." She did not share the warning the DEA agent had passed on to Tony. If she did share the threat with Withers, she feared he would pull her off the story.

Withers silently digested what Lesley was telling him before asking, "How much stock can we put in this undercover guy? Are we even sure he's a DEA agent?" He leaned back in his chair and looked thoughtful. "Why was he telling all this to the pilot and now the Brownsville reporter? It doesn't make sense. It's like he's using the media as some sort of conduit. What do you think?"

Lesley shook her head. "I honestly don't know, Mac. It is strange.

Maybe he's just trying to prompt us into investigating the story, especially since the *Daily Leader* did just that after he fed them some critical information."

"Could be." Mac sat forward. "Terrell will be back from Austin, or wherever the hell he is, by the weekend. He's supposed to be down there, double checking everything he learned on his last trip. Morales and Bottoms headed down there this morning to get whatever Witt's got on tape. Witt just told me he'll have even more for us when he gets back."

Lesley was puzzled. Mac had not mentioned he was sending a camera crew to Austin. She suspected he was not telling her everything Witt had found. It must be something pretty explosive to merit a camera crew. Why wasn't Mac being more candid with her? This was her story too. Indignation mixed with her anger.

"What has Witt uncovered?" she asked bluntly.

"He said it's the Dallas connection you two have been looking for. And it's all in the records down there. He hasn't told me much more," he lied smoothly. "When he gets back he'll be staying at my place. Maybe you could run by this weekend and we'll go over everything, the three of us."

So, perhaps Mac wasn't holding out on her. She felt relief and a tinge of guilt for momentarily doubting him.

"I'll clear as much of my weekend as I can. Grant's mother invited me to spend the weekend with them. We're supposed to pick out a wedding dress Saturday morning and Grant's sister-in-law is giving me a shower Saturday afternoon. They've also invited some of Grant's friends for a small dinner Sunday night."

"Sounds like some good reasons to get the hell away from all this for a weekend." Withers said.

"No, no," she immediately protested. Grinning, she said, "I *can* walk and chew gum at the same time. This is my story," she asserted with proprietary emphasis in her voice. "Just call me when Terrell gets in and I'll drop everything and come over, at least for a little while, even if it is the weekend."

"Sounds like a plan." Mac glanced at his desk calendar and looked back at Lesley, a broad grin lighting his face. "I guess I'd better get out and shop for a wedding gift."

"No hurry," she replied flippantly, as she started to exit his office. "You still have a little more than a month. Bring your savings account book when you shop. I'm only registered at the best places. See ya."

"Hey, Les," Mac called before she reached the doorway. "You looked like something was really bothering you when you came in here. Anything you want to add?"

"Oh, no," she said, mustering as much blitheness as she could into her voice. "I was only referring to hearing from Gomez after all these weeks. He and the others down there haven't been exactly cooperative with our efforts here."

She slipped out the door before Mac could respond. She had come to his office fully intending to tell him about the threat Gomez had passed on to her—the very reason he had called. It would only upset Mac. Worse yet, he might tell Grant. That wasn't something she wanted to happen. Grant had already proposed hiring round-the-clock security after her apartment was broken into, and had discretely asked the Dallas police to keep a closer eye in the neighborhood around her apartment building. Lesley had noticed a patrol car cruising along the street in front of her apartment twice this week as she returned home.

At Mac's insistence, she drove a rental car instead of her Mustang, with the station picking up the weekly tab. She was also taking other precautions, like driving different routes home. But Gomez's words still rang in her ears. *You better be careful. These people are killers.*

And there were five people dead to prove it: Manny, the pilot, the two Dallas warehouse workers, and now, apparently, Edmonds.

31

Blaine Stewart eased back comfortably against the headrest of the leather seat, extending his long legs under the desk on which the contents of his briefcase sat in neat stacks. It was sometimes pleasant to get away from Dallas, his father's intrusive questions, and Grace. Even if what took him away was something unpleasant.

Edmonds was a fool. And he was well rid of him, although the man had run his operation with quiet efficiency—up until now. But his constant demands had been vexing. And the marriage to the stripper was proving to be a problem. She was too much the grieving widow. Something would have to be done about that. Grace had warned him about the woman. He should have listened. Grudgingly, he conceded his wife was generally right. Edmonds' disappearance was a short article on the inside of the morning paper.

Now, he feared the story would find its way to the front page. That must be prevented at all costs, or at least manipulated, to make the disappearance look accidental. The cover story was being arranged; a tragic accident during a fishing excursion, by the wealthy businessman seeking a few days relaxation at a Mexican resort. Edmonds' name had already been registered at a posh hotel eliminating that small detail. His name was also listed on the manifest of a deep sea fishing firm. Another detail covered. *Damage control* was what his public relations head, Lance Jennings, advised, without being told many of the pertinent facts. Damage control—the same approach Grant suggested after advising his father of the prior criminal record of the now departed member of the Stewart Oil Company board. He absently rubbed his forehead, a habit he had acquired over the years to ease stress. Grantham Stewart had said nothing in response, but his keenly observant eyes held a look of silent disapproval. Blaine Stewart had been the target of his father's critical scrutiny many times over the years. That he was a disappointment to his father was something Blaine Stewart had sullenly, but silently harbored. The two men—father and son—never discussed their differences.

As for Grant, his father and older brother had assured him they were as floored by the revelations about Edmonds and his criminal past as he was. Despite their reassurances, Grant still had misgivings about how those unsavory disclosures could impact his campaign and how much political fodder it could provide his savvy opponent. He insisted his campaign—not Stewart Oil—handle any media questions about the scandal surrounding Edmonds.

Blaine Stewart closed his eyes. He did not doubt that Grant could handle any such inquiries with his usual aplomb. His mind wandered back to Danford Pearson; the dapper, silver-maned, former district court judge who brought Althea Oil & Gas into the Stewart Oil fold of companies. He had thought at the time there could not be greater damage than that done by Pearson's untimely suicide. *Lawyers were royal pains in the butt*, he mused silently, *particularly those who undergo a sudden change of conscience*. Now this! At least Edmonds had the foresight to shred records and remove hard drives that could have compromised their operation. The man was a pragmatist. Where Stewart Oil was concerned, a dead pragmatist, fortunately.

Even with the records disposed of, there was some cleaning up to do. Althea Oil & Gas must be dissolved legally. They would miss the convenience of using its oil holdings. Perhaps only a temporarily inconvenience. Althea would have to be replaced by another company, to be spun off from Stewart Oil's plentiful stable. Elliott would be directly in charge of accomplishing that. No more outsiders to deal with. An attorney among the five members of his inner circle was already working on the legal aspects. It would all be in place within a month. It was this good news he was bringing to the meeting ahead.

"Coffee, Mr. Stewart?" He opened his eyes and feasted on the sable eyes and light-olive complexion of Susanna Ruiz, who placed a delicate china cup and saucer with the Stewart Oil logo on the desk in front of him. She poured into the cup his favorite blend, imported directly from Colombia. Her breasts were level with his face and he reached out and softly traced the profile of the left breast and heard her breath catch.

"Thank you. I could use some coffee."

She smiled indulgently. "I stopped and picked up some Danish from that Greek bakery you like so well."

"No, thank you. Just the coffee for now." Susanna's smile was forced, masking the disappointment she felt at the abrupt way Blaine dismissed a kindness she went out of her way to provide. She retreated to the small kitchenette in the rear of the jet.

Susanna Ruiz was one of the luxuries his father railed against at annual meetings. "Too much fluff," Grantham Stewart called the expenses for a full time pilot and stewardess, for a company plane that spent far more time in a hangar than in the air. What his father did not know would undoubtedly raise the tenor of the old man's annual railing to a higher level of outrage; the Dallas apartment for Ruiz, the credit card, the car. For the comfort Susanna provided when he was in her welcoming embrace, Blaine Stewart would gladly have paid more.

"Mr. Stewart. We'll begin our descent in about five minutes. Should be landing in about a half hour." It was the voice of the pilot on the intercom above the partially shaded window.

As the plane rolled smoothly to a stop, Stewart glanced out at the bland landscape shimmering in the blazing heat of mid-morning.

Its dullness was interrupted only by the occasional green of a cactus or gnarled pine brush. The isolation of the place was comforting.

"Your jacket, Mr. Stewart." Susanna held the blue linen sports coat as he slipped his arms through each sleeve. He kissed her discretely on the cheek. The petulance he noted in her eyes disappeared. As he stood in the doorway of the plane, Stewart could feel the intense heat encircle him. *How in the hell do these people stand this heat? Texas is Montana in the mountains compared to this.*

The approaching black Mercedes looked almost grey under the thick layer of road dust covering its sleek finish. A second vehicle, a large black SUV, followed the Mercedes. As the two cars pulled up to the plane and stopped, Stewart stepped through the doorway and down the steps. He held out his hand to the man approaching from the Mercedes.

"Blaine, it is good to see you again, even if the circumstances that bring us together are unfortunate." Christo gripped his American partner's hand warmly. They had much to discuss.

"Althea Oil & Gas is a wholly-owned subsidiary of Stewart Oil," Witt Terrell said, getting directly to his point, saying no more to give Withers time to absorb the statement. Terrell's rheumy eyes mirrored exhaustion after he had driven back to Dallas during the early morning hours to meet with Withers on Friday.

"We can prove this?" The words were barked, as much as spoken, by Withers, who was closeted with Terrell behind closed doors.

"Yes." Terrell did not flinch under Withers' piercing gaze. It had not taken long to complete his work in Austin. He had been there and in Tyler for over a week, confirming what he had discovered earlier; nailing it down; having the KDLL crew videotape the records he had uncovered; arriving back in Dallas and coming straight to the station.

"Do we know if anyone at Stewart Oil knows about drug money being laundered through Althea's books? Or if when the wells ran dry, Edmonds was just trying to cover his ass?" Withers suggested.

Withers pushed back in the leather chair, folded his hands behind his head in a position he often assumed when he was weighing what was being said around him—his eyes, as well as his words, confronting Terrell.

"I looked up the engineer who signed off on field reports years ago," Terrell replied, meeting Withers demanding gaze. "He's retired. Still lives in Tyler. He told me the Allison field played out nearly two decades ago, long before Edmonds took over as head of Althea Oil & Gas. Something else he said that's interesting. Blaine Stewart asked him to continue filing his monthly reports showing oil production. That's when the guy retired. He said it's not unusual for an oil company to falsify production numbers, to spread the costs and cook the books, to show non-existent expenses. Helps boost the profit margin. He just didn't want any part of it. So he retired."

"Will he talk on camera?"

"He already has. He just didn't know the camera was rolling. I got it all."

Terrell had a proclivity for understatement—had for as long as Withers had known the man. A faint smile teased the corners of the news director's mouth. *What in the hell else did Witt tape during the last week?*

"Something else the engineer said," Terrell continued. "Other fields leased by Stewart Oil have played out. He gave me a list of possibilities, mostly in West Texas. I still have to check them out." He looked directly at Withers. "So, do I keep living off the expense account?"

"Your days of wine and roses continue. Good work, Witt. Take Hank and Hector with you. They're yours for as long as you need them."

"Let me check things out first, then I'll give them a holler. It doesn't take long to tape what we find. It's the finding that takes a spell."

"Where you headed?"

"I'll probably stay somewhere near Midland. I'm heading out right now."

"Look, you're exhausted." Mac noted the weariness on Terrell's face. "Why don't you go to my place and get some shut-eye before hitting the road. Midland's a long drive from here."

"Thanks for the offer, but I'd rather get going." Terrell paused at the door. "What's going to happen to Lesley if I find Stewart Oil is involved up to their boot tops?"

Withers looked beyond Terrell, toward his anchor's darkened cubicle across the newsroom. "I don't know. She could really get caught in a meat grinder by all this. It worries the hell out of me."

"How much more you gonna tell her?"

"I honestly don't know, Witt. It's definitely a problem."

Terrell nodded agreement and left, leaving Withers to ponder how much of what he had just been told he should relay to Lesley. If Stewart Oil was involved in something illegal, it created at least the appearance of a conflict of interest for her. Grant Stewart had resigned from the board of directors of Stewart Oil and severed any ties with the family business more than a year before he announced his candidacy for mayor four years ago. As far as Withers knew, those ties remained severed. Stewart had worked for a top Dallas law firm before entering politics. He did draw income from a trust set up by his grandfather, funded primarily with Stewart Oil Company stock. Withers recalled those particulars from the mayor's financial disclosure statement, filed when Grant announced he would seek a second term as mayor.

Lesley was caught up in all the wedding hoopla. Maybe he should take her off the story and turn it over to Jack Reilley. He seemed on top of things. And after all, she would be gone for a week after the wedding. Reilley could handle it, at least for the time being. He would talk to Lesley when she came in.

Lesley arrived at her office a short time later. To Withers' relief, she did not come to his office, giving him time to further consider removing her in favor of Reilley. It would be a tough call. *Tough but maybe necessary.* He needed more time to weigh all the considerations, everything that could affect the biggest story KDLL had dealt with since he became news director.

It was Lesley's habit to check her messages when she first arrived. As usual, there were several. It was the last voice that caught her attention. She replayed it again to be sure she had not missed anything. "This is Sally Edmonds. There are some papers I found that may explain why my husband is missing." The woman's voice was husky, as if she had just awakened or had been crying, or maybe it was just a smoker's rasp. "I'm afraid to take them to the police. He mentioned you were a reporter. Can you look at this stuff and tell me what I should do?" There was brief bout of sobbing. "I need to talk to you right away." More nose blowing and sobbing. "Please call me. I think something real bad has happened to Walt."

Lesley listened closely to catch the telephone number. She suspected it was unlisted. When she dialed the number Sally Edmonds answered on the first ring.

"Yes?" The voice sounded desperately tired. Maybe drunk or drugged.

"This is Lesley Rowan, returning your call. You wanted to see me."

"Oh, could you please come over, Miss Rowan? I've got to show this stuff to someone. I think something bad has happened to my Walt." She broke into uncontrolled, choking sobs.

"Mrs. Edmonds, I'm sorry you're so upset. I understand. This must be very difficult for you."

There were unintelligible moans from the other end of the line.

"Mrs. Edmonds, I'll come right over. Tell me how to get to your place."

Mac had been watching Lesley on the telephone and noted the alarm on her face. Then watched her with growing curiosity as she grabbed her purse and hurried out of the newsroom after shouting she would be back a little later. Mac picked up his phone and dialed the reception desk at the main entrance to the newsroom. When a voice said, "Yes?" Mac asked, "Hey Marta, did Lesley say when she would be back?"

"No, sir. Not a word. She just went sailing by me. Sure was making haste."

"Yeah. Thanks Marta." Mac's curiosity was now fully piqued. He dialed Lesley's cell phone. She answered on the second ring. "Mac, I apologize for rushing out like that. I'm on my way to Sally

Edmonds. She's very upset. Says she had some papers to show me which might explain why her husband disappeared."

"I'll be here when you get back," was all Mac said before ending the connection.

✝✝✝

The woman who opened the door to the large brick home in an upscale Dallas subdivision was dry-eyed and controlled. Only the swelling under her bloodshot, red-rimmed eyes betrayed hours of sleeplessness and intermittent sobbing.

"I appreciate you comin', Miss Rowan," she said as Lesley stepped into the wide, marble-tiled foyer. Sally Edmonds closed the door behind her. "I didn't know who else to call."

"I'm sorry about your husband being missing." Lesley deduced that Sally had not been told her husband was permanently missing.

Tears swam in the large green eyes. "I don't think Walt's coming back. He's not coming back ever." Sobs pulled at Sally Edmonds' throat. "This stuff I found…" Tears now streamed down the smooth pale cheeks, washed clear of makeup, making her oval face look like that of a scared little girl.

"Walt must've been in big trouble when he left. I'm so scared for him." More sobs. She extracted a tissue from the pocket of the oversized terry cloth robe she was wearing and blew loudly. "Sorry, Miss Rowan."

"It's okay. I'd be upset too if my husband were missing." Lesley reached out and patted the stricken woman's shoulder, thinking Sally Edmonds was probably about her own age.

"What is it you found that's so troubling to you?" Lesley asked, trying to focus the distraught woman's attention on the reason she had telephoned.

"Come in here." She led Lesley into a large den with a wide sky light above wood beams that partially followed the cathedral line of the roof. On a round, glass-topped coffee table, half-circled by an overstuffed, white leather sectional couch, sat several manila

212

envelopes and what appeared to be a computer hard drive. Still wiping her nose, Sally Edmonds pointed Lesley to a seat in the center of the couch nearest the folders.

"I found this mess in Walt's secret wall safe." She turned away looking unsure. "Ya know… the safe." Sally looked remorseful as she handed one of the manila envelopes to Lesley.

Another gusher of tears spilled down Sally Edmonds cheeks. "I'm worried about Walt. When you read this, maybe you'll understand why my Walt isn't ever comin' back."

Lesley looked startled. "Why is that, Mrs. Edmonds?"

"Because it looks to me like he's up to his eyeballs with some bad people. I know that now. That's why I don't think he's ever coming back. He hooked up with some really bad people in Mexico." Her sobs became louder as she covered her face with her hands.

"Please don't give up hope, Mrs. Edmonds." Lesley felt helpless facing such raw grief, even though she knew Sally Edmonds' fears were now reality. "The Mexican police haven't given up. I'm sure they'll try to find your husband," she added, hoping to reassure the sobbing woman.

Lesley pulled a group of crumpled papers from a worn manila envelope and began slowly scrutinizing each one. On each page were handwritten lists of what appeared to be account numbers, dates, and amounts. As Lesley's eye scanned down the list, she saw the numbers were amounts deposited into a bank in the Cayman Islands. There were additional pages with account numbers and deposits made into a bank in Freeport in the Bahamas. There were so many Lesley could not do the math in her head, but she knew she was looking at tens of millions of dollars placed in various accounts in these banks. There were no names written for any of the accounts, only account numbers for deposited amounts that went back five years. Lesley could barely contain the excitement welling inside her. Could this be the money laundered through the books of Althea Oil & Gas; the smoking gun; the Deep Throat; the evidence that could bring everything Terrell had uncovered together?

Lesley opened the second manila envelope with rising excitement. It was more lists of deposits to the same several banks, only these lists were neatly typed. The deposits went back another eight years.

Neither woman spoke during the long minutes Lesley perused the contents of each manila envelope. When she completed her cursory examination she turned to Sally. "These are deposits into banks in the Cayman Islands and the Bahamas. Do you think your husband was involved in hiding money in these accounts?"

"It wasn't his money. He was doing it for other people. I think he was working for that Castelero bunch in Chicago."

There was that name again—the Chicago crime family the Brownsville reporter had mentioned in passing. "Who are they?" she inquired, seeking affirmation.

"They're the bunch that mostly runs mob operations in Chicago. I used to work in a joint owned by them. Walt worked with some of them before he went to prison. He said he was through with all that when we got married and moved to Dallas. He promised me… He promised." More sobs choked off her words.

Terrell alluded to a possible mob connection, she recalled. *Could this be the same group?* "Why did he keep these records at home?" she asked, trying to redirect the woman's attention to the information she had found in her husband's safe.

"I think I know why, Miss Rowan. I think this was his insurance policy, so to speak." Sally Edmonds eyed the folders. "You know, like if they ever tried to do something to him, he could threaten to give the police or the feds this stuff." Her moist eyes swept across the folders strewn on the table.

"Mrs. Edmonds, we already know your husband headed an oil company that fabricated production records for wells that haven't produced oil for years. Were you aware of this? Did he ever talk about his business?"

"No. Walt never said much. Not to me, anyway. He liked the social stuff we did with the Stewarts, but he really didn't like any of them. He thought they were kinda snotty. Especially that Mrs.

Stewart… you know, Grace." She dropped her eyes and turned her head away from Lesley, twisting her hands nervously.

"I guess I'm talking out of turn. I know you're marrying into that family." Sally Edmonds was clearly embarrassed by her remarks. "By the way, I really like Grant," she added, attempting to assuage the disparaging summary of Grace Stewart she had shared only with her husband until now.

"Please, Mrs. Edmonds," Lesley said, reaching out to pat the woman's arm in a gesture of reassurance. "No offense taken." Lesley took a deep breath. "About these records. They could be helpful to the story we're pursuing. Would you allow me to make copies of these lists?"

"Yeah. But I don't want to go to the police. That's why I called you." Sally Edmonds was looking directly at Lesley, the pleading apparent in her eyes. "Back before me and Walt moved to Dallas, I had a past. He didn't know a lot about the things I did before I met him. We met in a strip club, but he never knew about the rest. Please don't get me involved."

Lesley gave her word to the woman now sobbing again beside her. "I'll take these to the office now and make copies. I'll drop them back by tomorrow, on my way into the station, if that's okay." Then Lesley looked at the small box she knew was a hard drive. "Can I take this as well and find out what's on it?"

Sally Edmonds nodded affirmatively. "You won't lose nothin', will you?" she asked, her voice again jerking with sobs.

"No, Mrs. Edmonds, I promise. I'll return all this to you tomorrow." She placed all the folders in a stack and slipped the hard drive into her purse.

Sally Edmonds held the door open for Lesley. "You won't let me down. It's just—I felt like I could trust you." The bright sunlight fell across her tear-streaked face and highlighted the brown roots of her blonde-from-a-bottle hair. "I knew before I called you Walt is gone for good. They probably killed him. I just know it. If he was alive he would've called me. We was real close, you know." She wiped her streaming eyes with the cuff of her robe. "Maybe this stuff will help me find out what's happened to my Walt."

"It could be crucial, Mrs. Edmonds." Lesley squeezed the woman's arm gently with her free hand. It did little to quell the sobs now shaking the buxom body. "I'll call you tomorrow before I bring these back. If you need me for anything, you can reach me at this number." She wrote her cell number on the back of a station business card and handed it to Sally Edmonds. "You can reach me at that number anytime."

33

Lesley could hardly contain her excitement on the drive through the late morning traffic back to the television station. She burst into a producers' meeting unannounced. "I'm sorry, Mac. Can you step out a moment? You've got to see what I just picked up."

"Gentlemen, I never disobey an anchor. Her wish is my command." Withers was unable to disguise the hint of irritation in his voice, and then tried lamely to excuse himself with humor. It drew knowing chuckles from the three men sitting in his office. Just outside the office door, Lesley handed one of the manila envelopes to Mac.

"Guess what's inside that envelopes?"

He shook the large envelope teasingly. "It doesn't sound like keys to a new Corvette convertible."

"It's no key. It may be our smoking gun. Look inside."

Withers pulled out the handwritten pages, looking momentarily puzzled at the figures. Lesley watched with growing anticipation for his reaction as his eyes scanned from the top of the first sheet to the bottom, and on to the next page.

"Where'd you get this?" His voice now reflected the excitement she was trying hard to contain.

"The widow Edmonds."

Withers interrupted her. "When did we find out she's a widow? Police confirm it?"

Lesley looked into Mac's eyes. "Not yet. She knows about her husband's background and is pretty sure he isn't coming back."

"How did Edmonds' wife come by this information?" Withers demanded after scanning the contents of the manila envelope, before placing the contents carefully back inside. Lesley had learned to tolerate Withers' impatience. He could be a curmudgeon at times. This seemed to be one of those times.

"She found it in a safe at her house. Thinks her husband was keeping this information just in case his friends decided to turn unfriendly."

"No question, Les. This is a huge lead. Now we've got to figure out how to check out the validity of this information. And, by the way," he added, a slight smile softening his flinty expression, "it was okay to interrupt the meeting for this." He waved the envelopes lightly and pressed them back into her hands. "What are you going to do with this now?"

"Make copies and take the originals back to Mrs. Edmonds tomorrow." She started to move away. "Oh, I almost forgot. What about this? I think it may be my hard drive. Anybody here who can check for sure?"

"Yeah. Me. I'll load it in my computer. Get Marta to help you make those copies. I'll call Witt and see how we can check out the numbers and make sure those accounts exist. Good work, girl." He squeezed her arm affectionately, then turned to enter his office where the men still waited, watching with gnawing curiosity the exchange between the news director and the anchor.

Withers sat back down. He noted the curious stares and dismissed them without a word of explanation. "What is it you guys say about Hal," he said, referring to the evening executive news producer, "he's a brick-shitter?" The three men laughed. "Sorry for being a brick-shitter. Now what's our lead for the noon news?"

✝✝✝

Grant sensed her restlessness. Always after they made love Lesley would snuggle next to him, limp as a kitten. Now, he could feel the tautness in her muscles when he caressed her arm and moved his hand to her neck. He slept briefly and knew when he turned over toward her, she had not. Something was bothering her—something more than pre-wedding jitters.

It must be a problem at work, he guessed, knowing she generally avoided discussing anything involving the station with him. It was one of the few things over which they had argued, when he asked her to consider leaving the station and her career. He had apologized later, acknowledging the selfishness of his request. His note had accompanied a dozen red roses that arrived for Lesley at the station. It was signed, "Your most adoring fan."

The prospect of his personal wealth was not a tempting enough enticement for her to quit and leave behind her own six figure salary. In the end he agreed she should continue her career.

Later, when Grant told his father he and Lesley had agreed she would continue working after their marriage it provoked a heated discussion between the two men. Grant brushed off his father's ill-temper as just a bad day at the office. The following weekend, when he and Lesley arrived at the estate, his father could not have been more charming. The subject of Lesley's career was never broached.

Grant leaned over and kissed her neck invitingly. She responded by turning to bring her face even with his.

"I love you, pretty lady," he whispered, kissing the end of her nose and then her lips. "You're far away. Where?"

"I'm right here and never want to be anywhere else."

"I hope not. This wedding is costing me a huge nickel," he said, and proceeded to tickle her until she yelled for mercy amidst her laughter. They were kneeling on the bed, facing each other, when Lesley's gamine expression suddenly changed, like a shade being pulled over the merriment that had lighted her face moments before.

"Grant, I've learned something else about Walt Edmonds."

He was jolted by her words, but kept his demeanor calm as he lay back and propped himself on one elbow. "What now?"

"His wife called me yesterday. I went to visit her. She's very upset about his disappearance and doesn't think he's coming back."

"Why would she call you?"

"She just wanted to talk mostly. She's fearful Walt was involved in something that may have landed him into some kind of serious trouble."

"Why would she think that? Walt seemed very capable, even though you said he had a prison record. He really knew the oil business from everything I've heard about him. That's why Dad put him on the board. Dad did say Walt could be a little recalcitrant at times." Grant looked down at Lesley, who had reclined back on the pillow. "It sounds like she's just worried. That's understandable." A smile creased his face. "Anyway, ole Walt will probably show up shortly with a new babe. Personally, that's my theory and I'm sticking to it."

"Grant." Lesley's expression deflected his attempt at humor. "Sally Edmonds showed me a list of off-shore bank accounts, all numbered, no names. She found them in a secret safe somewhere in their home. I told her she needed to give such information to the police, but she's insisting on not going to them. I think she fears Walt may have been embezzling money from Althea Oil & Gas." Lesley looked at Grant searchingly. "She wants me to check it out."

Grant was stunned. *Edmonds had off-shore bank accounts?* A nonplused expression wavered for a moment on his face. Then a mask descended. "I probably need to tell Dad if Walt may have been embezzling funds from Althea and squirreling it away in those off-shore banks."

"His wife doesn't think that. She thinks her husband is still tied in with mobsters in Chicago."

"Jesus, no! What else did you learn about this man who is so high in my family's company?" His brusque question stunned her.

"She really didn't say much else. Grant," Lesley said, looking pleadingly into the face of the man she loved. "I'm worried about the impact on your campaign if Mrs. Edmonds' allegations prove true."

"I'm sure they could hurt." Grant sighed heavily. "I'm sure they will. Anything of that nature is fodder for the Davis side."

"Grant, I've been working on a story for weeks now. It involves Althea Oil & Gas. I can't say any more. But it could be damaging." She hesitated, fearing she had said too much already. "Can your father distance the company from Althea Oil & Gas now, to blunt anything that might come out in the future?"

"I don't understand, Lesley." Confusion reigned in his eyes. "You've been working on a story about Althea? What kind of story?" There was a sharp demand in his voice.

"Please, Grant. I can't say anything else. I shouldn't have told you. I just don't want you hurt by anything I do for the station."

"Then leave there, Les." He lay back on the pillow and rested his head on his arm. "You don't have to work. I can take care of you. I can. I will." He turned over and pulled her into his arms, kissing her hard, his tongue probing, until she felt weak with the love and need of this man who she loved so fiercely.

In the morning, as she approached the door to leave, he walked over and kissed her lightly on the lips. "Think about what I asked. I want you with me all the time, Lesley. You'll never want for anything. Not for money. And most of all, not for love."

34

"Please hold. I'll see if Mr. Stewart is available." The formal voice was gone. Soft music now played in his ear. Gerald Tillis was a patient man. Never in a hurry. *It does no good,* he always told himself, *to spend your life being the hare.* All it did was buy an early heart attack for several of the guys he had worked with during his 35 years with Stewart Oil Company. Not him. He was 74 and still walked his usual two miles a day. He would hold off the nursing home as long as he could.

"May I ask the nature of your call, Mr. Tillis?" the formal voice inquired.

"It's personal. Just tell Mr. Stewart it's about a man that came round, asking a lot of questions about the Allison fields in East Texas."

"Thank you, Mr. Tillis." The formal voice was gone again, the music back. Tillis was a little miffed he had to explain the reason for his call. He felt his call—to alert the head of the company that sent him a retirement check every month—was a point of loyalty, a courtesy, and it shouldn't be questioned. He never liked Blaine Stewart much from the time the younger man took over the company.

Old Mr. Stewart would take his call and bend his ear for a half hour about the early days in the East Texas oil fields. During most of his years with the company, old Mr. Stewart had been at the helm. It was different when the son took over. Things changed. Tillis disagreed with a lot of the changes. And when the younger Stewart asked him to falsify productions statements, he'd had enough and decided to retire. He informed Blaine Stewart that very day he would be leaving. It was the best reason he could think of to avoid signing off on those inflated production sheets, and not tick everyone off. He really hadn't planned to retire. It was just the best thing to do under the circumstances.

"Jerry, how are you? This is a pleasant surprise." Blaine Stewart forced joviality into his voice.

"I'm doing just great, Mr. Blaine. Sorry to call in the middle of the day like this."

"Not a problem, Jerry. What's on your mind?" It was a gentle push to get Tillis onto the subject of his call.

"There was this fellow from a Dallas television station... I can't remember which one... I think Channel 15... who came to see me. Said his name was Witt Terrell. Used to work for one of the Dallas newspapers." Stewart printed the name on a note pad near his telephone. "This Terrell fellow was asking about production reports from the Allison fields. He said he looked me up because I was the engineer who signed off on them up until I retired. Been gone now 10 years. Doesn't seem that long, Mr. Blaine."

There was an awkward silence as Tillis waited for a response. "Anyway, I just thought Mr. Stewart would want to know about this guy going through our old production records."

Blaine knew he meant his father. Older employees always referred to the company founder as Mr. Stewart. Even many of the younger ones yet today. It was a respect he and Elliott were never accorded, except by the fawning secretaries and receptionists. Women always seemed to be more deferential.

Feigning a hearty good humor he was far from feeling at this moment, Blaine said, "Jerry, I appreciate your call. It was good to talk with you. My guess is the guy is from the Internal Revenue Service or the state, just checking us out. Keeping us on our toes, so to speak I'll let my father know you called. He'll be pleased, I'm sure."

Before Tillis could hang up, Blaine Stewart added, "I can assure you of this, Jerry. We don't have anything to hide. Again, I really appreciate your call. We should have more like you still working in this company. Loyal folks like you are hard to duplicate in this day and time."

Gerald Tillis smiled, basking in the compliment. His loyalty to Stewart Oil was appreciated. He did not expect such a reaction from the younger Mr. Stewart. It pleased him immensely. "If I hear anything else, or that fellow comes back around, I'll let you know."

"I'd appreciate that, Jerry. You call anytime. And make sure you ask for me. By the way, did he leave you a number to contact him?"

"No, he didn't, Mr. Blaine." The response disappointed Stewart.

"Thanks for calling me. And let me know right away if he contacts you again. I'll alert our lawyers at this end. As I said, it sounds like we may be under scrutiny by the IRS. You know that crowd in Washington doesn't like us oil folks very much, Jerry. They took away our depletion allowance and God knows what mischief they're up to now." Blaine laughed to underscore his attempt at humor.

"I sure will—let you know if he contacts me again, Mr. Blaine." Tillis hung up smiling.

"Goddamn it!" Blaine shouted the oath as he slammed down the telephone. Outside his office, Rachel Arrington flinched. It was not like Blaine Stewart to swear. The call must have upset him terribly. She should not have put it through; she should have insisted on taking a message. She castigated herself for her lapse in judgment.

"Rachel, get me Stu Aarons right away." The intercom clicked off. Mr. Stewart was upset and it was her fault. She prided herself on running an office that kept his day fluid, with no consternation to interrupt the flow of regular business. This telephone call from a former employee had clearly done what she tried rigorously to protect the head of Steward Oil against. Rachel looked up the number for Aarons Security Service. Aarons was on the line in seconds. "Please hold the line, Mr. Aarons," she said briskly. "Mr. Stewart is calling." After connecting the two men, she headed for the coffee maker. Maybe a cup of coffee would help assuage Mr. Stewart's irritation.

"Stu, I need you to check out a Witt Terrell. He's a reporter, currently working for Channel 15. Keep this confidential and get back to me quickly. Here or on my cell phone."

"Right away, Mr. Stewart."

As soon as the light went off indicating the telephone call was completed, Rachel knocked on the door and placed a cup of coffee, a teaspoon of cream and two sugar cubes, stirred, in front of her boss. "I thought you could use this."

"I can. Thank you, Rachel." He silently wished all employees were as dependable at Rachel Arrington.

Coffee was doing little to banish the tiredness dragging at Lesley. Frequent calls from Grace left Lesley feeling inadequate, and often at a loss in making decisions to finalize preparations for the wedding. Her pre-nuptial jitters were mounting. And her sleep was further shortened by their lovemaking every night.

Lesley felt the familiar rush of feeling at the thought of Grant. She loved him deeply, more than she thought it possible to love another human being. At first sight of him last night, as he opened the door of his grandfather's home and welcomed her into his arms, the wave of excitement caught her breath and caressed her heart. She looked at the five-carat diamond ring, bordered on each side with large emerald baguettes, now glistening on her slender finger. It had been enclosed in a small, blue velvet box embossed by its designer, Tiffany's of New York. Her eyes were awash in tears as he held her in a long embrace before leading her into the living room where his parents, Elliott and Emily, and his grandfather were waiting.

The two women were effusive in their delight and praise of

Grant's choice of an engagement ring. "It is truly a match for the lovely woman who wears it," Grace said as she released Lesley's hand.

"Come here, daughter." Grantham Stewart beaconed to her with a gnarled bony hand to where he sat on a couch. "Let's get a good look at this rock," he chuckled as he clutched her hand in his and peered closely at the ring. "This must have set you back a year's salary, Grant." The old eyes then fixed on Lesley's face. "But I think it was a good investment."

Lesley was momentarily overwhelmed by the warm embrace of Grant's family until Blaine lifted her hand to view the ring. His words were complimentary, but his expression remained cool and he remained aloof the rest of the evening.

How much of what she revealed to Grant had he shared with his father? This might explain his father's remoteness during dinner. Lesley refused to allow her sullen future father-in-law to diminish her enjoyment of the evening. She was about to marry a man she loved deeply, a man she never saw herself worthy of in her mind's eye, a man with whom she dared to envision a long and fulfilling life together that would be further fulfilled by children. Lesley had never felt such pride and happiness as when she looked across the table at Grant, but her joy was quickly dispelled by what she knew lay ahead. She was about to help break a story that could prove a new pinnacle of her career and bring about the possible downfall of his father.

The urgent light was flashing on her voicemail when she arrived at her desk—a message from Mac to see him immediately.

Withers motioned Lesley to close the door as she entered his office. There was an edge of excitement in his demeanor. "Witt has dug up some stuff he says will uncork one of the biggest scandals ever in the Texas oil industry," he told her in a hushed voice. "This is some heavy shit." He looked over apologetically. "Sorry, Les."

Then his voiced rose again excitedly. "We need to go with what we have. When Terrell comes back tomorrow, we'll meet immediately. Can you come in early?"

She nodded yes. Mac continued, "I want Reilley in here. And Hal Crockett. He needs to sit in this time, so he can start laying out the series and assign camera crews to get responses."

"I think you're already smelling a Peabody or two," she quipped.

"You're damned right I do," Withers replied, his intensity undaunted by her attempt at lightness. Then he sat back, scrutinizing her in a way that troubled her. "Les, this is your story. You brought it to us. I hope we don't lose you because of it."

What is Mac thinking, lose me because of it? She was marrying Grant. This was his home. It would be hers, as well. The question of her quitting her job had not been broached again, although Grant alluded once or twice to a strong preference for having her home with him every evening or at his side for the myriad of functions he attended as part of his mayoral duties. His concern, Grant quickly reassured her, was only her happiness. If working was part of her happiness equation, he would never again pressure her to quit. Of this she was now certain.

Mac's remark remained puzzling, unless—and her mind immediately recoiled at the thought—Terrell had found something that linked Grant's immediate family to the brewing scandal.

35

His private line rang. It was Aarons. Always a model of clandestine efficiency, Aarons would not be calling without information to impart. It was an attribute that distinguished him as head of security for Stewart Oil.

"We've started tailing the guy," Aarons began, without even a hello. "Witt Terrell's a former reporter for the morning newspaper. As far as we can tell he's not worked much since being fired—was in an alcohol rehab program for a few weeks after he got canned. Then he just got lost. Drives an old blue Pinto he bought from a Dallas lot a couple months ago. Paid cash. It matches the description of the car we saw parked near the station. This *is* the same hombre."

"Where is he now?"

"In Stanton, near Midland, in the Warm Breeze Motel. He's been there two days, according to the room clerk. Castelero had Estavar send two guys there to keep an eye on him. They blend better with the natives there than the Chicago crowd does. Castelero's calling the shots on this one. That's all I can tell you." Aarons remark was not lost on Blaine Stewart. He knew where Aarons' information came from.

"Is this man doing the same thing there he did in Tyler?"

"Yes, sir. Since he got there he's been to three fields. Same thing. Checking storage tanks. Checking pumps. He went to the courthouse in Midland this morning." There was silence at the other end of the line. "We're keeping an eye on him."

"All right, Aarons. Keep me posted. And for God's sake, tell those people not to be spotted," he said, taking no pains to hide his irritation at having Castelero and Estavar usurping his authority with his own security person.

"No chance, Mr. Stewart."

Terrell had spotted them that morning—two men in a dark blue, late model SUV, sitting off the two-lane highway, pretending to be changing a tire. From where they were parked they had an unobstructed view of most of the field he was checking. Terrell could only guess how long they had been watching him, but he was certain that's what they were doing. Cars were few and far between in this isolated part of the county. Everybody local seemed to drive a pickup. If it had been a pickup with its back tire jacked up, it would not have drawn a second glance from him. But seeing a car kindled his suspicions and invited his scrutiny. Spotting two burly Hispanics changing the tire sent a strong, almost electric warning to every nerve fiber in his gut.

When he returned 30 minutes later the car was gone. It had pulled out the same way he was headed, before he circled the Pinto back on a side road. It wound through hilly terrain, thickly dotted with ponderosa pines and scrub, through a long-deserted oil field, where rusted pumps still jutted at odd angles, long-stilled, some cannibalized, all silhouetted against a cloudless mid-day sky.

After getting back from Midland late that evening, he drove around the small town, looking for the dark blue car. No sign of it or its driver and passenger. Checking his rear-view mirror frequently, Terrell made sure the same set of headlights never stayed behind him too long.

This morning, the road leading into the last field he wanted to check was level and deserted. His Pinto was the only car amid a small sea of clanking oil wells. It was a now familiar cacophony of sound, as the long, thick pump arms rose and fell to the same rhythmic cadence. Morning was dissolving into the full heat of midday when he returned to his car, his methodical listing of well numbers complete.

Terrell returned to the county seat where he had stayed at a 1960s-style motel last night. Parking off the main street, he strolled over to the vintage, Bedford-stone courthouse. The old courthouse dominated the buildings circling a square, built around a statue commemorating the county's fallen soldiers from several wars. He emerged two hours later, his work complete. The wells listed on the pages of Terrell's crumpled legal pad belonged to five of the oil companies he traced in the records in Austin—all wholly-owned subsidiaries of Stewart Oil.

Hungry, he walked briskly across the landscaped square to a café on the other side. Terrell let his eyes adjust to the dim lighting inside before taking a booth toward the back where he could eyeball anyone coming in. He ordered the fried chicken plate lunch from a cranky waitress who was not pleased at having a late-lunch customer. He pulled deep on a cigarette as he waited for the food. He was back to smoking nearly a pack a day. But what the hell, he could afford it now. After consuming most of the heaped plate of fried chicken, green beans and mashed potatoes, topped with thick brown gravy, Terrell placed twelve dollars on top of the green bill and left the café feeling full and sleepy. He headed for a print shop he had spotted earlier. Mac had asked him to fax his notes, so he could review them before Terrell arrived back in Dallas.

It took the better part of an hour to fax the pages Terrell kept handing to the plump, drab blonde clerk to manually feed into the machine. He sent each yellow sheet to the fax number Mac instructed him to use before he left Dallas. Each page was filled with handwritten lists of oil-well numbers, each well's corresponding ownership, and some of his meticulously noted observations—long days of accumulated and careful research. None of the wells were putting out what was claimed in the county seat records. The last page was a handwritten note saying it would be late tonight before he got back to Dallas and could he meet with Mac tomorrow morning.

Terrell counted out the bills for the fax charges to the bored young clerk, included a $5 tip, than carefully placed the pages he faxed underneath the blank pages remaining in the pad.

Outside the shop, the August heat seared his face. He walked to the Pinto parked on a side street, just around the corner from the courthouse. Inside the car, where heat compressed behind closed windows, Terrell felt the chill that signaled a familiar need. He reached for the pint of Jack Daniels in the glove compartment, still wrapped in a brown bag, and allowed himself a long swallow, feeling the welcome burn of the liquor passing down his throat. It would have to hold him all the way to Dallas. A slight breeze brushed through the open windows, venting the stale, hot air inside the car. There was always wind in West Texas. It rustled his thinning hair and relieved the relentless mid-afternoon heat radiating off the windshield which faced the western sky.

Terrell pulled a wrinkled hanky from his pocket and wiped the taste of Jack Daniels from his lips. He suddenly felt ebullient. He did what Mac had asked him to do, he thought, as he wiped the hanky across his damp forehead. The documented facts just faxed; the discovered facts sitting inside a pad at Mac's house; it was accumulating into one helluva story. There were too many dry wells; too many empty storage tanks. And illegal drugs were making up for what Mother Nature no longer supplied. He was now certain someone at the top of Stewart Oil had to be involved. He sure as hell was going to find out whom.

Terrell was not a man to indulge in envy. He never measured his success against the success of others. He was what he was and accepted his lot in life—much of his life had been spent too drunk to change much anyway. But he could not shake off the nagging prickle of covetousness that clawed at him as the panorama of oil wealth rushed past his view on both sides of the highway, observed as he had driven from Dallas to Midland two days ago. Texas riches pumping into someone's bank account. In his entire life he never had more than a few hundred dollars in his wallet. Certainly not in those early days with the bureau. Later, rent, booze, and cigarettes claimed too big a share of his bi-weekly pay at the newspaper.

It was only after placing the pint bottle back in the glove compartment that he felt the presence of the man at the open window. Surprise flickered momentarily over his face as he felt the cold end of the silencer against his ear and the searing bullets forging into his brain, their deftly cut tips exploding through skull and brain. Witt Terrell slumped sideways in the car seat, dying without making a sound. A gloved hand reached across him and pulled the yellow legal pad from underneath his head.

The murder happened so quickly, so quietly, no one saw it; no one heard it; even in broad daylight, the town constable was told by those he later questioned. That puzzled him. The victim had been shot just off Main Street, in front of a row of businesses, in a car parked at a meter with its overtime arm up. Nothing like this had ever happened in a town which saw almost no petty crime, let alone an execution-style murder in broad daylight. Well, it would be up to the county sheriff or the Texas Rangers to figure it out. This crime was well above his pay grade as a constable.

†††

Mac Withers punched the off button on the television remote with his thumb, silencing the largest of several television screens lining a wide shelf, high on the wall across from his desk. It had been a good hour news block from five to six. He must remember to give kudos to Trace Abernathy tomorrow during the staff meeting. The young producer was filling in for the regular producer for that time block. He kept the newscasts moving seamlessly, making even the commercial breaks appear well produced.

Withers was reaching for his suit jacket on the coat stand by the door when the private line rang. He could always recognize its higher-pitched ring. It was sounding a second time before he reached the side of his desk where the telephone hung just below the top. The sheriff's detective at the other end explained this was one of several numbers found in a small book in the victim's shirt pocket. What was his name, the detective wanted to know? Mac Withers, he answered. Did he know a Witt Terrell? Yes, Withers responded.

"Sorry to tell you sir, but Mr. Terrell is deceased.

A long pause before the question— "how?"

"An apparent gunshot wound to the head. The coroner will know in the morning." No sound at the Dallas end of the connection.

"You all right, sir?"

"Yes."

There were no witnesses. The sleepy detective had been on duty since seven this morning. This kind of crime was few and far between in his neck of the woods. He yawned between each question. Did the victim have next of kin? *None that he knew of.* What else could he tell him about Witt Terrell? *Nothing much. A former federal agent turned journalist.* Do he know why the victim was in Yarrow? *Yes.* Can you tell me why? *No. Can I call you back?* Just a few more questions, the weary investigator's voice pleaded. *I'll call you back,* came the response.

Withers reached mechanically to hang up the telephone. His shaking hand fumbled, missing the metal cradle twice. On the third attempt, he slammed the receiver onto its holder as tears burned his eyes. He was still at his desk later, when several staffers went by. Some glanced absently at Withers as they hurried to their own desks and offices. There was always a sense of hurry in the newsroom. *So senseless,* he thought. The scene in the movie *Network* of a girl with the videotape, racing from the editing booth to the control room, leaping over obstacles, sliding under others, to get the tape on the air, played over and over in his mind, a mind numbing video that he seemed unable to turn off. *She doesn't die at the end of the race to get it on the air,* his mind screamed, *not like Witt.*

Jack Reilley was returning to his desk from an interview at the police department and started into Withers' office. He was waved away by the man sitting behind the desk staring at the wall across from him, tears now dried on his thick, rough cheeks. Reilley motioned to Lesley as she walked out from the studio. He whispered his concern. She glanced back at Mac sitting still behind his desk. When he saw her approach, worry written on her face, he abruptly waved her away. She turned, confused and somewhat hurt.

Later, Withers picked up the telephone and called Grant Stewart's condo. Stewart answered. "This is Mac Withers. I want Lesley to stay with you for the next few days. Something has happened. Don't ask what. I can't say. Just get her over there tonight, and make sure she's with you and protected when she isn't here." Withers' tone silenced the question forming on Stewart's lips. He agreed.

After another solitary hour in his office, Mac Withers left. Later, inside the darkness of his home, he checked the locks on all doors before going to his austere bedroom. He lay back on a pillow fully dressed. His eyes did not close until far into the morning.

36

Three mourners and a minister stood solemn and silent under a boiling Dallas sky, as the cemetery workers began lowering the casket into the neatly dug, oblong opening in the earth. Farewells went unspoken. Witt Terrell was being buried in the same manner he lived his life—with little fuss. No obituary announced his passing. No telegrams or telephone calls went out to notify family. There was no known family to notify, at least none the deceased ever spoke of.

Mac Withers crossed over to the broad-bellied, ingratiating minister who agreed to read some scriptures over the closed casket holding Terrell's thin body. A part-time police chaplain, he was doing a favor for Jack Reilley. Tucking his Bible under his fleshy left arm, he shook hands with Withers and discretely accepted the proffered envelope. A small stipend for a small favor. It would fill up the tank of his gas-guzzling, older model Mercury.

"Much appreciated," he said in a low voice, waving awkwardly to the mourners as he ambled away. The minister belatedly remembered good etiquette required him to shake the hand of Jack, and maybe the woman standing beside him. *Too late*, he thought, shrugging his rounded shoulders. He kept walking.

With no flowers to hassle with, the lone cemetery worker remaining climbed inside the small cab of the backhoe, impatient in the stifling heat for the trio standing silently by the open grave to leave. His impatience was quickly allayed. By the time the three reached Withers' car, parked nearby in the rolling, park-like cemetery, the backhoe was already pushing dirt onto the casket.

Jack Reilly held the door for Lesley as she sat in the front. Reilly then slipped into the back seat. No one spoke during the ride back to the station. When the ignition key silenced the motor, Withers turned to Jack and Lesley, his face drained of color and emotion.

"Some federal agents want to talk with us. I told them about what time we'd be back. I've already told them we won't turn over any files until the story airs, but we would tell them what we could. Agreed?"

"Sure, Mac. Whatever you think," replied Reilley. Lesley looked over at Withers and nodded.

Ben Worthington was slightly built, soft-spoken, polite, empathetic, and handsome in an almost effeminate way. His slender head sat atop an equally slender neck, the antithesis of what Lesley thought an FBI agent should look like. His incisive questions erased any doubt about the nature of his business.

The two DEA agents with him appeared content to let Worthington take the lead. They sat quiet but sharply attentive. Worthington explained their interest was kindled by a tip that a Channel 15 reporter was investigating drug smuggling by the El Poder cartel and had videotape of an actual drug drop in Texas. He offered no clue to the identity of the tipster.

Withers refused to confirm the tip without ever actually denying it, verbally sparring with the special agent. When Worthington attempted to direct his questions to Lesley she smoothly deferred to Withers. An hour later the three men walked out the main entrance to the bustling newsroom knowing little more than when they arrived, convinced the journalists knew far more than what they had revealed.

"How the hell did those guys find out we have tape of the drug drop in Tyler?" Anger was a rare reaction from Mac Withers, but now it flared in his gray eyes and hardened his voice. "Hell, the competition probably knows by now. Have either one of you been talking to anyone outside this station?" He looked demandingly at Reilley before his eyes moved to Lesley.

"I made notes about the videotape on my computer. An informant told Tony Gomez at the *Daily Leader* some of what was learned from my notes, and I may have confirmed it to Tony. I just don't remember. I'm sorry, Mac."

"Shit." The expletive made her flinch. He had forgotten the stolen hard drive. "Sorry, Les. But damn it, you shouldn't have confirmed anything about what we're doing here. You think he may be trying to undermine our story?"

"I can't imagine. After Manny's murder, they pretty well dropped everything, especially since Gomez left. I check the *Daily Leader* online almost every day and haven't seen any new stories."

Reilly chimed in, "If the *Daily Leader's* informant is a DEA plant, the guy is no doubt in touch with his own people, and maybe the FBI. That could also explain the visit today."

Withers nodded. It might have explained it, but it did little to dampen his exasperation. As he watched the three men disappear through the double door into the station's main hallway, Withers turned to Reilly. "Jack, thank you for coming with us to put Witt to rest. I need to talk with Lesley alone. Will you excuse us right now? But stay close. I'm going to have a meeting shortly. We're starting the series Monday."

"No problem. Can we..." Reilley's voice trailed off, his question, *could they get the series together that soon*, left unsaid. He turned and walked slowly to his desk.

"Les, I'm taking you off the series."

Lesley looked at Mac startled. She moved forward in her chair. "Why?"

"I made up my mind the same night I heard Witt had been killed."

"I'm not afraid, Mac. Nothing is going to happen to me. You can't remove me now," Lesley pleaded. She still had not told Mac about the warning from Gomez.

"I have to, Les. I have no choice. Witt faxed me his notes just before he was shot. They show more wells in West Texas that are dry as bones, with the pumps still running—same situation as you two found in Tyler. He traced ownership of every one of those wells, in East Texas and West Texas. They're owned by subsidiaries of Stewart Oil."

Lesley slumped back in her chair, Mac's words striking like a physical blow, the impact of his words slowly cementing in her mind. It was unthinkable. The company owned by Grant's family, founded by his grandfather, an icon of the Texas oil industry. How could this be?

"Do we know yet if Stewart Oil is involved directly?" she finally asked.

"No, we don't. It's apparent from Witt's notes that's where he was going. He speculated someone high in the company had to know. He uncovered the subsidiaries and traced them back to Stewart Oil when he was in Austin. They were expertly hidden, Les. Someone knows what they're doing. All but two of the companies traced to Stewart Oil carried the same registered agent, that same nonexistent law firm in Chicago. Witt found that out when he went to Chicago. The address for the law firm was a condemned building. It was empty. He also found the bodies of the two guys you followed to the Dallas warehouse. They were in a trash bin behind the Chicago building."

"Oh, my God!" The color drained from Lesley's face and she looked away. "How long have you known all this?"

"Witt went to Chicago right after you taped the drug drop in the oil field near Tyler. I wasn't sure where all this was leading. Witt didn't tell me a lot. Kept saying he was still putting it together. I didn't know about the Stewart Oil connection until Witt came back from Austin, the same morning he left for West Texas. He wanted to be certain. I agreed not to say anything to you until he got back." Withers paused, searching Lesley's face, now pale with shock. "Our widow, Mrs. Edmonds, supplied you with the possible motive for all this chicanery. After laundering the drug money through the books to make it look like income from oil, it was stashed in off shore banks, where the feds probably can't touch it."

Withers stood up and walked around his desk to where Lesley sat, her stare fixed on the opposite wall. He gently lifted her chin and turned her face toward him.

"Les. I don't know how all of this is going to shake out. We've got to talk with Grant's father. He's chairman of the board. And Grant's brother. He's an officer of the company. We need answers. And I need an answer from you. Have you told Grant about what you've been working on?"

She lowered her head under his demanding gaze. "He knows about Mrs. Edmonds giving us a list of off shore accounts. I told him about Edmonds' criminal record, but that was all."

Withers sat back down, folded his hands and rested his chin on his knuckles. It was all he could do to mask his disappointment. "Les, it's clear those federal agents believe someone found out what Witt was working on and had him killed. The notes he faxed to us are missing. Whoever killed him probably has the notes, so they know a lot of what he uncovered. Your name, my name, even Jack's name are mentioned in Witt's notes. They killed Witt. They've killed everybody we've come in contact with, just about. These are dangerous people with a lot at stake. And we probably don't know a flea egg's worth of information about them. But it was enough to lose Witt."

Lesley knew he meant it. He wanted her off the story. Her story. The story that first began to reveal itself in Brownsville. It seemed so long ago. The faces flashed across her memory. That first night when a police car, routinely patrolling, panicked the pilot—the pilot whose name she didn't know until she gleaned it from news reports of his murder—the audacious Walt Edmonds with the buxom Sally proudly clinging to his arm, inviting fulsome remarks from their hosts—Witt Terrell's pinched face, its thin skin pulled taut over prominent cheek bones; a face so spare you could see the outline of his skull; a face softened only by a crooked smile that reminded her of Will Rogers. Mac now feared she would join those faces.

No! The word resounded in her brain and immediately bolstered her resolve. "No, Mac. You can't take me off the story. It's our story—mine and Witt's. Wherever it goes, I want to see it through, for Witt as well as for myself. Please. I am a journalist first. I discovered the meaning of journalistic courage when I read *All the President's Men* in eighth grade." Her eyes locked on his face. "I won't fail you. Mac." *And I won't fail myself,* she thought. "I'll call Blaine Stewart and schedule an interview tomorrow. Can Hector and Hank work with me? We started together. We'll finish this together. I'll be in early."

Lesley stood up slowly and turned toward the door.

Withers started to say no—then relented. "Don't blow it, girl."

He barely heard her response, "No chance."

37

"Agent Worthington. Mac Withers at Channel 15," he announced brusquely the next morning. "I need to discuss something with you. First, I need your word this will remain private. No subpoenas. We'll share what we've got willingly, but I won't allow our story to be compromised."

"I'm not sure I can make that decision, Mr. Withers."

"Cut the crap, Worthington. You know damn well you can make this decision. We've been working on a story for weeks. It breaks Monday. We have facts. We have tape. It's big. Big enough to make the networks. I have one hole I need to fill and I want protection for my people. That's where you come in."

"I need to confirm what you have before I commit."

"Can't go there, Worthington. Your visit yesterday and your questions tell me you're aware of what we've been up to. If you think it's worth your while, then work with me—only me. Nobody else can know, at least not right now."

The pause was long and awkward before the federal agent finally said, "All right, Withers. I take you for a straight shooter. That's your reputation. If you prove otherwise, we come in with a helluva lot more than subpoenas."

Withers brushed aside the threat. "We have a list of banks in the Cayman Islands and Freeport with account numbers, dates of deposits, and amounts—big amounts, Worthington. Enough to give you tax evasion charges to pursue for the next decade."

"Jesus! Where did you get that information?"

"Can't say just yet. Can you match names to account numbers?"

"Christ Almighty! What are you guys running there? A mini-CIA? What else have you got?"

"Can you match the names with the numbers?" Withers insisted.

"Jesus!" Worthington's end of the line fell silent.

Withers waited, his nerves stretched like ice-coated utility wires ready to snap under the burden. "We may have enough to link a big oil company here with the El Poder cartel, and maybe with the Castelero family in Chicago. We'll turn it over to you after the series airs."

"We'll get you your names."

"How soon? Story breaks Monday."

"Two days?" Worthington exclaimed. "I've got to clear this through Washington, despite what you think."

"Worthington, we happened on to the story. A stroke of luck. Our luck's running out. One of our people is dead. I'm fearful for the other two working on the series. Can you provide protection?"

"Yeah. We'll notify the marshal's office. Who? The two people with you yesterday?"

"Yes. Make sure they're safe and we'll cooperate fully after the series breaks. Deal?"

"Yeah. Here are my numbers. Cell phone gets me quickest." Mac scribbled down the agent's cell phone number, home number, and pager.

"Now, fax me what you have and I'll get working on those names."

"By the way, Worthington, you've apparently got a DEA guy undercover. He's helped us indirectly..."

Worthington interrupted. "Not any more. They tossed what was left of him outside our counselor's office in Monterrey two days ago. That was one of the reasons we came to see you yesterday. He tipped the folks at DEA a while back that your station had taken up where the *Brownsville Daily Leader* left off. A reporter there verified as much."

"I'm sorry. I didn't know. All the more reason my people need protection," Withers repeated.

"They'll get it. I'll get someone over there shortly to arrange everything."

"Thank you."

Blaine Stewart answered in a hearty tone. "Hello, Lesley. To what do I owe this pleasant surprise?"

Lesley felt her stomach doing somersaults and willed it to calm. "I would like to interview you, this morning if possible. It's about Althea Oil & Gas and the disappearance of Walt Edmonds."

There was an uneasy silence at the other end of the line. "I'm not sure I can add anything to what we've already told police, Lesley. What's this about?"

"I'd rather not discuss it on the telephone. May we come to your office? I can be there in 30 minutes. I'm sure you'll be interested in what we've learned about Althea Oil & Gas."

I'm sure I would, he thought silently. "Yes. This has been most unpleasant. As I said, I don't believe we can add anything more than what we've told police." But his curiosity was piqued. "Come over now. I have a lunch engagement with my son, the mayor. I think you know him. Maybe you can join us." His voice dripped cheerfulness she felt sure he was not actually feeling.

"I can't think of anyone—besides you, of course—with whom I'd rather have lunch. See you shortly."

As she hung up the telephone, Lesley flashed an "okay" sign at Hank Bottoms sitting across from her. "He'll see us right now. Let's go. Let me tell Mac, and I'll meet you at the van."

Twenty minutes later Lesley, Bottoms, and cameraman Hector Morales and his young assistant piled into the van. Morales drove to a space in the underground parking garage near an elevator. It lifted them to the dramatic, floor-to-ceiling glass entrance of the executive offices of Stewart Oil Company, towering 30 stories above downtown Dallas, in the building the founder, Grantham Stewart, had added to the Dallas skyline nearly 40 years earlier.

A smiling receptionist behind a half-moon shaped, gilded French provincial desk announced their presence. Moments later, Rachel Arrington swept through the tall, mahogany double doors and walked over, looking chic in a turquoise two-piece silk suit with a matching striped, boat-neck blouse. She extended her hand to Lesley in welcome.

"Miss Rowan. Such a pleasure to meet you." She was equally effusive with Bottoms and Morales and the younger man who was hoisting one of the cameras on his shoulder, its light on, as it silently rolled, catching on video tape the elegance of the corporate headquarters. "Mr. Stewart asked me to show you to the board room. Please, follow me."

Rachel Arrington led the way down a wide corridor through more double doors. She ushered Lesley and the three men into an elegant room with two enormous crystal chandeliers poised over a seamless mahogany table. The table was surrounded by more than two dozen thickly upholstered chairs. The entire length of the room had an outside wall of floor-to-ceiling windows, providing a breathtaking panoramic view of Dallas. *This must be how birds see us when they fly over*, Lesley thought, looking out at other iconic sky scrapers reaching up into the cloudless blue sky. An early morning front, propelled by stiff winds, had cleared out the haze triggered by the scorching temperatures, typical of late August.

Lesley was impressed. It was a room resplendent with good taste, strength, and power. This was where Grant used to come for monthly board meetings. His disparaging description of board meetings always made them sound mundane, even boring. *Surely, nothing could approach mundane in such an elegant room*, she decided, gazing out at the view.

"Mr. Stewart will be with you shortly," Rachel Arrington

announced. "Please make yourselves comfortable. May I bring you some coffee, water, soft drinks?"

"No, thank you." Lesley politely declined on behalf of them all.

Morales had just finished setting up the camera and checking batteries in the cordless microphones when Blaine Stewart walked in. He looked impeccable in a dark blue suit with a small-patterned, maroon silk tie and matching handkerchief peeping the appropriate inch above his lapel pocket. A bland smile crept across his handsome, angular face. Lesley was again struck by how much Grant looked like his father. Walking slightly behind Blaine was a younger man, shorter, with a jovial expression fixed on his face.

"Lesley, my dear." Blaine grasped her shoulders and brushed each cheek softly with a kiss. "This is Lance Jennings, our corporate communications director. Who are your friends?"

"My producer, Hank Bottoms. Our cameraman, Hector Morales. And his assistant, Jeff Winston." The men shook hands and Morales directed Blaine to a chair at the end of the table, away from the windows. Lesley took a seat at an angle from Blaine. Jennings sat in a chair near the windows across from Lesley.

Morales quickly pinned a microphone on Blaine's tie, focused, and nodded to Lesley for the interview to begin.

"Mr. Stewart." She smiled at her own formality with this man who would become her father-in-law in just over two weeks. "An investigation by Channel 15 has found 504 oil wells—owned by Althea Oil & Gas and five other subsidiaries of Stewart Oil—in the Allison fields outside Tyler and in the Jefferson fields near Midland—are dry. But they are shown on state production records as still producing oil. Were you aware of these discrepancies?"

A faint smile creased his lips. "There is no way this could happen. Your information is mistaken. We review reports of all our petroleum holdings, from all over the world, weekly. If there were discrepancies, as you allege, we would have discovered them. Our people are very competent and very thorough." Blaine glanced at Jennings and received a subtle nod of approval.

"Then you are unaware of these falsified reports?"

"Yes, I am unaware of any discrepancies. But I certainly will look into the allegations, which I can assure you, are unfounded."

Lesley scanned her notes quickly and looked up at Blaine Stewart, who was observing her now with a hard glint in his eyes. "Channel 15 taped a plane landing on an airstrip in the Allison Fields. Suspected illegal drugs were unloaded from the plane and taken to a warehouse in Dallas leased by Althea Oil & Gas. We have learned the FBI is investigating the possible connection between Althea Oil & Gas and a Mexican drug cartel headed by Vincente Estavar. Are you aware of this probe?"

Blaine looked at her incredulously. "This is the first time I've even heard of such a ridiculous charge," he answered evenly, despite feeling his stomach lurch.

"You have no knowledge of such a probe?"

"I believe that is what I just said, Miss Rowan," subtle annoyance in his tone. "This company *has* never, and *will* never be involved in anything illegal."

"I understand your concern at these questions, Mr. Stewart." Lesley looked down at her hand-written notes and took a deep breath before looking up. She reminded herself how critical this interview was to the story.

"Channel 15 has obtained a list of accounts and deposits in off-shore banks in the Cayman Islands and the Bahamas, kept by Walt Edmonds, who served on Stewart Oil's board, and recently disappeared while on a business trip. We have information Mr. Edmonds may have been fabricating oil production reports for Althea Oil & Gas to account for income from illegal drug trafficking—and that this income was hidden in the off-shore accounts."

"Good God! Turn off that damn camera," demanded Blaine, pointing at Morales, agitation rising in his voice.

"Turn that camera off now." Jennings shouted, echoing the same demand, as he jumped to his feet, mimicking his boss. Morales looked at Lesley, nodded, and feigned hitting the pause button. The camera continued rolling.

"Lesley, what's going on here? This isn't an interview. This is a damn inquisition."

Taking his cue from Stewart, Jennings announced stiffly, "I believe this interview is over, Miss Rowan. If you have any further questions, I suggest you submit them in writing and we'll get back to you."

"All right, Jennings," Blaine said. He irritably waved the company spokesman to silence.

"Lesley. Walt Edmonds was my friend and associate. He was on our board of directors. We just learned this morning from the Mexican authorities Walt may have drowned on a fishing trip while vacationing in Cozumel. They've been investigating his disappearance. I'm sending some of our company people to Mexico to assist with finding out what happened to Walt. We hope to know more shortly."

Blaine stood up slowly, a pained expression replacing the anger that had hardened his features just moments before. "I'm sorry, Lesley. This interview is over. My secretary will show you out." He walked quickly out of the board room, Jennings one step behind.

38

"Lesley, what's going on?" Grant's voice was thick with raw anger. "Dad just called and said you came over to interview him and leveled a bunch of charges about illegal drugs and off-shore accounts. What's going on?"

"Grant, we're breaking a series Monday about drug-running under the cover of Althea Oil & Gas. Walt Edmonds appears to be..."

"Dad said you accused Walt of some of the same criminal activity you hinted at to me," interrupted Grant hotly. "Lesley, the man is missing on a fishing trip. He can't even defend himself. He may be dead." Grant heaved a sigh. "Lesley, you can't do this to my family."

"I'm sorry, Grant." She felt tears sting her eyes. At this moment she regretted ever pushing Mac to leave her on the story. "Let me tell you what we know. I tried to tell your dad. He wouldn't hear me out. We know Edmonds was falsifying oil production reports for wells in fields near Tyler and Midland. We obtained a list of off shore accounts the FBI is checking out. There were tens of millions of dollars listed in those accounts, Grant. Edmonds may have used Althea Oil & Gas as a front for running drugs. He disappeared after taking a plane to Mexico provided by a Chicago crime family. We also taped a drug drop at an Althea-owned field outside Tyler. The drugs were then taken by truck to a warehouse leased by Althea. I was there when that happened."

Grant was silent. She could hear his ragged breathing as he attempted to control his anger—anger that felt almost tangible through the telephone line.

"Lesley, I love you. But these are egregious allegations. They'll ruin my family. They'll kill my grandfather. If you've known about this, why didn't you tell me sooner?"

"Grant." She could hear the appeal in her voice. "We've only just learned more fully about Althea's connection to Stewart Oil. Our reporter, Witt Terrell, had been checking oil production records and found out Althea is a wholly-owned subsidiary of Stewart Oil. Witt only pinned all this down a few days ago. He's been murdered."

"Murdered! By whom?"

"The FBI is looking into that. We don't know. But Witt's notes are missing. Luckily, he faxed his notes to the station just before he was shot."

"Lesley, I'm going over to be with Dad. I've got to sort all this out. I don't know what's going to happen to us." Grant hung up abruptly.

So it had happened, what Mac feared, what he had warned her might be the outcome. Why hadn't she listened? She could have distanced herself personally. Pride had pushed her to hang on, to put her name on the story alongside that of Witt Terrell. The tightness in her chest gave way as she lowered her head, hiding her face in her folded arms, no longer able to control the sobs that convulsed her body.

From across the newsroom, Mac watched her head disappear from his line of sight and sensed a cruel choice had just been made for her. He picked up the pile of faxed notes. It was Witt's legacy. She needed to read them before writing her story. Mac Withers stood up slowly, feeling suddenly older than his years. He never dealt well with sadness or loss. Not when he lost his parents; not when he lost his toddler son to pneumonia; not when he lost his wife to another man years later. Now he must deal with a woman who may have just been told she would not be getting married next month. He was not certain what he would say to Lesley. What words of comfort could he summon? Maybe he should say nothing at all. It was the latter choice he made as he placed the pile of faxed notes beside her arm and patted her shoulder before walking away. In his mind, she had grit. Witt said so. Grit, not words, would overcome the spasms of grief that still shook her shoulders.

A short time later Lesley began reading Terrell's handwritten, sometimes roughly scribbled notes. It was a diary of facts, day-to-day, as he progressed from Tyler to Austin; from Austin to Midland. She turned to the blank computer screen and began writing.

"From black gold to white gold, this is the frightening odyssey of a proud Texas oil company that may have been made a pawn of Mexican drug smugglers and Mafia drug distributors in Chicago...." The dark words flowed onto the white screen.

An hour later, Mac's voice interrupted from the intercom on the telephone. "Les, can you join us for a meeting? We're going to put together a taping schedule."

"I'll be right there."

Moments later Withers noted the swollen eyes of the beautiful woman taking a seat in an empty chair in the crowded office. Hank Bottoms was sitting next to her. He looked at her sympathetically and patted her shoulder.

"This is going to be our team. Hank will produce the series and have final say on all segments." Lesley glanced up and saw Hal Crockett looking glum, and the usually sanguine Billy Burton looking equally glum. They had been shuffled to the rear on this story. The introverted, placid Bottoms would be the lead producer. Lesley liked that.

"Pete, you work with Jack. I want every police and FBI angle covered like a glove." Pete Kannady nodded, pleased he had been picked to work with the station's hardboiled police reporter.

"Jack, you set?"

Reilley nodded his head. "Yep! Just got off the phone with Worthington. Things should start pumping out of a federal grand jury early next week. The federal attorney is going to keep them meeting through the weekend." A smirk flitted across Reilley's ruggedly handsome features. He would get to share the glory on this one. He had busted his ass and had come up with some good stuff. This was great. Worthington would give him the break when indictments were announced. Worthington also promised they would kick ass from Chicago to Dallas. Reilley looked over quickly at Lesley. She might be a pretty piece of ass herself, but she would have to share this story with him from now on. He had the inside track with law enforcement and that's where the action would be from here on.

"Morales. You work with Lesley," said Mac. "As soon as you've scripted the first segments, Les, give them to Bottoms. He has the final call on everything. You're a good team. You started with this in Brownsville. You'll finish together."

Lesley reached over and laid the bold print first segment on Mac's desk. "See what you think of this for starters." Despite her puffy eyes, she managed a thin smile.

"Ahhh, Mac." Hank Bottoms rubbed his hand across his mouth. "I'd like to tape the first segments with Lesley in Brownsville." Withers had briefed the producers on a short list of facts before Lesley was called and Bottoms immediately recognized the scope of the story. "It might mean pulling her off the anchor desk Friday," the soft-spoken producer added.

"You've got the creative call on this one, Hank. Is that all right with you, Les?"

She nodded assent.

"I want the station attorney to review all scripts. Angelina?" Mac called out. A dark-eyed, dark-haired young face poked through a narrow opening in the door.

"Yes?"

"Call Bill Swanson and fax this over to him," ordered Withers, motioning Angelina into the room. "He's the station attorney. Tell him I need any questions in ten minutes and his faxed approval in a half hour."

"What if he isn't there?"

"Then, damn it, Angie, find him," barked Withers. "Or get the other attorney—I can't think of his name—his assistant."

She was nearly out the door when she turned around in the opening, a question forming on her pretty face.

"Angie—just do it. Okay?"

"Okay." The head popped out as quickly as it had popped in. Withers often wondered how much his secretary overheard. She seemed to have ears like a lynx when it came to knowing what was going on in his office.

"Hank, check the weather down south right away." Mac sat forward. "I think I want to keep Lesley's presence on the air. Let's hire a private plane to take you to Brownsville tonight, right after the early newscasts. Start shooting early tomorrow. Get a lot of B-roll then head back immediately. It's best if we don't tip our hand to anyone, especially our competition."

Mac turned to Lesley. "That okay with you?

She nodded her reply. "It'll make for some long days—and nights," Withers added.

"No problem."

Withers acknowledged her response with a thin smile of approval. "Morales," Withers started, directing his gaze to the stocky cameraman seated in the corner. "Get a list of background shots you'll need for Hank. And cut some promos while you're down there, or I'll have the promotions department all over my ass."

The news director turned back to Bottoms. "You have only the time it will take to shoot what you need and get Lesley back here for at least the six o'clock block. She can write the scripts on the way down."

Withers moved from face to face. "We can sleep after this series airs. Thank you, everyone. We have one helluva few days ahead."

Lesley stood up to leave with the other men when Withers said, "Les, could you stay a moment?"

She sat back in her chair as the others filed out.

"You've told Grant?"

"He called. His father had called him and told him about the interview." Lesley felt her throat tighten and turned away as tears welled in her eyes. "I don't think we'll be getting married."

"I'm sorry, Les. This may be the biggest story you'll ever break. I hope it doesn't break you. Don't let it."

"I love him so much," she said in a choked voice. The tears she tried valiantly to dam, flowed down her cheeks unchecked, as she buried her face in her hands. Withers walked over and sat in the chair next to Lesley, taking her hand in his. "Here, use this," he said, pulling a folded cloth handkerchief from his pocket. She wiped her eyes. "Go ahead and blow your nose. I won't need it."

A thin smile etched across his face. "You make me feel like Rhett Butler. What was it he told Scarlett? Something like, never in a crisis do you ever have a hanky."

Lesley laughed. "Something like that. How would you know about Rhett Butler?"

"I read the book because I give a damn about good literature."

"It's a chic book, you know," she said, blowing her nose gingerly.

"Are you questioning my manhood?"

"No. But I would be careful who else you tell. You don't want to ruin your crusty image, you know."

"Angelina," Mac called out again. The dark eyes looked through the opening in the office door almost instantly.

"What now? I'm busy calling the attorneys," she said petulantly. Withers' impertinent secretary had drawn many a shocked glance after she was hired two years ago. Her derisive humor, especially when it was directed at her often intractable boss, eventually became the stuff of legend among station staffers, over many an after-hours beer.

"Lesley is going to give you the keys to her apartment and directions. Go there and pack a bag with clothes appropriate for stand-ups in the boiling heat of south Texas. Put in anything else she tells you." Withers looked over slyly at Lesley. "I'm sure being the nosy person she is, Angelina will have no problem finding whatever you tell her you need. Right, Angie? And include pajamas. Lesley will be staying at a hotel near Love Field tonight," he added to suppress the curiosity that spouted on his secretary's face.

"We'll discuss all these extra duties I get assigned when it's time for a raise. Your car or mine?"

"Here. Take mine before you shipwreck my budget with gas mileage," he snapped, his face tightening in a scowl as he fished keys from his pocket and tossed them to his secretary who caught them with the adroitness of an outfielder.

"Thanks, yourself" she said flippantly. "Come on, Lesley. Tell me what you need and where it's at." The two women walked out the office door together.

39

Dear Manny. Lesley stared at the granite stone carved with the names of Manny Zammorra and his wife Alicia. *This is your story, Manny. They silenced your voice. They stilled your words. But not the story.*

She whispered a short prayer and touched the top of the gravestone. In the waiting van, Hector Morales watched her walk across the cemetery, the midday sun shimmering on her raven hair. It had been an arduous morning, rushing from one location to another in the stifling heat. This was the last shot, at Manny Zammorra's grave site. The martyred editor. Lesley had insisted he be remembered. They were finishing what he began, she said in the segment just taped: "Manny Zammorra and his staff at the *Brownsville Daily Leader* shed the first light on the multi-level corruption that allows a free flow of drugs across the Mexican border into this country. Zammorra paid a terrible price for his zeal and unflinching journalistic integrity. Lesley Rowan, Channel 15 News, Brownsville."

When Lesley arrived back at her desk shortly before four, there were several messages blinking on her voicemail—all from Ben Worthington, none from Grant.

"We have the names," announced Worthington, dispensing with any salutation. "I promised we would give you names in return for those account numbers. It goes without saying these did not come from us."

"You have my word on that, Mr. Worthington," Lesley replied.

"Got a pen?" he inquired. The names meant nothing to her. The only one she recognized was Walt Edmonds.

"Who are these people and companies?"

"I suspect they're fronts, Miss Rowan. Fronts for our friends in Chicago. Some of the names we've learned about have a familiar ring. E-M-S, Inc. is one we're already acquainted with. It's a front for the Mexican cartel run by Estavar. The initials match his and his two top henchmen. They're cousins and keep everything they do in the family. There are some accounts under a name we're not familiar with at all. They're registered to an outfit called Sepulveda, Ltd."

Worthington gave her seven more names the FBI was still tracing. "By the way," he said, his voice changing to inquisitor. "Did you learn anything more while you were in Brownsville?"

"How did you know I was in Brownsville?"

"We have our sources too, you know." Worthington celebrated his own joke with hearty laughter. "You've got a newscast to do. And I've got dinner waiting, if I make it home tonight. See you on the tube."

Despite her wariness of police in general, Lesley was beginning to like the gregarious FBI agent. He had just added significantly to the story. So the FBI could tap into numbered accounts in offshore banks. Interesting. *Was nothing sacred*, she mused, *even for the bad guys?*

✝✝✝

Ginny said nothing, but used a lightener to cover the subtle shadows and puffiness under Lesley's green eyes. *This girl is bone tired*, she thought, smoothing the masking stick with her finger. *Probably been crying some.* Ginny never pried. She was a good sounding board for many of the anchors and program hosts who sat in her chair daily before going on the air. She heard most of what went on in the newsroom without having to venture into that area of the station. Her well-lighted, mirrored cubicle was just off the main studio, away from the day-to-day action. But somehow, news and gossip always came to her. *For news people, they're sure loose-lipped*, she said often, but only to herself. Except for Lesley. She was usually happy, upbeat, especially lately, talking about her wedding plans. It was something Ginny hadn't known about until she read it in the morning paper. This one just didn't talk much about herself. *Now the happiness has disappeared*, Ginny thought, lightly dabbing powder over Lesley's face with a brush. She wondered why.

Ginny turned the leather barber chair around to study the finished product in the mirror. "I can't improve much on perfection. Go break a leg, girl."

"Thanks, Ginny."

Lesley *was* exhausted. Her inner turmoil was only dragging further at her physical well-being. Why did Grant not call—if for no other reason than to formally cancel the wedding? It was what she expected him to do; was convinced in her mind he *would* do; wished with all her heart he would *not* do.

At the end of the six o'clock newscast Lesley quickly left the station. She wanted only to go to her apartment, take a hot shower, gather the clothes she needed for the long weekend ahead and cry until her hurt and remaining energy were spent before getting some much needed sleep. The editing of the series would begin in the morning and would take the entire weekend. They had caught a break.

When she arrived at the apartment, she was startled to find Grant sitting in her living room. His head was resting against the back of a couch, his feet propped up on the table separating it from the matching couch on the other side, his profile silhouetted by the rapturous sunset streaming in through the picture window where the drapes had been pulled back.

"I let myself in. I hope that was all right." He did not stir or turn toward her. Only his words filled the space between them.

"Of course." She placed her beige leather briefcase and shoulder bag on an antique cherry hall table, and walked hesitantly into the living room.

"Where have you been?" At his question she turned toward the telephone on the bar separating the living room from the kitchen. The lighted number above the dial showed eight. Had he called that often?

"The calls. They're all from me. I checked." He turned his head toward her and she detected the slur of some words.

"Grant. I should have called you. I'm sorry. I was on assignment in Brownsville. It was a rush trip."

"Ace reporter returns to the scene. That's where this all started, wasn't it? In Brownsville. I've never been to Brownsville. Nice place to visit...." His voice trailed off, his last word almost unintelligible. She was certain now he had been drinking. Reaching down, Lesley turned on a table lamp.

"Turn that goddamned thing off," he demanded, jerking his face toward her, his eyes darkly ringed by fatigue and glinting with anger.

"I'll make you some coffee."

"Don't bother. I'm not that drunk." His surly voice mirrored the expression hardening his features. "I came here to tell you our wedding plans are on hold for the moment. The FBI came to see my father this morning at his office. They had a fistful of subpoenas. Seems they think he may be a drug dealer instead of an oil man. I'm not sure where they got that idea. Would you know anything about where they got that idea?" His words were edged with angry cynicism.

"Grant, I'll drive you home. We'll talk tomorrow. You need some sleep."

"We'll talk now," he commanded roughly. Grant stood up and tilted a glass she had not seen in his left hand menacingly toward her as he approached. For the first time, she felt fear prickling at her senses. He stood over her now and she could smell the liquor, heavy on his breath. He stared at her, unblinking, as she watched a range of emotions play across his face. After long moments he lifted his head, closed his eyes, and drew in a deep breath.

"I love you, Lesley. Whatever happens, I love you. I just want you to know that." A deep sadness replaced the anger in his eyes. He turned away and set the glass down on the lamp table. "I helped myself to a drink. Hope you don't mind. Goodbye, Les." He walked past where she stood frozen toward the front door. She pulled the engagement ring from her finger. "Grant." He stopped with his hand on the door knob and his back to her. She walked over and silently handed the ring to Grant. The large diamond caught the light and reflected a rainbow of colors that danced on the foyer ceiling.

Grant lowered his head and made no move to take the ring, holding fast to the door knob with one hand, his other hand at his side. When he raised his head, an indifferent smile floated briefly across his mouth, his eyes impassive. "Keep it. You can display it along side the Pulitzer Prize you'll probably win at my family's expense."

She started to say the Pulitzer was awarded to print journalists, but kept silent. The door closed softly behind him.

Even in the defused lighting of the editing room, Withers could tell Lesley had not slept. Her eyes were bloodshot. With her face devoid of any make-up, it only accentuated the deep shadows under her eyes. She had spent yesterday morning shooting stand-ups in the oil fields outside Tyler. Then she had flown to Midland for stand-ups there and in the oil fields documented in Witt Terrell's notes before returning late Saturday evening aboard the station chopper based at Love Field.

Withers was wrong. She had slept. She had finally fallen into an exhausted sleep early Sunday morning, troubled by dark dreams of Witt Terrell's dying face, and of Grant shouting blame at her and pulling a gun from inside his belt. When she awoke with a start, Lesley wasn't sure if he had fired the weapon.

"Hey, Les," Withers waved. "The gang's all here. Sit down. We're just getting started." The news director pushed a desk chair toward her. She rolled closer to the monitors and Sony editing units where videotape from the Midland oil fields, some of which had been shot by Witt Terrell, was being reviewed by Bottoms and two video editors.

By noon, the first six segments for the series were completed. Pizza was ordered. The work went on until late Sunday evening. The series was all there in neat, chronological order, from Manny's funeral, to the aborted meeting with the pilot in the Brownsville riverfront park, to the final segments shot in Chicago and Midland. With guidance from their FBI source, they named names—names that were also being secretly investigated by a federal grand jury empaneled a week ago.

Much of the video from Witt Terrell's mini-camera was poorer quality, which made it appear more realistic when interspersed with the color-balanced location footage and Lesley's stand-ups. There was only one hole. A Chicago network affiliate was filling that hole by shooting additional footage of the condemned building on Delacorte Street and the notorious trash dumpster in the rear of the building. They were sending the tape to Channel 15 by satellite in an hour. With that snippet of tape, the series would almost be complete.

Mac Withers leaned back in his chair, his arms linked behind his head. "It's good. It's really good. There's only one problem."

"What's that?" the voices around him asked, almost in unison.

"We're not in sweeps." That brought a burst of laughter from those gathered around the editing console. "Bart Henderson reminded me of that when he stopped by earlier."

"Ah, shit. Well, there's only one thing to do," said Hal Crockett, his usual dark humor tempered by the triumph he visualized from the series. "Let's hold this damn series till November. Gotta run it during sweeps."

His suggestion was greeted with more hoots of laughter. "Beer's on me, if anybody feels up to it." Withers' offer was greeted with more whoops. "We'll gather at the same ungodly early hour of eight o'clock to finish the final segments tomorrow morning. Any revisions to the scripts before we adjourn to the bar?"

Hearing none, Crockett said, "Let's fly this coop."

As Reilley was rising to leave, Withers stopped him and clapped him on the back. "Great job, Jack. Comin' with us?"

Looking pleased, Jack Reilley stifled a yawn before nodding yes. He was a night owl who covered a beat that often required him to work late.

Withers had told him the feds had already subpoenaed the scripts and videotape from the copyrighted series, something he had given his word to Worthington he would do. They were waiting for the series to start airing and for the station's Dallas attorney to sign off on the agreement. Withers acknowledged Worthington's help had been crucial. That would put him on Ben Worthington's A-list, reasoned Reilley, and give another trusted source. Best of all, he would be kicking the newspaper's ass big time. Reilley did not hold back the next yawn.

Lesley slipped out quietly amid loud plans on where to get a beer, and sought the sanctuary of her office in the dimly lit newsroom. It was almost over. At this moment she felt no satisfaction, only a desperate loneliness. She had not talked to Grant since he left her apartment. His office issued a terse news release late Friday saying, "For personal reasons the mayor and Miss Rowan have decided to postpone their marriage."

Lesley had called her mother, fearing she would hear about the breakup on a radio or television broadcast. Katherine Rowan was sympathetic and kind, keeping any advice she might have given to her beleaguered daughter to herself. She immediately offered to come to be with Lesley. Since her earliest years Lesley had recognized her mother's innate kindness, but never had turned to her mother as a refuge of comfort during any crisis. Pleading the press of work, mother and daughter agreed for the visit to begin when it was originally planned. Katherine Rowan would arrive next weekend.

Telephone calls from media outlets had come in from across the state. Lesley simply ignored them, allowing a pile of pink message slips to stack up on her desk and verbal pleas to return calls clog her voicemail. She opted out of the beer celebration with a weary smile and nodded to the two young federal marshals who were assigned to drive her home and keep her apartment under tight surveillance. As the government issue black SUV was approaching her apartment, Lesley spotted several television crews camped outside her building. There was no way to avoid them. As she attempted to rush the gauntlet of reporters and cameramen, microphones were pushed in her face, and questions shouted at her about the reasons for the cancelled wedding. Flanked by the two marshals, she kept her head low and said nothing.

Looking down on the street below from the shelter of her apartment, Lesley knew the tantalizing spots promoting the series were feeding the media frenzy surrounding her breakup with Grant. She presumed media crews were also staked out at the entrance of his condo.

KDLL's promotion director, Sid Lewis, zeroed in like a laser on the prospects of a ratings bonanza after reading the first two scripts. Stewart Oil was not mentioned directly by the announcer on the promos, but a tie to Mayor Grant Stewart was strongly hinted at, red-flagging the upcoming series to the viewing public. On Sunday morning, Lewis gleefully told the news people in the editing booth he had commissioned the station's consultants to take a special viewer sampling beginning Monday. Lewis was ecstatic. He had manually changed the weekend logs to insert more spots promoting the series, displacing most of the public-service spots viewers were fed routinely to appease the Federal Communications Commission.

It was unfair. They had uncovered no direct evidence linking Grant Stewart to the drug trade; and certainly nothing linking him to the machinations of Walt Edmonds with the Chicago mob or the Mexican cartel. Yet she knew her story would paint Grant with the same brush of guilt-by-association as his father and brother. *Collateral damage.* That was the term used by Ben Worthington. What about her own heart; her own happiness? Was she a victim of collateral damage?

Sleep was reluctant in coming. Dark dreams again wrestled in her subconscious, allowing little rest. She awoke more disturbed than when her eyes had finally shut just an hour before. The craggy face of Witt Terrell drifted in and out of her thoughts, along with Manny Zammorra. She could not keep at bay the intrusion of the unthinkable. That Grant may have, even indirectly, had a hand in the murders of these men. How many others had died to fatten the bank accounts of Stewart Oil, Walt Edmonds, the Mexican cartel heads, and the mysterious Sepulveda, Ltd?

✝✝✝

From inside a car parked unobtrusively under a tree, across the street from the upper-level apartment, a set of night vision binoculars were trained on the front windows to detect any movement inside the darkened apartment. Moments later, a light came on in the front area and he had a momentary glimpse of a female figure before the drapes shadowed the interior. The object of his scrutiny was apparently home. *Mighty late tonight, lady*, he surmised.

Stu Aarons lowered the binoculars and lifted the styrofoam cup from the dashboard holder to his lips. The coffee was cold, but wet. The strobe lights of the television crews had clicked off some time ago, allowing darkness to return to the neighborhood. The last of the satellite trucks had departed shortly after midnight, leaving him a clear view to do his job—except for a black SUV that moved slowly by the woman's apartment building every half-hour or so.

Bobby Castelero had been specific about what he wanted done. "Keep an eye on that broad. Don't make no move till I tell ya," he had commanded in a nasal voice thick with his native Bronx brogue. "You got it?"

Stu Aarons knew when to say yes. He had learned that important lesson as a kid growing up Jewish in an Italian neighborhood, where the mob controlled drugs and protection, unions and trash collection, and just about everything else from which a dollar could be squeezed through intimidation.

When Roberto Castelero muscled his way into a Chicago crime family, Stu Aarons moved west to sniff the wind for his childhood chum. When Bobby took control of the Chicago arm of the mob, Aarons began the security service that protected enterprises with which the Castelero organization owned or had dealings. Dallas was almost a perfect midway point between Mexico and Chicago; the right place for Aarons to relocate and keep watch over the family's growing drug operation, from behind a perfect cover.

Aarons had an ingratiating manner, especially with cops. Private badges could do that. It was only in the movies that private eyes were resented by the guys in blue. A little cash here, a little cash there, bought a lot of information. For the price of a cup of coffee, Aarons learned only yesterday the feds had convened a grand jury to hear evidence about the Stewart's drug operations—a lot of it gathered by the woman behind those closed drapes upstairs. Aarons wasn't sure yet how much the lady knew. She had showed some of her hand when she came to interview Blaine Stewart.

Egotistical bastard should have declined the interview. Bobby was furious, yelling at him. Blaming Aarons. But how could he have stopped it? He didn't even know the snobby bastard had agreed to an interview. At least Stewart had the good sense to cut it short when the questions got too hot to answer.

The woman was not sleeping. Was the sleeplessness over her work or her boyfriend? Knowing women, probably the boyfriend, he decided. At least it was a problem that had resolved itself. He gave the mayor credit for having more smarts than his old man. He still didn't like either of them. Too damn condescending. The father was containable. The older son—that was a different matter. He was weak. The FBI would probably be able to flip him against his father and everyone else. Bobby would have to call the shot on that one.

Aarons wanted a cigarette. It helped him think. He couldn't think now, not with nicotine on his mind. He needed to get to the woman. He had earlier checked out the back of the apartment. Tough area. A six foot tall wood fence ran along the back of the apartment building, enclosing a manicured courtyard and pool. The fence was rigged with silent alarms. *Good set-up. Effective too.* Best access would still be through the front. But getting that access was a challenge he had been weighing most of the night without an answer. It would have to be someone she knew or was expecting—maybe a repairman of some kind. *He needed a cigarette.* He'd figure it out later. Aarons turned the key in the ignition and drove slowly away.

✝✝✝

Lesley stared at the steaming cup of tea. Her second. It ensured no more sleep. With every fiber of her being, she resisted picking up the telephone to call Grant. He would probably hang up on her, only deepening the hurt clawing away inside her. She wished her mother were here now. Maybe they could talk; something they had done so little of when she was growing up.

Her grandmother explained to Lesley many years before that her mother had always been quiet, reserved, painfully shy, especially with men. Which was why her parents were shocked when Katherine introduced them to a tall, dark-haired man, whom she had married. Katherine Rowan had done the first unreserved thing in her life. She had eloped while she was still in nursing school. By the time she graduated, Lesley was taking shape in her protruding belly.

Lesley was barely two when Lloyd Rowan left in anger one night, never to return. Katherine Rowan's smile, which was the first thing Lesley saw in the morning when her mother lifted her out of her bed and the last thing at night when she bent to kiss her cheek goodnight, seemed to dim with each passing year. Katherine retreated behind her natural reserve and there she had remained for all the years of Lesley's childhood. Only her grandparents provided an outflow of gregarious affection she could never expect from her mother.

They lived on a cattle and produce farm outside Paris, Texas, raising mostly beef, and acres of tomatoes they sold to a canning factory on the outskirts of town. Katherine Rowan had fled to San Antonio following the divorce. Trips to her grandparents' home became more infrequent. Only in summer was Lesley allowed to spend prolonged periods with the aging couple who so doted on her.

She'd romp through the fields of the farm they owned. Some days, she would saddle the old mare, Cherokee, for a long ride along the creek bed, and stop to rest under the shade of a cottonwood tree, relishing the freedom of each summer's day, that always seemed to end too soon.

Never, in all those formative years, did Lesley recall her mother ever mentioning her father's name. Even when she queried her grandmother, her questions were artfully dodged by the effervescent woman who had a passion for baking and an equally determined passion to put some meat on her granddaughter's thin frame. The sweet aromas of homemade bread and cinnamon rolls filled the vintage two-story farm house with delicious scents—scents Lesley still associated with the elderly couple who had been taken from her and her mother by a drunk driver on a quiet Sunday morning as they were returning from the rural Baptist Church they had attended as children and remained members of through their adult years. It was a loss that Lesley still mourned.

It was only after Lesley found pictures of her father in a box hidden underneath her mother's bed, was she able to put a face to the man in her daydreams. There was a curious, yellowed newspaper clipping—short, like a business brief—announcing Lloyd Rowan had been named sales manager of a car dealership. It mentioned his wife, one child, and his membership in a Baptist church. That was the sum total of what she knew about her father. Did she have a half-sibling? She had never bothered to find out.

She had hoped the engagement to Grant would stimulate a closer relationship with her mother. She had attempted to involve Katherine in the wedding plans, inviting her to a luncheon, to the shower hosted by Grace and Emily, or just to spend a weekend. Her mother declined, citing her schedule at the hospital which had her on duty most weekends. Lesley suspected the real reason was her mother's intense shyness. Katherine did agree to come several days in advance of the wedding to help Lesley with final arrangements.

Lesley glanced at the wall clock. Nearly 6:30. She wasn't sure how long she had been at the kitchen's island bar, lingering over her tea. Light was softly filtering through the casement windows in the kitchen, the opening act of what she knew would be a pivotal day in her career—the day the series was fully completed. And another day without Grant.

41

Ben Worthington nodded agreement. No question. No doubt in his mind. This was their man. Despite the exhausting hours spent working the past two weeks, he felt his blood pumping faster with excitement. "Who got these?"

"A guy working for the Mexican national police got a tip and was hanging out near a private airport when the Stewart Oil plane came in. The Mexicans passed it to the DEA a couple of weeks ago. It just got to my desk this morning. They say this is Christo," replied Mace Harding, sliding the grainy black and white security camera photo toward Worthington and propping his feet up on his desk. The young assistant U. S. Attorney seemed pleased with the Special Agent's reaction.

The FBI veteran had seen only one other picture of the elusive Colombian, suspected of being something other than a respectable businessman. It was taken years before, when Christo married. He stared at the image. Not handsome. Tough. Eyes like coal. Older. It was a face now indelibly printed in his memory. No question about the man next to him. It was Blaine Stewart. Stewart's tie to the suspected Colombian drug kingpin looked firm, but more evidence would be needed to solidify those ties.

"For the grand jury," ordered Worthington, handing the photograph back to Harding. "Terrific!" Harding was presenting evidence gathered by Worthington's team of agents to the grand jury. He was brash and had little experience in the job he now held, having been appointed only three months ago. But so far, he was living up to his own braggadocio.

"Bad news for Stewart. Got to be careful who your friends are in this world," observed Worthington smugly. He turned abruptly and walked out of the office whistling a low, indecipherable tune. He knew the photograph could seal the decision of jurors; seal Blaine Stewart's fate. They had already viewed the 10-part series Channel 15 began airing yesterday. Telling evidence. He saw it on the faces of each juror. But it was the list of off-shore accounts, squirreled away by Edmonds, which registered more with the jurors. With reluctant cooperation by banks in Freeport and Georgetown, accounts had so far been traced to Stewart Oil and five of its subsidiaries, along with personal accounts in the names of Blaine Stewart, Elliott Stewart, Walter Edmonds, Roberto Castelero, Vincente Estavar and Estavar's two cousins, and another entity, Sapulvida, Ltd. That last one remained a mystery. But Worthington was working hard to pin down an identity. The tentacles of his suspicions about who or what Sapulvida, Ltd. might be were reaching out strongly toward a single man whose picture was now in his hand—Juan Christo.

It was evidence that could never be used at trial unless verified by someone who handled transfers into those accounts. Worthington had found that someone—Irwin Simonton. He was the assistant comptroller for Stewart Oil. Except for not wearing a green eye-shade and not having a garter on his sleeve, Simonton could have played an accountant in any classic old movie. Slightly built, with an oversized, aquiline nose on which rested double-bifocal eye glasses, the little CPA was, in Worthington lexicon, "squirrelly."

Initially belligerent and unresponsive, refusing to answer any questions, Simonton finally agreed to cooperate when threatened with a possible conspiracy charge. It was enough. Simonton then filled several hours of audiotape with key information about the financial machinations of Stewart Oil Company and its several subsidiaries—information Worthington, the federal attorney, and Mace Harding agreed could seal the fate of Blaine Stewart and his associates.

Testifying with a promise of immunity, Simonton spent most of one day and part of the next tracking deposits listed on computerized statements. The spare-built, Woody Allen look-alike became Harding's star witness. The grand jury was expected to hand down an indictment after lunch.

By the end of the day, a sealed federal indictment listed a litany of charges, from facilitating drug smuggling across state borders, to falsifying company records, to conspiracy to commit murder, to income-tax evasion. Conspiracy to murder would be the tough charge. No real, hard evidence there against either Stewart or any of his immediate associates. Grand jurors could be easily swayed to bring a charge, and they had. What was that phrase? A good prosecutor could get a grand jury to indict a ham sandwich. It was now up to Worthington and his team to get the concrete evidence the federal attorney and Harding would need before defense attorneys began issuing discovery requests.

There were eight names on the indictment—the same names that had been secretly traced to numbered accounts in Freeport and the Cayman Islands. They included Blaine Stewart, Elliott Stewart, and the five CEOs of Stewart Oil subsidiaries. Walt Edmonds was indicted *in absentia*. Sally Edmonds was named a material witness. She was already in protective custody. Worthington had taken that precaution immediately after the Channel 15 news director shared with him that she was the source of the off-shore accounts information.

It was shortly after 4:00 before Worthington found time to call Lesley Rowan, from the privacy of his office. He knew she was waiting on his call and had earlier elicited her promise to protect him as a source. Worthington knew the consequences if he was traced as the source of the leak. It was a crime. At best, it could cost him his job and his pension. But he had given his word to Mac

Withers, and he owed it to the woman. He would break neither promise. His case had been built on her work and the work of the dead reporter.

He read the names on the sealed indictment and the list of charges against each of the suspects. His teams of agents were already on their way to serve the warrants and begin making arrests.

Lesley copied the names and addresses quickly and thanked Worthington. "Yes, Mac is standing right here," she told Worthington before hanging up, after Withers had rushed across the newsroom at the urging of her waving arm.

Worthington laid the receiver slowly back on the telephone and leaned back in his chair. He ran one hand through his flaxen hair as his dark brown eyes gazed at the top of his cluttered desk. Legal-size folders of differing thicknesses were scattered across the desk. He was feeling the fatigue he had managed to keep at bay through the crush of the last few days. It overwhelmed him now.

He had to salute the constraint in the voice of the young woman who had been at the other end of the line. He knew from the marshals guarding her she had spent the long weekend at the television station and was probably more exhausted than he. She was paying a high price for the story she had already broken to the Dallas market, a story the rest of the nation woke up to this morning. He shrugged off his fatigue and grabbed his suit jacket, pulled it on wearily, and headed out the door of his office. They were awaiting him at the scene. This would be another long night.

Mac Withers went back in his office. Reilley and two camera crews were quickly dispatched to the Stewart compound and other reporters and camera crews to the homes of Stewart associates named in the indictments. The videotaping of *perp walks* would now begin.

Withers alerted the six o'clock producer to expect Reilley's report live from the field and put the late news producer on notice for a fresh story at ten.

Discipline was the principle that directed Lesley in everything she did. It transcended emotion. It had guided her actions since childhood. It obviated her tears now. She opened the folder bearing her name on the computer, clicked her cursor to a blank page, and began to write. She had the 15 minutes left in the network news block to write the story and copy it to the six o'clock producer and to the teleprompter operator. For Mac, she printed a hard copy and walked it into his office on her way into the studio. He quickly scanned the entire text before looking up, mentally saluting her ability to capture the drama of a breaking story in her script and to encapsulate the detail to fit the time constraints of television.

"Reilley is headed to the Stewart house," Withers told her. "We'll take him live as soon as he gets set up."

Mac noted the pain on her face. "Fitzgerald can read this," he offered.

"No, I'll do it," she said, then turned to leave.

"I'm sorry, Les," Withers said, sighing heavily. "I can only imagine how hard this is for you."

She turned in the doorway. "Can you call Grant? I don't want him to hear about his father's arrest from us."

The mayor had left early, replied his secretary, and left word not to be disturbed. Withers called Grant's home and left a message on the answering machine. "Grant, if you hear this in time, we've just learned a federal grand jury has indicted your father and brother and some other executives of Stewart Oil subsidiaries. Lesley wanted you to hear it from us before it's on the news coming up." Withers found his voice faltering. After a short pause he added, "Mayor, I'm sorry for you and your family." He hung up.

Grant was just opening the door to his condo when he heard the news director's voice. He listened with dismay as his hand rested on the knob of the front door he had just opened. When it finished, he rushed back out the door and sped through the knot of late rush hour to the Stewart compound. A Channel 15 van was parked just outside the compound gate, its satellite dish aimed at the sky. Other satellite trucks were arriving. His own arrival at the front gate of the compound was met with the flash of cameras and shouts from the gathering news media. He rolled down his window and picked up the phone to notify the security guard to open the gate. In his side view mirror, Grant spotted Jack Reilley rushing toward him with an outstretched microphone. He reached his hand out to fend off the police reporter as the large wrought iron entrance gates began to open. Grant was appalled by the scene before him. A chain of large black SUV's, with blue and red lights flashing in their back windows, were blocking the curved drive in front of the mansion.

He left his car nearer the gate and as he was ascending the wide front steps of the home, a hysterical Grace burst out the front door, her face streaked with tears. "You can't let them take him, Grant." Her voice choked with sobs. "You can't let them take him," she repeated as he pulled her into his arms, circled her shoulders protectively, and guided her back inside.

In the expansive living room, just off the wide foyer, Grant was stunned to see a man in a blue windbreaker emblazoned with large yellow FBI initials on the back reading Blaine Stewart his Miranda rights as he stood stoic and straight. Another similarly clad agent was securing his father's wrists behind his back with handcuffs. The snap of the metal restraints made Grant flinch.

"Call Willis Johnson," Stewart ordered his wife in a measured tone. When his request was met with a blank stare, Blaine repeated his demand more sharply. "My attorney, Grace. Call him immediately. His home number is in the Rolodex on my desk. Do it now," he demanded curtly.

Energized out of her inertia by her husband's sharp command, Grace slipped out of her son's arms and disappeared across the foyer. Blaine Stewart turned to a tall, angular man in a dark suit and asked, "Where are you taking me?"

"To the Dallas County jail, sir," Ben Worthington replied.

From above the elegant entrance hall, the old face peered down at the distressing drama below, his voice silent, his mind screaming, *What is going on in this home?* Wiley Jefford had been dozing in front of the television and was awakened by the commotion. He rushed from his bedroom next to Grantham Stewart's room. The meal that he had put in front of the old man an hour ago was untouched. Grantham Stewart was sitting in a chair, tears tracing tiny rivulets through the deep furrows in his hollow cheeks. Jefford took a robe from the closet and draped it over the frail shoulders, then stood beside the man for whom he had worked these past 50 years, as they waited for someone to come upstairs and explain what was happening below.

42

In the large southern colonial home sitting behind the shelter of a coppice of towering oak trees behind the Stewart mansion, Emily Stewart watched in panicked shock from the balcony overlooking the wide foyer. One shaking hand covered her mouth, not comprehending the scene below. A wailing toddler tugged at her leg, as two U. S. marshals, flanked by several FBI agents, led her husband to a waiting car. The nearest marshal reached out a hand to protect the top of Elliott's head as he was guided into the back seat. Elliott had not looked up to where his wife now sat on the floor behind the ornate balusters, trying to comfort the frightened child in her arms, as tears flooded her own eyes.

Sarah Stewart stood watching from the top step of the wide-arched porch of her home, drawn by the long line of flashing lights on the black cars she had seen pull up in front of her former in-laws' mansion as she was returning from a yoga lesson. She had rushed inside and dialed the mansion. The persistent ringing went unanswered. With rising alarm she checked the children in their bedrooms upstairs. Both were loudly competing with their rapid fingers in a video game, oblivious to what might be happening at their grandparents' home. She was relieved to see no ambulance among the row of cars lining the circular driveway. *Maybe something involving Grant, she speculated silently—a fundraiser. Who knew?*

Since the divorce, she had maintained a reserved distance from Grant's family, allowing the children to visit often, but avoiding any unnecessary contact with her former in-laws. After several minutes of standing in the humid heat of early evening, she went back inside. If there was an emergency, she was certain Grant would call her.

Jack Reilley spotted a Dallas detective he had a long acquaintance with arriving and was about to ask him if the mayor was going to be arrested, along with his father and brother, when his cell phone rang. "Get video of Elliott Stewart. They're about to leave with him," Mac instructed tersely, before abruptly hanging up. Reilley knew Mac was monitoring the FBI frequency that Worthington had provided the station after receiving Mac's assurance no one would ever know how he was able to track the raid on the Stewart compound. Reilley sent a second camera team scurrying out of the chilled satellite truck to stake out the entrance gates.

As the evening wore on, more media arrived, until there was a small army of reporters and cameramen nervously milling about like a herd of cattle in a thunderstorm outside the Stewart mansion.

Mace Harding turned into the drive leading to the Stewart compound and his temper flared at the media chaos just inside the gate. He rolled his window down, flashed his credentials and ordered two Dallas policemen parked inside the gate to move the noisy throng of reporters and cameras back beyond the entrance road leading to the compound's gate. He parked his own car behind the police cruiser, stepped out and flashed his credentials at an approaching Dallas policeman, who then waived him through the gates. Worthington had called him to be on site during the search—a search that was expected to take several hours, given the size of the physical premise.

Jack Reilley fumed inwardly as he was forced away from the front driveway along with other members of the media. But at least the second camera crew was still in position just outside the gates, unobserved by the two Dallas policemen attempting to herd the recalcitrant and loudly complaining gaggle of newspeople back to the perimeter street. Since the Channel 15 truck was the first to arrive and had a prime spot, it would be the last one able to turn and relocate. Reilley decided to just bide his time.

A short time later the front door opened and Blaine Stewart, flanked by FBI agents and U. S. Marshals, was escorted down the wide steps and placed in the back seat of a dark blue unmarked Crown Victoria parked beside one of the SUVs. Reilley's camera crew had the telephoto lens of their Sony poked through the iron slats of the fence, following the activity.

Another car moved slowly into view from the far side of the mansion, carrying a sobbing Elliott Stewart. A crush of cameras and reporters were scrambling back toward the gates to focus on the new object of their collective attention. Jack Reilley spotted Grant Stewart standing at the top of the front steps with two other men Reilley recognized as Ben Worthington and Mace Harding. Reilley heard the gate lock sound. He tapped a KDLL cameraman on the shoulder and motioned for him to follow. Reilley pushed open one of the unlocked gates and was stepping inside when a beefy arm reached out to stop them. "Sorry gentlemen, you'll have to stay outside the gates."

"I'm Jack Reilley, Channel 15. I just want to speak with the agent in charge over there," he said, pointing to Worthingon. "He knows I'm coming."

"Sorry, Jack," the officer said, recognizing the police reporter. "He told us to keep the media back."

"Look," insisted Reilley, "he knows I'm here and told me to come down. But not the rest of them." Frustration rising in his voice, Reilley said, "Check with Worthington, Findley," he urged, pulling the name from the brass tag above the policeman's shirt pocket.

"Okay, sir. Let me check first." The officer moved a few feet away and began talking into the radio on his shoulder. Reilley whispered to the cameraman, "Keep your baby running, Jake. Don't stop for anyone. And keep it trained on Stewart and those guys around him. Get in as close as you can."

Moments later, Grant Stewart disappeared inside. Worthington tucked a small notepad into an inside pocket of his jacket and walked slowly down the wide steps, with several agents at his heels.

Worthington had refused Grant's request to accompany his father to the federal detention center or even to speak with him. "That's bullshit," Grant had angrily tossed over his shoulder as he stormed back into the mansion.

You're on shaky ground, Mr. Mayor, Worthington thought, as he approached the car where Blaine Stewart sat staring straight ahead. Opening the door and leaning inside, his face was brushed by the cool air from the interior of the Crown Victoria.

"We're going to drive you downtown, Mr. Stewart. You can meet with your attorney there, after you go through booking. We have you scheduled to appear before the magistrate tomorrow morning at 9:00. Tonight, you'll be housed in the county jail."

Blaine Stewart nodded only slightly and continued staring ahead, unblinking.

As Worthington straightened up and closed the door, Jack Reilley called out his name from across the wide drive-way. He walked between cars to where Reilley was standing, a microphone in hand. "How the hell did you get in here, Jack."

"Charm, brother, pure charm. I laid it on thick and the gates parted."

"Bullshit, Jack." Worthington's voice was thick with exasperation. "Alright, what?" His answers to Reilley's question were brief and terse, revealing no details of the grand jury indictment other than the charges. When Reilley pushed for more, Worthington looked tiredly at the eager reporter and said, "I'm sorry. That's all I can say at this time."

Worthington turned and walked wearily back to the house where a swarm of agents, were meticulously scouring through desks, drawers, and files—in a home with more than two dozen rooms. *This would take all night.* Worthington had slept very little the past few days and had not seen his family since Friday night, when he left work briefly to attend his oldest son's first varsity football game in the mid-August heat. He couldn't remember when he had last had sex with his wife. She was pissed all the time lately because he was gone so much. *Tell that to the on-call psychobabblers*, he thought. *Or tell that to the honchos in Washington who think all the action is there, not out in the bureaus.*

He would leave the agents to their search. Worthington walked back to his car and slid into the front passenger seat. He had glimpsed Stewart's grim profile in the back seat of the waiting car. *He'll be a hard nut to crack.* But pulling information from intractable suspects was a part of the job at which Worthington excelled. If Stewart talked, he knew it could lead to Chicago, and that was the real target. There was little they could do about the Mexicans. Money spoke too loudly on the southern side of the border. Vincente Estavar and his cousins would remain well-insulated behind the cartel's millions—maybe billions by this time, he thought savagely, while he had to struggle to keep enough money out of his paycheck each month to feed a college fund for three kids, who would follow each other into that cash-draining environment about every two years. Maybe his wife could go back to work. Give her something to do besides bitch about his hours.

With a mesmerizing rhythm, the white lines separating the freeway lanes flashed rapidly by in the side-view mirror. Ben Worthington felt encumbered by a lot of superfluous emotion. He was feeling something akin to pity for the man in the back seat of the car he was following.

He sighed softly. *What is it that makes rich men want even more wealth, whatever the means, whatever the cost?*

43

The old eyes glistened with tears. Without interrupting, he listened to his grandson's explanation of why his only son had been led away in handcuffs. From time to time he would look back helplessly at Wiley Lefford's empathetic ebony face, as if hoping to find understanding of the tragedy they had witnessed.

"What will happen to my son?" Grantham Stewart asked finally.

"I don't know, Grandpa. We'll have to wait to hear from Willis Johnson." Grant rose from the chair where he sat facing his grandfather and walked toward the fireplace. A large oil portrait of his grandmother smiled down at him, painted when she was still a young and beautiful woman. She had died well before her husband edged into old age, the lost partner of his youth, the love of his life, his only love. Grantham Stewart never remarried.

Grant Stewart felt an overwhelming sadness shroud his senses. He bit his lower lip hard and jammed his fists roughly into his pockets to hold back tears swimming in his own eyes. The telephone call from Withers, not much more than two hours ago, had sent his life crashing around his feet. The sheer tragedy of seeing his father and brother taken away in handcuffs to jail was enough to immobilize his spirit.

From halfway across the room, Grantham Stewart watched his grandson's shoulders drop and realized he was also puzzled and paralyzed by this situation. Seeing the despair engulf his namesake acted like a tonic on the old man's flagging spirit. He pushed himself up from the chair and walked slowly to where the younger man stood with his back to him. Placing a liver-spotted hand on his grandson's shoulder, gently patting with fingers gnarled and bent by age and arthritis, the 92-year-old patriarch looked up at the woman he had loved so long and so deeply, drawing strength from the familiar smile.

"Whatever is the truth, we'll get at it," stated the old voice, sounding resolute as it addressed the younger man next to him. "Truth we can deal with, no matter how painful. First, we must comfort the women. You go see about Emily and the children." he added. "I'll tend to Grace. They need us, son. They need us," he repeated sadly. Tying the belt of his burgundy silk robe, the old man walked back toward his long time valet. "Wiley, while I talk to Grace, get me some clothes laid out. I'm going down to the police station to check on my son."

Waiting for his grandfather to finish bathing and dressing, Grant watched the television crews from a window seat in his old bedroom, which faced the front lawn. The Channel 15 crews were setting up lights and cable, making preparations for the live shot during the ten o'clock newscast. Other satellite trucks were still arriving. By morning, Grant suspected there would be even more media at the gates clamoring for statements and photos of the house where the wealthy oil barons lived, grabbing video of Stewart family members in their comings and goings. They could expect a siege of media attention in the coming days.

He picked up the telephone to call the security service whose number was on the back of the receiver and requested an extra guard be sent as early as possible in the morning to help man the front gate.

Emily Stewart's tears had dried by the time Grant arrived. Only her red, swollen eyes betrayed the sobs that had convulsed her chest as she watched her husband being led away in handcuffs. "My parents are on their way to pick up the children. They'll stay there for a while," Emily said, referring to her parent's sprawling ranch outside Mineral Springs, where she had spent her own childhood. It would be a safe refuge for the children from the chaos swirling around their home. She explained a tutor would be hired to school the two older children. They would be fine with her parents, she assured Grant.

Grant stood watching her racing through the house, gathering toys and other children's items. He was at a loss to know what to say or do in the wake of her dervish energy. The two older children sat on a couch looking bewildered, each clutching a stuffed animal. Grant hugged each child and tenderly touched the cheek of the sleeping toddler in a brightly padded chair swing.

As Emily came sailing through the living room heading for the stairs Grant pulled her into his broad arms, holding her close, feeling the heaving in her chest as she fought to hold back tears that threatened her tight control.

"I'll try to see Elliott tonight, or in the morning. I'll call you as soon as I know something," he promised, kissing her lightly on the forehead. "Call me if you need anything. I'll be staying with Grandpa tonight."

He then hurried out the back door, to take a bridle path that cut across the rear of the three properties, to his former home. Sarah was waiting in the kitchen, a cup of coffee in front of her. She had been expecting him and poured him a steaming cup as he stood inside the doorway—silent. "I'm sure you need this," she said, as she handed him the cup and pointed to a chair across from her at the kitchen table, encircled on three sides by a bay window. Security lights illuminated the back yard which stretched to the edge of a creek that meandered through the property.

Grant sat down gratefully and looked out toward the narrow stream. It was a picturesque scene he often missed since moving from his grandfather's estate, especially the morning view from the wide windows of the mansion, looking out beyond the creek to the thick woods at the rear of the property. It was in those woods he and Elliott had roamed as children, playing soldiers, darting behind the big trees for cover as they stalked each other. It was a private, sheltered retreat, even in an area of sprawling estates that had built up around the Stewarts' secluded acres.

In between sips of coffee, he shared what he knew about the charges leveled against his father and brother. Throughout their marriage Sarah had disliked both men. It had often been a source of conflict between them. Now she was silent and uncritical, the only solace she could offer this man she had loved and still held close in her secret heart, for what he was going through.

They agreed the children should not begin school next week. This would help shield them from any media encroachment into the protected, happy cocoon in which Sarah sheltered her children, with Grant's tacit concurrence. He visited with his children before leaving a short time later, refreshed by the coffee and Sarah's unspoken support.

✝✝✝

"Can you arrange for my grandfather to visit my father tonight?" Grant asked. There was no anger, no pleading in his voice.

"It's a little late," replied Ben Worthington, looking at the large clock on the far wall of his office. "Anyway, his attorney was there when I left. They may still be meeting."

Grant sighed heavily. "He's an old man, Worthington. You can arrange this."

There was a pause. "All right," the FBI agent said with a sigh. "I'll make the arrangements. Don't plan to stay long. It's nearly midnight now."

"Thank you."

An hour later, Grantham Stewart, on the arm of his grandson, was ushered into a small room by a khaki-uniformed sheriff's deputy. Several minutes later, the door opened and a handcuffed Blaine Stewart was led in by the same deputy. The sight of his only son in a bright orange jump suit, his hands constrained in front of him, his salt and pepper hair askew, was a dagger striking Grantham Stewart's heart. He could not speak and only gripped his grandson's arm tighter.

"Hello, Dad." Pain and despair were betrayed in Grant's voice. "How did it go with Willis?"

"All right, I guess. He didn't stay long. Just said he would get a copy of the indictment and try to postpone any hearings for a few days. And request bail." There was resignation in Blaine's soft spoken words, barely audible to his father and his son.

"How is Elliott?" Blaine asked in a low voice, devoid of any emotion.

"They won't let us see him tonight," said Grant. "Willis met with him right after he left you. I'm to call him first thing in the morning to arrange bail for you and Elliott."

"We'll post bond and get you out of here tomorrow," the older man stated with the same resolute tone Grant had noted earlier. *The body may be frail, but the spirit undaunted*, Grant conceded as he listened to his eponym. Grantham Stewart reassured Blaine that Emily and the children would be taken care of, and he would take back over operating the business he had entrusted to his only son nearly two decades earlier.

Blaine did not ask about Grace.

Thunder sounded in the western sky, now ominously dark, as Grant pulled to a stop in front of the wide front veranda steps leading to the main entrance of the mansion. A strong wind stirred the tops of the towering trees around the home, shaking loose leaves and small limbs, a prelude to the approaching storm. Wiley Jefford hobbled toward them, his knees victims of his own advancing age and arthritis.

Leaving the two elderly men at the elevator on the second floor, Grant went to his mother's room. The lights were out. He knocked softly on the door. There was no response. Jefford had mentioned she took a sleeping pill and retired shortly after they had left to drive to the jail.

Grant went down to the study. He loved this room, framed on three sides by floor-to-ceiling mahogany bookshelves and smelling of seasoned leather. Even as a child, this had been his favorite room, where he could escape and climb one of the three movable ladders, to reach the books secreted on the topmost shelves. He spent hours exploring the titles on those forbidden shelves. It was on one of the top steps of a ladder he had been sitting one rainy, summer afternoon reading *Lady Chatterley's Lover* when his mother had spied his hiding place and ordered him down, then angrily denounced his choice of books.

He moved to a high, intricately leaded casement window, where the drapes had not been drawn, and watched the frequent flashes of lightning spark across the sky. The lightning illuminated dark clouds gorged with heavy rain and loud thunder, advancing toward them from the center of the city.

He felt a kinship with the storm's rage. Like the lightning lashing from the dark heavens to earth and the thunder bellowing the storm's anger, he wanted to rage against his father and brother for imperiling all his grandfather had built. He wanted to shout his anger from the depths of his soul, and ask the question for which there seemed no answer—*Why?*

The storm continued to rage, extending darkness well into dawn before its energy was spent, its meek remnants passing to the east. Like the exiting storm, Grant's anger was replaced by a lethargy that thwarted his ability to focus on the day ahead. It was the telephone ringing that forced his weary mind back to reality.

Willis Johnson. Was Grant prepared to put up cash for the bond or should he contact a bondsman? Grant realized he had no idea how much money his family now had or how he could access it to post a bond. But his grandfather did. He was awake and dressed when Grant stepped into his bedroom. Jefford arrived moments later, balancing a tray with a carafe of coffee.

Grantham Stewart had a number of cash accounts and a list of securities that could be pledged as collateral. After several telephone calls to bankers he had dealt with over many years, the old man arranged for the amount necessary to post the bond.

Following a brief hearing, Blaine Stewart and his oldest son were each released on a $10 million bond, and each surrendered his passport. Johnson implored the magistrate for a bond half that size, to no avail. Both men left the Dallas county jail before noon, shaken and subdued, surrounded by marshals who formed a ring around the pair and their attorney. They struggled forward against the crush of cameras and shouted questions from the throng of news media, congested in a small area between the federal courthouse and the parking lot.

Sheltered behind the darkened glass of Willis Johnson's Lincoln Navigator, the men were steered through the gauntlet of camera-mounted strobe lights to the safety of a main artery leading to the freeway. "Sons of bitches," Elliott muttered bitterly.

Emily ran from her home to the mansion as the Lincoln pulled to a stop. She was embraced by Elliott as he exited the car. Grace remained in her bedroom, watching the homecoming with deep resentment from behind a sliver of opened drape.

When Grant arrived an hour later, the three generations of Stewart men and their attorney withdrew to Blaine's study to deal with the crisis confronting the family. Willis Johnson verbally drew a bleak picture of their situation. The assistant U. S. Attorney had outlined the government's evidence in succinct terms. Willis Johnson was himself a blunt, plain-spoken man, and he did not spare the two clients sitting across from him. The charges were serious—very serious—and were underscored by the strong evidence revealed so far, he told them grimly.

Worse, a state grand jury would soon be investigating many of the same allegations. It was possible that grand jury might try to tie Grant to the conspiracy angle because he had once served on the board of directors and had signed off on annual reports for the skeletal companies, even though it was nearly a decade ago.

Grant was an attorney who had left his law practice behind when he chose to run for mayor. He retained enough knowledge of the law to assess his vulnerability. That the election was lost he accepted. Facing possible criminal charges for something he was an unknowing party to stirred deep feelings of resentful anger, which he quickly repressed.

Grant stood up from where he sat on a leather couch, across from his father and brother, and walked over to a large mullioned glass bay window, his hands shoved deep in his pockets, listening to Johnson behind him. What the attorney did not say was the five men arrested with the Stewarts were probably being offered deals, or even outright freedom, to testify against their former employers and friends. It was common strategy to flip lesser players in a case likely to be as complicated as this, especially given the possible Chicago mob connection.

"I've only heard the bragging points in the fed's case," said Johnson. "They don't point out their weaknesses. They leave those for me to find. And there will be some. There may be many such weaknesses, gentlemen," nodding his head and pursing his lips as he looked at each of his clients to emphasize his point. "What I'm trying to tell you is, don't despair." He rose to leave, scrunching his iconic Stetson on his head and clasping the expensive leather briefcase that served him like an extra appendage. "We're going to bring a Sherman tank to this fight. Make no mistake about that."

Even outside a courtroom, Willis Johnson's demeanor of absolute confidence ensured his reputation as an attorney of choice. Especially if you were in deep shit, as he liked to call the situations in which many of his clients found themselves. A thick mane of silver-grey hair, piercing blue eyes, manicured nails, and $3,000 tailored suits, gave him a distinctive look to match his performance in a courtroom. He was a studied, tenacious, legal viper, ready to strike at any weakness in a courtroom opponent. It was that fierce tenacity that grew his reputation into legend, even beyond the borders of Texas.

"Not for a moment must we minimize the seriousness of this situation," he concluded with a lusty voice. "Once I know fully what the other side has," he said, "or doesn't have, then we'll look at our options. That could include a plea bargain." His eyes measured the impact of his words. "But it's a little early to consider that."

Grant still stood with his back to Johnson and the others. *Plea bargain?* Had Johnson reached the same conclusion he had in the past hour—that his father and brother were guilty of the unthinkable? His father and brother connived with thugs to turn his grandfather's legacy into a drug-smuggling front, and make a lot of money—money piled on top of the considerable wealth his grandfather had already amassed? The same question churned again in his mind—*Why?*

After Johnson left, Grant walked over to his father as he stood up to leave. "Could I talk with you privately, Dad?"

Reluctance was written in Blaine's eyes, but he said nothing and sat back down on the couch. Grant waited for the door to close behind Elliott before sitting down across from his father. He leaned forward, his elbows on his knees, his chin resting on his clenched hands, his eyes lifting from the marble-topped table in front of him to his father's pale face.

"I want to know the truth, Dad. I can handle it. Just tell me why."

Blaine Stewart rose wearily and left the room without answering his son.

44

This was the day on which Lesley Rowan should have been in London, finishing dinner at the Savoy, before taking a cab to the theater for the 8:00 p.m. curtain. They would have slept late to ward off the lethargy of jet lag, made love, showered, made love again, and finally dressed just in time for dinner. It was a scenario that played over and over in her mind as she lay awake staring into the nighttime darkness of her bedroom. The same scenario intruded on the drive to work, and as she entered the elevator that took her to the second story newsroom. Each time her mind wandered to what might have been, she savagely forced it back to reality.

Instead of beginning her honeymoon, this was the day the state grand jury was being empanelled to hear evidence presented by the Dallas County Prosecutor whose reputation for brashness exceeded even his federal counterpart, Mace Harding. Lesley feared it was evidence which could implicate Grant as a co-conspirator in drug trafficking and money laundering—charges his father and brother were already facing.

Foreboding washed over Lesley as she pushed open the door to the newsroom. She had taken several days off, on Mac's orders, and spent those days with her mother. For the first time since launching her journalism career, she dreaded going to work.

Her mother's presence this past week had been a surprising

comfort. A woman she felt she had never known as a child or adolescent emerged during their long hours of conversation, hanging out in Lesley's apartment, going out to dinner, a movie, and even shopping. Her mother was, at the same time, consoling and uplifting. A sense of humor—never revealed during her growing-up years—alighted at pertinent moments, injecting much-needed levity, even giddiness; helping assuage the morass of sadness into which Lesley found herself sinking at times. They made a pact—mother and daughter—before Katherine returned to San Antonio, to take a cruise together in January. And to meet in Austin next month for a weekend get-away and shopping spree.

The woman who had arrived unannounced to comfort her daughter was someone Lesley had always loved with the kind of claim made by blood and maternity. The woman who left was somehow different; as much a trusted confidant and friend as a parent. Thinking about her mother helped banish the sense of dread she felt returning to the newsroom for the first time in a week.

Hal Crockett was coming out of Mac Withers' office when he saw Lesley heading across the newsroom toward her office. He was not usually a demonstrative man; generally reserved, occasionally humorous, sometimes gruff and impatient when he was under stress. Crockett tucked the early news budget under his arm and began clapping his hands slowly.

Stepping out of Withers' office just behind Crockett, Billy Burton and Jerry Simms also began clapping. Throughout the large newsroom heads raised and chairs were pushed back, as the source of the applause was sighted and staffers stood up to join in. Photographers and video editors heard the commotion and stepped out of their dimly lit editing bays, joining the crescendo of applause reverberating throughout the newsroom, loud enough to turn curious heads in the sales and billing offices one floor below. Bart Henderson heard it and stepped into his secretary's office. "What the hell is that?"

"I would guess the news folks are giving Miss Lesley a

well-deserved ovation," Marcella Gallagher, his secretary replied, knowing this was the first day she was expected back at work. She noted the blank look on Henderson's face, and for about the one-zillionth time, questioned how Bart Henderson ever got to be manager of a major Dallas television station.

"You suppose I should go up there?" he asked.

"No. It's their tribute for her. You can do something later," she suggested, barely managing to squelch her sarcasm. It was a discipline she learned early-on in dealing with her boss.

Mac Withers stood framed in the door of his office, joining the applause, a lump forming in his throat. *This is better than a Peabody*, he thought. He watched Lesley look out at the newsroom, her eyes directed by her ears to the applause, staring at her fellow staffers with a bewildered expression as the slow realization spread across her face—the applause was for her. Tears sprang to her eyes, a drop, another drop, then a cascade down her cheeks as she looked out incredulously at the applauding journalists, not sure how to acknowledge the spontaneous tribute. No acknowledgment was expected. When it was over, those who stood during the prolonged ovation sat back down and went back to work.

Downstairs, Marcella Gallagher was relieved when Henderson finally turned and walked back into his office. She whispered her own tribute to her blank computer screen, "You go, girl."

Blaine Stewart looked around his bedroom, separate from his wife's—separate for a long time. He could not remember when they had last been intimate. Or when he had quit loving her. Or if he had *ever* loved her. He propped the painstakingly written letter in the envelope on the night stand and absently drew his fingers through his disheveled grey hair. He sat down on the side of a high, four-poster Tudor-style bed, draped in an elaborate canopy of moss green silk. Grace had hired a chatty, obsequious decorator to refurbish the bedroom, after Blaine took refuge there from her disdain and frigidity.

It was time. He was ready. A fitting end to egregious behavior. He wondered if Grace would even bother to bury him properly, with a minister and prayers. Would anyone come? *Probably not*, he answered himself derisively. He was disgraced; the power he craved from his father, the prestige that accompanied that power, and much of the wealth entrusted to him, were gone. Evaporated. He was alone. A pariah. *A coward*, he admitted, too ashamed to face the only man whose opinion he ever valued. The letter on the night stand was addressed to him. Blaine Stewart lifted the 16-gauge shotgun to his open mouth and, without hesitation or time to reconsider, pulled the trigger.

It was Wiley Lefford who heard the loud discharge of the gun and found Blaine Stewart moments later. Blaine's body lay prone on the bed. He was already dead, his face partially obliterated by the shotgun shell's brutality. Blood was soaking the silk coverlet and had splattered the canopy above. Bits of flesh and bone and brain clung precariously to the high headboard, a site so gruesome and sickening Lefford turned his head away. It was then he saw the envelope propped against a lamp and knew instinctively it was a suicide note. He clutched the envelope, itself splattered lightly with blood, and stuffed it hurriedly inside his suit jacket. He rushed to the door and closed it behind him to prevent the others who were pounding up the stairs from seeing what he just viewed.

Grant was in the library sharing a rare cigar with his grandfather and Elliott when he heard the sharp crack of the shotgun. He raced down the broad hallway, Elliott at his heels. Lefford blocked the door to the grisly scene inside. "Don't go in there, Mr. Grant. Please," he appealed. "Don't go in there. There's nothing left to do for Mr. Blaine."

Grant attempted to push past Lefford, but felt himself restrained by the older man's surprisingly strong arm. "He's passed, Mr. Grant. He would want privacy. I'll call an ambulance. Then I best go and be with Mr. Stewart."

Tears rolled down Elliott's stricken face. Grant turned to his older brother—always the weaker, always the more dependent, and pulled him into his arms. Only then did he feel the sting of his own tears.

Grace stood watching her sons from just outside the door of her bedroom at the end of the hall. Her face was void of any expression. Blank. She could feel no pain. *I should feel pain,* she thought without emotion. *It is the right thing to do to feel pain when your husband dies.* But she felt only emptiness inside and could summon no remorse. Blaine had been lost to her for too long. She turned and slipped back into her bedroom, shutting the door quietly behind her.

Within a half-hour of Lefford's call, a dozen uniformed police and detectives swarmed over the mansion, herding the sobbing servants into the living room, taking statements from the valet, Grant, and Elliott. When Grace was summoned from her room she appeared pale and listless and remained detached and silent when asked questions by a team of detectives.

After an entreaty from Grant, Grace was allowed to be led back to her bedroom by her two sons. Elliott remained with his mother while Grant went back downstairs to be with his grandfather, who was sitting pale, dry-eyed, and alone under the canopy of elaborately coffered ceiling in the library.

Later, after the police left, and the body of Blaine Stewart had been removed to a funeral home, Wiley Lefford pulled the letter from his inside coat pocket in the privacy of his bedroom. He stared at it for a time, hesitated, then finally opened it and began haltingly reading the two pages. His eyes blurred as he wiped away tears with a shaking hand.

Outside the Stewart estate, television satellite trucks angled their round dishes at the sky, drawn like large technological vultures by police scanner reports of a shooting at the Stewart compound. The descending media were forced to remain outside the high black wrought iron gates that blocked entrance to the compound, now guarded by additional security personnel, hired by Grant to keep the curious away.

Reporters holding slender notepads and television cameramen craned to see what was happening in front of the main home, through the narrow view between the black bars of the ornate gate. Sheltered by distance from the main road and large trees, they saw little of the activity inside the mansion. After a hearse carrying Blaine's body pulled through the gate, a police spokesman walked out of the mansion to brief the media.

A low voice in her earpiece alerted Lesley to go live to the scene outside the Stewart compound where a police spokesman had just arrived to brief the media. KDLL was interrupting regular programming to take the news briefing live. A light on the camera in front of her clicked red. "There is new information on the shooting at the home of pioneer oil magnate Grantham Stewart," she ad-libbed smoothly to the camera. "Let's go live to Dallas police spokesman Darrell Mason, who is about to make a statement outside the Stewart compound near Park City."

Mason was ringed by more than a dozen microphones, smartphones and small tape recorders pointed at his mouth.

"I'll tell you what we know at this point and then take questions. Police were called to the scene at approximately 3:20 this afternoon, where the body of Blaine Stewart, 60-years-old, was found in a bedroom. He was deceased at the time the first officers arrived, from an apparent self-inflicted gunshot wound."

The statement was brief, the questions which followed more prolonged, until Mason cut short the shouted mayhem.

Jack Reilley stepped in front of the Channel 15 camera to summarize the facts revealed by the police spokesman, detailing yet another scandal swirling around the family of Dallas Mayor Grant Stewart. Reilley reiterated the grand jury indictments and arrests of the head of Stewart Oil, his oldest son, and several top executives.

Lesley felt numb listening to the narrative and left the set quickly when the special report was over and headed for the sanctuary of her cubicle. She was startled to see Mac Withers sitting behind her desk. "Mac!"

"How about going out with an old man to get a drink? I could use a good, stiff whiskey," he smiled. "You can have your usual soft drink. Date?"

"I could use some company."

"I figured that."

Shortly after seven, Mac was driving to a small restaurant in the near downtown that he frequented. He directed the hostess to seat them in a private booth at the back of the dimly lit eatery. "I've got to hide you in the rear, now that you're such a celebrity. I have a real aversion to autograph seekers."

Lesley knew she was being teased. Withers was aware of her own discomfort with the recognition and celebrity accorded news anchors. Age might separate them by a generation, but their shared feelings for the integrity of their craft bridged the canyon of years and experience. As they waited for the ordered drinks, Lesley looked across his shoulder at the couples and groups circled around tables. She watched them eating, lifting beer glasses to their lips, talking, laughing. Would she ever again be carefree like the people she was watching?

Mac noted the sadness in her eyes. "It will pass, Lesley. Most things in life do. Right now you can't get past the feeling of loss and despair you feel for Grant. But you will. It all eases at some point. It takes the passing of time. Time's really the only healer."

"I know that, Mac. I wish I could fast-forward or rewind. Either way. Just not be stuck right here, right now."

A tall waiter placed a Coke in front of Lesley and a smaller glass, half-filled with amber bourbon, and a glass of tap beer by Mac. "Can I get you anything else?"

"Not right now, thanks," said Mac, pulling several bills from the silver money clip he fished from a pocket. The young waiter held up his hand. "No charge. My boss, Mike, the guy behind the bar? He says he's proud you came in, Miss Rowan. Enjoy."

"That was nice. Bart will be grateful," Mac said after the waiter was gone. "One less round of drinks on my expense account this month."

They sat silently for a time, with no awkwardness, Lesley sipping her cola, Withers sipping the beer to chase his bourbon. Lesley smiled each time the foam left a mustache on his upper lip, which he quickly cleared with his finger. "Best part of the beer,' he said lightly.

There was another prolonged silence between them until Withers said, "You should go to the funeral. Grant would want you there."

"You're wrong, Mac. He would be embarrassed. I haven't talked with Grant since he called off the wedding."

"So? He could use a friend." He took another swig of beer and prompted another smile. "How'd you two meet anyway?"

"At a news conference. Fitting, huh? We had dinner. And all through dinner I kept worrying about what I would do if he tried to kiss me or make some other move."

"You must have said yes."

"I did." He watched the tears gather in her eyes and slip slowly down her cheeks.

"Go to the funeral, Les. He could use a friend. So could you," he added, downing the last of his beer.

"I have one." Lesley said. She reached over and laid her hand on Withers'.

45

The man watched the retreating sun from the spacious veranda overlooking the lush gardens planted on the steep terraces sweeping down the back of the sprawling hacienda, secluded atop its mountain sanctuary. It was a view he never tired of. And tonight he would enjoy it without the intrusive rancor from his Mexican partners. It took much persuasion to calm their concerns. It was an effort bolstered by news of Blaine Stewart's suicide.

Christo sneered silently at the man's lack of courage. Stewart had chosen an easy end. *Only cowards choose such paths*, he concluded, watching the great red ball descending behind the western mountains. It, of course, forestalled what Stewart must have known was inevitable. If he hadn't taken his own life, Christo would have had to accomplish that same end for him.

All things considered, it was a good end to what was proving a difficult situation for him and his remaining partners in Mexico and America. But there was damage control still left to be done.

Blaine Stewart was wrong. More than a hundred people attended the austere graveside service: business acquaintances; longstanding friends; even several city officials. A few Lesley recognized from where she stood, unobtrusively, at the back of those gathered around the mahogany casket. The casket was bedecked with only a small clutch of yellow roses. No other flowers were on display.

Grant stood by his mother. Her right arm was linked tightly in his, her face obscured by a thin, black veil. Grant's two children stood on his other side, looking up at their father occasionally, receiving a wan smile of reassurance for being there to honor a man who had shared so little of himself with them.

Elliott clung to Emily's arm, their free arms pressing each of their two oldest children against them. Grantham Stewart stood alone, leaning heavily on a wood cane, his thin shoulders slightly bent, just behind his sons and their families. He had refused Wiley Lefford's proffered arm and declined the offer of a folding chair

No eulogy was spoken for Blaine Stewart, no spoken tributes from his wife or children, only a reading of psalms and a brief prayer offered by the minister Lesley recognized as the clergy-man she and Grant had asked to officiate at their wedding. An overwhelming sense of loss swept over her. The loss of Grant; the loss of a life with him that would never be. Most of all, the loss of love. So much loss; so much grieving; so much agony still ahead. Raising her bowed head as the minister intoned *amen*, she turned and began walking back toward her car.

Her mother had called prior to the funeral; encouraging, empathetic, proud. Conversation by conversation, Katherine was becoming even more a welcomed friend, and less a distant mother. But Lesley's best friend was still lost to her. Was any story worth this price?

Stepping into her apartment, she pushed the button on the answering machine. It was Grant's voice. "Thank you for coming today." The machine beeped the end of the message.

Lesley was just stepping out of the shower when the telephone rang. It was on the third ring before she reached the telephone on the bed stand. "Hello," she said breathlessly.

"It's Mac. Grant has called a news conference for four o'clock. We're carrying it live. Can you make it in time to co-anchor the coverage here?"

"I'm on my way."

Throughout the city, people grouped in front of television sets as Grantham Stewart II, nearing the end of his second term as mayor of one of the country's most storied cities, stepped in front of the cameras, placed a copy of his statement on the podium, and looked straight into the glare of lights hitting his tall frame from every angle. Behind him stood several staff members, including his executive secretary Helen Grissom, who clutched a Kleenex in her hand, raising it frequently to dab tears which threatened to betray her normally stoic control. The grim-faced press secretary reached over to pat her shoulder.

"In the wake of the tragedy that has befallen my family, I am resigning as mayor, effective immediately, and withdrawing from the campaign for reelection. I did so in letters sent this morning to the Mayor Pro Tem and the city manager. I want to wish Dennison Davis Godspeed in the months ahead as he takes the reins of office. I appreciate his consideration and restraint in not using, for political gain, the difficult and tragic circumstances that force me to this decision today. He has shown himself to be an able and caring man, for which I am grateful."

Grant looked away from the prepared text and into the cameras in front of him. "My grandfather and I will cooperate fully with the investigations into the allegations made against my father, my brother, and executives of several Stewart Oil subsidiaries. We are in the process of making available all records pertinent to the investigation of Stewart Oil, and all our subsidiary companies and any individuals who may be implicated in any wrongdoing while employed by these companies. My grandfather is coming out of a long retirement to again head the company he founded. I will be at his side and work in whatever capacity I can to restore the integrity of Stewart Oil, and rebuild its resources as a formidable competitor in the oil business."

Grant paused, and Lesley watched his hands grip the podium tightly as he fought for control. He lifted his head slowly and turned his eyes to the camera lens directly in front of him.

"I wish to thank the people of Dallas for the honor they have accorded me to serve as their mayor. I will miss the people I've worked with in the City of Dallas, particularly the very able staff that made being mayor so enjoyable each day. We have a great city with enormous pride in its history, its people, and its institutions—a city eager to address a future that holds promise of even greater accomplishments." His voice failed him for just a moment before he ended the news conference with a simple, "Thank you."

He turned from the podium amidst a hail of shouted questions, his broad shoulders the last thing Lesley saw as Grant walked out of the conference room, followed by his press secretary and other staff members.

Lesley turned her head toward the camera that had just clicked on in the studio, "A somber and premature end to a political career," she began. "Mayor Grant Stewart announcing his resignation, effective immediately, to join the oil firm his 92-year old grandfather founded more nearly 70 years ago, and will once again lead. Lynn Delaney is live at the news conference. Lynn, describe for us the mood in the mayor's office when they learned what was about to happen."

The coverage continued for the remainder of the hour. Political pundits crowded the news set to pontificate on the political fallout from the mayor's resignation; and the apparent anointing of Dennison Davis as the next mayor. The filing period for launching a new candidate to replace Grant Stewart had long passed. There were more interviews with government and business officials, all reacting to the resignation and its impact on the city.

Then Dennison Davis stepped before the microphones at his

law office in downtown Dallas to issue a statement punctuated with sympathy for the Stewart family. Davis also mixed in a gracious acknowledgment of the now-former mayor's contributions to Dallas. Even the acerbic Davis conceded Grant Stewart was handling, with laudable dignity, a cataclysmic situation for himself and his family.

†††

Grant watched Davis from the privacy of his inner office. Dennison Davis was an old school political animal, a product of the political precincts that still ruled city elections. If given a choice, Grant would have selected a less partisan man to succeed him, a mayor who walked more comfortably down the middle of the road, where both sides of an issue could be heard more clearly. But fate had interceded. *You play the cards you're dealt*, he reminded himself. Dallas would have to make do with Dennison Davis come November.

After embraces and tearful well-wishes from his aides and staff, Grant tucked a cardboard container under his arm. It was filled with small personal items he had brought to the mayor's office. He slipped down the back elevator to the parking garage and drove toward the Stewart estate. It would be his home for the immediate future, a place to find refuge from the shattered life from which he now retreated, a more convenient place to help his grandfather overhaul a family business beset by scandal. And to wait. Wait for the decision of a county grand jury, he learned only today, was also investigating his possible involvement in the drug-smuggling that drove his father to suicide, and likely would send his only brother to prison.

It was Jack Reilley who learned the target of the grand jury. It led the news that evening, and rated top-of-the-fold play in the newspaper the following morning. "Ex-mayor's possible role in drug empire target of grand jury" screamed the headline.

As she read the story, citing the same unnamed sources that

Reilley had quoted, Lesley began to feel the first stab of doubt. The pain of her doubt deepened as the days passed and Grant's indictment appeared imminent. Her sense of betrayal and loss grew, as well.

Television vans and reporters had been ensconced outside the front gates of the Stewart compound following Grant's resignation and in anticipation of charges being brought by the investigative panel. But after several days passed with no announcement of an indictment, one by one the media vans gradually vacated the scene. Grant Stewart remained secluded. He was even absent for his brother's arraignment.

It was his mother who kept Grant within his grandfather's home some days and away from the downtown offices of Stewart Oil. Grace refused food and now spent her days in bed; weakened by her refusal to eat, drifting in and out of reality, her mind clouded by paranoia. She was becoming so weak the doctor who came by each evening suggested she be hospitalized and a feeding tube inserted. Grant and Elliott agreed. The physician would make arrangements for Grace to be moved to a hospital in the morning.

After sharing a meal in the kitchen with his grandfather and Wiley Lefford, Grant went up to his mother's bedroom. She was asleep. He sat down in a chair near the bed and lay back, allowing his eyes to close, if only for a moment. He was lost in thought when he heard Grace moan. He reached for a light by her bedside and saw his mother's eyes had rolled back in her head. He felt for a pulse. He could find none. Shouting frantically for help, he threw back the covers and began CPR.

Elliott was pounding up the wide staircase as an ambulance siren shrieked in the distance, disturbing the evening quiet. When it drew up to the gated entrance of the compound, followed by a single Dallas police car, the security guard stepped out to speak to the driver as the heavy gates were opening. The siren was stilled. Grace Stewart was already dead.

Sarah Stewart had heard the siren's sharp wail from the den

where she was helping her children with their homework. Then it fell silent. She urged the children to continue their work and hurried out the door and across the lawn to the large mansion. Grant stood outside his mother's bedroom, his face ashen. Seeing his despair turned Sarah's heart. It was Sarah he was clinging to as his mother's body, covered by a white sheet, was removed on a gurney. For the first time since misfortune had wrapped its smothering cloak around his family, Grant gave in to deep sobs that wracked his body. Sarah could only hold him as she cried softly herself.

The sudden death of another Stewart family member spurred reporters and cameramen, working nights at the newspapers and television stations, back to the scene. By the ten o'clock news, satellite trucks and news vans were again clustered near the entrance to the compound. Reporters and cameramen stood outside the iron gates, microphones at the ready.

It was that scene Lesley saw after flipping on the television set under the kitchen cabinet. She planned to be at the office early, after being alerted late yesterday the grand jury could hand down an indictment of Grant Stewart today. She stared at the screen, jarred deeply by what she was hearing. She sat down at her computer desk and pulled up the webpage for a flower shop she had used in the past. She ordered a vase of Grace's favorite flowers, yellow roses and baby's breath.

"This arrangement just arrived, Mr. Stewart. Shall I place it by the casket?" a funeral director inquired of Grant the next afternoon. Grant was sitting in the manager's office, finalizing arrangements for the burial of his mother. *What difference does it make where you put it?* Grant wanted to scream at the quiet spoken man who hovered above him. Seeing the arrangement of yellow roses separated by baby's breath the man was holding, Grant knowingly reached for the card and opened it. *I am so sorry. Lesley.*

46

"**A**n old man dropped this off for you a little while ago. I told him you'd be in shortly, but he said he couldn't wait."

The front lobby receptionist handed a white envelope to Lesley as she came through the employee's entrance from the parking lot, just after 9:00. Waiting for the elevator, she unsealed it with her finger. There was a short note paper-clipped to the two pages. "I have the original letter," was all it said. She pulled out the pages of a handwritten letter that had been copied, a letter which began with the simple salutation.

Father,

The charges against me are true. Elliott was an unwitting part of my plan. He was just following my instructions in all of this. Please help him as much as you possibly can. Grant was never a part of any of this, and, like you, knew nothing of my dealings. All the others charged are deeply involved in every aspect.

I know you are asking why I did it. I erred in buying Hancock Drilling Supply from a Colombian businessman named Juan Christo. I paid too much to become a player in that arena. When the recession hit, the company's debt load was dragging us down and I had to subsidize from other areas of cash flow. I feared I would lose everything you entrusted to me. Christo offered a way out of our financial losses. He proposed a plan that allowed us to use our non-producing oil assets as a cover for raising new income, by acting as a go-between to ship his products. He grows and processes drugs and smuggles them into the states. The product is brought across the border from Mexico under the protection of the El Poder cartel run by three cousins, Vincente Estavar, Pietro Salador, and Eliud Mendoza. They shipped the drugs to us through Mexico, usually by plane or by truck. They are thugs and killers. Mostly I dealt directly with Christo and his Chicago partner, Robert Castelero. Castelero heads an organized crime group in Chicago that ultimately distributes the drugs on the streets. He is not much better than a street thug.

I now fear for you and Grant and the rest of our family. Elliott will need protection, because they will be afraid he might tell all he knows to the authorities. Except for Walt Edmonds, the other heads of our subsidiaries were told only as much as they needed to know to run their divisions. I was forced to hire Edmonds by Castelero.

Do not call Stu Aarons, who heads the protection service we use at the company. He is an associate of Castelero and is ruthless. Aarons was placed in Dallas to ensure we did what Christo and Castelero expected of us. It was made clear to me that my family would face retribution if I ever attempted to sever our business relationship. It was Aarons who carried out the murder of a reporter working for KDLL. He used two men provided by the El Poder cartel to shoot the reporter. It was the same group that killed the editor in Brownsville and a pilot who flew for Althea Oil & Gas. The pilot was Sarah's father. He was married to Sarah's mother, but they divorced soon after Sarah was born. I do not think she is even aware of his existence. I knew nothing of this until after the man was dead, or I would have tried to intercede.

My arrest has placed you in great danger. I appeal to you to seek protection from the police. In a wall safe in my bedroom you will find information that could help investigators seeking evidence against Aarons, Castelero, Christo, and the three leaders of the Mexican cartel. The combination to the safe is in the left bottom drawer of my desk in the bedroom.

Grant asked me why. I could not answer him. I only know I wanted you to be proud of me, and when you appointed me your successor, I wanted to show you I was worthy. You were the legend I could never live up to.

I know I am your son in name only. You allowed Mother to adopt me only to indulge her, because you were away so much. It is too much to ask forgiveness of you and Grace.

You asked me once why Grace was so distant. It angered me you even noticed. I was in love with someone else a long time ago and asked her for a divorce. She refused to divorce and we were never close after that. Take care of Grace. I let her down. I let you all down. I am very sorry. Please forgive me.

Blaine

When the elevator doors opened onto the second floor, Lesley emerged slowly and stood outside the newsroom door, re-reading the long letter. It was the candid and remarkable confession of a man whose final words assigned both guilt and blamelessness as his final bequest. It clearly exonerated Grant.

The same day Grant resigned as mayor, Worthington had called Lesley to confide the evidence against Grant was flimsy. He said he told the county prosecutor as much, and that the investigation against Grant should be dropped. Worthington said to expect the federal grand jury to hand down a no bill against Grant, but he wasn't sure about the local grand jury. This letter could ensure a no bill from that grand jury as well. And lift the cloud that had hung over Grant since his father and brother were arrested.

An old man, the receptionist said. *It must be Wiley Lefford,* she thought. And he must have the original letter. She rushed to her computer and began scanning the computerized morgue files and found the copy for the story on Blaine Stewart's suicide. It was Lefford who found the body, according to the police spokesman. *Did he find the letter and not turn it over to police?* she speculated.

Mac read the letter, and read it a second time before looking up. "See if you can get this verified, Les. Call the valet. If he has it, see if he will talk to us on camera."

"He won't," she interjected quickly. "I wouldn't even try."

He searched her face. The old man was her source and she would protect him. "Fair enough. Call the police and the prosecutor. See if they know about the letter. My guess is they haven't seen it. We'll lead with it at five," he said, and handed the two pages back to her. Before she was out the door, Mac's voice was on the telephone intercom summoning Hal Crockett to reshuffle the line-up for the early newscast. There would be a new lead story—a big lead story.

"Stewart residence." Lesley recognized Wiley Lefford's reedy voice.

"Wiley, this is Lesley Rowan. Are you where you can talk?"

"Yes, ma'am," came the hesitant response.

"I got the letter you left for me. It *was* you who dropped it by the station?" There was only silence from the other end of the line, except for the old man's breath rasping into the receiver. The old voice was barely a whisper. "I never wanted to hurt Mr. Stewart. He's been hurt enough, that's for sure."

"I know that, Wiley. This will clear up many questions." More silence at the other end. "Wiley, why did you not give this to the police earlier?"

"I was scared, Miz Lesley. I didn't know what to do. I was 'fraid they might haul me away. Then what would Mr. Grantham do? And then there was what Mr. Blaine said about Mr. Elliott. I feared for him. Feared the police would come and haul him away again. So I hid it in my room. Safe place there. Nobody but me knows the place."

Lesley could hear the old man's breath coming faster. "You ain't gonna tell the police I hid the letter from them, are you?"

"No, Wiley. No one will ever know it was you who brought the letter to me. But thank you, and protect that original."

"I will, Miz Lesley." The old man hesitated, than asked, "What you think they'll do to Mister Elliott?"

She heard the pain in his voice. "I don't know, Wiley." Lesley felt her heart lurch for the old man, who had known both sons since they were born. She sensed he was feeling remorse for turning the letter over to her, knowing while it would clear one son, it would clearly implicate the other.

"Wiley, you did the right thing. Just remember that." She hung up quickly.

†††

Dallas County Prosecutor Drew Michelson finished reading the faxed copy of Blaine Stewart's letter Lesley had faxed him and tossed it onto a stack of other files awaiting his attention. "Shit," he muttered in disgust. "Do the police know about this?" he demanded sharply, picking the letter back up and waving it at his chief deputy, Lyle Stevens, who had just returned to the office in response to an urgent summons from Michelson.

"I don't know. The crime scene guys gave the bedroom the once over. Nobody at the police department said anything to me about a suicide note."

"This isn't just a suicide note. It's a damn confession. Goddammit, somebody saw it," he yelled at Stevens, "and gave it to the television station."

Anger propelled Michelson out of his chair. He stood looking down on noon-hour traffic crawling below his county courthouse office. "Get the goddamned police working on this. We need that original before the feds get their hands on it. This is a shit-load of evidence," he said, slamming back down in his chair and waving the two faxed sheets at his assistant's retreating back. "And call that goddamned woman at Channel 15 and tell her no comment."

The door to his office opened. "Here's that indictment Mr. Stevens told me to put a rush on, Mr. Michelson." She stood in the doorway, confused by the angry scowl on the county attorney's face. "I thought you wanted this right away?"

"Yeah. Just put it on my desk," he ordered peevishly. Michelson sat back down after she closed the door and cursed his luck. This was the case that would have accelerated his career into a lucrative law practice; even possibly elevate him into a judgeship.

Morosely, he picked up the telephone and dialed the judge he had asked to sign the indictment. "This is Drew Michelson. Tell

Judge Kearney the grand jury won't be filing that indictment today. Some new information has come in." He made a second call to Mace Harding.

†††

Stu Aarons held the faxed copy of the letter in his hand, as he dialed Roberto Castelero's office in downtown Chicago.

"Good morning, Castelero Enterprises," the sultry, breathy voice announced.

"I need Bobby."

"Mr. Castelero's in a meeting. Can I take a..."

"Cut the bullshit, lady. Get me Bobby. Tell him Aarons is on the line."

Soft music played in his ear for several minutes before a gravely male voice interrupted it.

"Yeah, Stu. What's so fucking important you have to fart off to my gal like that?"

"A letter. I just heard about it from a clerk in the DA's office who thinks I work for Grant Stewart's attorney. It could be bad, Bobby. Real bad."

"Bad, smad. What're ya talking about?" he asked, making no effort to cover his irritation. Stu Aarons was a downer in Roberto Castelero's eyes, always had been, since they were kids. Aarons saw thunder clouds in a clear blue sky.

"Your partner. Stewart. He wrote a tell-all letter before he pulled the trigger. It names names, Bobby. Yours, mine, Vincente, and just about everyone else. It names our names, man."

"Ah, shit! That sonabitch." Castelero slammed his fist down on the desk. "Look Stu, they got the letter, but they ain't got a witness, not if we take out Elliott. He's the only one who ever saw me and his dad together. Him gone, the police ain't got shit. You take care of it, okay?"

"Let's hope so," Aarons muttered as he hung up the receiver. He admitted to himself, Bobby was right. Street smart. That was

Bobby. For problems Bobby Castelero had answers, always. His savvy showed early, Aarons remembered ruefully, in their boyhood days in their old Brooklyn neighborhood. It was Stu Aarons who pored over his school work at night, under the watchful eye of his widowed mother. *An educated man is a successful man,* she would remind him whenever he carped about homework. Stu Aarons went with his mother to synagogue. Bobby skipped Mass to hang out with his friends.

When they moved from adolescence to adulthood, it was Bobby who led and Aarons who followed, always saddled with the dirty work. A lot of good an educated mind did him. He was still a lackey for Bobby Castelero. Always had been. The only place it was likely to change was behind bars or in a grave. Castelero issued the orders. Aarons used his well-schooled mind to figure the best way to carry out those orders. Elliott Stewart would be a particular challenge.

47

Grant answered the telephone. "A repairman from Aarons Security is here to check out the alarm system," the guard at the front gate announced. "They called earlier and said it was malfunctioning."

"Okay. Does he need in the house?" Grant asked.

"He might. But I told him to go around back, where the outside box is, and check that out first. If he does need into the house, I told him to ring the back doorbell."

"That's fine. Thanks, Jim." replied Grant, hanging up the telephone.

Grant walked over to his grandfather, who was reading the morning newspaper. He looked diminutive and frail in the high wing-backed leather chair that was the old man's favorite seat in the library.

"I'm going to the office to do some work on the computer. Call me if you need anything," said Grant. A thin, spindly hand waved him away.

Mid-afternoon shadows crept across the room that had been transformed into a makeshift office. On weekends, this was where Grant spent much of his time, often with his grandfather. As was his habit when he knew Grant was working in the office, Wiley Lefford knocked lightly and entered. "I have some coffee, if you would like some, Mr. Grant."

Grant leaned back from the computer and stretched his legs. "Sounds good, Wiley. How's Grandfather?"

"Still reading in the library. Marcy says dinner will be ready at 6:00, if that's agreeable with you?"

Grant smiled at the question. Dinner was always served at 6:00 and had been for years, unless it was a special occasion. But Lefford never failed to ask each day and never failed to get the same response.

"Hey, Wiley. Did that repairman finish checking out the security system?"

"I don't know, Mr. Grant. I haven't heard anything about a repairman. Marcy didn't mention no repairman when I was in the kitchen."

"Jim called from the guardhouse a while ago and said a repairman from Aarons Security was here to check out a malfunction in the system. Would you mind checking to see if he's still here and if everything's okay?"

"I'll be glad to." Lefford was half way to the door when he turned around. "Did you say someone from Aarons Security was here?"

"Yeah. That's what Jim said. Why?" Grant swiveled around in the computer chair.

"Aarons was one of the names in Mr. Blaine's letter." Grant saw alarm flash on the old man's face.

"What letter, Wiley?"

"In the letter Mr. Blaine wrote before he shot hisself. He mentioned an Aarons who was working with them drug fellows. I remember that name."

"Wiley, I'm sorry," said Grant, totally confused by Wiley's statement, and the fear imprinted on the old man's face. "What letter are you talking about?"

"I was going to tell you, Mr. Grant." There was hint of panic in the old voice. "I found a letter on the dresser when Mr. Blaine shot hisself. I hid it from the police." The old eyes were glistening with tears. "Please God, forgive me, Mr. Grant. I opened the letter. It told all about what Mr. Blaine was doing with those drug folks. I was afraid to give it to the police. When I overheard you and Mr. Willis talking, and him saying you might be indicted, I took the letter to Miss Lesley because I knew it'd clear your name. Your daddy said in the letter you had nothing to do with anything."

"When was that?"

"Last week. When you was afraid that grand jury was going to charge you with a crime."

"Oh my God, Wiley. You should have told me sooner. What you did could be considered withholding evidence." Grant walked over to the distraught old man and patted his shoulder. "It's all right. There's nothing to be done now. Tell me again about this Aarons."

"Let me go upstairs to my room and get the letter. You can read it for yourself." Lefford set the coffee tray on a table and shuffled out of the study. Grant reached for the phone and dialed the guardhouse. "Jim, its Grant. That guy from Aarons security service. Has he left yet?"

"No sir, not yet."

"Get down here right away. The guy may be trouble. I'm calling the police."

"Right away, Mr. Stewart."

Grant dialed 911 and gave his name and address to the dispatcher, saying only there could be an intruder on the property near the main house. He directed the dispatcher to have the police come to the main gate. He could open it remotely from the mansion. He then dialed Sarah's number. She answered immediately. "Are the kids inside?"

"Yes, why?" She could hear the urgency in his voice.

"I can't explain right now. Lock all the doors, and you and the kids get upstairs and lock yourselves in one of the bathrooms. Try to keep really quiet. Just tell the kids to do what I say, please Sarah. I'll send the police over to check things out as soon as they arrive."

Grant could almost hear Sarah's lips forming the first questions. "Just do it Sarah, now!" he snapped.

Sarah called to the children. They were sitting at a table spread with books in the den, along with the tutor she had hired to teach them at home. With a fierce determination she kept her voice calm as she hurried the elderly tutor and the children upstairs to the large bathroom in the master bedroom. She locked the bedroom door behind her, before herding the confused children and their tutor into the bathroom and ordering them in a harsh whisper to stay very quiet.

Grant dialed Elliott's home. The line was busy. He slammed the receiver down and rushed to the library, where his grandfather sat reading. "Grandpa, we may have an intruder on the grounds. Please come upstairs with me to your room."

Grantham Stewart stood up slowly, testing his stiffened knees. "Where's Wiley and Marcy and Anna?" he asked.

"Wiley went up to his room. Marcy and Anna are in the kitchen. Let's get you upstairs and I'll take care of them. Police are on the way."

Grant gripped his grandfather's arm and helped him toward the elevator in the front hall. Lefford was coming out of his bedroom as the elevator door opened onto the second floor. "Take Grandpa. I'm going down to get Marcy and Anna."

"I found the letter, Mr. Grant."

"Good. Hang onto it. I'll be right back." Grant bounded down the stairs three at a time, leaping over the banister at the quarter landing just as Jim Santino, the front gate guard, came in the front door.

"Jim, thank God. Get Marcy and Anna out of the kitchen and take them upstairs with Grandpa and Wiley. Put them in Grandpa's room and make sure they lock the door behind them while I try Elliott again."

He dialed from a telephone in the living room. A busy signal sounded. He rushed into the office and looked around for his cell phone. "Shit!" he muttered, as he grabbed for his cell phone on the desk next to his computer. It rang four times before Elliott's voice started speaking saying he was unavailable. Exasperated, he tried Elliott's home number again. Still busy. He slammed down the telephone, just as Jim was propelling the rotund, nearly hysterical cooks through the dining room doorway.

"Don't be afraid you two. Everything's going to be okay. Jim will take care of you." Grant patted each wailing woman on the shoulder. "I can't reach Elliott. The line's busy. That repairman may have gone over there. Give me your gun, Jim. Grandpa keeps a loaded shotgun by his bed. You get that one."

"Sure thing, Mr. Stewart." Santino drew his .38-caliber pistol from a stiff black leather holster and handed it to Grant.

"Is it loaded?" Grant asked.

"Yes, sir."

"Mr. Grant. There was a man who came to the kitchen door a few minutes ago. He asked which way to Mr. Elliott's," said Marcy, her breath coming in gulps.

"Okay, Marcy. I'll take care of it. You go with Jim," he said, trying to keep his voice calm despite the panic he was feeling. "Jim, get them upstairs with the others. Call the police again on your cell phone. Tell them to go to Elliott's first."

"Let me come with you, Mr. Stewart. You don't need to go over there by yourself." The guard dropped his grip on Marcy's arm and started toward Grant.

"No, Jim. You stay here. Just get that shotgun and keep everybody safe," Grant commanded. He turned and bolted out the front door, racing toward Elliott's home, at the same time he released the safety on the pistol. He had cleared half the distance between the mansion and Elliott's home when he spotted a white van with two ladders on top parked in front of the three-car garage on the far side of his brother's home. He knew that must be Aarons or whomever he sent. *Please God, don't let me be too late,* he pleaded silently.

Grant heard a distant siren as he sprinted the remaining distance to Elliott's house. His breath was coming in gasps as he vaulted up the porch steps two at a time. The front door stood ajar. From deep inside the home came a shrill, wrenching scream. He felt the twin fingers of fear and panic clutch at his insides and knew instinctively he was too late. He followed the screams to the den at the rear of the home, where an anguished sound echoed from one of the two people in the center of the large room, dominated by a high cathedral-ceiling. Emily was kneeling over Elliott, who lay on the wood floor, his chest heaving as his lungs struggled for air.

Grant fished his cell phone from his pocket and ordered an ambulance. He looked at his brother and the blood now puddling around his head and realized there was nothing he could do. He pulled a stricken Emily to her feet and helped her to a chair.

"Where are the children?"

She looked at him with doleful brown eyes. "They're not here. They're with my parents." He remembered his own children.

"That's good, Emily. You stay here until the ambulance arrives while I check on Sarah and the children."

She nodded feebly.

Grant rushed out of the house and was racing back across the wide expanse of lawn between Elliott's home and the home on the other side of the mansion when a white van flashed past his view on the long drive leading to the main entrance. The van was nearing the entrance gate, left open by the guard, when he saw a police cruiser screech into the path of the van. The collision slammed the van sharply to the right and into the heavy iron fence. It struck with such force the driver was thrown through the windshield, impaling his neck on the jagged remains of the shattered windshield.

He saw two police officers leap out of their crumpled car, apparently unhurt. Only when he ran to where the two officers were standing in front of the van did he see what had happened to the driver. He would pose no further danger to his family.

Grant rushed back to his brother's home. By the time he knelt over Elliott, his brother's struggle for breath had ceased. He felt the tears smart his eyes as he gently folded Emily into his arms.

As Grant turned the key in the lock he felt the weight of the day's events descend on him like an iron shroud. It seemed to grip his chest and threatened to strangle his breathing. It was then he saw her, in the shadow of a table lamp across the room.

"I still have a key," she explained in a husky voice. Lesley held open her arms.

He wanted to reject her overture, to fling words of blame and rebuke, to order her away. Instead he walked across to where she sat and sank down on his knees as her drew him to her.

$$48$$

Six months later

Christo motioned to his son, who was chatting animatedly with one of the young field workers. He was a gregarious boy, so unlike his father. *That will have to be tempered*, Christo said to himself, as he watched the smiling young face running toward him. At nine, he was still a child, but a child old enough to begin learning about what would one day be his, the vastness of the rich fields, filled with the tropical shrubs that yielded such a lucrative crop. Just as Jacoby had taught him, he would teach his son.

The lesson lasted much of the morning. Christo was pleased by the rapt attention of the youngster. This was good. The boy would learn quickly.

The new American partner would be arriving shortly, a businessman like himself, not a street thug in a three-piece suit. That was his disdainful assessment of Roberto Castelero; a pernicious man, in Christo's eyes, and stupid. Castelero had been arrested after ordering the murder of Elliott Stewart on a phone not scanned for wire-tap devices. It was stupid beyond any words Christo could fling at Castelero from his considerable vocabulary.

The market share of drug trade lost by the dismantling of the Castelero family must be regained. The means to take back what he had spent years securing would be joining him for lunch on the veranda shortly—the man from Las Vegas, whose business interests stretched from California and Arizona, east to Texas and Florida. Christo visualized wider avenues of distribution to feed the growing American appetite for drugs. The plans forming in his head in recent weeks would be accomplished by this new partner as long as the Mexican center of their network remained stable. And that was something Estavar seemed always able to accomplish as long as the money kept flowing. *Cooperation is easily purchased in Mexico,* Christo thought contemptuously.

It was approaching noon. He hoped Vincente and his cousins were awake and ready to dine with his guest.

"Come, Jacoby. Papa has a friend we must welcome soon." Christo motioned to the bodyguard as he began walking toward the villa, pulling the dark-eyed handsome boy to him affectionately. *This will always be my most loyal partner,* he thought, squeezing the boy's shoulders, which were forming broadly like his own. Looking down at the young face that showed such eagerness to learn, he felt a strong surge of love and satisfaction. *He is his father's son,* he noted with silent pride.

As the father and son approached the main gate of the sprawling villa, the distinct sound of helicopters could be heard in the distance. Christo felt a spike of apprehension. The sound was unmistakable—like the slow roll of thunder announcing a coming storm. He turned toward the sound just as another sound infiltrated from below the villa—vehicles ascending the mountain. Not the refined growl of SUVs that would bring his American guests, but the intrusive rumble of trucks. Large trucks. The kind of trucks used by the military. Christo grabbed the shirt sleeve of the bodyguard. "Take Jacoby and see that he gets safely to his mother."

The bodyguard's young face flashed with sudden alarm and he appeared immobilized.

"Now! Do as I say," Christo barked. The order penetrated the bodyguard's inertia. He grabbed the boy's hand and moved swiftly toward the villa. Christo followed a short distance behind. He leaped up the wide front steps three at a time just as several heavily armed men appeared from the rear of the villa. Glancing back, Christo could see the first trucks lumbering into view a quarter-mile down the mountain. Christo's agile mind assessed the danger. He felt a sudden calm descend as he estimated the time it would take for the trucks to cover the distance to the villa entrance and the helicopters to be hovering overhead. *Only minutes—four, maybe five—no more.* Christo shouted for the men to take up positions near the entrance before entering the cool interior of the villa.

Christo had anticipated this scenario—years ago. It was time to initiate the fail-safe plan he had put in place—escape through the tunnel. His most trusted bodyguard now stood at his side, his hands gripping an automatic rifle. "Gather my family, Eduardo, and bring them to the tunnel. I'll meet you there. Hurry, my friend. We have little time."

"I can't leave you."

"Go now," Christo ordered calmly. Christo patted the man's shoulder. For a large man, in height as well as muscular bulk, Eduardo moved away with the stealth of a shadow.

Inside the house Christo hurried to his office and from a floor safe planted under a rug in front of his desk he lifted a canvas bag filled with American cash and something far more valuable—a list of numbers for access to safety deposit boxes in countries that guarded the contents of those boxes with laws and discretion. From his desk drawer, he took a 45-caliber handgun and shoved it into the small of his back. He quickly dialed a number and in terse words ordered the means for their escape to be made ready. In the distance he could hear shouting, the sudden commotion now punctuated with sporadic gunfire.

Christo raced across the courtyard past its bucolic fountain and gardens to the kitchen at the rear of the sprawling villa. The tunnel was hidden behind a false panel of shelves in a wide closet which served as a pantry. Bette stood white-faced by the pantry door gripping Jacoby's hand. Fear wrestled with panic on the boy's face. Christo patted his son's face reassuringly and kissed his wife softly on the cheek to quiet the fear in her large eyes. They would all be safe soon, he assured them.

Eduardo had sent the two cooks and their helpers scurrying out the rear door, telling them to flee to the safety of their homes in the village below. He yanked open the shelved entrance and guided his wife and son into the dimly lit passageway which descended to an exit nearly 800 meters down the mountain. A large SUV with bullet proof windows awaited the passengers, camouflaged under a canvas painted with the green shrubs that grew all around it. From the air Christo knew it was nearly undiscernible. A dirt road would take the all-terrain vehicle onto the main road below the mountain villa and to a private airfield where a plane would be waiting to take the Christos and their bodyguard to a destination in the Caribbean, to a secluded seaside villa which promised comfort for the exiles and a non-extradition treaty with both Columbia and the United States.

As Christo followed Bette and his son up the steps of the Cessna Caravan, he felt a silent tsunami of rage and bitterness rise in his chest, a surge so strong it left him breathing heavily. From the doorway of the plane, he looked back at the distant villa on the mountain from where they had fled and felt a deep sense of loss. Would he ever return to the home on the mountain, the only real home he had ever known? Bette's birthplace? His son's birthplace? Christo shook his head sadly as he entered the cabin. Eduardo quickly pulled the door closed behind him and signaled wheels up to the pilot.

Christo buckled himself into the plush leather seat across from his wife, who was clutching their son tightly as the plane began gliding down the runway, her beautiful face tense with fear. He blew a kiss at Bette and saw her expression soften into a wan smile.

Someone had betrayed him, he reflected bitterly as the Cessna lifted smoothly toward the eastern sky. Was it someone within the organization over which he had held tightfisted control for nearly a decade? Or someone from the outside? The Mexicans. They would be caught up in the raid but claim to be innocent bystanders and have the cover of their country's endemic corruption, as well as their own, to ensure their untethered return to Mexico. *Money buys many things,* Christo thought sardonically, *most especially freedom to operate.*

He leaned back against the headrest. His money would buy the same. He would return. He would rebuild the empire that had been entrusted to him by his mentor. Then he would exact his revenge.

London traffic was in its usual snarl. Lesley envied the motor scooter messengers, who darted in and out of the crawling cars like frightened hares fleeing a fox. She wondered absently if they had a death wish. Discouraged by passing cabs, which seemed always to be occupied, and the constant sound of discordant horns, she had decided to walk. The Savoy was only a mile or so distant.

Diving between cars to cross at the first intersection, Lesley decided she much preferred the bucolic side of England. She had just spent several days in the Cotswold's and the Lake District of Beatrice Potter. Driving past the hillside pastures, where sheep grazed placidly, she remembered feeling like she had been stepping onto the pages of a Thomas Hardy novel, expecting Tess of the D'Urbervilles to come skipping down the lane toward her.

In the evenings, before dinner, they had walked the country roads, past quaint stone houses with thin spirals of smoke curling up from chimneys. Some of those stone homes had sheltered farmers for longer than the United States had been a country. They had spent two nights in just such a farmhouse that served as a bed-and-breakfast during peak tourist months. Everything was old, or quaint, and famously historic in England, even the angled portico just ahead.

A light drizzle began falling, tapping her face like tiny, gentle feathers, before she stepped under the sanctuary of the Savoy's iconic portico. He was waiting just inside.

"I'm sorry. I went shopping and couldn't find a cab," Lesley said, feeling her breath catch and her cheeks warm at the site of him. *The flush of love*, her mother called it. He pulled her into his arms.

"I just got in myself a short time ago," Grant Stewart said, as he lifted her face to meet his lips and embraced her for a long enough time to evoke curious glances from bystanders in the lobby. "I missed you, Mrs. Stewart."

"Me, too," she whispered, her finger tracing softly across his lips.

"Do you need to freshen up?"

"No, I dressed for dinner before I went out this afternoon. How was the trip?" she asked as he led her toward a cocktail bar off the far side of the lobby.

"Over wine, I shall tell you about my adventures on the sands of Oman, where I battled heat, fended off scorpions, and went thirsty—but only for you. Actually, the Al Bustan Palace was quite nice. Not a scorpion to be had," he added lightly. "And I returned with the contract signed, sealed, and in my briefcase—actually in our lawyer's briefcase. But never mind the details. I will be making almost as much money as you do now." His eyes were teasing.

"Not when I renew my contract next month," she countered smugly. "Peabody Awards garner big bucks, you know." Lesley turned away, her expression wistfully pensive. She had insisted on sharing the award with Witt Terrell, which pleased Mac. She wondered, had Terrell not been murdered, if he would even have shown up for the award presentation. Probably not. Not the Terrell she knew. His thin, fissured face still came to her at odd times. And each time she felt a sense of enormous regret that she had so underestimated him. Mac was the one person who had known the true measure of Witt Terrell. His murder remained unsolved. Lesley surmised the perpetrators had probably fled across the Mexican border before investigators even finished processing the crime scene.

She turned back to Grant and forced a smile to dispel the sadness that momentarily washed over her. Grant seemed to sense where she had gone and after they sat down at a more private table in the back of the lounge, he reached over and took her hands in his and drew them to his lips. "Thinking about your friend, Les?" She nodded. A shadow of anger passed over his face. "They'll get the bastard. At some point Christo will crawl out from under his rock in Columbia, and an unpleasant surprise will be waiting for him." The shadow that clouded his features was banished by a knowing smile not lost on Lesley but quickly deflected by the approach of a waiter, who slid glasses of chilled Pinot Grigio in front of them. "Will there be anything else, sir?"

"Thank you. That's all for the moment." Grant raised his glass. "To my beautiful wife… who will shortly sign a contract that should ensure she can support me in a manner to which I want to remain accustomed."

Lesley laughed and lifted her own glass and tilted it toward him. "With pleasure, my good gigolo."

"And something else. Something just texted me by our friend at the FBI."

"Good news, I hope, for a change."

"It is." A droll smile broadened his lips. "Our Columbian friend has been forced into exile to a place where the FBI will have an easier time tracking his movements. One of the side benefits of foreign aid."

ALICE A. JACKSON

Alice Jackson is a retired journalist, broadcast professional and world traveler, having visited more than 123 countries since 2002.

She majored in journalism and political science, at the University of Tulsa, married the editor of the university newspaper, and raised four children and a younger brother. She worked in local television as a reporter, anchor and news director for 20 years before purchasing a small radio station in Franklin, Tennessee, which she sold in 1997.

When her dearest friend died of cancer in 2000, she adopted his adult, special-needs son, Robert. It was the first adult adoption in Williamson County, Tennessee. In 2007, she moved with her adopted son to Indianapolis to be near her daughter to insure care for Robert.

Robert passed away in 2011. Since then, Alice has traveled and focused her attention on her writing.